Praise for Larry Watson and
White Crosses

Praise for Larry Watson's
Justice

"A worthy collection, filled with rugged prose sometimes as biting as a northern plains wind, the next page as inviting and lyrical as a well-stoked wood stove. . . . *Justice* explains much of the history of *Montana 1948* . . . [and] demonstrates . . . that defining one's manhood, bearing a name, and achieving a fragile balance between race and gender is a challenge to all Americans. . . . Watson writes of people universal in their flaws and virtues, a community that cannot be defined or limited to one region or genre."

—Tim McLaurin, *The Washington Post Book World*

"Gracefully constructed. . . . With prose as unassuming and a narrative style as authentic as a Montana landscape, *Justice* will inevitably have a reservation at the select table set for only the very finest . . . fiction."

—Jo Gilbertson, *Minneapolis Star-Tribune*

"Beautifully written. . . . Some of the stories about men in *Justice* evoke the feeling of *A River Runs Through It,* but it's Watson's description of the Hayden women that gives the reader the sweetest gift."

—Carol Knopes, *USA Today*

"This fine book is billed as a 'prequel' to Watson's earlier book, *Montana 1948,* but don't be fooled—[*Justice*] stands quite well on its own. . . . From the way fresh snow illuminates a moonless night, to the way a gun feels in a man's hand, to the way a baby rolls and moves inside a pregnant woman, Larry Watson makes us feel Montana life."

—Laurie Hertzel, *Minnesota Monthly*

Praise for Larry Watson's
Montana 1948

"This story is as fresh and clear as the trout streams fished by its narrator. . . . As universal in its themes as it is original in its peculiarities, *Montana 1948* is a significant and elegant addition to the fiction of the American West, and to contemporary American fiction in general."

—Howard Frank Mosher, *The Washington Post Book World*

"Montana 1948 stands out as a work of art. . . ."

—Susan Petro, *San Francisco Chronicle*

"Wonderful. . . . Be prepared to read this compact book in one sitting. Start at 10 P.M. By 11, you're hooked. You finish in the wee hours, mesmerized by the fast-moving plot, the terse language, uncompromising characterization, and insights into life. . . ."

—Mike Bowler, *Baltimore Sun*

"Montana 1948 is a superbly rendered novel. The writing is clean, the characters finely drawn, the whole book deeply felt and honest. . . . It is a spare, unpretentious, but riveting book . . . with great sensitivity and subtlety. . . ."

—Fritz Lanham, *Houston Chronicle*

"Larry Watson is one of those good writers few people know about, a writer whose work is worthy of prizes. . . . The style of *Montana 1948* is as thin, clear and crisp as a North Dakota wind."

—Annick Smith, *Los Angeles Times Book Review*

"A beautiful novel about the meaning of place and evolution of courage. . . . A wonderful book."

—Louise Erdrich

Books by Larry Watson

In a Dark Time
Leaving Dakota
Montana 1948
Justice
White Crosses

white crosses

a novel by

larry watson

WASHINGTON SQUARE PRESS
PUBLISHED BY POCKET BOOKS

New York   London   Toronto   Sydney   Singapore

To Susan

In appreciation of their encouragement, advice, and support, I would like to thank agent extraordinaire Sharon Friedman, Emily Bestler, Gina Centrello, Michael Siegel, and Bill Grose.

I also wish to thank Ruth Watson, Amy Watson, and Elly Heuring.

And the greatest thanks, beyond words, to my wife, Susan.

WSP

A Washington Square Press Publication of
POCKET BOOKS, a division of Simon & Schuster Inc.
1230 Avenue of the Americas, New York, NY 10020

ISBN: 0-671-56773-X

First Washington Square Press trade paperback printing April 1998

10 9 8 7 6 5 4 3

Cover design by Brigid Pearson
Front cover photo by Victoria Goldman/Graphistock

Printed in the U.S.A.

1

WHEN SHERIFF JACK NEVELSEN GOT THE CALL FROM THE DISPATCHER about the accident out on Highway 284—single car, two fatalities—his first thought was, kids. Teenagers. Oh, sweet Jesus, somebody's babies.

It was ten o'clock Sunday night, May 28, 1957, and Bentrock High School's senior class had graduated that afternoon. Mercer County's roads and highways were going to be traveled that night by kids going from party to party. And they were going to be drinking.

This was Jack's fear every year at graduation, that a kid—or worse, kids, a whole car full of them—would get drunk and try to beat a train to a crossing, or weave across the center line, and some parents' proudest day would turn into their worst. On graduation night kids drank; the ones who never drank would probably pick that night to start, and the ones who drank regularly would try to do it up bigger than ever.

So far Mercer County had been lucky. No graduation-night tragedy for them. But three years ago they came close, damn close. The kids held a big party at an area north of town known as The

Haystacks, and in all the driving back and forth, a young woman missed a bridge and landed her car in a creek bed. Jack could never figure out if it was good or bad that the creek was dry.

At any rate, the drop from the bridge was not far, less than fifteen feet, and everyone got out of the car unhurt. Only minutes later, another carload of kids—speeding around the same curve— missed the same bridge. They didn't fall as far as the first car because they landed right on top of it. A giant hand couldn't have balanced the second car more precisely on the first.

The next morning when the tow truck winched the cars up the slope, and when Jack saw the crushed roof of the first car, Kathy Hessup's white Ford, he wondered how much luck Mercer County had used up the previous night.

So every year, come graduation time, Jack, along with Chief of Police Bagwell, tried to put the word out: Stay put and we'll leave you alone, but if you drive drunk, we're going to be on your ass.

Now it sounded as though someone hadn't gotten the word, or hadn't heeded it, and Mercer County's luck had run out.

Jack took the call on the phone in the kitchen, and before he went out to his truck, he stuck his head into the living room where his wife, Nora, was sewing and watching television.

"I've got to go out," he said. "Accident out on two-eighty-four west of town."

She didn't ask how bad the accident was, or if he knew who was involved. But that was Nora. She would know soon enough; everyone in town would. She was not in any hurry to hear bad news, and the fact that his job kept bringing it to their doorstep, like a stray dog or cat that, once fed, won't stay away, put some strain on their marriage. It was nothing serious. But often Jack could not talk with Nora about his work. If it was in the least sordid, ugly, brutal, or even unpleasant, Nora did not want to hear about it.

Starting at midnight on Friday nights, the television station in Williston broadcast *Shockerama*, a double feature of old horror movies, and Nora would not even stay in the room when those movies played. Jack loved them, especially the werewolf features, and if he wasn't out on patrol (he and his deputy alternated Friday nights), he brewed a pot of coffee and sat down in front of the set. He kept the volume low, but Nora, in the bedroom, still kept the door closed.

Their ten-year-old daughter, Angela, on the other hand, loved scary movies almost as much as Jack, and she would often put her blanket and pillow on the floor in front of the television and watch with him. She seldom lasted through the second movie, and Jack would finally carry her to bed. He remembered thinking one night, as he watched the movie's light and shadow flicker over his daughter's face, about the contrast between mother and daughter. While Nora was in the bedroom with her pillow over her ears so she couldn't hear the monster's roar, Angela slept peacefully while above her the Wolfman claimed another victim.

Ah, it was just as well Nora was the way she was. He shouldn't bring his work home with him. Wasn't that the advice he read in the law enforcement newsletter every month?

Tonight even the family dog seemed to know that it was bad news calling Jack out of the house. Muley, an aging shepherd mix, who usually ran excitedly to the door as soon as he heard the jingle of Jack's keys, did not move from his station by the stove, but merely tilted his sleepy gaze in Jack's direction.

Before he left, Jack shook three Chesterfields out of the pack, slid them into his shirt pocket, and carefully snapped the flap. He was trying to cut down on the number of cigarettes he smoked in a day, and he could best do that by not carrying the pack with him. If he had a full pack out at the accident site, he knew he'd light one right after another. He liked to smoke outside, liked the way the wind tore the smoke off in its own direction no matter how hard he exhaled, or how, when the air was cold, the smoke and the steam from his breath combined and billowed around him like a miniature cloud. He also liked to use his cigarettes to give himself a little distance. While he tried to think of what to do or say, he could strip the cellophane from a fresh pack of cigarettes, slit the foil with his thumbnail, exposing those perfect brown circles of tightly packed tobacco, knock the pack on his index finger until one cigarette jumped apart from the rest, take it out, and tap it on his lighter or the face of his watch. If he still needed more time, he could light the cigarette, inhale, exhale. . . . By that time,

3

he usually had considered the alternatives and their consequences and knew what course to follow.

When a particular moment became too much—the drunk was cursing you out or the farmer was telling you why you had to arrest his neighbor—lighting and smoking a cigarette gave you something to concentrate on besides the moment at hand—like the look of a car or the bodies at an accident site. Jack reconsidered and put the entire pack in the pocket of his denim jacket.

As he drove out of town, Jack tried to keep his gaze aimed straight ahead. He was fighting the urge to speculate who might be lying dead out there along Highway 284, and he didn't want to start looking around for citizens, or their sons and daughters, to eliminate as possible victims. He had already caught himself once. Less than a block from the house, Jack saw Arletta Whitcomb standing under a streetlight with her dog, and he thought: There. It's not Arletta. When was she scheduled to graduate? Next year? Two years? Thank God. He would not be knocking on the Whitcombs' door tonight. But that line of thinking was no good; eventually he would land on someone's name about whom he might say to himself, why not, why not let it be him? He's been in trouble since grade school; he's going nowhere, except perhaps the state penitentiary in Deer Lodge. . . . That line of thought, as far as Jack was concerned, was damn near the same as wishing someone dead. And how Christian was that?

Jack let his thoughts spin for a moment until they settled themselves on a subject that allowed him to think about the accident but not the victims or their identity: he wondered where the white crosses would be. Whenever a fatality occurred in a highway accident, a white cross was planted at the site, one cross for each death. Cautioning other travelers was the idea, to tell them that someone had died here, because of speed or carelessness or hazardous road conditions or simply bad luck. No doubt it made sense and had an effect—you approached that railroad crossing and saw five crosses bristling up from the weeds alongside the tracks and perhaps you looked carefully before proceeding. But were those five crosses from five separate accidents, indicating that here was a crossing where trains came out of nowhere, or were all the crosses from only one accident, from the night five teenagers heard the *Empire Builder*'s whistle and saw its light but still thought they could beat it to the crossing? What if you drove a highway only once, and by the time you noticed that single cross in the ditch you were already past it—what lesson could you take from that? Jack had seen bouquets of those crosses in places so dangerous they made you nod your head and say silently, yes, no question but that a heedless driver could meet his death here. But he had also seen crosses in places that brought nothing but puzzlement, that left you scratching your head and wondering what the hell a driver must have done to get himself killed along this ribbon-straight stretch of road.

Now two more crosses were going to be stuck in the soil of Mercer County. And who stuck them anyway? Was there a special highway department crew whose only responsibility was to visit those death sites? Or was it a regular sign crew who just kept a few white crosses in the back of the truck along with the Falling Rocks, Yield, Cattle Crossing, Dangerous Curves, and Soft Shoulder signs? Who—or what—marked the spot until the permanent cross was posted? What about the deaths that occurred in winter, when the earth was often frozen so deep April couldn't even finish the thaw, when the mortician had to stack the dead in an unheated Quonset hut until spring—was there a special spring detail that traveled Montana's highways, pounding in all the white crosses that were owed the previous winter?

He couldn't help it. Those crosses made him feel as though he hadn't done his job. Each one could just as easily be flying a little pennant that said, "If Sheriff Jack Nevelsen had kept the county roads free of drunks, speeders, reckless or incompetent drivers, this cross wouldn't be here." He knew there wasn't a man, woman, or child in the county who held him accountable; nevertheless, he would take those two new crosses personally.

2

WHEN JACK LOOKED DOWN FROM THE TOP OF THE HILL TO WHERE THE accident had occurred, he let his hopes rise just a little.

Below him were the lights of three cars—his deputy's, the tow truck, and a third car that looked like a highway patrol vehicle but which could as easily have belonged to a civilian, a witness who had waited around to report on what he had seen. The cars were parked near the bottom of the hill, at the exact spot in the county where an accident was most likely to occur. There, less than five miles from the Bentrock city limits, the road made a steep descent, coming down from the bluffs west of town. As the road dropped, it curved gradually toward the northwest until, almost at the base of the hill, it veered hard to the southwest. If you missed the curve, you were off the road in an instant and sailing toward a slough. Beyond was the meadow where Jonas Sprull pastured his prize Appaloosas. If you were going slowly when you went off, you were going to slide and probably roll down that steep, crumbling embankment.

If you were going fast? Well, you just might soar out and land in the branches of one of those huge, old cottonwoods. That was on the right side of the road, the open side. The other side was a sheer rock face, ready to bounce you right back over the edge. Because of the rock wall and the slough, the road was narrow, with a tight shoulder and no guardrail. Jack believed he was as skilled at driving on snow and ice as the next man, but if the roads were slippery he might go out of his way so he wouldn't have to negotiate that hill and that curve. No two ways about it—it was just a treacherous piece of highway. If Mercer County weren't up there in the corner of the state that nobody gave a damn about, Jack was sure the highway department would have long ago straightened or widened the road. Or condemned it altogether and rerouted the highway. Everyone in the county knew how dangerous the hill was, knew you had to respect it, regardless of the season, and slow way down, coming up or going down. If you drove it any other way, you were probably drunk or suicidal. Or from outside the county. And that was what Jack hoped for—that the bodies down there did not belong to his county. Or—and he damned himself immediately for this thought—were Indians from the nearby reservation. Either way—Indians or residents from another county, another state, another country (the Canadian border was less than twenty miles away)—the dead would be someone else's problem. He could call the tribal police or the sheriff of another county or the Mounties and let them take over.

There was no part of his job that Jack dreaded more than notifying the next of kin. He even hated the word. *Kin.* It sounded like a word out of another time, a word that survived up in their remote part of Montana. *Kin*—it reminded him of the backwoods, of cousins marrying cousins. And maybe what bothered him most was the fact that he never had to ask: he always knew who the next of kin was.

During Jack's first term in office, for example, when old Harold Many Bulls was found frozen to death behind the Fremont Creamery and no one knew if Harold had any kin, on the reservation or off, Jack knew. Harold and Rhoda Cleer had once been husband and wife, and Jack had a hunch they were never divorced. He drove out to Rhoda's little farm to tell her about Harold, and damned if she didn't break down in tears. Seventy-five-year-old Rhoda Cleer, as tough as prairie fescue, and there she was weeping over that drunken town Indian. Yes, she admitted it; she and Harold were married years ago, back when she was trying to work the place alone. She had first hired Harold to help out, one thing led to another, and before you knew it, the two of them were heading for Havre to find a justice of the peace to marry them. And no, they were never divorced, even though Harold didn't actually live in the house more than a year. Once they were married, Rhoda said, Harold wasn't as good a worker. His drinking worsened, and soon she had to tell him to get out. But how did Jack know about the marriage? Jack's father used to own a hardware store, and Jack and his brother had worked in the family business from the time they were old enough to sweep a broom. Jack was working the day Harold Many Bulls came into the store and tried to buy an assortment of goods—hammers, saws, wrenches, coils of wire, lengths of rope. Harold had no money but tried to have the items put on Rhoda Cleer's account. Jack's father refused Harold's request, telling him it looked as though Harold meant to trade the merchandise for whiskey. Harold was already drunk, and he became belligerent, insisting that Jack's father had to let him take the items. Bring me a note from Miss Cleer, Jack's father said, and you can charge anything in the damn store. Harold pounded the counter with his fist. He didn't need no note, he said—I'm her husband. Jack's father laughed, and did not stop laughing until Harold shuffled from the store. Jack witnessed the incident and, like other moments from his childhood, stored it away in one of those regions of his mind that he was unlikely to visit again— until the day Harold's frozen body was found and no one was quite sure who should be notified. Rhoda not only immediately confessed to the marriage, in her rambling way she tried to explain it to Jack. Living out on the prairie . . . No one who lived in town could know how lonely it could get. The brevity of those winter days, the length of the nights . . . You felt you were so alone in the world you had to make your pleasure any way you could. But when Jack asked about the disposition of Harold's body, Rhoda's tears stopped. That wasn't her problem, she said. Call his tribal leaders. Harold was a Cheyenne; let them decide. And once her tears dried up, Rhoda Cleer, in a voice as stern and full of menace as she could manage, told Jack that he needn't bother blabbing this marriage all over the goddamn county.

Although Jack drove away with Rhoda Cleer's curses and threats echoing in his ears, he felt that day that he was doing the job he was meant to do. No other man in Mercer County was elected to serve as sheriff, and no other man knew to draw that line from Harold Many Bulls' corpse to Rhoda Cleer's farmhouse.

That feeling was rare. On most days Jack felt as though he was doing a job that others could do and do as well. The position was Jack's only because his best friend from childhood, Steve Lovoll, had a perforated eardrum and could not serve in the military. While most of the other males of Bentrock were going off to fight in Europe and the Pacific, Steve went to college and law school. After receiving his degree, Steve decided to return to his hometown and run for public office. Jack had been in the military police, and it was Steve's idea that the friends run on the same ticket—Steve for state's attorney and Jack for sheriff. Jack didn't think he made a bad sheriff. Not at all. He understood the concept of duty, that it meant facing up to and doing unpleasant tasks, but mostly it just meant doing the job, all of it, and doing it as well as it deserved to be done. He had, apparently, an authoritative air about him, though Jack believed what others saw as authority was actually the way shyness was perceived in a physically large man. People respected him, but that too seemed to Jack merely the consequence of his policy of never speaking ill of anyone in the county. He held plenty of them in low regard, but he kept his opinions to himself. Other men in the county might also possess these qualities, but for better or worse, the name on the courthouse register was Jack's.

And part of his job was notifying the next of kin.

He usually took someone with him—a priest, a relative, a close friend, a doctor. In the presence of grief—of any strong emotion, for that matter—Jack was often without resource. He could think of little to say beyond, "I'm sorry," and even that phrase, repeated often enough, began to sound less and less like consolation and more like a child whining for forgiveness. Some people, when they received bad news, needed the comfort that only a physical embrace could provide, and this was something Jack couldn't do. He could hand over his handkerchief or pat a shoulder, but hold someone, let her sobs gradually subside in the circle of his arms—no. But if the widow's sister or the father's minister was there, they could furnish the hugs or the promises of God's mercy, and Jack could simply relate the facts of the accident and back quietly away.

It didn't always work.

Last fall when Walt Flightner accidentally shot himself in the leg on a hunting trip high in the Bitterroot Mountains and bled to death before a damn thing could be done to save him, Jack took Father Howser along to break the news to Walt's wife, Marge. But Marge must have had an uneasy feeling about the trip her husband was on, because when she saw the car with the sheriff's insignia on the door pull up in front of the house and the sheriff and the priest get out of the car and walk slowly up her front walk, Marge locked her front door and ran out the back door.

Father Howser spotted her as she cut across the neighbor's yard, and the two of them called out and ran after her. In that part of Bentrock, a newer subdivision, almost none of the residents fenced off or hedged their yards, and each lawn ran right into the next. Finally, however, Marge came to a fence that she couldn't get over before the two men caught up to her. She cowered before them as if they were assassins. And they were. They were about to take from her the life she had known. Sobbing, shaking her head, Marge held her hands clamped tight over her ears. Father Howser reached down, took hold of her wrists, and pulled her hands away so she had to hear what he was about to tell.

"Walt's dead, Marge. He's dead."

Jack, first of all, could never have grabbed her the way the priest did. And he couldn't believe the way Father Howser gave her the news. Where were those words and phrases—*in the Lord's hands, watching down from heaven, at peace*—that were supposed to make the truth easier to bear? But Marge calmed somewhat and let herself be led back to her home.

Jack followed along behind them. With Father Howser's arm around her, Marge looked like a little girl who had fallen at play and was being taken home to have her wounds washed and bandaged. Jack could have lifted her up and carried her the way he held his own Angela. But she was not Angela. She was Marge Flightner, a short, pretty, energetic woman with full breasts and sturdy legs and a deep tan from all the hours she spent on the golf course. She had grown up in southern California, and when Walt brought her to Bentrock, she came with talents and interests that few Montana women shared. She loved to swim and play tennis, and she was a better golfer than almost any man in the region. Rather than scorn the women who couldn't do what she could, Marge tried to convert and teach them, and because of her enthusiasm and patience, many women followed her lead, and soon there were enough female patrons at the Knife River Municipal Golf Course to justify having Ladies' Day. But Jack couldn't allow himself to lift her up or embrace her or touch her in any way because he couldn't be sure why he might be doing it: because he wanted to comfort her, or because he wanted to know what it felt like to touch a woman like Marge?

Walt made enough money in his construction business to allow the family (Walt, Marge, their two sons and daughter) to spend two weeks in Florida every winter. They made that trip at just about the time Marge's summer tan was fading away, and she returned as bronzed as she was in midsummer.

Jack wondered, as Father Howser helped Marge back into her home, when winter came would Marge turn as pale as every other Montana woman?

And he wondered now, as he tapped his brakes, shifted into second, and eased down the hill toward the accident site, if before the night was over, someone would try to lock the door on him and the bad news he brought.

3

He parked behind his deputy's car, but farther up the hill, where the road and the shoulder widened slightly. Even so, he had to have two wheels on the pavement and two on the soft, crumbling shoulder. His deputy, the highway patrolman, and the driver of the tow truck had all left the lights of their vehicles on, so Jack turned his off. If he left the lights on with the engine off, the truck's battery would run down in no time.

Once he got out of the truck, he saw that earlier the scene had been lit even better. Stuck in the dirt next to the road were two burned-out flares. They had to be the work of his deputy, Wayne Schirmer. Wayne was a first-rate deputy, reliable, hardworking, ambitious in the best way, but he was like a kid when it came to flares. Any excuse at all and he'd fire one up. Last summer when they were directing traffic on the last night of the county fair, showing people where they could park so they wouldn't block the way of the exhibitors and livestock owners and carnies who were tearing down and moving out, Wayne took it in his head to indicate where cars were supposed to go by putting up flares. The summer had been dry, and a grass fire started in a field next to the fairgrounds.

Fortunately, a fire truck was at the fair—letting kids clang the bell and start the siren—and the fire was put out immediately. The next day at work, Wayne was so ashamed of what he had done that he offered to resign. Jack told him he wouldn't hear of such a thing, that he couldn't run the department without him. Wayne was so grateful he was on the verge of tears. But he still lit flares every chance he got.

Both Wayne and the highway patrolman walked toward Jack. The driver of the tow truck—Jack couldn't see for sure but figured it was Gordon Van Allen, who owned the Mobil station—was easing himself down the embankment, probably where the car went off. The patrolman was Milt Paugh, a man Jack knew.

Milt was an even bigger man than Jack—close to six feet six and well over two hundred fifty pounds. But where Jack never felt quite comfortable with his size—it seemed like one of God's cruel jokes to make a man who didn't like to be noticed that large— Milt made the most of what he had. He had a big jaw, a big chest, and a big belly, and even in moments of relaxation, he found a way to push one or more of them forward. He was close to sixty years old and probably began with the patrol when more roads in the state were dirt and gravel than blacktop and concrete.

Wayne and Milt had flashlights, and Jack tried to remember if he had one in the truck. He did, but its batteries had almost no juice. He went back to the truck and got the flashlight anyway.

Milt stayed back while Wayne came to Jack's side.

"Kids?" Jack asked Wayne.

"Beg pardon?" Wayne had an annoying habit; when he didn't understand something, he widened his eyes, cupped his hand to his ear, and pretended the problem was his hearing. Or the speaker's voice.

"Kids," Jack repeated, louder. "Teenagers. You know, graduation today."

"Oh." Wayne looked back over his shoulder. "Oh, yeah. One. Junie Moss."

The name was immediately familiar to Jack as most names— adult's or child's, white or Indian—in the county were, but nothing accompanied this name, no face, no reputation, no anecdote. This happened from time to time, just as, occasionally, someone's face might be familiar to Jack, but he could not attach a name, occupation, or history to it.

Nevertheless, Jack felt that if the entire population of Mercer County were gathered in an auditorium with the people on one side and their names written on slips of paper on the other, eventually, he would be able to match them all up.

Junie Moss, Junie Moss. Something would come.

"She was laying up against a tree," Wayne said. "I guess she must have flew out of the car and rolled down the hill and just landed there, but it looked like she curled up on the spot and went to sleep."

With that image—of a dead girl lying against a tree—something suddenly came to Jack. Junie Moss—but to him she was June Moss. A tall, thin girl with wide eyes and hollow cheeks, a serious girl with a perpetual expression of bewilderment and sadness. She and her mother belonged to the First Lutheran Church, the same church Jack and Nora attended. June's father had been killed in the Second World War. And now Mrs. Moss had lost her only child as well.

"Her shoulder was up against the tree," Wayne continued. "Like she was just leaning. But when the ambulance attendant pulled her away, her skin just sort of peeled off. Like her shoulder was glued to the tree."

While he talked, Wayne had been walking Jack farther away from Milt Paugh and the accident scene. Now Jack stopped.

"The ambulance attendant?"

"Vern Wrede, I think. He's new—" Bentrock's hospital was less than three years old. No one was yet completely familiar with all its personnel or procedures.

"The ambulance has already been here?"

"He said her neck was broke. One look and you could see that angle—"

"Jesus, Wayne. How long ago was this?"

"I don't know. Fifteen minutes maybe. When they left."

"You called them first?"

"Shouldn't I? I mean, I didn't know how bad . . ."

Jack was glad the bodies were gone. That was something he'd just as soon not see. As it was, he knew he would carry with him a good long time the mental picture of that young woman's long delicate neck, broken, and her head drooping at an angle not possible in life. He thought of a dead goose, the way its neck simply collapsed upon itself. Hell, he might as well have seen her; the sight couldn't be any worse than what was happening in his imagination. But he didn't want to see the tree; he could look at her shoulder with the skin peeled away, but he didn't want to see any flesh sticking to bark.

"That's all right," Jack told Wayne. "Ambulance first. But how long after—"

"I told Darlene right away." Darlene was the night dispatcher. "But you know how she can be. I'm surprised you didn't drive past the ambulance."

Jack waved his hand. "Doesn't matter." He started to walk back toward Milt Paugh, but Wayne grabbed his arm.

"Jack. I've got to tell you . . ." His voice dropped almost to a whisper, and he looked back over his shoulder again. "It was Leo Bauer."

"Leo?" Jack shook loose of Wayne's grasp.

"The other one. The other fatality. Junie Moss and Leo Bauer."

Wayne's voice had become soft and urgent in the manner that Jack associated with women and gossip. He had an urge to tell Wayne to speak up, to stop acting like a goddamn schoolgirl. That was one impulse. The other was to tell Wayne to shut up, that someone might hear him.

"You said one car?"

Wayne nodded. "That's Leo's white Chevy down there."

"But him too—right? Not just the car?"

"He wasn't so bad I couldn't i.d. him. Leo Bauer."

With this name Jack had no trouble summoning up a picture of the man and a good deal more. Leo Bauer—a man who reminded Jack of himself in certain ways. Leo was about Jack's age, tall, soft-spoken, a veteran. Leo had thinning hair combed straight back over his large head. A serious man. Jack pictured him in the clothes he always wore—black Wellingtons, dress slacks, a short-sleeved

15

white shirt, and a narrow dark tie. This was Leo's uniform. He was the principal of Horace Mann School in Bentrock, grades one through eight, but even off the job—at a barbecue or at a town council meeting or at a high school basketball game—he was likely to be dressed the same way, perhaps without the tie. Oh, yes, Jack could see Leo Bauer clearly. And he could see Leo's wife and son.

Then Jack wondered if he had made a mistake, a miscalculation. Were there two Leo Bauers in Mercer County? Could Wayne be talking about Leo Bauer the wheat farmer and not Leo Bauer the principal? Was there a name that sounded like Leo's that caused the confusion in Jack's mind? Somewhere in the county was there a Lee Bauer? But Wayne had said a white Chevy. Leo Bauer drove a white Chevy. Jack wanted a cigarette now, but he was afraid to light one because his hands might shake. Leo Bauer. Leo Bauer and June Moss, dead on the Sprull ranch curve.

Jack felt that if he moved, just took a few steps, got his legs and feet working, he might get away from this moment he was stuck in and find some perspective that would let him see and understand what was completely baffling. Leo Bauer and June Moss? Leo Bauer and a teenage girl?

But Jack couldn't make his feet work. He still had his flashlight in his hand, and he turned it on, shining its feeble beam straight down at the dirt and gravel he stood on. Something green was improbably sprouting from that rocky, sandy soil—perhaps a dandelion's first struggling efforts. He had an urge to reach down and pluck it, pulling slowly so its roots came out clean.

Wayne whispered again, "Did you hear me, Jack? It was Leo Bauer with her."

Jack moved the flashlight's ray to the toe of his boot. Even in those rings of alternating dim light and shadow you could see how scuffed, worn, and cut the leather was. They had been good boots, more expensive than Jack could afford, but they were badly in need of repair—new soles, stitching in places, a good workout with saddle soap and boot wax. His weekend boots, he called them, but they were so damn comfortable he wore them almost every day. Hardly the kind of footwear an elected official would wear; more like something you'd see on a down-and-out cowboy. At that moment, those worn boots and that miserable excuse for a flashlight seemed to be telling Jack how poor a choice he was for public office. He had to agree. If he could resign right now, he'd do it. He snapped off the flashlight before its beam faded out completely.

"What do you think they were doing out here, Jack," Wayne asked. "Leo and a girl. What do you think?"

"I just got here, Wayne. I haven't the damnedest idea. Let me see what Milt has to say."

Jack walked over to the patrolman, mostly to get away from Wayne's questions.

Milt stuck out his hand. "Jesus, you got one here," Milt said.

Milt's hand was larger than Jack's, and Jack could tell, as he shook it, that Milt deliberately kept his grip soft. That little bit of consideration was enough to make Jack want to give up, to hand it all over to Milt, to say, Here, I can't carry this load; I haven't the strength or the will. And Jack felt so much gratitude and tenderness toward Milt at that moment that he imagined Milt would take over. Like a father who sees that his son is not yet ready to assume his adult responsibilities, Milt would lead Jack back to his truck, get him in behind the wheel, and tell him to go home, get some sleep; he'd clean up this mess. When Jack took his hand away, he jammed it in the back pocket of his Levi's.

"That's what Wayne tells me. How do you see this?"

Milt strode a few paces back down the hill. He shone his flashlight at a spot off the road's shoulder where the stones and gravel were scraped away, leaving a smooth slash of soft dirt behind. "This is where they went off."

"Uh-huh. Skid marks?"

"Not a long track. They just missed it, looks like. Not hard to do."

"No, it's a son of a bitch."

"That it is. And they were moving. You can tell by how much air they took." He directed his flashlight beam up and out over the black empty space. "Then they hit and hit hard. Rolled a few times."

Jack took a step back. "Hard to know what happened."

"That's right," Milt said. "It sure as hell is. Even when there's a witness. Or a survivor. They never can remember quite right. First thing they say is, 'It all happened so fast,' and then you just know you're never going to get the whole story."

"Could have been a deer in the road," Jack suggested. "No matter how hard you think you're not going to swerve, you do. Instinct, or something."

"Sure. A deer. Or a horse or a cow. I've seen that. Or another car might have been coming from the other direction, swung around that curve too wide, and this fellow had to swerve. You knew him, you said?"

"I knew him."

"Sorry. He have a family?"

"Wife and a son."

"Jesus. Don't let them see the car."

Jack squinted into the darkness. "They'll want to."

"They always do. Or think they do. But keep them the hell away, if you can."

"Bad?"

"He didn't tell you?" Milt nodded toward Wayne, who was skidding and sliding down the embankment to where the owner of the tow truck was trying to figure out how to get the wrecked car back up to the highway. "Lot of blood. That young gal was thrown clear, but he rode it out. Hung on like a bastard. Bent the steering wheel like it was wire. Anyway, the side window caved in on him and really sliced him up." Milt made a cutting motion at the side of his neck with the tips of his fingers. "Wouldn't be surprised if he bled to death. What the hell. Accident as bad as this, it's a race to see what kills you first."

"Maybe we should leave the car down there," Jack offered. "Permanently."

"They'd just jam up the goddamn road out here. They got to see it."

"Yeah. Crazy, isn't it?"

"I think sometimes we ought to burn 'em. Light a match and let 'em go. Bodies too maybe. Save everybody a lot of goddamn grief."

"You won't get any argument from me."

Milt turned off his flashlight and put it in his pocket. "I might

18

write up my report tonight. Anything you want me to leave in or out?"

Jack shook his head. "Can't think of anything."

"Give me a call if you do. We can get the thing coordinated."

"Thanks, Milt."

Wayne struggled back up to the road. "Gordon wants to know if it'd be all right to come back tomorrow. He says it's too dark down there to see what he's doing. Plus he's maybe going to need some help getting it up all in one piece."

Jack knew Gordon Van Allen to be an honest man and not one to shirk any job. If Gordon said it was too dark, it was too dark. Yet Jack was tempted to say that he didn't give a damn if the car came up in one piece or a thousand. They could carry it up one hubcap at a time for all he cared. "Tell Gordon that's fine," was what he said. "Tell him there's no hurry."

Wayne edged closer to Jack. "Something else I have to tell you about," Wayne said, his voice dropping down once more as though he were talking to a conspirator. "I found something down there."

4

JACK HAD REFRAINED THIS LONG FROM LIGHTING A CIGARETTE. HE HAD stood out here in the chill night air and taken the news of the accident and heard pronounced the names *June Moss* and *Leo Bauer*. He had listened to the descriptions of their bodies. He had listened to Wayne's and Milt's voices and the murmur of the cars' engines, all hushed in the presence of the miles of silence surrounding them. But now he had to light a cigarette and hope that act would stop Wayne from telling him any more.

It did not.

"Suitcases," Wayne said. "They had suitcases in the car."

Jack held the smoke in his lungs and then blew it out hard. "How many?" he asked, as if the number mattered.

"Three. Two of them was Junie's."

Jack wanted to tell Wayne to stop whispering. What was the point?—anything that was a secret out here tonight would not remain so for long.

"People pack suitcases when they travel," Jack said. If only that statement of a small truth—a fact as hard, common, and ordinary as the pebbles at their feet—could somehow return the night's event to a track of normalcy, to something as tragic and simple as an auto accident that killed two people—two people who had no business being in the same car together and no business being out on this road, not tonight, not any night.

Across the road from Jack and Wayne, Milt Paugh put his car into gear and drove off. He was headed toward town, and if they listened carefully, on a night as still as this, they could probably hear the thrum of that powerful engine all the way to the city limits.

"Jesus Christ, Jack. Leo Bauer and Junie Moss—"

"I know, Wayne. I know." He wanted to tell Wayne never to utter those names again within a minute, an hour, a day of each other. They didn't belong together on the tongue.

"With suitcases. Where were they going, do you think?"

"I told you before, Wayne. I don't have an opinion. It's not like they bought tickets."

"They were running off together, weren't they?"

As bad as that fact was, it was made worse by Wayne saying it out loud.

"Yeah. Yeah, I reckon they were." Jack stared up at the night sky. The stars must have been up there all along, the Big Dipper hanging over the Sprull ranch just as it always did. "Heading west."

And what was *west* going to mean for them? After hundreds of miles of wind-humbled prairie, Great Falls perhaps? Or the mountains beyond and Missoula? Maybe they were going to drive all night and unfurl the whole damn length of highway and not stop until Seattle and the Pacific Ocean. Or perhaps they were planning to cut north as soon as they could and cross into Canada. Not that it mattered. They weren't going to find a direction to travel in or a border to cross where they wouldn't be looked on as father and daughter. Or lecher and young fool. No, if they had a destination in mind, Jack couldn't imagine what it might be. He wished he knew. God damn, what he'd give to know where that might be.

"What will folks say when they find out?" asked Wayne.

"They're going to say what they're going to say. Nothing we can do about it one way or the other."

21

"When you think what this is going to do to those families . . ."

"Why should we? They didn't." Jack put his hand on Wayne's shoulder and shoved him gently. "Now, go get those suitcases. I don't want them sitting in the car all night. And bring up anything else you can find that might be important."

"Do you think they were ever coming back?" Wayne asked as he backed away.

For an instant, Jack misheard Wayne's question, and he thought Wayne had asked, Do you think they *are* ever coming back? and Jack felt he was in the position where he had to answer his young deputy's question about the inexplicable behavior of human beings not only in this life but in the afterlife as well. In that instant, Jack had time to think a prayer: God, yes, let them come back and undo what they have done.

"I don't know what was in their heads," Jack replied.

"But I don't suppose they were packing for a vacation."

A car came down the hill, and Jack was torn between wanting to look at the car, to try to identify it and its driver, and wanting to look away toward the wreck, to see what might be revealed in the quick sweep of headlights.

In the end, he did neither. He pulled his hat low, took a few careful steps down the embankment, and stood still. He kept his gaze lowered, as if he were looking for something in the weedy brush. He had been hit with a sudden sense of shame at being here, at being associated with this accident, these people and what they had done, even in this official, after-the-fact way.

Behind him, Jack heard the car slowing, the engine lugging as the driver geared down to find out all he could about what had happened out on Highway 284.

Don't stop, Jack thought. Don't stop and make me try to explain what happened out here.

The car accelerated and moved on.

Gordon Van Allen had climbed back up to the road and was standing by his tow truck. Jack dug his boot heel into the soft dirt and stepped up onto the blacktop. To Gordon, he said, "I hear it's a mess down there."

"You could say." Gordon was a squat, unsmiling man who had

the most muscular forearms Jack had ever seen. "I'll get 'er up though. I just need a little daylight."

"There's no hurry."

"I wasn't sure how much investigating you needed to do."

"Two people dead . . . That's about all the investigating I feel like doing for now."

Jack offered Gordon a cigarette, and for a moment the two men smoked in silence.

"You saw who was down there?" Jack asked.

"I saw."

Jack hesitated, blew a lungful of smoke toward the sky, then made his awkward request. "I'd just as soon keep it quiet for a while. Until I make sure it's everything that meets the eye."

Gordon tapped the ash from his cigarette in an odd way. He held the cigarette between his thumb and index finger and lightly rubbed the glowing ash with the tip of his little finger. As well as owning and operating the Mobil station, Gordon did a little iron work out of a shop behind his home. His father had been a black-smith back in the days when that occupation was one of the busiest and most necessary on the frontier, and Gordon felt an obligation to keep the trade alive, even though, as he told Jack, its days were numbered.

When Gordon touched his finger to the cigarette's tip, Jack wondered idly if Gordon, because of his work at the forge and in the auto garage, had a tolerance for fire and heat that other men lacked. Certainly he did not seem to feel much; Gordon was the most expressionless man Jack had ever met.

Sparks from his cigarette fell, and Gordon said, "I won't tell Patsy."

Jack knew what Gordon was telling him. Patsy was Gordon's wife, a tall, dark-haired woman originally from Fort Pierre, South Dakota, and the worst gossip in Bentrock. Nora didn't like to be around Patsy because of the way she talked about people. Worse still, Nora suspected that Patsy lied. When the rumor was only a fragment, Patsy was willing to concoct the rest of the story in order to make a complete package of her gossip. Nora also believed that Patsy made her friends according to how much access they

23

could provide into the lives of others. Nora was an important conquest because of Jack; in his position he must know the worst that was to be known about the citizenry. For Patsy, only knowing the wives of the town doctors might be more useful than friendship with Nora.

Jack was embarrassed that Gordon knew this truth about his wife. "Probably just for a few hours," Jack said. "Until I talk to the families. Get things settled down a bit."

Gordon nodded. "You let me know." With the fingers of his free hand, he pinched the end of his cigarette, just above the live ash, and the tiny ember fell to the ground. It was what a person did who wanted to save what was left of a cigarette, but Gordon dropped the butt and stepped on it.

"Once you get the wreck up, if you could find someplace for it that's not in plain view . . ."

"Behind the station okay? Inside the fence?"

"Fine. Sure, that'll be fine. I guess you can tell—this one's got me jumping." As soon as he made that admission, Jack wished he could take it back.

"Yeah, well. You got a hell of a way to make a living."

Jack shrugged. "That's what people always say about the other guy."

"Not tonight they don't. Tonight they're all saying it about you."

As Gordon walked away, Jack called out to him, "Call me when you get it hauled up. Or if you need any help."

Gordon waved without looking back. Once he drove away, only Jack's truck and Wayne's squad car were left, and only Wayne's headlights were still on. They seemed to be growing fainter, and Jack wondered how much life was left in the car's battery. Maybe before he drove away he'd have to swing his truck around and attach the jumper cables to Wayne's car.

Jack turned around and there was Wayne, standing beside the road looking like a stranded traveler. He held one large, scuffed pullman suitcase and two others, one large and one a smaller, overnight size, both a pale bone color and new looking.

"Something kind of funny here," Wayne said.

Jack didn't want to ask. He knew it wasn't really going to be funny.

"This don't seem to be Leo's suitcase."

Shortly after he was first elected, Jack came home from work one evening, and Nora gently brought Angela before him. "Go ahead," Nora prompted. "Ask your father what you asked me." Angela, who usually had no trouble asking anything, turned suddenly shy. "Ask him," Nora urged again. "Ask your father." Angela's question was so softly, hurriedly asked that Jack barely heard her. "What if someone shoots at you?" Angela wanted to know. Jack's first impulse was to joke. "Why, I'd duck!" he said. He pretended to feint left, then right. "If I see a bullet coming at me, I'll move the other way." When he saw Angela's jaw was set in seriousness, Jack stopped joking. "It's not going to happen, honey," he told her. "Not here. People don't shoot at each other here. In the movies. But not here." His answer reassured her, but shortly after that conversation he had a dream that he had never had before. People were shooting at him, or at least in his general vicinity. He was moving through a building of some sort, full of brightly lit halls and corridors of various lengths and widths. Somewhere guns were being fired, and though bullets were not exactly whizzing by him, he knew he was in danger of being shot if he did not get out of the building. But he couldn't find a door anywhere! Jack wasn't sure if it was his years in the service or Angela's question that breathed the dream to life. For most of his tour of duty he was stationed in Texas, shipping out to the Philippines only after the island was retaken by Allied forces. And while Jack never did go into combat, he knew that it was a possibility at any time. Guns were firing, and with one order he could become a target. Over there it wasn't a question of ducking but of waiting. When the war ended, it was only days before Jack's unit was scheduled to ship out. They were to have been part of the Japanese invasion force. In the dream, he escaped without knowing exactly how. At one moment he was groping along a wall—a wall that wasn't really a wall but something that seemed to have its own life, like a tree, but with a wall's smooth texture and dimension—

and then he was outside, standing free and clear where even the air and light were benevolent. Safe, he was safe, with no reason to duck or fear.

Jack had the same feeling when Wayne announced that one of the suitcases was not Leo's. He felt that he was, at least for the moment, miraculously out of the line of fire.

5

"LOOK HERE." WAYNE SET THE SUITCASES DOWN AND TRAINED HIS flashlight on top of one of them. "What it says."

Jack bent down and read the luggage tag. In three carefully printed lines it said, "Richard Bauer, 611 Fourth Street, Bentrock, Montana."

"Rick," Wayne said. "He's Junie's age, ain't he?"

Jack had to think. Rick Bauer was the son of Leo and Vivien Bauer, their only child. Yes, Rick would have graduated today. He could even have been the valedictorian. Then Jack remembered: That honor went to Gus and Mary Camp's girl, but Rick must have been close, bright as he was.

"That's right," Jack answered.

"What the hell's Rick's suitcase doing out here?"

"You keep asking me questions, Wayne, and I don't have any answers."

"But maybe this isn't what it looks like. Rick's suitcase and all."

"What does it look like, Wayne? Suppose you tell me." He didn't mean to sound harsh.

The air was still and that was rare. The wind blew almost continually—and blew hard—in their corner of Montana. Years ago, when Jack's father was trying to sell his hardware store, one prospective buyer, a one-eyed man from the Pacific Northwest, pulled out because he couldn't tolerate the weather. "I can take the cold," he said. "And the snow. And the heat. And the dry. But not that wind. Jesus, it just never stops. You must be the goddamn wind capital of the world. You could put up a sign on the outskirts of town to that effect. But you probably couldn't keep the damn thing standing."

Another outsider had an odd way of speaking about the wind. For a while, the owners of the Coffee Cup cafe employed a Mexican as a short-order cook and sometime counterman. Everyone referred to him as Pedro, and though Jack doubted that was his name, he called him that as well. Pedro didn't seem to mind. One day while Jack sat at the counter smoking and drinking coffee, Pedro used a phrase Jack had never heard before. "The winds are strong today," Pedro said. Now, Jack was accustomed to hearing the wind described as strong—or as cold, hot, icy, dry, and damn near everything in between—but no one he knew ever referred to the wind in the plural. It was always *the* wind, whether it came cold and hard out of the north or warm and mild off the eastern slope of the Rockies or hot and dry out of the south. Jack tried out Pedro's notion of the many winds, but he couldn't adjust to it. To him it was one wind, and it was generally of one mind: making life miserable for anyone in its way. If he ever left Montana, it would be to escape the wind.

Tonight, however, the wind was calm, and those tall weeds and grasses in the ditch that were usually bent low were standing upright, and those new cottonwood leaves that would usually be flipping up their whitish undersides were hanging motionless.

And tonight, from the moment he found out who was killed out here, Jack had felt that Montana wind had been blowing inside his head, gusting and whirling with questions and explanations about what Leo and June were doing out here. And only one explanation had caught and stuck: they were running off together. It had to be. But now this suitcase. Rick's . . . Let Wayne say it, and maybe what would come out of his mouth would be a possibility that Jack had overlooked. And maybe it would just be more wind.

Wayne took a step back from the suitcases. "It ain't really for me to say."

"It's just us out here. This might be your last chance to say it."

"Leo and Junie . . . God damn. If you could've seen them. But Leo can't do something like this. I mean, he couldn't."

Wayne's first choice of words struck Jack as exactly right—Leo *can't* do this. This was prohibited behavior, as widely known as any law of the land. And for a man of Leo's age and status, June Moss was off-limits—and that was as clear as the signs that farmers and ranchers nailed on fence posts: No Trespassing.

"Something like what, Wayne?"

"Like taking off with a young girl. How much older is he than June?"

There. He'd heard it said. Perhaps that mind-wind would stop swirling. "Old enough to be her father, that's sure. If she's Rick's age."

"Rick. Now, that'd make some sense. And this suitcase . . ."

Wayne fell silent and Jack waited. If the wind were blowing, it would fill in that silent space, moving through the cottonwood leaves with a sound like a hundred decks of cards being shuffled. The grass on the other hand would bend without protest.

"Are you sure that was Leo? Milt said the accident—"

"Hell, Jack—how can you ask me that? That was Leo, all right. Don't you think I looked at that face long enough, hoping it wasn't his?"

Jack held up his hands. "I'm sorry. Okay."

"But what are they doing with Rick's suitcase? Where's he, you suppose?"

Jack thought for a moment. "Any chance you missed someone? If June got thrown out . . ."

"Nope. It's dark down there, but I gave it a good going over."

"Could someone have gotten out? Walked away maybe."

"And you wouldn't ask that either if you'd seen the car."

Jack nodded. "All right, Wayne. I'm not doubting you. I'm just thinking out loud here."

"Death car. That's what folks will call it. And that'll be right. It sure as shit looks like death."

Jack looked up again at the night sky. He wished he knew the constellations, something beyond the Big Dipper and the North Star. His mother knew all those starry configurations, and when he was a boy she tried to teach him. They would stand outside on summer nights, and she would point up at the sky, trying to help him see the rams and horses and soldiers and women and children and swords and shields. Jack would line himself up behind his mother's pointing finger, and while she held him close, she would slowly connect star to star, explaining what they shaped. To the frustration of both of them, however, he could never see what she sketched in the heavens. "You have to use your imagination," she would say. But all he could see were stars, stars, and more stars, some faint, some bright, some clustered, some spread out. If they had simply been flung into the sky like a handful of gravel, they would have no more pattern than they had to his youthful sight.

Jack's mother died when he was overseas, and on the night of the day he got the news, he went out and stared up at the Pacific sky, once again searching in vain for his mother's constellations. Another soldier approached him and asked what he was doing. "Just looking at the stars," Jack said. Although the soldier was a friend, Jack couldn't quite bring himself to say his mother had just died. "They're not the same here, you know," his friend said. "This far south they're all turned around. The constellations, I mean. They've got their own down here." Jack wasn't sure if he believed him; nevertheless, his remark was enough to keep Jack from looking any further. He went back to his tent to compose a letter of condolence to his father. He knew this was a letter he would never complete, but the effort of trying to make words obey, to get them to line up in sentences, would keep him from tears. The work was hard. It was nothing like looking at the stars.

Yet in the years since his mother's death, Jack felt that he had finally reached the stage where he would be able to recognize the constellations, if only someone would point them out to him once again. He kept meaning to check books out of the library that he could use on his own, but he never got around to it.

He swung his vision back to his deputy, who was waiting as patiently as any star.

"Throw those suitcases in the back of the truck, would you, Wayne? I'll take care of them."

"What are you going to do?"

"It's not exactly the right order, but first thing I'm going to do is talk to Rick. I've got to find out if he's got any light to shed. That suitcase has got me thinking."

"Thinking what?"

"Oh, not any one thing in particular. Just chasing thoughts around. But I don't want to be telling people one thing when they know it's another."

Wayne picked up the suitcases and obediently started for the truck. "Wait up," Jack said. He took the largest suitcase from Wayne, and the two of them walked together. "Where's the big party tonight?" Jack asked. Wayne was the oldest of six children, he still lived at home, and he had a younger brother and sister in high school. That was another reason Wayne was a valuable deputy: he often knew—or could find out—what was going on with the younger crowd.

"Concannon's? Does that sound right?"

Darl Concannon, who owned the Cattleman's National Bank in Bentrock, had a big, new house on the northern outskirts of town and a loud, wild daughter who would have graduated that afternoon.

"Darl and Mrs. going to be home?"

"I believe so."

"Not that it makes a whole lot of difference."

In Jack's opinion, the Concannons indulged and spoiled their children, and he doubted they would make any effort to supervise their daughter's party. Hell, he wouldn't be surprised to learn that they bought the beer. He let himself savor, just for a moment, how good it would feel to arrest Darl Concannon on a charge of furnishing alcohol to a minor. The thought would have to do. Short of a felony offense, a man like Darl Concannon was immune from arrest. No one ever told Jack this, but no one ever told him

31

on which side his badge was supposed to be pinned either. In this job, some things you just knew.

"Before you head out," Wayne said, "can I ask you one more thing?"

"Fire away."

"When you bring your own vehicle, like tonight, when it's official business, do you turn in a voucher for mileage? I mean, I know it's only a few miles out here, but what if you were going further?"

"I never have, Wayne, no."

"But you could though, couldn't you? You'd be within your rights and all."

"I reckon."

"I never have either."

"And you figure the county owes you?"

"Maybe. Not much."

"You do what you think is right, Wayne. Don't go by me."

"But you'd sign it? The form says a supervisor or some such has to sign."

Jack looked once more at the stars. Off to the right, the darkness at the horizon seemed to be developing itself in folds and wrinkles. Northern lights? A trace? Now, there was something he could identify in the night sky. And Wayne had finally asked a question Jack could answer.

"Hell, you know I'll sign anything you stick in front of me."

6

JACK DID NOT LIKE LEO BAUER. ONLY IN THE PRIVACY OF HIS TRUCK could Jack admit that. He knew he was supposed to have liked Leo. No—more than that. He should have *admired* Leo. Leo was a respected educator, a deacon in the church, a member of the school board and the town council. He was chairman of last year's March of Dimes campaign, and in the past he had been an officer in a statewide organization that oversaw high school athletics. Jack couldn't think offhand of a Bentrock civic or charitable group that Leo wasn't connected with one way or the other.

This activity went all the way back to high school. When Jack was a sophomore, Leo, who was two years older, had been president of the senior class, captain of the debate club, head of student council, first chair trumpet in the band, valedictorian, winner of a fistful of scholarships. Only in sports did Leo not excel. He was on the football and basketball teams, and he lettered in track, but these accomplishments were more the result of persistence and hard work than of talent or skill. The male population at Bentrock High was not large. If you were willing to try out for a team, attend the practices, and do the work, the coach would probably find a place for you. Especially if you were Leo Bauer. Jack remembered Leo on the basketball court. He was uncoordinated as hell, he had an ungainly two-handed set shot that wouldn't go in the basket, but he knew how to get in the way. He shuffled his big feet, waved his arms, and stuck to his opponent like a burr. Of course, Jack made teams because of his size as well, and he didn't have much more ability than Leo.

Leo's successes were all the more remarkable because of the start he got in life. Leo was raised on a small farm on the county's eastern edge. The land was not good to begin with, but for all the luck the Bauers had, the soil may as well have been salted. Their years of poor crops alternated with outright failures. They must have held the county record for harvests that were burned out or hailed out. But they stayed with it, even when they barely got back enough to put food on the table and keep clothes on their backs. There were four Bauer boys—Leo was the second to youngest—and their willingness to work hard helped keep the place running. "Poor but proud" was the phrase Jack heard his mother once use in reference to the Bauer family. "Maybe if he wasn't so goddamn proud, he'd be willing to ask someone to help him get his windmill working," was his father's response.

Then the Bauer family luck turned from hard to stone.

The oldest Bauer boys got a day off from chores, and they decided to go on a fishing trip with friends. They drove to North Dakota, rented boats, and set their oars into the Little Missouri River. It was a warm, early spring after a deep winter, and the river was close to flood stage. The Bauers tipped their boat, and the current carried them under and away. Neither could swim, but in that swift water, it probably wouldn't have made a difference.

After her sons were buried, Mrs. Bauer took the baby and went back out to Wolf Point to stay with her parents and grieve. She didn't return for two years. Leo, suddenly the oldest son and saddled with all the responsibilities of that position, had to stay behind and work the farm with his taciturn, sorrowful father. Only a boy himself, Leo bore that weight, though it rode him hard.

Because he didn't break, was he made stronger? Did any trial, any challenge, seem easy after those years? Even as a teenager,

Leo was serious, determined, forward-looking. Summer and after-school work and scholarships paid for two degrees at Montana State down in Bozeman, and when he returned to Bentrock to start working in the schools, it was with a new bride—Vivien Wallace, from Salt Lake City. Was she Mormon? everyone wanted to know. They sighed with relief when they learned she was not, for once one Mormon came to your town, others were sure to follow. Vivien was quiet and pretty and Presbyterian, and the town was as glad to have her as it was to welcome Leo back.

So why didn't Jack like this man to whom so many pointed in admiration? For some reason, Jack came to regard Leo as a rival, although as far as Jack knew they had never competed for any-thing—not a girl, not a place on a team, not a school or political office. Perhaps it was simply because Leo was so damn good, a constant reproof to Jack of all he hadn't measured up to. Worst of all, Leo seemed aware of his superiority, though he also seemed to know he shouldn't flaunt it. Leo simply had a look, tight-lipped and faintly scowling, that said he was judging you. And finding you wanting.

As far back as Jack could remember, Leo had that air. Once, when Jack was twelve or thirteen, he was hanging around the train yard with a few friends and older boys, Leo among them. Someone got the idea of climbing inside an empty boxcar and riding to the next stop on the line. From there, they would either hop another freight or hitchhike back to Bentrock. Jack had misgivings; what if the train didn't stop or slow down for hundreds of miles? What if it were days before they could get a train coming back? What if they got kicked off the train far from the highway? Nevertheless, he planned to climb in the boxcar if his friends did.

Leo stepped up to the boxcar's open doors and hoisted himself up so he could see into all four corners. When he dropped down, he said, "You shouldn't do it." Not *we* shouldn't, but *you* as though Leo not only knew he wasn't one of the group but also that they wouldn't listen to him. And they didn't. Who was the first to shoulder past Leo and climb into the boxcar—Daniel Sem? Jack was the last to get in, and he looked around carefully, trying to figure out if Leo actually saw anything to make him advise against the venture. Nothing was in the car but his friends, a little loose straw in the corners, and a charred spot in the middle of the floor where it looked as though someone had once built a fire. Leo walked away, but no one yelled after him, calling him a pussy or chicken shit. The train bumped and lurched forward and backward a few times before it really began to roll.

Leo had been right. Once the train picked up speed, it never slowed down enough for them to jump off. With a few whistles, the train barreled through Schooler and Runbuck and Milk Butte, and the boys began to wonder, first aloud and then silently, if the train would stop before Cut Bank, more than halfway across the state. The boxcar's doors remained open, and the hot wind rushed in, mingled with the smell of diesel fuel and uncut alfalfa. At first Jack stood by the door and looked out on the blank undulating Montana prairie they were rolling over, but when they shot by a crossing where a car waited for them to pass—an old man and old woman with a small boy between them were sitting on the front seat—Jack went back to a corner and sat down on the straw. He had never been that far from home without his father and mother. Had he been alone, he might have cried at that moment, being carried farther and farther from his home against his will.

But the train did slow down at last, just after dark, in the little town of Granville, and a fortunate stop it was. The older brother of one of the boys, Lyle Kellner, was part of a crew that summer that set up prefabricated outbuildings on ranches and farms in the region, and they were working out of Granville. Lyle found his brother at the hotel—tired, dirty, and well on the way to drunk— and Lyle's brother agreed to take them back to Bentrock, although he was none too happy about it. During the long drive back he seldom stopped cursing the boys, berating them for their foolishness and their selfishness.

It was worse when Jack came home. It was close to two A.M., and the lights were on, so he knew his parents were waiting up. He swallowed hard and walked through the front door, but he didn't get far. Jack's father had been standing behind the front door, and he kicked Jack so hard in the ass Jack was almost knocked over. His father kept kicking, driving Jack toward the kitchen, so he could "see the woman you scared the hell out of." The look of his mother's tear-reddened eyes was worse than any number of kicks in the ass, though Jack's father's boot once struck him so squarely on the tailbone he felt it for months. Leo Bauer, Jack kept thinking, Leo Bauer is home in his bed.

Then there was the time only a few years back when Jack, Leo, and a few others decided, after a town council meeting, to stop in at Don Hogan's Flying Liberty Saloon for a drink. As soon as they got out of the car, Leo asked, "Does this place have a back door?"

"Sure," Dick Earling said, "right down that alley. Behind Wester's Jewelry."

Leo separated himself from the group and headed in that direction. "Where you going?" Dick asked.

"I don't think it would look too good for a school principal to be going into a saloon, do you?"

Like that day at the train yard when Leo walked away from the group, no one laughed or mocked him. You hypocrite, Jack thought; you're willing to take a drink—you just don't want anyone respectable to see you doing it. Yet at the same time Jack felt chastened by Leo. Perhaps the sheriff shouldn't be seen going into a saloon either?

As Jack drove away from the accident site, he felt the old Leo Bauer resentment leaking out, as if a patch, where he had tried to seal up his jealousy, had failed. Maybe it would serve Leo—that self-righteous bastard—right. Let his memory get mud-stained, which was exactly what would happen when the town found out he died in the company of a teenage girl. And maybe it would serve the town right too for believing that Leo Bauer was as noble as he pretended to be. Leo never strutted, but you could tell he was a proud man. Proud? Again, alone in his truck, Jack would use a different word. Leo was an arrogant man, and now it was up to Jack how low Leo would be brought in death.

Jack turned on the truck's radio, and after its tubes gasped and popped for a few seconds, music came forth so clearly it startled him at first and he turned the volume down. Angela was always trying to tune in one of the rock-and-roll stations that could occasionally be pulled in at night. One was in eastern North Dakota—

Jamestown?—and the other was all the way down in Oklahoma City. Most of the time nothing came in but static; you certainly couldn't make out the words of the song, and even its rhythm wasn't much more than louder or softer crackling and hissing. But that was close enough for Angela. She loved the music and could identify a song and its performer when only the smallest fragment, a guitar's chord or a singer's wordless wail, jumped free from all that interference. But once Angela tuned one of the stations in, she didn't want Jack to play with the dial, even if weeks might pass before she was in the truck again. "Just leave it here, Dad. No matter how bad it comes in, just leave it. It might be there the next time I turn it on."

Tonight, it was there. Jack was tempted to try to find a ballgame. On a clear night like this one, he might luck into a White Sox game coming in on WGN. He could sometimes find a Cincinnati Reds' game, though that was more likely in late summer. And on a rare night, he could pull in fragments of a Tigers' game. But now, when he reached for the radio, he heard Angela's voice. "Just leave it here, Dad."

And there was no question, this was her music. Those electric guitars whose sound reminded him of wires whining in the wind, the drumbeat with a rhythm so steady it seemed timed to the truck's rolling wheels. And that singer—you wouldn't think a man would want to sing that high even if he could. But Jack obeyed Angela, just as surely as if she were in the seat next to him, batting his hand away.

The next song came on, and it was one Jack recognized. He couldn't remember the name of the brothers who sang it, but Angela had the record and played it over and over.

Bye-bye love . . .

The local music store, Frieger and Son, who had for years sold pianos and sheet music and rented band instruments to the schools, had only recently started carrying the records the kids wanted to buy—they didn't have to go to Williston to buy their music any more. Angela already had a stack of them so high Jack sometimes wondered—it was his sheriff's mind—where she got the money for them.

Hello loneliness . . .

The young people who were driving around tonight were listening to this same song. Loneliness? What the hell did they know about loneliness? Jack sometimes saw couples sitting so close together it looked as though they were both driving. More than once he had been tempted to pull them over and tell them it wasn't safe to drive that way. But he never did, perhaps because he couldn't be certain if it was genuine concern that motivated him or jealousy. More than once, Jack had noticed a young couple riding around, and a thought, as sharp as a pain, hit him. What must it be like to be one of those teenagers, one hand resting lightly on the steering wheel, the other arm around a pretty girl in a soft pink sweater?

Now another thought pinched him hard.

Tonight that was Leo Bauer. Tonight Leo Bauer had a pretty young girl in the seat next to him.

Were they together, really together, the two of them? Was it possible? June Moss sitting tight next to Leo, her thigh pressed against his, his arm around her, pulling her close until the smell of her hair spray filled his nostrils. Maybe there was more. Maybe June reached her hand over and slid it between Leo's legs, and Leo, Leo couldn't stand it: the pleasure was so intense it crowded out all the pain and duty and hard work of his whole life, so that nothing, nothing he had or ever would have, could match having this girl by his side, her hand there, *there*, the music coming in so clear tonight—

There goes my baby . . .

—and Leo just gave it all to the moment, he threw his head back, Jesus, sweet Jesus Christ, he gave it all, and there was the curve—how could he not have seen it coming? he had driven this road a thousand times, but never with June beside him, much less

39

with her hands all over him, pressed into his crotch, or working in between the buttons of his shirt—and by the time Leo knew he had to slow down or turn the wheel, it was too late to do either, and the instant the car hit, something got jarred loose—a tube or a wire—and the radio snapped off. . . .

All he had to do, Jack thought, would be to drive back to the accident, scramble his way down to Leo's car, and shine his light in on the radio dial. If it was tuned to the same station Jack was listening to now, he'd know. He wouldn't have to talk to Leo's boy, he'd know it was Leo, Leo and June.

Jack kept driving in the direction of the party.

7

DARL AND ELOISE CONCANNON LIVED ON TOP OF A HILL OUT IN THE Harlan Hill section (named after Boyd Harlan, the developer) where, less than five years before, there had been no houses. In fact, Jack remembered hunting for arrowheads and shooting gophers and jackrabbits out there when he was a kid. Rumor had it that the area had once been the site of an Indian village, a tribe like the Mandan or Hidatsa that lived in earthen mounds. Jack's uncle, who knew about such things, doubted that was so; he said it wasn't likely that those tribes, mound-dwellers, would have lived so far north.

Now that was the exclusive section of town, the area where a few wealthy people tried to get themselves a hilltop where they could see twenty or thirty miles in any direction. Back in Bentrock, the houses were built close together, in spite of all the open prairie on each side of town, as if it were important to be close to your neighbors, for whatever help or heat or shelter from the wind they might offer. Jack's and Nora's house was a single-story wood-frame affair on Cheyenne Avenue. They had three small bedrooms, a driveway that wasn't paved, and a garage that wasn't attached to the house. The house wasn't expensive—Jack got a break on the down payment because he was a vet—but there were months when it was touch and go making payments. How did those people out on Harlan Hills do it? Jack often wondered; where did they find the money in dirt-poor Mercer County to live that much better than anyone else? Hell, Darl Concannon was only a few years older than Jack, yet he was already on his third house, each one finer than the one before. Could there be that much money in banking? Could you build yourself a house as fine as Darl's by refusing loans to people who wanted to buy a home of their own— or by foreclosing on those who fell behind? Thank you all the same, but Jack would take his little cracker box any day; he'd have trouble looking in the mirror if he owned a house like Darl's.

Cars lined the hill leading up to the Concannons. More cars, it seemed to Jack, than there were graduates of Bentrock High. When the hell had it come to pass that all these kids had cars? He recognized many of them as the cars of parents—the Collinses' Hudson, Kleists' Studebaker—but still these kids had access. When Jack was in high school, there were kids who came in on horseback or rode in on a horse-drawn wagon. It was the lucky kid who had a bicycle or a short distance to walk.

There he went again. Soon the words would pop out—"Kids nowadays . . ." If Angela could hear his thoughts, she'd say what she'd said to him before: "Dad, when you guys were kids, weren't you . . . *kids?*" They were, of course they were. They smoked, they drank, they smarted off, they screwed up, they got in trouble. But no girl from his class, or from any other Bentrock graduating class, got killed in a car accident with an older man.

Jack was looking for Rick Bauer's car. He thought the boy drove a Plymouth, 1948 or 1949 maybe, but he couldn't be sure. He didn't see anything that looked like it, but that didn't mean anything. So many kids and cars. . . .

He knew he could just pull into the Concannons' driveway and march up to the front door, but he would likely be seen and a commotion would start before he even knocked on the door. Jack parked alongside the road with the other cars. He got out and walked up toward the house.

It looked as though every light in the Concannon house was turned on and every curtain was pulled back. Each window shone with its bright rectangle of light, two floodlights stared down at the driveway, porch lights, yard lights in back—Jack almost expected the house to give off heat as he got closer.

Before he got to the driveway, he changed his mind. There was a coulee behind the Concannons', and he could leave the road, cut through the field, drop down into the coulee, and come up on the backyard without being seen. He wanted to see what kind of party the Concannons were hosting, and maybe he could get Rick Bauer away without interrupting the entire proceedings.

He hadn't taken many steps into the field before the high, dew-wet grass soaked his jeans through up to the knee. The grass soon thinned, however, and he was picking his way through rock and what must have been sagebrush, judging from the odor that rose to his nostrils. The smell reminded him of the dressing his mother once made for Thanksgiving dinner. The dressing he could not make himself eat. "What's that?" he asked, wrinkling his nose. "That's sage," his mother answered. "A seasoning." "And too damn much of it," his father added. "It's what the recipe calls for," his mother replied. His father looked around the table. "It's not what we call for."

Then Jack was walking across alkali, or so he guessed from the whitish glow the ground gave off. A night with nothing but stars overhead—where did the earth find any light to reflect? But there it was: he could not only see where to put his foot, but, looking back, see where his foot had been, a dark print as if he were tracking mud.

Jack's heel came down on something hard that rolled under his foot. His ankle twisted but not dangerously so. He reached down to find what he stepped on. A golf ball. Did Darl Concannon hit golf balls from his yard down into his coulee? Must be nice, to hit a golf ball without caring about retrieving it. Although he didn't golf, Jack put the ball in his pocket.

Jack sensed something in the darkness before him but ducked an instant too late. A branch. Twigs raked his face and one caught him in the eye. Tears ran down one side of his face. His hat fell to the ground, but he couldn't reach for it until his vision cleared. He tried to move forward and stepped in muck that threatened to pull his boot off. What the hell are you doing out here? he asked himself. Playing detective? Why won't you walk into all that light up there and simply ask for Rick Bauer? No, not you. You'd rather sneak around out here, hoping you can see or hear something not meant for your eyes or ears. And to that end, Jack began to hike up the hill toward the sounds of the party.

As he neared the edge of the yard and the brick retaining wall that Darl had built to separate his groomed lawn from the dry weeds and brush growing up the hillside, Jack heard breathing. Not ordinary breathing, but amplified, like someone who had just run himself out of breath. No, it was more pronounced than that. Someone joking—imitating a panting dog?

Five or six kids stood on the lawn out of reach of the yard lights. They weren't more than twenty feet from Jack, and crouching behind the wall, he could see and hear them clearly. All but one of them held a can of beer.

It looked as though the heavy breathing was coming from a boy squatting in the middle of the group.

Someone—could it have been Billy Lindy?—said, "Okay, remember: When you stand up, you have to do it fast, really fast, and blow on your thumb as hard as you can."

In between his panting breaths, the boy said, "I know, I know."

The boy stood, and Billy said, "Get behind him! Catch him!"

He blew on his thumb—Jack saw his cheeks puff out—and he fell backward as swiftly as if he had been shot. Two of his friends had positioned themselves in time, and the fainting boy fell into their arms. They lowered him to the ground.

Once the fainter was on the grass, he began to twitch and convulse as if he were having a seizure.

Or dying. Jack had never been in battle during the war, but he had seen someone die. He and a few other soldiers had been building an observation tower, a wooden structure from which officers could supervise drills and formations. A two-by-four fell from the top of the tower and hit an Oklahoma boy square in the back of the head. He died on the spot, but before he did, his body twitched and spasmed as if he were trying to burrow himself into the sand.

Jack was ready to reveal his position, to jump up from behind the wall and shout at those kids to help the convulsing boy. But before he could, Billy Lindy started doing a little dance, hopping up and down and saying, "See! See! God *damn*—I told you! He does it every time!"

"Make him stop," one of the girls said.

"He'll come around," Billy answered.

"I can't stand to see him do that," she said.

"Jesus. Okay." Billy bent over and slapped the fainter across the face. "Hey—*hey!*"

His twitching stopped. He lay perfectly still.

"Is he okay?" the girl asked.

Jack stood, prepared to step over the wall.

"He's all right," said Billy.

"Are you?" asked the girl.

The boy sat up slowly. "How long was I out?"

"A couple seconds."

"No shit? It felt like an hour. I think I had a dream even."

A new voice asked, "What did you dream?"

The boy on the ground bent over and rubbed his legs. "I can't remember already."

Billy asked, "Who's going next?"

"You mean who wants to twitch around like a fucking spastic?" the girl replied.

She was smoking a cigarette, and she inhaled, took a sip of beer, then exhaled.

"Not everybody does," Billy said. "Not every time."

Someone else said, "I said I was going to get shit-faced tonight. I didn't mean that way."

"Let's get to it."

Billy raised his beer can to his lips and drank until the can was empty. He crushed and bent the can in both hands, then threw it out over the coulee. Jack heard the *ding* as it bounced down the slope. That seemed to be the signal for them to move off toward the house, all except the boy sitting on the grass.

4 5

Jack stepped over the wall and walked across the lawn. Every few feet the grass felt ridged and uneven, as if he were stepping on hardened seams. Sod. Darl Concannon didn't seed his new lawn; he had sod trucked in and unrolled. He couldn't wait for grass to grow.

The boy looked up at Jack's approach, and as soon as he did, Jack recognized him. That perfect circle of a face—he was a Hogue. Every member of that family, from both father and mother on down, had a head as round as a basketball.

"Douglas?" Jack said.

"Sheriff Nevelsen?"

"Are you all right, Douglas?"

"I'm pretty sure."

"Can you get up?"

"I thought maybe I'd just sit here a spell."

"You need some help?"

Douglas reached up, and when Jack gripped the boy's hand he was surprised at how small and delicate it felt. He pulled and Douglas bounced to his feet.

"I ain't been drinking."

"No?"

"I tried fainting once when I'd had a few, and I got sick when I came to. Puked all over everything."

"You were outside?"

"Yessir. I don't like to faint inside. I will, but they got to clear the furniture out of the way. Ain't no law against it, is there? Fainting?"

"None that I know of."

Jack couldn't be sure if the boy was staring at him in defiance or if he was still having trouble focusing.

"Douglas, is Rick Bauer at this party?"

"Rick?"

"Rick Bauer. Yes."

"I believe he is. He was anyway."

"I tell you what, Douglas. You can do me a favor. You can go in there and try to find Rick Bauer and very quietly tell him I'd like to talk to him outside. Tell him to meet me at the bottom of the driveway. And don't make a big deal. I don't want to ruin the party for everyone."

"Just for Rick, huh?"

"Just tell him to meet me."

"What if he ain't in there?"

"Then you come out and tell me."

As Douglas walked away, Jack noticed the boy's gait was off. One foot came up higher off the ground, as if one side of him was trying to hop while the other side wouldn't allow it. Had the fainting something to do with this or had Douglas always limped?

"Douglas?"

The boy stopped and looked back at the sheriff. "Yeah?"

"Did you graduate today?"

"Next year. If I make it."

"Stop passing out and you probably will."

8

FAINTING. FOR CHRIST'S SAKE. JACK STOOD AT THE BOTTOM OF THE
driveway and tried to make sense of what he had just seen. He
could barely remember his own high school graduation, but he
knew no one was fainting then. Not on purpose anyway. And
none of the girls was smoking or drinking beer out of a can. Or
saying "fuck."

What had he done that night? He knew he went to Nora's, to
her family's farm. Nora was the first high school graduate in the
family, and her folks did it up big. Aunts and uncles and cousins
came from as far away as Great Falls. Food—God almighty, did
they have food! Makeshift tables were set up in the yard, and they
could barely contain all the food those people brought. When they
weren't eating, they were congratulating Nora or Jack for their
achievement. Nora deserved it. She was a top student, but Jack had
just scraped by. She wore a white dress that day, and when she
blushed—and she couldn't stop blushing—the color moved upward
from her chest and throat to her face. She looked as though she
had broken out in a rash.

Jack left early, giving as his excuse the fact that he was scheduled to begin working the next day with a construction crew that was setting up oil rigs in their part of the state. Graduate on Sunday and go to work on Monday—and feel damn lucky to have a job at that.

But Jack didn't go right home after he left Nora's. At first he simply drove around, up one county road and down another, heading no place in particular but just driving, smoking, and drinking the quart of warm beer he had hidden under the front seat.

Eventually he found himself back in Bentrock, but he kept driving, going up and down the streets, starting systematically at the north end of town and moving south. He remembered going past his own house. No lights were on. He was a high school graduate. His parents no longer waited up for him. Hell, they hadn't for years.

What was he looking for that night? At the time he couldn't have said, but now, standing at the bottom of Darl Concannon's driveway, he thought he knew. On the night of his high school graduation he was looking for a girl who drank beer and said "fuck," and not some hard-drinking slattern who hung around the Northern Pacific Hotel or somebody's foul-mouthed mother who liked to shock her son's friends or some back-alley barfly who panhandled anyone who passed for the price of a drink. No, he was looking that night for someone who couldn't be found, at least not in Bentrock, someone young and cool and pretty who wouldn't wrinkle her nose when a beer was opened or blush when the word "fuck" was uttered, a girl who didn't act as though sex was only for a boy's pleasure, to be avoided if at all possible and to be borne stoically if not.

He was through with school, but he should have kept up with his lessons. That night could have taught him something. He left the side of the girl he said he loved, the young woman he would marry, to aimlessly look for a girl who didn't exist.

Had June Moss been such a girl?

Was that house up there full of such girls? Or was there only one?

Jack still drove the county roads just the way he drove them on his graduation night. Now, of course, it was his job; he was on patrol. But the fact of the matter was, he usually drove without direction or purpose. Asphalt hummed under his tires or gravel clattered up against the undercarriage, but Jack just drove, piling up the miles but ending every night exactly where he began. On some nights Mercer County could feel like a giant cage; he was free to range as far as he liked as long as he stayed within its boundaries. And on nights when the moon was full and the highway's white lines glowed far into the distance and the station on the radio came in as if there were no such thing as distance . . . maybe on those nights he was prepared to understand Leo Bauer and June Moss.

A slouching figure came down the driveway, his shoe soles slapping against the concrete as he tried to walk slower than the driveway's slope wanted him to move. The night air was cool enough for Jack to see his breath, but Rick Bauer was not wearing a jacket. His white T-shirt glowed in the dark.

"Howdy. Rick?"

"I didn't think you were really out here. I thought it was a joke. But Douglas said I better go. . . ."

"It's no joke."

"What's wrong?"

Scarcely a day went by when Jack didn't wonder if there was a way he could alter his job so occasionally he could bring something other than bad news. He'd give anything if he could walk up to someone, or let them know he wanted to see them, and not automatically stir up worry or dread or suspicion or guilt or fear. But again and again he saw that look when he approached, even in the eyes of the innocent. My God, was no one's conscience clear?

"Let's go sit in my truck."

"I'm not cold."

Jack knew what Rick was thinking: If I don't get in the truck, if I stay out here, I won't have to hear what he wants to tell me. If I can stay out here in the open air . . .

"Well, I am. And I'm getting colder seeing you out here with those bare arms."

Jack purposely took the lead as they walked down the hill. It was a technique he had developed to help put people at ease. If he was walking ahead, then he wasn't taking them in custody, following closely behind to make certain they didn't try to escape. But as long as Rick was behind him, Jack couldn't reach back to see if he had a handkerchief in the pocket of his jeans. Rick was probably going to need one. Maybe Jack had a few clean napkins in the truck from the last trip he and Angela made to the Dairy-O for milk shakes.

Jack started the engine as soon as they got in. The radio came on—the reception still as clear as starlight—and Jack quickly switched it off. He turned the heater fan on medium, and immediately the smell of the fraying, overheated rubber of the heater hoses filled the cab. And beneath that, Jack could smell Rick Bauer, the young man's aftershave splashed on too heavily and a hint of body odor, the yeasty smell of a child who has been playing in the sun. Jack cracked his window an inch.

Then he lit a cigarette. Why was he hesitating? Why didn't he come right out and tell the boy why he had called him out of the party? Did Jack believe he was sparing the boy in some way? This was torture, torture as surely as if he were pulling out the boy's fingernails.

Jack exhaled sharply, letting the stream of smoke shatter against the windshield and fan out in both directions. "I've got hard news for you, Rick."

Jack didn't wait but followed that warning immediately. "Your dad got killed in a car accident tonight."

Rick lurched, as though the truck had started to roll and he needed to brace himself.

"How long?" the boy asked quickly.

Too quickly. Jack didn't understand the question, and Rick probably didn't either. He was talking just to be talking, to demonstrate that he could. Jack had seen it before. People who got hit with bad news and then wanted to talk about the weather, anything to show they were fine, still in control. Before long, Jack was sure, this polite young man would thank Jack for telling him his father was dead.

"I meant," Rick said, "how long ago was this accident?"

"Can't say for sure. A few hours probably."

"How long . . . I mean, how long . . . Did he die right away?"

"Right away. He didn't suffer."

Rick put his hand on the protruding ridge of the dashboard and began to rub at the metal with short, hard strokes as though he were trying to wipe out a stain or mark on the surface.

Jack waited. To give Rick what little privacy the truck's cab afforded, Jack looked straight ahead.

What Jack wanted to do, however, was to stare intently at Rick Bauer, to see if he could determine exactly how the boy was handling the news. No, that wasn't quite right: what Jack really wanted was to watch Rick without being seen himself. He wished the glass in his truck's windows were like those two-way mirrors, and Jack could stand outside and watch how Rick behaved while he was alone with these brand-new thoughts and feelings. Jack made do with peeking over at Rick's reflection in the windshield. That didn't reveal much—a pale, barely there, ghostly image that the darkness was trying to wipe away completely. You could no more read that reflected face than a blackboard that had just been erased.

Without looking up from his dashboard rubbing, Rick asked, "How's my mom?"

"I haven't told her yet."

Rick started to say something, stopped, and then asked a question that probably was not the one he was going to ask. "How did it happen?" But surely that was one of the questions waiting in line.

"Your dad went off the road out by the Sprull ranch. Looks like he missed the curve."

Rick went back to rubbing the dashboard. "My dad was a good driver. . . ."

Was—Jack marveled at the speed with which people adjusted. For Rick Bauer, his father already *was*, even though the man had only been dead a few hours and his son had only known a few minutes. Why didn't the mind make its own insistence and keep him alive a little longer—put him to sleep in his favorite chair or put him out on the porch smoking a last cigarette and staring up at the same stars that shone above Jack Nevelsen's truck? No, Leo Bauer already *was*.

52

"I had to talk to you before I talked to anyone else, Rick. Some things I need to get cleared up."

The boy's head jerked up as if it were pulled on a string. "What things?"

Jesus, how many times had Jack seen this in his years in office. He could be talking to someone, asking for information or an opinion, and then if he shifted the grounds ever so slightly and hinted—no more than hinted, mind you—that that person might know more than he was letting on, everything changed and as suddenly as if a switch were thrown. Just as now, with Rick, something would change between them. Like Rick's, their eyes would widen. Their voices would rise. Their answers would become too short or too long. We're all afraid of arrest, Jack long ago concluded; whether on charges false or true, we're all afraid we can be run in at any time. And when we're up against that fear, it's ourselves we think about first; the hell with our dead daddies.

"June Moss," said Jack.

"June?"

"You know June?"

"Sure, she's . . . Sure, I know her."

"She graduated with you today?"

"Yeah. Yes."

"Anything more?"

"More? I mean, I know her. I know June."

"You know June pretty well?"

"Sure, I—" Rick cocked his head to one side as though he were listening to a far-off voice. "Did something happen to June?"

Now Jack paused, and he wasn't quite sure why. Was he trying to put pressure on Rick, trying to see if he would blurt something out to fill in the silence? Was he giving the boy a chance to think? Or was he simply trying to slow things down, trying to let himself catch up?

"June was killed tonight too."

Rick leaned toward Jack the way people do when they don't understand and are trying to listen to you even with their eyes.

"June?"

"June Moss was killed in the same accident as your dad."

53

Jack planned to count silently to ten before he spoke, but he only got to six. "She was in the same car."

Rick barely moved or changed his expression, yet Jack could sense how the grief and anguish and confusion were twisting him hard. The boy squirmed a little, as though they had been sitting in the truck for hours, as if he were trying to find what little comfort was possible after traveling a great distance. Jack felt sorry for the boy. A part of him wanted to reach over and open the door, like opening an animal's cage, and just let the boy run.

He leaned toward Rick and spoke the boy's name until Rick looked at him and Jack could be sure he had the young man's attention. "Rick. Rick. *Rick,* are you listening to me?"

The young man nodded, but that wasn't enough.

"Are you *really* listening? Goddamn it, this is important. You have to pay close attention."

Rick nodded again, this time more vigorously. He was afraid of what Jack was going to say—Jack could see that—but he was listening nonetheless.

"All right. Now, I'm going to tell you some things about what happened tonight, and you're going to listen. Just listen. When I'm finished, don't answer right away. Think first."

9

"You're listening? Okay. Good. Now, remember. You're just following along right now; you don't worry about saying anything for the time being.

"Tonight your dad got killed when his car went off the road at the Sprull ranch curve. Nobody knows exactly what happened. Most likely he just missed the curve. God knows that's easy enough to do out there.

"Your dad wasn't alone in the car. June Moss was with him. June was killed too. Both of them instantly, so there's no need to worry on that score. They didn't suffer any.

"Now, any time there's an accident, there's always questions, and sometimes you can piece together some answers and sometimes you can't and you just have to leave it go. Your dad being who he was and all, there'll likely be even more questions than usual.

"I'm not talking about a crime. You be sure you understand that. Nobody's going to be charged. I'm just after information. Like I say, trying to clear up a few matters. And if I don't come up with all the answers, so be it. There's a good many things in this world that remain a mystery to me. One more isn't going to make a hell of a big difference. But if you can help . . .

"Here's the thing. Out there at the accident site we found suitcases in your dad's car. Couple of them were June's. And that made some sense—June had her luggage with her.

"But the other suitcase didn't have your dad's name on it. It had yours.

"I don't even remember what I was thinking, but whatever it was, it changed all around when I came across that suitcase with your name.

"You and June being the same age and all—that somehow made it right for your suitcases to be together.

"I don't know anything about such a history, but maybe you and June were a couple. And maybe you decided, as soon as school's out, we're taking off, leaving Bentrock. Making a life somewhere else. Hell, you wouldn't be the first ones thinking along those lines. Maybe you were coming back, maybe you weren't. But see, this theory makes some sense. Some. It's just got a few pieces out of place: You here. June out there. Your dad, of course.

"Even so, I can make it work. I just need a little help, and I can make it work. You're following me, aren't you? Good, good. I'm not used to talking this much, but just let me gallop ahead here and try to get somewhere.

"See, I can imagine your dad maybe trying to help you out. Like I said, you and June a couple. With your plans. You have to know you're going to get some argument. But your dad . . . Your dad maybe understood and wanted to help you out. He—I can't quite get through this part—he was going to get June out of town. You were planning to follow later. Leaving separately—that would be a way to throw off suspicion maybe. So, I don't know . . . Your dad was just taking June down the road a ways. Where you'd meet her later. It's—what time now? Close to midnight? You were going to stay at the party awhile. Let everyone see you. Then slip away to meet June. You'd be halfway across the state before anyone noticed neither one of you was where you were supposed to be. And your dad . . . The kind of man your dad was, maybe he said he'd come back and talk to your mom. June's mom too. Smooth it over for both of you.

"Now, I'm not saying this is the way it had to be. God almighty, there's got to be any number of ways to explain what June and your dad and your suitcase were doing out there tonight.

"But I don't have the kind of mind that can come up with much. I need to see things right there in front of me, and even then I can't see much more than that. So you need to tell me. How did I do with this?"

Beyond the *Mercer County Tribune* and an occasional issue of *Argosy* and *True*, Jack was not much of a reader. And never of books. He had, first of all, difficulty sitting still for long periods of time, and an open book before him only made him more itchy; it reminded him of school, of assignments due, or having to sit for endless hours. And it seemed such an unproductive use of time. Sitting and reading—what good would come of those hours? If he stood on a street corner or stared out a window or drove around aimlessly, he could at least pretend he was doing his job. He was present, he was watching; his presence alone could conceivably prevent a crime. But staring at the pages of a book—never.

Nora, who read all the time, tried to encourage him by suggesting books she thought he would like. Novels, mostly, stories of adventure or mystery. They were worst of all. Jack couldn't get past the thought: This is all a lie elaborately built to make us believe it's a true story. Every board, shingle, and window that went into making this imaginary house was only there to deceive us about its reality. It wasn't only Jack's profession that made him dig in his heels, but that was part of it. When Jack questioned someone about a crime, and he heard an alibi or an explanation that was complicated and detailed, he was immediately suspicious. People's memories simply weren't that good.

But beyond that, there was something about the act—the very idea—of making up stories that made Jack uneasy. It didn't strike Jack as a particularly manly or responsible activity. And especially he couldn't understand a mind for which an imaginary world was more ponderable than a real one.

Yet now, as Jack questioned Rick Bauer, he couldn't help wonder if he was doing exactly what those authors whom Nora admired did. How many of the planks holding up the theory that Jack offered Rick were real?

As soon as Jack finished talking, Rick opened his mouth to speak.

"Wait!" Jack held up his hand as if he were stopping traffic. "Just hold on. Remember what I said before? Take a minute here. . . ."

Rick held his tongue. He turned away from Jack and looked out his side window. His shoulders rose but didn't fall, as though he took a deep breath but never exhaled. He's holding in more than air, Jack thought. God help him if he never lets it out.

A minute passed, and Rick Bauer continued to stare out his window, although there was nothing on his side of the truck but rocks and brush and the dark gully behind Concannon's.

Jack grew impatient. Yes, it was his idea that Rick think carefully about what he said in response to Jack's questions, but at a certain point, Jack became aware of the world outside this truck and how difficult it was going to be to prevent news of the accident from getting out—and once it did, it would be impossible to control. Once out, it would take on its own form, and that shape could be as enormous and inexorable as the night that pressed against the truck from every side.

To break the spell, Jack said, "Okay if I roll down my window a little more? I can't seem to get my own thermostat regulated. That's what it means to get old—you can't decide if you're too hot or too cold."

"That's the way it was," Rick said, his face still turned away. "The way you said." He spoke so slowly that each word's steam upon the window glass faded before the next word's fog took its place.

"What do you know. I guessed right for once."

"Everything. Everything was just the way you said."

"And you could say it all back to me—or to anyone else who asked?"

"Yeah." There—the boy's shoulders dropped at last.

"If someone wants to know where you were going?"

"California. We were both going to get jobs in California."

"Was this a big secret, you and June?"

"I don't know. I guess."

"Did any of your friends know about the two of you? Or June's friends?"

This time his shoulders rose and fell.

"So if I go up to that party and ask those people if they knew Rick Bauer and June Moss were running off together, is anyone going to say yes?"

"Probably not."

"Will anyone know you were going together?"

For the first time, Rick wiped away tears. With the back of his right hand he rubbed swiftly and roughly once under each eye. "People don't always know everything about each other."

"No, you got that right." Jack wanted so badly to let this boy go, not just from the truck, from this interrogation, but from this life Rick had landed in—and would live in for the rest of his days. He wished he could tell Rick to go on back to the party, to drink beer until everything he had learned from Sheriff Jack Nevelsen was washed away.

"How old are you, Rick?"

"Eighteen."

"And how old was June?"

Rick hesitated. The truck was absolutely still, yet they had a destination and they could only reach it together. Could the boy see it?

"She was eighteen too."

"When was her birthday?"

"March. Both of our birthdays were in March."

"That's easy enough to check."

"Go ahead."

"And did you know you can get married in Nevada when you're eighteen, without needing a parent's consent?"

"Yeah, we knew."

"So that's where you were headed?"

"Eventually."

"California first or Nevada first?"

He shrugged, and then turned toward Jack. Since he had last

looked into Rick's eyes, the boy's expression had changed utterly. Even in the dim light of the truck's cab he could see that Rick Bauer had passed over to some new place, a place beyond bewilderment and confusion, beyond anger and grief—and a place where he could not be touched by those feelings, not tonight and perhaps not ever again. He was resolved, he would do what was necessary—say what should be said, even feign some tears if they were required—but he would not feel. He had found a self that would not be shaken, and he was dedicated to its survival. It was just as well Leo Bauer wasn't alive; he wouldn't recognize this young man as any son of his. Would his mother?

"Did your mother know about this plan of yours, yours and June's?"

He shook his head.

"You're sure?"

"She knows where I am. She'd be calling after me if she thought any different."

"When were you going to tell her?"

"I wasn't. Dad was. After we got away."

"So he was going to handle that too."

"Yeah."

"June's mother?"

"Her too."

"That was a hell of a load he was going to carry for you."

"I guess."

"And now it's yours. *Whew!* After your loss—your double loss. Jesus. Well, maybe people will give you a little room on that account. When they see how hard this is on you. . . ." Jack shook another cigarette from the pack and brought it to his lips. He offered one to Rick.

"No thanks."

"Don't smoke?"

Rick shook his head. "I just don't want one."

The draft from the open window caused the smoke to drift Rick's way. Jack waved his hand between them. "Still something I don't understand. . . ."

Rick took his own turn waving the smoke away.

"I don't understand why your dad was driving June out of town. Why didn't the two of you—"

"We were going to trade cars. My dad was going to let me— let us—take his car. Mine's been having transmission problems, and we didn't think we'd get too far. So he—so my dad—was going to meet me in—" he paused; he could have been calculating distance and direction—"in Rifle Gap, and we were going to switch cars."

Rifle Gap was not much more than a bar, a gas station, and a few trailers twenty-three miles west of Bentrock. But right on the way. And just across the county line.

"I told people I'd go to some stuff tonight," Rick continued. "So I'd leave later. And no one would see us leaving town together."

Like they'd see Leo and June, Jack thought, but he let it pass. "Stuff like this party?"

Rick shrugged. "Why not? I wanted to go and June didn't."

"Sort of a farewell-graduation-stag party all rolled into one."

"I guess."

"She didn't want to celebrate before you pulled out?"

"She just wanted to get going."

"You and June have different friends?"

"Not really."

Jack looked toward the Concannon's and their bright lights. Right now he preferred darkness, and the blank of his closed eyes would have been his first choice. Barring that, he'd take the night sky, all that dark, dark blue and the pathless pattern of star, star, star. . . . "Well, I'm sorry to break up the party. For you anyway. I reckon we better get the news to your mother."

"I'll tell her," Rick said quickly.

"You sure? I've got to tag along anyway."

"No, I'll do it. Maybe I can talk to her first?"

"If that's the way you want to do it. I just want to make this as easy as possible. For everybody. You too."

"What about my suitcase? Can I get that?"

"It's in the back of the truck. Help yourself. It's yours."

Rick pointed toward the party. "My car's up there."

"Go ahead. I'll follow you to your place."

The young man walked around to the back of the truck and lifted out his suitcase from the three that were lying back there. As soon as Rick was up the road a ways, Jack turned on the truck's headlights, casting so much light on the young man's back that the outline of his close-set shoulder blades was visible under his T-shirt. His shadow leaped out in front of him, but Rick did not turn around. He continued his progress up the road, though the suitcase's weight so unbalanced his stride it looked as though the earth itself were shifting under his feet.

10

SECRETS. JACK KNEW HIS TOWN HAD SECRETS; EVERY TOWN DID. . . .

One of his first duties in office had been to respond to a call from a farmer who reported tools stolen from his barn. When Jack drove into the farmyard, the farmer's wife stepped out onto the porch and signaled him to come inside. Mrs. Carney was a stout, lively, red-faced woman who looked and smelled as though she had been baking bread. As she held the door open for him, she said, "I told Morris not to bother you. Just go on over to the Yeager place and shake those boys until they let loose what they took from you. And don't bother talking to the folks. They'll lie right down the line to cover up for their kids."

"Did you see the boys in the barn?"

"Might as well have. Those little bastards walk by every day. Giving us the eye. Come on in the kitchen. I wrote out a list of what's missing."

The Carney home was filthy. The floors were tracked with mud. Underfoot, the mismatched, overlapping rolls of linoleum bubbled and curled at the corners. Light had to struggle through the grime on the windows. The kitchen smelled of brackish water. The spout on the sink's rusty pump dripped; rags and washcloths were draped over the pump handle. There were dirty dishes and an overflowing ashtray on the kitchen table, and empty cans and jars and food wrappers littered the counters.

Jack glanced down a hallway and noticed that the walls were nothing but unfinished drywall panels nailed to the studs, the seams and nail holes untaped, uncovered—and these walls in a house the Carneys had lived in for close to twenty years.

Mrs. Carney had written her list of missing items in pencil on a strip of butcher paper. A drop of what looked like dried blood dotted one corner. Nevertheless, Jack thanked her for the list and told her it would not be necessary for him to look in the barn. If the inside of the house looked like this . . . He assured her he would talk to the Yeagers right away. Yes, he would lean hard on them with his suspicions.

Jack grew up in a home completely unlike the Carneys'. His mother's day consisted of relentless washing, wiping, polishing, and scouring, and while she was busy trying to keep everything spotlessly clean, his father was concentrating on order, on conquering and banishing clutter wherever possible. He organized every drawer in the house; he had the spaces of the basement and garage, those areas so often given over to overflow and thoughtless storage, shelved, partitioned, allotted, classified. During the years when Jack's father owned the hardware store, it was a model of how a bin, rack, shelf, or hook could be made or found for every item, no matter how large, small, odd-shaped, singular, or irregular.

Nora seemed more the offspring of Jack's parents than he. She was as fastidious as his mother and as orderly as his father. Their home was always clean, and it was almost totally without decoration. Even a magazine and an ashtray on an end table could seem to Nora to be opening the way to a life of litter and confusion.

Jack, on the other hand, could hang a jacket on a chair or leave his boots by the side door and not be bothered by the sight. He let his truck go unwashed, and if he noticed the garden hose snaking across the driveway, he didn't feel a need to roll it up. Yet for the most part, he too preferred neatness. He made a point of straightening his desk before he went home for the day, even if it meant putting work in a drawer. The army's insistence on every-thing in its place—soldiers *and* their equipment—was a difficult adjustment for many men, but for Jack it was one of the few things that reminded him of home. Even if his house and yard was no showplace, he still kept his grass cut and his sidewalk shoveled.

He supposed he could have gone the other way. His brother had. Phil lived alone in a trailer outside Bentrock. His place wasn't dirty—Jack would never say that—but it was . . . full. Phil was a saver—of books, of magazines, of phonograph records, of car and truck parts, of building or electrical or plumbing supplies, of all kinds of oddments he came upon in his long walks: a sheep's skull, a rattlesnake skin, the handlebar of a bicycle, tobacco tins, a fishing reel, mateless gloves and shoes . . . Jack could never figure why Phil didn't just leave these things where he found them. Perhaps Phil was like their father in his collecting, trying to recreate that feel of the hardware store that seemed to have everything, but without their father's talent for organizing. Or maybe his pack-rat habits represented another way that Phil couldn't quite fit in this world, another truth about his brother that Jack had long known. Phil never finished high school, never married, never held a regular job. He worked when he had to, but he'd take a handout, too; it was all the same to him. He wanted to keep his days as free as possible, he once told Jack, to try to make sense of things, yet as far as Jack could see, Phil had made no particular progress on that front either.

But the Carney household did not shock Jack merely because it was unlike the homes he had come from. He had seen messy houses before. One of his childhood friends was Karl Werner, and the Werners were poor. To make up for the food they could not afford to buy, they had a huge backyard garden—a small farm was more like it—and Mr. Werner and his sons hunted and fished at every opportunity. Their house was always full of the sights and smells of this food scavenging. Mr. Werner and the boys were often out in the shed plucking feathers, skinning or gutting some creature, cleaning fish, or hanging carcasses to bleed or cure or dry. Bones and hides littered the yard, and stray dogs prowled constantly, hoping to make off with a bone or scrap. Inside, Mrs. Werner was always boiling or canning or rendering or reducing something, and her pots and pressure cookers simmered and bubbled and hissed on the stove, aromatic steam filled the air—the very walls dripped—and the counters and tabletops were lined with her canning jars, lids, and spices. So much of the household's energy went into the procuring and preserving and preparing of food that not much was left for cleaning up after. Besides, it was all going to start over again the next day. When Jack's father asked Jack where he was going or where he had been and Jack said, "Karl's," his father might ask, "And how are things at the cannery?" or "What are they butchering today?"

So if cleanliness was not the issue, what was it that so unsettled Jack about his visit to the Carneys?

It was his job. His badge brought him to that house. His badge opened their doors. His badge made Mrs. Carney feel she could trust him to be quiet about their home's interior.

That incident made him realize that his badge was going to let him see into homes and lives. The question was—the question no one had asked him when he was running for office, the question he had not thought to ask himself—what was he supposed to do with the knowledge of what he saw in those secret places? If he carried this knowledge alone, would it make him stronger, the way lifting nail kegs in the summers strengthened him when he was a boy? Or would he find himself weakened, brought low by the weight? And what was right for his townspeople? What should they know?

Of course, the matter was sometimes trivial and the answer easy. What was to be served by telling people of the squalor in which the Carneys lived? Of revealing that old Henry Rambach often walked the town's streets in the middle of the night—drunk? Of making known how long Owen Jeter's car was parked in the alley behind Mrs. Furst's house or whether his car being there coincided in any way with Ben Furst's three-day runs as a brakeman with the Northern Pacific? And who, outside his own house, needed to know about Nora's dark, silent spells, when she spent hours, day and night, simply staring out the window, when it was all anyone could do to get a word, much less a sentence from her? Whose business was it that Nora seldom wanted sex, that he had to wait not only for one of her rare bright moods but even then had to lull and romance her all day long, as though pouring her coffee and asking her about her garden in the morning were the first tentative gestures of that night's foreplay—and then enter her at exactly the right instant, when her passion was at its crest (and God help him if he asked her if it was time because the sound of his voice would guarantee it would not be), and then to take her could be frightening because her need might suddenly be far, far beyond his? What would be served in revealing that he had not seen Nora's naked body for years, and even then by accident, having walked into their bedroom on one of those nights when she was willing but when she had not yet turned out every light and pulled every shade and drawn every curtain? And that body was beautiful, pale and luminous and slender and supple, even more beautiful to actual sight than he had imagined it under her clothes or under the sheets or under his touch, and if she chose to keep that loveliness hidden from her husband—from every human eye—if she chose to keep that body secret, who was to say she could not?

Plainly, there were matters of concern to the larger community, and it was frequently given to Jack to know the difference and act accordingly. When he was first campaigning for office, his friend Steve Lovoll told him to use the words "judgment" and "trust" as often as he could when he talked to the voters. Jack tried, even though he wasn't quite sure what he was saying. Was he saying in code that he could keep their secrets?

When he found out that Kenny Gilland was the one who had been setting fires around town, most of them small and harmless— gasoline poured onto newspapers and cardboard boxes in garbage cans and lit behind schools and a few businesses—he could have arrested Kenny and opened up that secret to the civic air.

But everyone knew Kenny was not quite right in the head, so what was to be served by arresting that poor, troubled boy—why put him in jail when Jack could talk to Mr. and Mrs. Gilland in their living room, when he could sit on their new davenport under the oil painting of a herd of wild horses done by their talented daughter Carla, and tell them what Kenny had done and receive their assurances, their hand-wringing vows, that their son would never set another fire in Bentrock? (As indeed Kenny did not; within a month he was sent off to live with Mrs. Gilland's sister in Salem, Oregon. Jack considered calling the sheriff out there to let him know of Kenny's past, but in the end he thought better of it. Why shouldn't Kenny have his fresh beginning too?)

Of course, with Kenny—as with Dr. Iverson and the way he drove drunk that night, or with Chet Gerlach and his penchant for beating up on his wife and children—Jack had the law to guide him if he wasn't sure of the way. When a law was broken, he could stiffen his neck and say he hadn't any choice, he took an oath. And more than once, that was exactly what he told the person he arrested: Don't blame me; you're the one broke the law; I can't do a thing but bring you in; that's my job. (Though he had arrested neither Dr. Iverson nor Chet Gerlach but had warned them both that next time he would.) And if the man or woman needed arresting, that was exactly the line Jack followed. Then the secret—which to an extent every crime was—came out.

Yet even where the law was involved, matters were not always clear. Take the time a few years back when he was transporting a prisoner to another jurisdiction. This fellow came in on the train from Kalispell, having been arrested out there for drunk and disorderly. But he was wanted down in Glendive on a more serious charge, armed robbery, and the Kalispell authorities were letting Glendive have him. A deputy escorted the prisoner to Bentrock, and though a deputy from Glendive was willing to drive up for him, Jack said he'd transport him. He was glad to get out of the office and out of town, even for a chore like that one. Jack had it planned; he'd hand the prisoner over, then head for the Wagon Wheel and have himself a steak at the county's expense. He'd take his time driving home, watching the sun set and the evening creep out across the prairie with its shadow shades of pink, tan, lavender, and gray. He'd pull in after dark, happy to be back home after his little one-day vacation.

But Alvin Booth, his prisoner, a short, sharp-faced man with skinny arms, slicked back hair, pale blue eyes, and a wispy mustache, had other ideas. They had traveled less than twenty miles when Booth spoke up from the backseat.

"I had one of your women," Booth said in his high, scratchy voice.

They were driving past sun-lit fields of wheat, the dusty gold of which always seemed to Jack exactly the color of late summer sunlight. Just watch the wheat, Jack told himself; watch to see if the rush of the car is enough to cause those heavy heads to wave on this windless day.

Booth went on, and though Jack couldn't see him in the rearview mirror, he could hear the sneer in the man's voice. "Yeah, I was through your little commu-ni-tee a few months back. Stayed over a few days. Long enough to have me one of your women."

Jack ran out of wheat fields to watch, so he concentrated on the way the heat-baked asphalt shimmered in the distance.

"And I'm not saying I asked," Booth said. "I'm saying I took."

Jailhouse talk, Jack told himself. Just the brag of a man in handcuffs. Let it go.

"But I gather she didn't report it. Maybe it turned so she liked it too much." One end of the handcuffs was attached to the man's wrist and the other locked around the car door's armrest. He rattled the chain's links as if he were testing for slack.

"She took some convincing though," Booth said. "Maybe you seen her on the streets. You'd know her. Marked up some, she was."

Jack finally broke. "And when's this supposed to have happened?"

"Hell, I'm not too sure of the month right now."

"*Where* did it happen then? I reckon you can remember that, can't you?"

"What I can remember and what I can say ain't the same."

"Mister, I believe less than a single word from you."

"That suits me, Sheriff. That suits me fine."

Jack tried to turn his attention back outside, but the bare ravines and dry washes, the treeless hills and the empty grasslands couldn't hold him. "You got a name to go along with this tale?"

Booth laughed. "Man, you want me to do all your work for you, don't you?"

"Young woman?"

Booth laughed again.

"White or Indian?"

For an answer Jack got nothing but the rattling of Booth's chain, the mocking clink of steel on steel.

Jack pulled over onto the shoulder of the road so suddenly he felt his wheels slide in the soft dirt and gravel. When he looked to his right, a tan cloud of his dust, faint as smoke, drifted slowly out over the field.

"How about," Jack said to Booth in a voice pitched as low and menacing as he could make it, "we get out of the car here and discuss this further."

Booth stopped rattling the chain but simply pulled it as tight as he could. Jack saw where the cuff gouged into Booth's wrist.

"I want some specifics to go along with that story of yours, and goddamn, I'm going to get them." Jack's anger was genuine, but as soon as he began to threaten, that anger subsided. He had never beaten a prisoner, not to punish, not to extract a confession. No matter how deserving the criminal might be, once a law enforcement officer beat on a prisoner, the prisoner became a victim, and the cop or the sheriff or the deputy or the marshal was using his badge to bully. Jack had moments—and prisoners—when he felt both the impulse and the temptation, but those feelings were so ugly he resolved he could never give in to them.

Booth gave the chain one more jerk. "You going to keep these on me for our little discussion?"

Jack had a vision of Booth taking off once he was out of the car, running hard over that sun-baked stubbly field. Jack doubted he could come close to catching him, and then what would his recourse be? Call for help and have to explain how he let his prisoner get away? Get the .30–.30 out of the trunk and shoot Booth down? Jack's anger turned even hotter over his lack of options, but reason, the cool wash of reason, kept wetting down his anger until its fire was out.

When he pulled back onto the highway, he noticed that the day was so dry he could taste the dust that he had stirred.

Jack didn't stay long in Glendive. He handed Booth over to the sheriff and then headed right back to Bentrock, leaving the Wagon Wheel and his steak for another day.

He couldn't say he believed Booth's story, but for the next few weeks he tried watching the women of Bentrock closely, searching for a sign, a scar, or a look of shame that hadn't been there before. He finally gave up. He wasn't going to get close enough to see a scar, and as for the other—too many women walked about with their eyes lowered for him to know if shame could be the reason.

The deaths of Leo Bauer and June Moss were a different matter altogether. Necks and bodies were broken but no laws. And if the accident itself were a secret now, it wouldn't be for long. Before the week was out, the *Mercer County Tribune* would be running Leo's and June's obituaries. Maybe Jim Brazelton, the paper's editor, had already tried calling Jack for a full report. Jack was never quite certain when Jim was trying to get information for a story and when he was simply looking to slake his own curiosity. Jim had his own decisions to make about the information he received.

But no newspaper was going to run the story that Jack had just gotten from Rick Bauer. That was up to Rick—and Jack—to spread.

And was that the tale the town needed to hear—that Leo Bauer was not actually running off with June Moss but only assisting a pair of young lovers? Would that account satisfy people's longing to know the secrets behind those deaths? Would that give them something to shake their heads over and then go on with their lives? Was that the version that would allow Bentrock to return to itself as quickly as possible, to be the town it was before the accident, a town where school principals didn't carry on with teenage girls? Was it going to be enough for people to know that the suitcase in the car had Rick Bauer's name on it? Or would they want that secret unlocked too? And if they could look inside, as Jack had done before he drove to the Concannons', what would they do with the knowledge that although the name on the suitcase may have been Rick's, the belongings inside—the white shirts and black slacks, the skinny ties, the pale blue pajamas, the electric razor, the toothbrush and Mennen aftershave, the zippered Bible, the envelope with three hundred forty dollars—were Leo's? Oh, yes, they were Leo's.

If they knew that, then where would they be?

11

THE BAUER HOME WAS DARK, WHICH JACK TOOK AS ANOTHER HOPEFUL sign. Surely if Vivien Bauer believed that either of the house's males had gone away for a life with June Moss, Mrs. Bauer would still be up, walking the floors and trying to figure out how she had arrived at this moment and what other shocks the future might have in store for her. And if she had somehow gotten the news of the accident, would she be sitting in the dark with that knowledge? Jack doubted it.

Rick drove into the driveway, and Jack shut off his lights and pulled in right behind him. He deliberately blocked the boy's exit, though Jack wasn't sure why.

Rick got out of his car and came around to Jack's window. "Is it okay if I go in first? My mom's probably in bed."

"If that's the way you want it. But I'm willing to break the news if you'd rather. And then you can fill in."

Rick looked back at the darkened house. "I better go in. If she's asleep . . . It's hard to wake her up sometimes. And I'd kind of like to put this suitcase away. If she sees that . . ."

"You do how you think is best. I'll be right here when you want me."

The boy turned toward the house.

"Rick? Wait up a minute." Jack felt around in his jacket pocket. He brought out a pack of Black Jack gum and offered Rick a piece. "On top of everything else, your mom probably doesn't need to smell beer on your breath."

Rick took the gum and looked at it as though he had never seen gum before. After this moment of inspection passed, he unwrapped the stick and put it in his mouth, biting it in half on its way in. "Yeah. Thanks."

Rick went back to his car and got the suitcase out of the front seat. Jack shook his head. No one put suitcases in the front seat. No one.

Even after Rick went in, the Bauer house remained dark. Jack imagined the boy inside, feeling his way along, trying not to bump into anything and wake his mother before he could put the suit-case—where? In the back of a closet? Under a bed? Hidden some-where until he could unpack it and put his father's things away without his mother knowing.

There—a light in a window at the far end of the house. Was that Rick's room? Leo's and Vivien's? Had Rick wakened his mother?

Jack got out of the truck in case Rick might soon call him in. Jack shut the door of the truck as quietly as possible.

No, nothing indicated he was wanted inside. After a few more minutes passed, he lit a cigarette but kept it cupped in his hand so the glow of the ember couldn't be seen. He had adopted that method of smoking in the service, when men were preparing for combat in small as well as large ways.

He looked up and down the block but could not see another light in any window.

But why would he? It was after midnight and a Sunday night at that. These people had to go to work in the morning, or if not, they still had the habits of a working lifetime telling them to retire and get up early.

Fourth Street was as old as any in Bentrock, but this side of the street was mostly newer homes, small, plain, compact, single-story dwellings that looked modestly across the street at Bentrock's first grand houses, large, two- and three-story affairs with their wide porches, cupolas and turrets, dormers and big brick chimneys. (Where did they get the wood to burn in their fireplaces? Jack wondered for the first time in his life. Bentrock sat on an almost treeless prairie. From what distance was the wood hauled in—to build *or* burn?)

How many lights would be on if the residents of Fourth Street knew one of their own was dead? How many curtains would be thinly parted, how many pairs of eyes would be watching him now? How many voices would be whispering, "Is that Sheriff Nevelsen out there?" "Why do you suppose he's just standing there—doesn't he have duties?" "That poor woman . . . that poor, poor woman." "What's going to become of her now that her husband is gone?"

Jack didn't want to be unfair to these people. If they knew Vivien Bauer's husband had been killed, they might already be here, bringing whatever comfort they could (as it was, tomorrow the pies, cakes, and casseroles would be on their way). But what if they knew only that Leo had died in the company of a teenage girl—would a single ham sandwich, would a single date bar find its way to Vivien's door?

The streetlamp cast enough light for Jack to see that Leo had already done a considerable amount of work on his yard this spring. The bushes looked clipped and shaped, the grass cut, and the driveway and sidewalk carefully edged. Leo's place always looked neat—shrubbery and trees neatly trimmed, house and garage freshly painted. It was one of the smaller homes on the street—a principal couldn't afford much—but the Bauers had made the most of it. The breezeway between the house and the garage Leo had built himself.

Jack tried to think of what work he had done on his own yard. He had mowed but maybe only once; winter had taken its time leaving this year. He meant to rake and scrape up what was left of last fall's leaves and last summer's thatch, but he hadn't. Nora no longer asked him to spade up the garden or fertilize. Even when he got around to those tasks, it was generally too late, so now she and Angela tended the garden. The window wells—my God, they were full of at least three years' worth of debris, and Angela said a family of salamanders lived in one. No, his yard never looked as good as Leo's. But then Jack was standing out here assessing the grass that Leo would never mow again.

What would this place look like in the future? Vivien would get plenty of help at first, and maybe Rick would even postpone going off to school, but that aid wasn't likely to last—her neighbors on this block were generally too old to tend her place as well as their own. Before long these trees would carry their share of dead branches, the shrubs would lose their symmetry, the uncut grass would tassel, hawkweed and dandelions would bloom, paint would blister, flake, and peel, cement would crack, the foundation droop. . . .

Jack walked around to the front of the truck, dropped his cigarette to the driveway, and after watching the brief display of tiny sparks, crushed the butt with his boot heel.

A neighbor could be looking out right at that moment, see him in the Bauers' driveway, and call the police—or the sheriff's office—to report a prowler. "Somebody suspicious-looking lurking around the Bauers' lilac bushes." The lilacs had not yet opened, but Jack could smell their swelling sweet perfume.

No, anyone looking out would see his truck and know. Sheriff Nevelsen was at the Bauers', and if they knew his oath as well as he did, they'd know he was there to do his duty: to serve and protect.

And just whom was he protecting? Certainly not Vivien Bauer. He might as well be mounting an assault on the Bauer household. An explosive couldn't do a better job of bringing down the family than the news of Leo's death.

Leo? Was he protecting Leo? He supposed he was, he and Rick. . . .

Yet what if Vivien had called him earlier in the evening, called him and told him that Leo had run off with a young girl? Although no law was broken, Jack would probably have lit out—on Vivien's behalf—and tried to track Leo down. If Jack had caught up to them before Leo left the county—Oh, hell, Jack would have kept going into the next county for this one. Or the next. As far as he had to go to stop Leo and ask him what the hell he thought he was doing. Get your asses back to Bentrock, the both of you, before you do something you'll regret forever. And maybe the sight of his badge would have been enough to shock them to their senses. Or would they have been too far gone?

For Vivien Bauer? What was he thinking? He wouldn't be chasing them down for Mrs. Bauer but more likely for Mrs. Moss. She was the one who would call him, to tell the sheriff that a man had stolen off with her baby and couldn't Jack please please bring her back. That he hadn't gotten a call like that and, as far as Jack knew, neither had the police might mean that June had sneaked away without telling her mother where she was going. Or with whom. It was a reasonable hope, and Jack held tight to it. Later, when he broke the news to Mrs. Moss, then he could find out for sure if she knew what her daughter had been up to tonight. If she did, well, he would deal with that when the time came. Maybe in the confusion of her grief she could be persuaded to believe that she had gotten wrong the name her daughter gave her. No, no, not Leo Bauer; Leo Bauer's *son*. If she couldn't be convinced of that, maybe he could make her see the importance of going along with the version of events that he and Rick were trying to establish. Her daughter was already dead; nothing would change that. But maybe the news of her death could be presented in such a way that it wouldn't do as much damage to the town. If he had to, that would be the argument he'd make to Mrs. Moss.

In the handbook put out by the National Sheriff's Association were these words: "The sheriff is required to protect the person, property, health, and morals of every citizen in the county, and these rights and possessions must not only be protected, they must be made continuously safe." The book was bound in bright yellow, the color of a traffic warning sign, and Jack kept a copy on his desk. When he first got the book—it came in the regular round of materials distributed to civic and county offices, most of them coming from the office of the mayor, who couldn't pass up a handbook, pamphlet, or brochure—Jack was scornful of the publication. What were those words printed on a page who-knew-where going to tell him about being a peace officer in Mercer County, Montana? But he kept the book, opened it again and again, read without meaning to, and before long had a few passages by heart.

"Any condition detrimental to the public welfare . . . may not be overlooked. The sheriff *must* correct these conditions. . . ."

That's what he was doing tonight: protecting the morals of as many citizens as possible, and he was doing it by correcting a condition that couldn't be corrected any other way, at least not after the fact.

Why, right over there, that was where old Esther Birdleigh lived, a resident of Bentrock probably from its very first days as a town. Over the years she had spent a good deal of her money—money left to her by her husband and his farm-implement business—on making Bentrock a better place to live. She had helped the library put up its own building. She had donated money for an auditorium when they were constructing the new high school. Her generosity made it possible for Bentrock finally to have its own hospital. Rumor had it she was going to fund a swimming pool this summer. Would she have done any of these things—would she even stay in Bentrock—if she thought she lived in a town where Leo Bauer could take June Moss away in the middle of the night?

The people of the county needed to believe in certain things, and that belief was necessary to their—to the whole county's— welfare. Bentrock couldn't go on being Bentrock if the citizens didn't know that grown men, married men, educators with young people given to their care, didn't run away with schoolgirls. Or girls barely out of school. By God, you had to know that. In every house on this street lights were off, the windows were dark, people were in their beds, sleeping peacefully because they knew what kind of town they lived in. They *knew*. And they knew that the men they respected deserved that respect. The townspeople needed to believe in Leo Bauer and his decency. Jack was too late to stop Leo and save his life before he drove out of town, but maybe Jack could save Leo's life after . . .

The Bauers' porch light blinked on, and its sudden illumination so startled Jack that he thought for an instant that it must have come on with a sound.

But the sound soon followed. The inner door pulled open with a clunk and then the screen door swung out. Rick's voice was barely a whisper. "Sheriff? Can you come in here?"

12

THE BAUER HOME HAD THAT SMELL THAT JACK ALWAYS ASSOCIATED
with the houses of older people, a peculiar combination of cooked
cabbage and the dust of rooms where windows were seldom
opened.

He followed Rick down a hallway toward a room where a bright
strip of light glowed under the closed door. It seemed to be the
only room in the house with a light on. Before the bedroom door,
Rick stopped.

"I had to wake her up," he said. "And when I told her what
happened. You know, what we talked about. How Dad was helping
me and all. She got sick! She . . . she got sick all over . . .
everything."

"Did you already put your suitcase away?"

Rick nodded.

"She's in here?"

He nodded again.

"And you want me to go in and check on her?"

Rick looked away. "You better," he said.

Jack took a deep breath, turned the knob, and opened the door a couple inches. "Mrs. Bauer? Jack Nevelsen." He was answered with silence. Perhaps a mistake had been made, and he was speaking to an empty room. "Mrs. Bauer? It's Sheriff Nevelsen. Can I come in?"

He looked at Rick, and the boy said, "She's in there."

Jack took his hand from the door and stepped aside. "Maybe you better go in first."

"I was just *in* there," Rick said impatiently, but he took the lead once again and pushed the bathroom door open. "Mom? Sheriff Nevelsen is coming in."

Vivien Bauer was sitting on the bathroom floor, leaning back against the tub. She was wearing a white cotton nightgown, and though the fabric was thin, she made no move to cover herself or to pull up the strap that had slipped from her shoulder or to tug down the hem that had ridden up above her knees.

Tendrils of hair were stuck to her glistening forehead, and her cheeks were flushed as if she had a fever. When Jack entered, she did not move. Her arms hung motionlessly at her sides, and her head remained tilted back over the edge of the tub. Her eyes were rimmed in red, yet strain and exhaustion seemed as much the cause as weeping. Those eyes, wild and dark, followed Jack as he came closer.

The room stank sourly of vomit, and Jack looked for a window.

"Mrs. Bauer? How are you doing?"

She made no reply.

"Are you all right?"

She still said nothing, but she kept her eyes locked on him. If she recognized him, she made no acknowledgment. Something in her expression, her general demeanor, reminded Jack of the time years ago when he took Angela to the zoo in Minot, North Dakota. When they entered the cat house that day, the lions did not get up or stir in any way, yet they watched Jack and his daughter with eyes completely focused, wary yet knowing, as if they understood these two-legged creatures better than the humans could ever hope to know them. In spite of the cats' indolence, Angela saw something that prompted her to ask if the lions could get out. Jack assured her they could not, but Angela still insisted they leave.

Something now told him to stay a few paces back from Vivien Bauer.

"Are you going to be okay?" he asked again.

She laughed. The sound came out weakly and almost caught somewhere deep in her throat, but it was definitely a laugh.

"I will never," she said softly and stopped, swallowed, and licked her lips before going on, "be 'okay' again."

Jack reached down toward her, but he wasn't sure why. To help her up? To touch her in consolation?

His outstretched hand helped her move on her own. She shut her eyes, turned her head, and raised her hands to ward him off.

Jack was tired. The night had gone on too long already and too much of it still remained, so when Vivien Bauer flinched at his approach, Jack became irritated. Me?—he wanted to say—You're cringing from *me*? Christ, woman, I'm here to help you. I'm trying to make the pain of this night manageable, something you can find your way back from. I'm here to get you up off the bathroom floor.

He glanced in the toilet to see if it needed flushing. The water was clear.

Jack backed out of the room to find Rick. The boy was waiting outside the door, leaning against the wall.

"I think we better get more help here," Jack said.

"Is she okay?"

"She's having it rough right now. What do you think—get your doctor over here? You saw her. Or maybe Pastor Ellingsen?" Jack realized he was wrong to ask Rick Bauer to make this decision; he'd already asked the boy to carry more than his share. But goddamn it, Jack wanted her off the bathroom floor and right now. He knew he couldn't manage it alone.

"Mrs. Andersen's a nurse," Rick said. "She lives a couple doors down."

"Can you call her?"

Rick nodded. "She and Mom are pretty good friends. I bet she'll come over."

"Okay. Tell her however much you're comfortable telling. I'll sit with your mom until."

Vivien's eyes were still closed, so he couldn't tell if she knew he was back in the room or not. That was fine. He lowered the toilet lid and sat down. He didn't know what to say to her anyway, so he'd keep quiet. For now, he'd just watch. . . .

He'd spent so many of the night's hours in the darkness that this room's bright, sharp light made everything look strange. Was Vivien Bauer's flesh truly that pale? He looked at her bare shoulder up against the tub and damned if her skin didn't look almost as white as the porcelain. Her legs were as pale as her shoulders, but the flesh of her extremities was faintly mottled, like marble. She must be cold, Jack thought, lying on the linoleum like that. As long as she wasn't going to get up, maybe he should cover her with something, a towel, his jacket. . . .

But he didn't move. He couldn't remember when he had had an opportunity like this, to study another human being, a woman, under light as bright and shadowless as the high noon summer sun.

He had never heard anyone describe Vivien Bauer as beautiful, but why not? Even now—exhausted, sick, without makeup, her eyes and forehead and cheeks covered with one bright pink blotch so it almost looked as though she were wearing a mask—she looked lovely to him. Those high cheekbones, that clean sharp jawline, the large eyes, the full lips . . . and this woman wasn't good enough for Leo?

He kept staring, and he couldn't be sure exactly when her eyes opened, because his gaze had dropped and he was examining her body, moving down from that bare shoulder and searching for where her nipples might show their shadows through the night-gown's fabric.

When he realized she was watching him, he looked away quickly. His eyes came to rest on the rubber-tipped doorstop sticking out from the baseboard, and he kept his vision locked there. He felt his face heating into a deep blush. He had seen Vivien Bauer—how often? every month? every week?—for years and years, yet he had never looked at her the way he was looking at her now. The widow Bauer—the words leaped into his brain from he knew not where. The widow Bauer. He had been ogling Vivien Bauer's body in the first hours of her widowhood. My God, what kind of man was he!

"Sheriff Nevelsen." Her voice was hoarse, faint.

"Yes, ma'am." He kept staring at that doorstop.

"Keep him away from me."

"Keep—?"

"My. Son." The words barely got out, but the difficulty seemed to come less from emotion and more from whatever apparatus in her throat and mouth that made sound into words and got them out into the air.

"Rick? You don't mean Rick. He's worried about you. He—"

"My . . . Leo's dead. My husband." He let himself look at her once again, at her face, at nothing but her lovely, sorrow-riven, grief-pinched face. "And he . . . I can't talk to Rick right now."

"Oh, ma'am. I talked to Rick, and he told me . . . He . . . This is hard on Rick too. He's just holding up for you—"

She put her hands up defensively, just as she had before when he reached out to her. Jack stopped talking.

Why shouldn't she hold her son responsible? If Rick offered his mother the same story that he and Jack had worked their way through earlier, why wouldn't she believe that, if not for Rick, Leo would still be alive, would be home right now, sleeping in his own bed? But didn't a mother love her child no matter what? Perhaps there was a zone that a mother's love couldn't enter, and it was that region where the child has taken a mother's mate away.

Jack had done enough damage. He'd wait for Rick to return.

He patted his cigarette pack. "Do you mind if I smoke, ma'am?"

She finally shifted her position, sitting up straighter, pulling her nightgown further down her legs. Her shoulder remained bare. "You used to call me 'Viv.' "

"I used to—? I'm sorry . . ."

"From the time we were first introduced. You called me 'Viv.' Everyone's always called me Vivien. Except my grandfather. He . . . Even Leo called me . . . And now suddenly it's Mrs. Bauer. My husband . . ." Her voice rasped to a stop, and she pressed the heel of her hand to her eye to stop the tears. "My husband has died, and I've turned into Mrs. Bauer. . . ."

How could he have missed it? The room smelled of liquor, and Mrs. Bauer's—Vivien's—breath was the only possible source. Yet the house had been dark, and Rick had had to wake his mother. Did that mean she drank herself to sleep hours ago? Maybe she took a drink after she got the news? No, there wasn't time. Besides, the odor didn't seem sharp or fresh. This was the kind of whiskey breath—as heavy and warm as the smell of a room in which bread had been baked—that came out with the very air you exhaled, not merely off the tongue or out of the mouth alone.

Vivien Bauer drank? No reason it could not be so—people, after all, drank whiskey, men and women both, and perhaps more than usual up in this often cold and joyless corner of the world. But Vivien Bauer? Who sang solos in the First Lutheran choir. Who organized a drive to ship food and clothing to the flood victims out in Crosley, Montana. Who volunteered her hours to help the slow readers in grade school. Who was married to Leo Bauer. . . .

"You don't want to go blaming Rick, Vivien. Listen to me. He's your boy. That hasn't changed."

She closed her eyes and tilted her head away once again. "Go ahead. Smoke your cigarette."

Now he wasn't sure: should he go back and reread everything Vivien had done and said and make adjustments for what was truly her and what might have been the whiskey?

And where should he stop? At the point where he walked into this house? Why not keep going back? Why not go years back to the Fourth of July picnic when Vivien tried to insert herself and a few of the other mothers and wives into the softball game played by the fathers and sons? Why not readjust the night of the Christmas party at the country club when Vivien tried to talk the celebrants into going outside and singing carols in the falling snow? Why not hand over all those moments to whiskey? Why not give her life with Leo to whiskey—and not just this grief?

Ah, he didn't have the strength for any of it. Let it stand, let it all stand. Her husband was dead. She blamed her son. She could not get off the floor. What did it matter where you found cause for any of it?

Jack didn't light a cigarette. He looked around the room. On a metal bar across from the toilet hung a single white bath towel. He stood and pulled the towel from its rack. It was made of terry

85

cloth, but it was thin from years of being used and laundered. The material was rough and stiff, no doubt from being hung in the sun to dry. Jack sometimes wanted to ask Nora to please not dry the towels outside; hang everything else on the line but put the towels in the dryer. Please, let's have just this little touch of softness in our lives. Of course he said nothing. Laundry was Nora's domain.

He lay the towel gently across Vivien Bauer's back, taking special care to cover that bare porcelain shoulder.

"It's cold in here, Viv. You can't feel it, but it is."

13

MRS. ANDERSEN HAD SIZE AND STRENGTH ENOUGH TO GET VIVIEN Bauer off the bathroom floor without assistance.

She came into the house wearing a frayed wool robe and slippers, with her hair pinned up in curlers, yet she looked wide awake and alert. Her first concern was caring for Vivien Bauer, and both Jack and Rick stepped aside for Mrs. Andersen's nurselike assurance.

"Oh, Vivien. Oh, you poor thing!" Her voice, the loudest Jack had heard all night, ricocheted between the bathroom's walls and its fixtures. "Let's get you back in bed immediately."

Vivien rose without protest and shrunk into the big woman's embrace. On their way to the bedroom, Mrs. Andersen raised her eyebrows at Jack as if to say, See, this is what you should have been doing all along. As they passed, Jack smelled Mentholatum. And bourbon.

Jack asked Rick, "How about it? I suppose you'd like to go to bed too right about now."

The wall seemed to hold the boy up. "I'm not tired."

"You ought to get some rest anyway. There's not going to be

anything else to do tonight, but tomorrow will be busy. And your mom will need—"

"She'll be okay. Tomorrow."

Should Jack tell him that it would take a hell of a lot more than tomorrow to make his mother okay? He decided against it. Rick and his mother would have to find their own way.

"What did you tell Mrs. Andersen?"

"That my dad got killed. In a car accident."

"Anything else?"

"I couldn't remember where you said it happened."

"Sprull ranch curve. You didn't remember where you were going to meet your dad and June?"

"We didn't really get that far."

"You told her about June?"

"Sort of. . . ."

"Sort of? Jesus, Rick. We can't have everybody running around with their own story on this."

Rick pushed away from the wall and began to walk toward the bedrooms. He stopped suddenly and turned himself halfway around toward Jack. "I told her enough, okay? I told her it was me and June, okay? That it was all our goddamn fault. Okay?"

Even in the darkened hallway, Jack could see how close the boy was to tears. "Okay, son. Okay. Go ahead. Go see your mom." Rick looked directly at Jack, his tears halted by sudden anger. "Or just go on to bed. Get some sleep if you can. If it's all right, I'm going to use your phone before I head out."

"It's in the kitchen," Rick said.

Jack found the telephone book on top of a china closet. The Bauers kept their directory inside the same brown plastic cover printed with the names of local merchants that Jack and Nora used. Perhaps it was that similarity—that and the lateness of the hour, his fatigue, his reluctance to make this call—that impelled Jack to look up his own name and number before he looked up Mrs. Moss.

There it was—Nevelsen, John. And their address and number: 420 Cheyenne Avenue; 3964. *John?* How did that happen? He had been *Jack* since infancy. Had he told the telephone company

"John"? Had Nora? He had never looked himself up before, but it occurred to him now that when other people did, they would know his real name—and as something other than what he called himself every day of his life.

He turned back a few pages, Bauer, L. No mention of Vivien or Rick. No name, no special lettering, no signal to alert people that Leo might not be who he said he was.

Jack tried to remember how long this directory had been out, and when it would be time for a new one. Would Vivien be able to change their entry? Bauer, V.? Bauer, L., Mrs.?

Stalling. He was just stalling, and he knew it. Calling Mrs. Moss instead of going over there was cowardly enough; he was making it worse by delay. He turned to the *Ms.* Moss, Celia; 4232. The ratchet and return of the telephone's dial seemed unusually loud in this house awakened then hushed by the arrival of death news.

Someone answered on the third ring.

He guessed it was Mrs. Moss, but here it was, the middle of the night, and her voice had none of the huskiness of sleep. That single spoken word came from a voice pitched high, but steady and clear, like the twang of a tight wire. Could she have been awake, waiting for her daughter's return? Was it possible she had already heard what happened to June?

"Mrs. Moss?"

"Who's this?"

"This is Sheriff Nevelsen."

The line was quiet for no more than three seconds. Time enough. She knew now. Jack closed his eyes.

"What's wrong, Sheriff?"

"There's been an accident. A bad car accident."

"June?"

"I'm afraid so."

More silence. Many people in Bentrock still had party lines, and Jack listened for that vacant sound—silence echoing silence—that might indicate someone else was listening in on the line. It wasn't likely, especially at this hour, but he knew there were people in town who routinely listened in on their neighbor's lives whenever they had the chance.

"You said it was real bad."

"It was a fatal accident, Mrs. Moss. I'm sorry."

Jack heard a faint hiss, which could have been a problem with the connection or Mrs. Moss trying to draw a breath.

"Did she suffer any, do you know?"

There was that question again. Since there was little else left to wish for—all hopes canceled but this one—why not hold out this small favor.

"She died instantly, Mrs. Moss." It was the answer he would have given no matter what. "Her neck broke." He could not bring himself to say June's name.

"What about the circumstances?" The taut wire pulled a little tighter, but it had not yet snapped. Jack guessed it never would.

"The accident happened just west of town. Out on Highway two-eighty-four by the Sprull ranch." He knew it was not the answer she was looking for, but he hoped it would satisfy her for now.

It did not.

"June didn't have a driver's license."

What was that remark for? Was she trying to trap Jack into some inconsistency? June didn't have a driver's license so she couldn't be dead? Why did people still hold on to reason when reason was gone, useless? Death could not be argued away, no matter how illogical, absurd, or unfair its circumstances.

"No, Mrs. Moss, she was a passenger in the car."

Once again Celia Moss said nothing. Was this a strategy of hers, a tactic of stubbornness calculated to make Jack so uncomfortable that into the quiet he would shove something he really didn't want to say? Well, he had grown up on this snow- and heat-hushed prairie himself; he could keep its silence with the best of them.

My God, what was he thinking! The woman had just learned that her daughter was dead! Stubbornness? Strategies? From what hidden valley in his brain was this suspicion coming? When Celia Moss fell silent, she was probably turning away or covering the phone so he wouldn't hear her weep. The shock—the attempt to believe this unbelievable thing—no doubt made it almost impossible to find words, words to direct to this stranger who called her in the middle of the night.

Celia Moss finally managed this much: "Someone else was driving."

"Someone else. Yes." He wasn't going to give her any more. Not now. He couldn't.

"Just the two of them."

"Both of them killed instantly. Yes."

He thought he heard a little sniff this time before she spoke. "What's next, Sheriff? What do I need to do?"

"I don't believe there's anything tonight, Mrs. Moss. But if it's all right, I'd like to come over and speak to you for a few minutes."

Jack could imagine what she was thinking: You're speaking to me now; what more do you have to say?

"I know it's late," he added. "If you'd rather wait till morning, I can understand."

"No, come on over. If you've got something to say, I want to hear it."

"Is there someone else you want me to call? I know you go to First Lutheran same as we do. I could phone Pastor Ellingsen. . . ."

"No, let him sleep."

"I'll be there shortly."

Jack kept the phone pressed to his ear. He wanted to hear Mrs. Moss hang up first. Then he would listen for someone else breaking the connection.

Celia Moss's phone clattered against the cradle, but then that was all. No one else on the line. He pressed the button down on the Bauers' phone, then gently replaced the receiver.

He stood and stretched. He was tall enough that he could touch the ceiling easily. Reaching overhead like that was a habit left over from childhood. Jack and his brother used to jump and try to touch the ceilings in their home. Jack was as tall as his brother, but his brother was older and the better leaper and his fingertips brushed first. Jack soon spurted past his brother in height, and before long they were both touching the ceiling so often their mother had to tell them to stop; she needed to climb on a chair to wash off their fingerprints. To this day, Jack could not resist the impulse: if the ceiling was within reach, he had to give it a tap.

Leo was almost Jack's height, so he would have been able to duplicate this feat.

Had that been Leo's problem—ceilings too low and walls too close? Was that what propelled him from these rooms and sent him speeding from town with a teenage girl?

There were days when Jack left his own house and went to the office where no work waited, or to the yard or garage where no chores needed to be done, because he had to get out, he had to move. He always thought it had to do with the air in the house, how, in the fall, winter, and spring, when the furnace was on, every warm, dry breath he drew seemed so stale it had to be the air he had exhaled just the moment before, or how, in summer, the dusty heat refused to leave the house, no matter how many windows were opened, no matter how many fans turned on, or how hard the breeze blew. On those days Jack had to get out, to pull into his lungs air that had never passed through the mesh of a window screen or the vents of a heat register.

After a few minutes of pacing the house, Jack would announce that he was leaving. Nora never argued with him, never asked him why or where he was going, but as he thought about it now, he seemed to recall a certain look she would give him before he left, a look both disapproving and wise. Did Nora know? Was she aware of something in his nature—in the nature of most men—which he barely recognized himself? Was that the knowledge that swam in her eyes as he said good-bye—that perhaps this time he might not return, that when he slammed the truck door it might be for the last time within range of her hearing, that under that canvas on the truck bed was a suitcase packed full enough to carry him away forever? Did every woman understand this—and understand as well that this was knowledge she could not reveal but must bear within? She—Nora—could never grab his wrist and say, Not this time. Not now. Not tonight. She might know that if he left this time he might stay away forever, yet she could only say good-bye. And tonight Vivien had to listen to Leo say he was going out for cigarettes, he was going to the auditorium to help supervise the cleanup after graduation—folding and stacking the chairs, rolling back the bleachers—and she had to hear him out and then say, only say, "Good-bye."

Jack turned out the light in the Bauers' kitchen. The room did not darken completely. A small light on the back of the stove remained on, its soft luminescence doubled as it bounced back off the porcelain's sparkling surface. The appliance looked new. A Kenmore. Electric. Had Leo made this purchase for the home before or after he decided to leave?

On his way out, Jack took a last look down the hall that led to the bathroom and bedrooms. Every door was closed.

14

Jack stood on Celia Moss's front porch, a cement slab no big-ger than a coffee table, and stared up at the light over the door. It was a bare bulb, yellow-coated to keep the bugs from clustering around it. That was the idea anyway, though husks of dead bugs stuck to the yellow light as well as to the surrounding overhang and fascia.

But it was not the color of light that amazed and transfixed him but the simple fact of its being on.

Inside this house was a woman who, after taking a call from a man who said he wanted to come over to talk to her about her daughter only hours dead, had thought to turn on the porch light to help him find the right door. What kind of mind was it that could find its way through sorrow to the switch that illuminated this yellow bulb?

Wait. June had been out. Perhaps Celia Moss left the light burn-ing every night her daughter was out. Then, a minute before mid-night, staying out as close to her curfew as she could, June would step through the door and, without thinking, turn this light off. Up and down the block, neighbors who were concerned or just plain nosy could look out and rest easy: the light was out; June was home.

Jack reached up and touched the tip of his finger to the bare bulb. It was warm but not hot. The light had not been burning long, certainly no longer than it took to drive from the Bauers' to here.

He pulled open the screen door and knocked softly. There was a doorbell, but its sharp electric burr was not for this hour or occasion.

Mrs. Moss was dressed, but of course there was no way Jack could know whether she had put clothes on for his visit or if she had not yet gotten undressed. She had only one child; perhaps she made it a practice to stay up and dressed until her daughter came home. *Had* one child was right. Whatever Celia Moss's practice had been, nothing would interfere with her bedtime now. If she could sleep at all.

Whatever the reason, Celia Moss was wearing scuffed, beaded moccasins, dungarees, and sleeveless white blouse. She was a tall, thin woman, and as soon as she opened the door, she wrapped her long arms around herself as if she were cold.

She didn't ask him to come in; she just stepped back and allowed him to enter.

No one with eyes or sense would call Celia Moss anything but a homely woman, and she did nothing to hide or deny the fact. She wore no makeup on that long, angular face, nothing to put color on the sallow skin or the wide tight lips, nothing to cover the moles, the bumps rising from her chin and cheek as if there was a pea under the first layer of skin. Her eyes were small and sunken, so it seemed as though simply looking out at the world required effort. Her long, lank hair hung past the bony points of her shoulders. Its color was the colorless shade of tree bark, not yet gray, no longer brown.

Jack spoke first. "I'm sorry about all this, Mrs. Moss."

She merely nodded, and then there they were, stuck just inside the front door, neither of them with any idea how next to proceed.

To avoid staring into Mrs. Moss's face—which on her best day seemed sorrowful enough—Jack looked around the living room.

It was tiny, and held little worth commenting on: A couch and two chairs, all with lace doilies, all old enough to have been handed down to Celia Moss from her mother. A television set. Two end tables with lamps and more doilies. In the dim light it was hard to see for certain, but it looked as though the painting over the couch was of mountains, a range that probably existed nowhere in the world but in the painter's mind. What was it with Montanans and mountains? Up in this corner of the state, hundreds of miles before you could hope to glimpse a far-off peak, there were still people who acted as though they had settled here because they loved the mountains and would never think of living anywhere far from their cool stony heights, their shadowy blue haze. And once you got out of the state, why, it was no use. The rest of the country seemed to believe every Montanan had a snow-capped peak right out his back door. Jack used to try to explain: We're more like North Dakota, the plains, the prairie; but the mountains were too high, too solid in people's minds to fade away. Besides, Jack couldn't come up with anything to replace the image of mountains. What was he supposed to say? Imagine . . . nothing? No mountains. No water. No trees. Just try to clear your head and when you've got it empty, you've got it. That's where I live. And winters weren't far from that truth. A faint pencil line dividing the gray-white sky from the gray-white earth.

Was that why June was leaving this tiny house and its doily-covered surfaces? Was she heading for another landscape, away from these tabletop prairies that no artist ever painted and toward the mountains, toward the real thing and not this corny, two-dimensional imitation that she had to look at every day of her life? If she left because she thought mountains looked like that, God help her.

And there *was* June, her graduation portrait anyway, sitting on another doily on top of the television. She wasn't smiling, but that wasn't required. Graduation was supposed to be a serious occasion; it was all right to put on a solemn expression for it, a look of purpose and determination, as if you knew the years ahead were going to ask more of you than a smile and a pretty face.

And June's was a pretty face. It had the length of her mother's but without the harsh planes and angles. June's lips were fuller, not so tightly set. And the eyes—there was the real difference. June's eyes were large and dark, knowing yet slightly amazed.

For a moment Jack tried to forget that the girl's mother was there, and he stared back at June's wide-eyed gaze, trying to determine if there was something special there for a man his age to see.

Did those open eyes mean she wanted to learn what an older man could teach her? That connection didn't work, not for Jack anyway.

He couldn't think of anything in his years of experience that a young woman might want.

Would she expect some skill at lovemaking that boys her age wouldn't have? Jack couldn't imagine how he would respond to such an expectation. With a graceful, pretty young woman in his arms he would feel even clumsier than he usually did. After all their years of marriage he still felt with Nora that he wasn't doing certain things correctly in bed or on their way to it. His kisses were too wet—or too dry. His caresses were too rough—or too light. Women didn't like to have their breasts touched this way—or this way. Women didn't want men to enter them this way—or that way. Women expected sex to last this long—or longer. His salvation was that Nora came to their marriage with even less experience, and she had done nothing over the years—read no books, overheard no barroom conversations, watched no stag films—that would increase her knowledge of how things were supposed to be between a man and a woman. If Jack were doing everything wrong, she'd have no reference to know. Nothing but her own pleasure. Or lack of it. An expert! Good Christ, he felt like a teenager himself in bed. If he had learned anything from experience, he forgot it all with the first flush of desire. He knew he pressed himself too eagerly on Nora at times, that he sometimes frightened her with his need. A teenager would frighten him in the same way.

A teenager? A woman! He would be afraid of any woman.

Afraid he couldn't please her or, worse, not even get to the stage where he could try, that she would rebuff him immediately.

Down at the courthouse in the Register of Deeds office worked a woman named Betty Stodd. She was raw-boned, broad-shouldered, and just over six feet tall. She had bright red hair that always had strands and tendrils sticking out no matter how tightly she pulled it back. Redheads are usually fair-skinned and freckled, but Betty always looked tanned, even with her office job. Her hair and her size brought her plenty of teasing—it turned into insult when she was not around—but Jack thought she was a shapely, pretty woman.

Betty came to Bentrock from Wyoming, and though she wasn't married, there were rumors she had been and was divorced. Or widowed, as the talk once had it in the Paper Dollar Saloon one warm fall night.

Jack was sitting at the bar. He was half finished with his patrol and had taken a break to get something cold to drink. Betty and four or five friends had stopped in after their bowling league.

A pair of cowboys from the Neihardt ranch were giving the women a hard time, alternating flirting with and taunting them. Jack knew the cowboys were trying to make time with the women, but in the way of young men it was easier for them to be mean than straightforward and pleasant.

Betty came in for the worst of it. "Big Red," they called her, though they knew her name. Was it true, one of the cowboys asked, that she killed her husband by hugging him too tight— that she splintered his ribs and they punctured his lungs? That wasn't quite the way he heard it, the other cowboy said. The busted ribs were right, but it was her legs she was wrapping around him.

Betty gave as good as she got. "That's right," she told them, "he just wasn't man enough for me. But the two of you still wouldn't add up to one of him, so don't be getting any ideas." That quieted the cowboys some, and Betty left for the ladies' room.

When she returned, she didn't go back to the table with her friends but sat down at the bar next to Jack.

His cigarettes were sitting on the bar, and she pulled one out of the pack.

"You mind?" she asked Jack.

"Help yourself," he said. "You earned it." He lit a match for her.

She asked the bartender for another Miller High Life. "How about you?" she asked Jack. "Maybe a shot in there? I'm buying."

He put his hand over the top of his glass. "Just Coke. I'm on duty."

She took a deep drag on her cigarette, and with a backward nod of her head, indicated the two cowboys who were now playing pool. "Local color," she said.

"I don't know what gets into them. . . ."

"Oh, shit, Jack. Same thing as always. Don't tell me you haven't got some of it in you."

He and Betty had an easy, bantering relationship. They ran into each other in the halls of the courthouse, at the post office when the mail came in, at Roller's Cafe, where so many people from the courthouse went for morning coffee. They bummed cigarettes from each other (they both smoked Chesterfields), they traded baseball scores (they were both Yankee fans), and the fact that she was a woman he found attractive was a secret Jack kept locked tight. Or so he thought. Now she was staring hard at him as if there were a haze in the air that prevented her from seeing him clearly. Or perhaps the haze had cleared and she finally saw him aright.

"Hey, Jack. How come you and me never got matched up? We're about the only ones around the right size for each other."

In the days, weeks, and months that followed, Jack thought of a good many things he might have said to Betty Stodd that night.

He might have tried a joke. "Hell, Red, you'd probably bust my ribs too. But I'm willing to take a chance."

He might have tried playing the gallant. "Betty, those cowboys could still give you trouble. You better let me escort you home."

He might have given her space to reconsider. "Why don't you ask me that tomorrow, when the light of day has shone on the matter?"

Oh, he could have said anything, and anything might have been better than what he did say.

He slid his pack of cigarettes toward her and said, "Keep 'em. I've got another pack in the car."

It occurred to him now, standing in Celia Moss's living room, that there was something else he could have said. "Leo Bauer's about your size too, Betty. And he just might take you up on your suggestion. It appears he's that type of fellow."

A teenager frighten Jack! Hell, any woman could throw a scare into him.

But not Leo. Not Leo. Apparently he believed he had something to offer a young woman, that she wouldn't mock him for his appearance or his attitudes. But how did Leo arrive at that confidence? What made him think he could put out his hand and touch her in that way and not have her flinch in disgust or anger? How did he find the courage to bend a kiss down to her when it was possible she might laugh at his advance? How did he know that she wouldn't do worse than spurn him—tell her friends, "Hey, do you know what Mr. Bauer did—yeah, Mr. Bauer the principal—he tried to grab me. Yeah, like *that.* Can you believe it? Mr. *Bauer.*" Jack could hear how a teenage girl would tell it. And he could imagine how the other kids would have made fun of Leo. "Mr. Bauer is a dirty old man! Mr. Bauer can't keep his pecker in his pants!" Christ, they would have driven him out of town.

Of course a woman—a young woman—could want something other than sex from an older man. Protection. Security. Wisdom. And June didn't have a father to provide those things. (Is that why Leo chose her, because if he made a pass at a girl with a father and she told her daddy, he'd come after Leo with a shotgun?) Maybe that was what she saw in Leo; in her mixed-up thinking she was running off with a father.

A father—sweet Jesus Christ, a father! Suddenly June's face seemed to change, change as surely as though a different photograph had been placed in that frame.

Now those delicate features, that pale complexion, were not signs of youthful beauty but only of youth, of childhood, of that age when every child in her nearness to innocence has a luster that the years have not yet dimmed. Over time perhaps June's smooth cheeks would, like her mother's, crease and sink with worry, those round eyes narrow with suspicion, the full lips clamp tight with words unsaid. But there in that frame now—that was not yet a woman. That was still someone's daughter, someone's child. That was Celia Moss's baby.

And a grown man—a father—was not supposed to carry a child away from her mama.

My God, Jack had been on the verge of envying Leo Bauer, and now he was heating up not with embarrassment but anger.

He thought of his own Angela, and without trying at all he could see her face—her sweet round face split by her wide smile, her smile that showed her two upper teeth especially, longer than the others and with the serrated bottoms that reminded Jack of teeth on teeth. Soon her pudginess—really just baby fat—would melt away, and she'd learn to keep her thick dark hair brushed and combed, and to wear makeup, and she'd be as pretty as any girl in her class. One day a photographer would pose her just right—head tilted up or to the side, fingers below her chin or along her cheek—and her face would be in a gilt frame like the one on Celia Moss's television set.

Jack felt he had to grab on to the back of the chair. He had let too many of the differences between Angela and June slip away, and now he not only had his daughter about to graduate from high school, he also had a vision—less than an instant and barely a sliver of a fragment but enough, enough. He saw Angela, *his* daughter, *his* baby, lying dead in a ditch. No, not all of her—a forearm, turned as white and cold as the bone beneath the skin, smeared with blood. Enough? No, too much, too much. . . .

"Sheriff? Sheriff?" It was Celia Moss's voice trying to find him.

Was there a man or boy in this town who would one day take Angela away? Someone who drove too fast, who wanted what he wanted, who didn't care that she had a mother and father who loved her, who kept only one hand on the wheel and with the other tried to pull Angela close. . . . The road dipped and curved, but the car, the car, the long black car, had a mind like its driver's and swerved at nothing. . . .

Jack groped his way around the chair and fell back into it.

He couldn't do this—he couldn't! He couldn't carry on like this in front of Celia Moss. She was the one who had lost a daughter.

He leaned forward and hung his head down between his knees, and when he did, he noticed that he was bowing in the direction of June's photograph. What the hell—as long as he was down there: Forgive me, miss, forgive me for my thoughts of you. Forgive me for any damage I've done to your memory. Or will do.

15

THE PRESSURE OF CELIA MOSS'S HAND UPON HIS BACK WAS VERY LIGHT and, at first, motionless. Then she began to pat and rub in tiny circles.

That touch, that small act of kindness, was almost more than he could bear. His embarrassment was doubled. *He* should have been comforting *her*—as earlier he had been willing to comfort Mrs. Bauer. But then Celia Moss was a less attractive woman than Vivien, whose white nightgown barely covered her. . . .

He quickly sat up straight and took a couple deep breaths. "Don't know what that was all about. Probably too many cigarettes and coffee in a day."

"I was about to ask you if you wanted a cup. I made a fresh pot."

Amazing. This homely woman thought to turn on the porch light and brew a pot of coffee for her guest, for the man who called in the middle of the night with the news that her daughter would not be coming home.

He rose slowly, letting his unsteady body unfold itself in stages. "I guess one more cup isn't going to make a difference."

"I figured it was going to be a long night."

Jack followed her into the kitchen and sat where she indicated he should, in a straight-backed wooden chair at the head of the table. The table was spread with a white cloth so clean it looked freshly laundered. Its folds were still visible, so Jack wondered if it too had been brought out for his visit. No—how could she have had time? Turn on the porch light, brew the coffee, get out a clean tablecloth—all since she hung up the phone. Not possible.

But how Celia Moss acted so quickly wasn't what bothered him. It wasn't time—it was her mind, her mind that could make room in this moment to set her daughter aside for a porch light, a pot of coffee, a tablecloth. . . .

An even more confounding thought struck him. What if these were not sudden, last-minute preparations? What if she had known about the accident for hours, the news having found its way to her by a route more direct than Jack's? The ambulance attendant told a nurse at the hospital about the accident and who was in it. She told her sister-in-law, who lived just two doors from Celia Moss. . . . Or Wayne told his sister, who told her best friend, whose mother belonged to the same church circle group. . . . Or, worst of all, Gordon Van Allen didn't keep his word to Jack and told his wife, Patsy.

Oh, Christ, he didn't want to think anymore! He wanted all these choices, all these possibilities that kept lining themselves up like an army of foot soldiers, he wanted them all to fall away, to leave him with nothing, nothing but certainty.

He ran his finger lightly along the crease, half-raised, half-sunken, in the tablecloth, trying impossibly to determine by touch what he could not know any other way: how recently had Celia Moss taken this cloth out of storage, shaken it free of its folds, and spread it upon this table? If he were in his own home, he could have used another sense. Nora kept her fine Irish linen tablecloth, a gift from grandmother to first grandchild, in their cedar-lined closet. Jack could always tell how long the tablecloth had been out by how strongly it smelled of cedar.

Celia Moss set Jack's coffee in front of him in a small china cup and saucer. The cup, decorated with a pink-and-green floral design and trimmed with fine lines of gold gilt, was so delicate Jack could not fit his thick fingers through the handle. He pinched the handle to lift the cup to his lips.

Mrs. Moss made one more trip from the cupboard to the table before sitting down herself. Beside Jack's arm she placed another saucer, this one obviously from the everyday dishes, a thick cream-colored plate with a chipped edge. "For your ashes," she said.

Jack brought out his cigarettes and laid them on the table but did not light one.

Mrs. Moss sat opposite him and crossed her bare arms once again.

If he did not get to the matter quickly, his courage might run out completely. "Mrs. Moss, did June have a boyfriend?"

"She might have."

With each question and answer, Jack felt himself buffeted by another gust of fatigue and doubt. Was she saying she didn't know if her daughter had a boyfriend or that whether June had one or not wasn't any of his business?

Jack swirled his coffee in his cup. The dark liquid caught and threw back the light from overhead. "Don't you know?"

"June went her own way."

"Rick Bauer?" He kept his eye on his coffee.

"The principal's boy." Was it a statement or a question?

"Rick. That's right."

"I thought she might have had somebody in her life from time to time. But she didn't say."

"Nobody coming around the house?"

"She went out."

"To meet somebody?"

"Could be." Celia Moss stood and walked to the stove. She lifted the coffeepot from the burner. "Can I heat you up a little?"

The gesture reminded Jack: Celia Moss worked behind the lunch counter at F. W. Woolworth's, where she put cups of coffee before customers all day, filling and refilling all those cups. He also realized why he hadn't recognized her from her workplace. In addition to her waitress's uniform, an aproned pale green dress, she and all the counter workers were required to wear their hair under a snug net that made it look as though they were wearing helmets.

No, hair nets had nothing to do with it. Jack no doubt saw Celia Moss in church too—and perhaps once a month or more in Nash's grocery store or in the post office. The truth was, Celia Moss was one of Bentrock's invisible, someone you ignored because you could: she had no power or influence; she minded her own business and made no great contribution to or trouble for her town. Someday she would die in Bentrock just the way she lived there—so quietly that the *Mercer County Tribune* would have trouble filling two inches of obituary space for her. Now her long hair, free of its daily encumbrance, seemed a reproach to Jack. Well, he was not ignoring her now. . . .

He lifted his cup, dispensing with the handle, clawing his fingers around the top. "No, I'm fine."

She returned to her chair and brushed the edge of her palm across the tabletop as if she were wiping away crumbs.

"June didn't talk much," Mrs. Moss said. "Liked to keep to herself."

"They can be like that."

"She was never any other way. I think some folks figured, her not having a father and all . . . But that's just the way she was. From when she was little. That was her nature."

"So you don't know if she had a boyfriend."

"I had my suspicions. But they don't come right up to the door anymore. That's not the way."

"I can't keep up with how they do things nowadays."

Celia Moss rose still another time and went to the stove, but once there she must have realized she had nothing to do. She bent over as if she were checking the flame under the coffeepot. She turned it higher then lowered it to its original height.

"Rick Bauer, you said. He the one driving?"

There. She finally asked. Jack wasn't sure if it was pain or pride that had prevented her from inquiring earlier. Just as he was not sure what kept him from telling her. Was he afraid of opening that chapter because of its complications—fear that he might be unable to convince Celia Moss of the circumstances surrounding the accident? Or had he come to regard Celia Moss as an adversary, someone not to be comforted but overcome? He hoarded his information because Celia Moss might be holding on to hers—maybe June told her mother everything before she left—and this woman was trying to outwait Jack, hoping to catch him in a mistake or an outright lie.

He had reason for that line of thinking. The people of Mercer County thought highly enough of him—trusted him, judged him capable—to choose him to be their sheriff, but after the election something changed. They began to resent him. They wanted him to stand apart from them, to give them a little distance for their day-to-day dealings, and then they disliked him for being aloof. They wanted him to stand for something, but they didn't want him to act superior to them. They wanted him to be fair, but they expected their transgressions to be overlooked.

After a few months in office, Jack finally figured out why they saw him this way. Once he was elected, once he was in office, he was no longer one of them. Now he was the government, even in this minor, rural way, and Montanans drank in with their mother's milk fear, suspicion, or, in many cases, outright hatred for any representative of the government, a government that existed, as far as they could see, for only one reason: to make their lives more difficult by telling them what to do. And if there was anything Montanans didn't want, it was to be told what to do. It was no mere oversight that Montana had no speed limit posted for its highways.

Jack eventually adjusted. The resentment was, for the most part, not personal. If he left office, it would probably vanish, except in a few especially rancorous cases. And if he remained in office, he could continue to be reelected; it was easier for voters to cast their lot with him than to arouse themselves to a new round of indignation.

In the meantime, Jack shouldn't be surprised if people were secretly—or not so secretly—pleased if he slipped up or looked foolish in any official capacity.

And he shouldn't be surprised if he learned that Celia Moss felt that when the sheriff was in her home, he was not there as a friend but as someone from the other side, whatever that side might be.

He waited until she returned from the stove. This time he wanted to see her face.

"It wasn't Rick," said Jack. "It was his father. Leo Bauer was driving."

16

CELIA MOSS GAVE A LITTLE SNIFF. HER MOUTH TWISTED UP THEN DOWN, and she blinked slowly.

It was an expression Jack found impossible to read. Was she trying not to show her surprise? To stifle a sob? To hold back a knowing laugh?

She went back to checking the flame beneath the coffeepot. Was it the memory of her touch on his back, his embarrassment at breaking down in front of her, that caused him to treat her so cruelly? She was not the town. She was one woman, and on what was quite possibly the hardest night of her hard life, he was making matters worse by parrying with her, trying to see if he could get her to reveal any secrets before he had to give up his. For the second time inside of an hour, he felt ashamed.

"Come on over and sit down, Mrs. Moss. Let me tell you what happened as best I can."

She shuffled back to her chair.

"I already talked to Rick and he gave me the story." Jack tried to keep his voice from sounding official. He wanted this scene to be as close as possible to what it could never be: two people sitting at the kitchen table and talking over coffee.

"Rick said him and June were going to run off together." Jack quickly added, "To get married. They were keeping it quiet. Planned on sneaking away before anyone noticed they were gone.

"Rick had someplace he had to be tonight, so his dad was taking June on ahead to Rifle Gap, and Rick was going to meet up with her later. Leo was going to give them his car. Let them get started with a dependable vehicle. The accident happened west of town, out by the Sprull ranch on that bad stretch. Just the one car involved, as far as we can tell." Jack liked the sound of "we"; it made it seem as though many others were behind these words.

And then that was it. He had told the story, and it ended so quickly he wondered if he had forgotten something. No, it was all there, all the essential information. If the incident could be presented so succinctly to June's mother, why, maybe this wasn't going to be so complicated to put over after all.

After another small, thoughtful sniff, Celia Moss asked, "Was she going to be waiting alone in Rifle Gap?"

"Alone?"

"I been to Rifle Gap. Dirty little town that's nothing but low-lifes. Was he just going to leave her there amongst them?"

He answered so quickly he surprised himself. "Leo was going to wait. Rick was going to be along directly, but Leo was going to stay with her until."

She nodded in approval.

"I'm not saying they thought everything through. Young people never do. But they tried to use their heads in some matters."

Celia Moss jammed her hands down upon the table with such force the tablecloth slid an inch or two. "And who was going to tell me what was going on? When was I going to get in on this?"

"Leo was going to talk to you. And to Mrs. Bauer too. After the kids were away."

"When?" It was only one word, yet it came out like an accusation.

"I don't know. Tomorrow morning maybe."

"And let me fret all night through?"

Jack leaned forward himself. "I can't say I'm too pleased with how Leo tried to handle this. God knows I wish he could have found another way. I don't know what was going on his head. But he did what he did." Jack felt a measure of relief that he could finally say something and be certain of its truth, no matter what the truth was.

Celia Moss seemed to accept the immutability, the finality of Jack's statement. "Well, I hope she found herself someone to talk to."

Did she mean Leo? Rick? God? Jack couldn't make himself ask.

She squinted down at the floor as though the words she spoke were printed on the linoleum. "Ever since June was old enough to talk—oh, God, maybe even before. That's the way I sometimes think. Like she could've talked before, maybe she knew how, but she just wouldn't. . . . She started so late. . . . But from the first, right to this very day, I knew she had things to say that she wasn't saying to me."

"But that's kids. They've always got their secrets."

Celia Moss kept her gaze down and shook her head slowly. If a man wore that expression, Jack would expect him next to spit in the dirt.

"She wasn't a pouter. It's not like she was mad or trying to punish me."

"They'd rather talk to their friends—"

She shook her head no faster but turned it further in each direction. "June was never much for friends. No. No, she just wasn't talking. Maybe thought no one would understand so why bother. I know what that's like. I know what that'll cost you. But she wouldn't let it out, not for anything. . . . I remember one of those Sunday school programs. Or grade school maybe. Whichever. I came in late and sat in the back and couldn't see too good. They were all standing up there, singing and looking so serious, afraid they'd forget the words. They held these little flashlights in front of their faces, so I couldn't see which was June. Must have been Sunday school. With those flashlights they were singing 'This Little Light of Mine.' Then they stopped singing and said a little poem or some such, and I saw this one little girl there on the end

111

and her lips weren't moving, and I knew, that's my June. That's the way I saw her all her life. Her lips not moving." Celia Moss's own lips trembled as perhaps she thought of the connection between what she said and her daughter now dead—not her lips, nor her hands nor feet nor eyelids moving, not ever. But Mrs. Moss's spell did not last long. She clapped her hands on her knees and, as if that was all the help she needed to get back on her feet once again, rose.

"So, Mr. Nevelsen," she said, widening her eyes the way a sleeper might upon waking, "that's why I say what I say. I hope this Rick was someone she could talk to. Or Mr. Bauer maybe. On the way out of town. Whoever. I hope she got a chance it get out what she had in her to say. Because she had it stored up. Believe me. She had a whole life stored away."

As if it were the only direction she could move in, Celia Moss took those familiar few steps back to the stove. She lifted the coffeepot. "You going to want any more?"

"No, I'm fine."

She put the pot down, turned off the burner, then bent down to make sure the flame was out.

Jack's lower back gave him trouble from time to time, especially when, as now, he was tired and let himself slump. He stood now, not because he was about to leave (though he had been hoping, since Mrs. Moss began talking, that he could soon find an opportunity to excuse himself), but because he needed to relieve that ache—a sensation that felt as though the bones of his lower spine were pressing and scraping together and pushing each other out of line.

But once he rose from his chair, Celia Moss quickly volunteered more information.

"I sometimes thought she was on the phone late. It would ring at all hours, and she'd answer right off, like she was trying to get it almost before it rang. I suppose that could have been the boyfriend. . . ."

"Did you have a private line?"

She nodded. "Junie had us switched over about a year ago. Said she'd pay for it herself."

"You never answered any of those late calls?"

She shook her head. "I knew it wasn't going to be for me."

Jack stretched and arched his back in an attempt to relieve the stiffness and the ache. "I'm going to have to get moving, Mrs. Moss. I've still got to attend to a few things before I call it a night. Thanks for the coffee, and again, I'm sure sorry about everything."

She waved her hand as if to dismiss his apology.

"Could I call someone for you? Someone to come over and stay awhile?"

"How's Mrs. Bauer? You talked to her already?"

"She's been notified."

"How's she taking it?"

"She's not too steady right now."

She nodded as if she was not surprised. "News like this hits a body hard. . . ."

Yes, you'd know, Jack thought. You've heard it more than once. Could it be that Celia Moss was proud? She had taken this news and was still standing. Unlike Vivien Bauer, Celia Moss was not about to break. Sure, that explained the coffee, the good china. My God, what kind of a place was this, where a woman who just heard her daughter had been killed might have the same pride as a man with a reputation for another kind of toughness?—hit them as hard as you can, they aren't going down.

"Like I said, I could call Pastor Ellingsen."

She sniffed contemptuously. "And wake him up and give him a heart attack? No thank you."

"Someone else? I hate to leave you alone. . . ."

"I was alone before you got here."

"A friend maybe? Someone in the neighborhood?"

"This ain't that kind of neighborhood." She waved him toward the front door. "You go on, Sheriff. I'm going to call my sister out in Spokane but not till morning."

He stopped before he got to the door. "I didn't know you had family in Spokane."

She looked at him as if she could not quite understand how this man came to be in her house. "I got a brother out in Long Beach too, but no reason you'd know that either."

Celia Moss's hand was on the doorknob before his.

"If I find out any more about the accident . . ."

"Maybe you best keep it to yourself."

When he pulled the door shut behind him, he had to give an extra tug to get it tight into the frame. One year the wood's warp would be so severe that it wouldn't close at all. Another winter might do it.

Had Celia Moss pushed on the other side of the door when he pulled? Was she in that much of a hurry to get him out and keep him out? What did she mean—he should keep it to himself?

When he got to the truck, he remembered—he still had June's suitcases. He lifted them out, a little surprised at how light they felt in relation to what he knew were their contents—a life, a new life, in only two bags. . . .

He hurried back to the porch and knocked again, this time on the screen door. This time Mrs. Moss didn't open the door wide in an invitation for him to enter, but only looked out at him through an opening most dogs would have trouble squeezing through.

"I almost forgot. I've got June's suitcases." Mrs. Moss looked so stern Jack had trouble getting his words out. "I'll put them in her room for you."

She opened the door a bit wider. "You can put them down right here."

"They're heavy. I'll—"

"I ain't a weakling, Mr. Nevelsen."

"No, I know that. I know. But . . . I was wondering. Would it be all right if I looked in June's room? Just for a minute?" When it first occurred to him, the request didn't seem unreasonable, but now, formed in words and presented to Celia Moss, it seemed in need of an explanation. If only he had one. . . .

"I'm sorry. If I can just look. I'm not going to take anything. This whole thing . . . it's just too . . . It's hard to understand how a thing like this happens. I thought if I looked in there . . ."

"What's to understand?"

"Nothing. I don't know. Please."

Wordlessly, Celia Moss let him in. She stood with her back

114

against the door and her head hung down. Then she pushed away and swiftly led him down a darkened hallway. Jack followed with the suitcases. The hall was so narrow, he had to turn sideways to keep the bags from banging against the wall.

The door to June's room was closed, and when Celia Moss hesitated before it, Jack wondered how long it had been since she was last in there. Jack suddenly had a vision of a young woman whose insistence on privacy was so complete that her mother didn't dare enter her room even after death.

Celia Moss opened the door, reached in to switch on the light, but did not go in. "Help yourself," she said.

The overhead light was too much for the tiny room. It left nothing for shadows, for secret corners. It revealed every flaw, every irregularity—the chipped paint on the dresser's knobs, the cracked veneer on the vanity table, the sagging springs on the narrow bed, the missing tufts on the white chenille spread. . . . No, June would never use that light. She'd click on that lamp with the yellowing shade on the bedside table. Or the smaller globe lamp, not much bigger than a softball, on the vanity. Jack was so convinced he was right that he almost asked Mrs. Moss if she ever had to change the overhead bulb. He was certain she'd answer no.

The closet door was not shut tight, but as much as Jack wanted to look inside, he did not, nor did he ask permission to do so. He believed the closet would have been close to bare. Her suitcases were packed tight with everything June needed, or thought she needed, to start a life far away from this one.

Jack wasn't sure where to put the suitcases. If he put them on the bed, it would seem as though June might have just gotten back from a trip and hadn't gotten around to unpacking yet. He set them down by the closet door.

On the dresser was a framed, eight-by-ten, sepia-toned studio photograph of a young man with jug ears and a lopsided smile. He wore an army officer's cap and what appeared to be a full-dress uniform. June's father. And now that Jack saw the photograph, he remembered: Calvin Moss had not been killed in World War II but in Korea. How could Jack have forgotten? Bentrock had not lost anyone during the Second World War, but three men, all from the same National Guard unit, had died in Korea. Six years ago? Celia Moss had not been widowed long, and certainly June had to have memories of her father. But none of them pleasant enough, important enough, to make her pack this photograph. Did Mrs. Moss have a picture of this man on her dresser as well, or had she tried to put his image and memory behind her as her daughter had planned to do?

On the floor beside the bed was June's record player with a small stack of 45s piled up on the fat spindle and waiting to drop down on the turntable. Waiting forever now. Jack tried to read the top record's label but could only make out the company: Capitol.

Had Leo been in this room? Had June been able to sneak him in when she knew her mother would be gone for hours? Had Leo found a way to get in without a neighbor spotting him?

Once Leo was in, did June play these records for him? Perhaps they danced, here on this gray-green, threadbare rug. Could you call it dancing, what they did in a space this small? Or did they just stand in one place and sway, as if the music were wind and they were little more than two grassy stalks obeying its will?

What about this bed? Could they have lain here together? The mattress, to someone Jack's size, barely seemed wide enough for one, and it hardly looked as though it would hold the weight of two. . . .

Celia Moss, as though she knew the way Jack's thoughts were turning, said, "You seen enough?"

Enough? Jack felt that if he spent the night in this room—no, more than a night, a week, ten days; yes, a ten-day sentence in this cell of a room—if he listened over and over to those records, if he lay on that narrow bed and stared up at the ceiling and the cracks in its plaster that looked like rivers on the map of a continent never visited, if he could look in that closet, then it might be enough to begin to understand the young woman who once lived within these walls.

Jack turned to leave and saw what he could not see before. Hanging from the inside doorknob dangled the tassel that not so many hours before had swung from June's graduation cap.

116

Enough? That was enough. Now he knew what was in that closet. June's graduation gown was in there, black as a funeral dress, and waiting for Mrs. Moss to find the courage to look through her daughter's things, discover the gown, and return it to the rental company.

"Yes, I've seen enough," Jack said. "Thank you."

17

JACK DROVE BACK TO THE BAUERS' STREET, NOT TO VISIT THEIR HOME again, but to begin searching for the telephone that Leo might have used when he called June Moss late at night. Jack could not imagine Leo picking up the phone in his own kitchen for such a purpose. Even if Rick was out of the house and Vivien sound asleep in her bed, even if Leo could be certain no one would overhear him as he murmured into the receiver, he would still leave the house. Of that Jack had no doubt. These houses—Leo's, his, almost all of them up and down Bentrock's streets—belonged to the women who spent most of their days in them. You wouldn't even whisper a declaration of love for another woman within those walls. No, Leo would have left the house.

As he drove, Jack counted eight blocks from Bauers' to Horace Mann, where Leo was principal. Leo would have a key to the building, and he could let himself in late at night, lock himself in his office, sit down at his desk, and from there talk to June to his heart's content. That plan wouldn't even have required a lie to Vivien. "I have to go back to school," he might have said, "I have work I have to catch up on." Jack had used the same excuse himself to get out of the house, though not for any reason as shady as Leo's.

But Leo may not have been alone in the building. A custodian was likely there, sweeping and mopping floors, scrubbing toilets, rubbing dirty words off the bathroom walls, cursing those kids whose messes gave him a job but made it a difficult one. What if he were right outside Leo's door when Leo called June? What if he saw the light on another phone that indicated a line was being used, carefully picked up that extension, and listened not only to Leo's every word but June's too? This custodian—a man Jack did not know, a man probably ignored by most—might be the one person in Bentrock who knew what was going on between Leo and June. Maybe he knew what they planned to do tonight. . . .

Jack *could* question him. It would be perfectly natural for him to ask around following an accident involving two fatalities. But interrogate a school janitor? For what possible reason? The questioning wouldn't have to be official of course. Jack could simply stop by the school after hours some day and strike up a conversation. Pretend he was there to talk about a problem with the older kids—about their smoking perhaps. Did he ever catch any of them smoking in school or find cigarette butts in the building? Jack wasn't much good at these conversations that pretended to be about one thing when they were about another, but maybe he could manage this one. Talk about kids and their behavior could lead to a discussion of discipline, which would move to teachers and principals and what they would tolerate. Now, Leo Bauer: how about when he was principal . . . ?

But where would it stop? Yes, he could question the janitor. And the teachers. After all, they might have observed their principal behaving unusually. And why not the older students of Horace Mann? Why not bring them in one by one and ask if they had ever heard Mr. Bauer talking familiarly to a young girl? Hell, he could knock on every door in Bentrock and ask every man, woman, and child if they'd ever seen June Moss in the company of Leo Bauer. And after asking time and time again, maybe eventually he'd find someone who had seen or heard something about those two, someone willing to talk, and maybe then Jack would be able to graft a beginning and a middle onto the story whose ending took place on the Sprull ranch curve.

But maybe there was no such person. Leo and June were careful. They knew the town and its darker corners, they knew where people were likely to be watching, and perhaps their caution paid off. The point was, Jack had to give up his curiosity, not only because the truth might be impossible to know—shattered forever like Leo Bauer's windshield—but because Jack needed to act as though the truth were already available, spread out for everyone in the form of his and Rick Bauer's story. Jack would be better off if he could convince himself no other truth lived to be told.

He had come this far, however, so he drove once around Horace Mann School, watching for a light on in the building that indicated a janitor might be inside waxing floors or washing windows. But on a Sunday night? Besides, the school year was over. They had the whole summer to get the building clean. The only sign of someone possibly present was a battered old Ford in the parking lot, although that might have belonged to a teacher who left it there on Friday when it wouldn't start. Jack sped off the way he had come, planning this time to count the blocks from the Bauers' in the opposite direction.

Yes, just as he had thought. Even nearer than the school was the telephone booth across from the Texaco station—only six blocks from the Bauers'.

Perhaps Leo didn't go to his office to call June but came here and used this telephone. Or maybe he alternated nights: school on Mondays and Wednesdays; pay phone across from the gas station on Tuesdays and Thursdays. And perhaps another location, or two or three—an entire network of telephones secreted around town— for the other nights. This booth was close enough to walk to from home. He might tell Vivien he was going out for a stroll and then come here. Jack didn't believe the Bauers owned a dog, which would give Leo another reason to leave the house. Jack was thinking now of what would be his own strategy for getting out. He'd bring Muley along, since the dog had to be taken out every night.

The booth sat on the corner of an empty lot. Jack had a vague recollection of a greenhouse occupying this space when he was a boy, but he couldn't be sure. There had been a greenhouse around here somewhere, because this was the route he and his friends walked to and from elementary school, and when they were a safe distance from the building—but still within throwing arm's reach—they would heave rocks in the air, concentrating on a high, arcing trajectory that would bring the stones down on—and break through—the greenhouse's glass roof. The glass must have been strong because they seldom heard the sound of it breaking (but took off running when they did). One of his friends, Allie Bascomb, always talked about how he'd love to sit up at the end of the block with a .22 and enough ammunition to shoot out every window in the greenhouse.

Bentrock's nursery and greenhouse was now Cooper's Floral, out on the west end of town. A year or two ago when they reported that someone had shot out a few of their windows, Jack's first thought was, Allie Bascomb, though Allie had long since left Bentrock. But what was Allie doing? Did he have a job that kept him on the road? In his travels did he pass near enough his hometown that he decided to buy a .22 and fulfill his boyhood dream?

Whatever had once stood on this spot had long ago been leveled. The lot was rutted, potholed, and unpaved, lightly covered with pea gravel and crushed rock to provide spillover parking for the Texaco station.

Jack parked next to the telephone booth and got out of his truck. Sure, Leo could have come here to call June. He'd have his privacy here. Here he could say anything he wanted to June. Here he would be free to tell her—what? What did a middle-aged man have to say to a teenager? Did he speak of his love for her, of his hopes for their forthcoming life together? Did he complain to her of his life's difficulties, of how hard his childhood was? Of how his wife didn't understand him or allow him full expression of the passions he had inside? Did he talk to her about his work, of dealing with unruly children and dissatisfied teachers? Or maybe he confessed to her a dream he told no one about, of leaving

Montana for good and finding someplace to live where it never snowed, where trees kept their greenery all the year round. Or perhaps the conversations were more personal still, full of the details of what they would do once they were alone. Or had already done. But to speak of these matters to a girl, a schoolgirl—Jack couldn't understand that.

What would she know of what it meant to go to work every day, of having to put the welfare of others, a wife, a child, before your own, of accumulating years and simultaneously shedding dreams? But maybe that was the point, to talk of these things to someone who as yet had no understanding or experience of them and who therefore wouldn't say to him what every adult Montanan was eventually broken in to say, silently or out loud, to another's complaints: Don't complain. Shoulder your load. Don't wish your life away. Don't make excuses. Jack's grandmother's entire vocabulary seemed made up of these phrases, each of them supposedly containing a recipe for successful living when in fact they were barely disguised scolds, even if his grandmother could deliver them with a cheery countenance. Be grateful for what you have. Don't make too much of things. You've got no cause to gripe. Others have it worse. And the one his grandmother especially liked and which Jack hated, at first because he didn't know what it meant and then because he did: If wishes were horses, then beggars would ride. He swore that as a father he would never say any of these to his child. He had already broken his vow.

So if Leo found someone with whom he could talk and never hear in return some stale advice about how he should be satisfied with his lot in life, then yes, Jack could imagine talking on long into the night, even if it meant standing in a telephone booth while a cold wind pried at the box's four corners.

Jack stepped into the booth and pushed the door shut. Instantly the light went on overhead. Now he wasn't so sure. Would Leo want to make calls like this, lit up and exposed for anyone driving or walking by to see? They couldn't hear what he was saying, yet this light was so bright it made it feel as though even your thoughts could be discerned. The "isolation booth"—that's what it was called on one of those television quiz shows—the glass cage where they put you so you could sweat and stew and try to come up with an answer while everyone watched. Jack pulled the door open a few inches, just far enough to shut off the light.

He dropped in his dime and told the operator, "Two-two-three-two," the number of the sheriff's office.

Wayne Schirmer answered on the second ring.

"Wayne? How's it going there?"

"Jack, hey. Where are you?"

"In a phone booth."

"In town?" Wayne's voice was a little too bright. Jack guessed the phone woke him.

"Across from the Texaco station."

Wayne laughed. "You paid a dime to call your own damn office!"

"I can always turn in a voucher, Wayne."

"A voucher for a dime! Would you—"

"Never mind. Listen. Has anything come in about the accident?"

"Leo's?"

Wayne's single-word question, as foolish and mindless as it was, revealed a truth, newly hatched but, Jack was sure, destined for a long life: the accident was Leo's, ceded him not only by the fact that he was the one driving but also because, of the two killed, he was the more prominent. Even in the country of death, status and reputation still mattered.

"Yes, Leo's. There hasn't been another, has there?"

"Accident? Nah, I could've arrested Ronnie Tall Bear though. Maybe I should've. When I come back into town, I saw him sitting on the curb in front of the Paper Dollar. He was so drunk he couldn't even sit up straight, so he was leaning up against the bumper of a parked car. 'Ronnie,' I says, 'that car drives away, your shoulder ain't going to be enough to stop it.' He just grinned at me like it was all a big joke. So if a call comes in that says Ronnie Tall Bear got himself run over, I wouldn't be surprised."

"Neither would he. But nothing more about Leo and June?"

"No-o-o. I thought you was looking into that."

"And I've found out a few things. But I thought I'd check in first." Jack wished he were handling everything alone. It wasn't that he doubted his deputy's competence, but Wayne was one more hindrance to be gotten around or worked through.

"Did you ever talk to Rick? What did he have to say?"

"He . . . What about the bodies? Are they still at the hospital?"

"They been shipped over to Undset's already." Undset and Sons was the town's funeral home. "Waiting interment."

"Whose idea was that?"

"Was what?"

"Undset's."

"Idea? Wasn't anybody's idea. That's the way it's done. That's where they wait interment."

Jack decided to go in a different direction so he wouldn't have to hear Wayne repeat the phrase one more time. "Rick explained the suitcase."

"I bet. What'd he say?"

Jack knew it was his obligation to report this conversation as convincingly as possible. Unlike Mrs. Bauer or Mrs. Moss, Wayne was not going to be so overwhelmed by emotion that he couldn't hear the story clearly.

"It was Rick and June who were running off together, and—"

"But Leo, Leo was driving—"

"Let me finish, all right? Leo was just helping them out. He knew they wanted to elope—" The word surprised Jack as much as Wayne's use of "interment," yet it also immediately pleased Jack in its rightness; it sounded accurate, official, and romantic all at once. And how much easier explanations suddenly seemed now that there was one word that covered so much. "—and Leo was sneaking them out of town—"

"Before their mommas could put a stop to it."

"Something like that. He was taking June to Rifle Gap, where Rick was going to meet up with her a little later. Leo was going to switch cars with them so they'd at least be setting out in a dependable vehicle."

Wayne made a small tapping sound with his tongue and his front teeth that was obviously meant to indicate disapproval. "Sounds mighty complicated."

"Well, you know. Given a choice between hard and easy, some people will pick hard every time."

Wayne's voice dropped down low. "You reckon you ought to order an autopsy?"

Jack's fatigue was coming in waves, each one gaining force from the one behind it. With the fat fleshy part of his thumb, he rubbed his eyelids. It felt as though grit were stuck behind the right one. "Why would that be, Wayne?"

"You don't think she might have been p.g.?"

"I can't say that occurred to me, no."

Wayne blew into the phone. "First thing I thought of."

"Is that right? I guess we'll never know."

"All you got to do is say the word. You can get it done."

"And what would be the point, Wayne?"

"The point? Jesus. We'd *know*. The truth would come out."

"Would it?" Jack's eyes were closed, and he leaned hard against the phone. Someone driving by might think he had fallen asleep in the middle of a conversation and was using the phone as a pillow. "I'm not so sure. . . . Anyway, I'm not going to be the one to tell Mrs. Moss that her daughter's going to be split open so we can find out if there was a baby in her baby. No, sir. There's nothing on earth I want to know that goddamn bad."

"Maybe you ought to think on it, Jack. You could still change your mind. While she's waiting interment."

Jack stuck a finger in his free ear. The hum of his own blood rushing was louder than the breath of the entire night surrounding him. "You know, Wayne, you're going to make a good sheriff someday."

"Nah. I couldn't do the politicking. Too much bullshit."

"You'll be able to handle it." Jack could have added, just use phrases like "awaiting interment" often enough; you'll be a shoo-in.

"I don't know. Maybe." Jack could tell Wayne wanted to mull over this statement. It should have been a compliment, yet it didn't quite feel that way.

"You can call it a night, if you like," Jack suggested. "I'm going to make another call or two and then turn in myself."

"You talked to Junie's mom? And Mrs. Bauer?"

"I did."

"Two in one night. God damn."

"Makes politicking sound easy, doesn't it?"

"Hey, I'd rather wrestle Ronnie Tall Bear into the car than have to walk up and ring Mrs. Bauer's bell tonight and give her the news."

"Ronnie always comes easy."

"But you know."

"Yeah." Jack flipped the coin return box up and down. "So go on home. And sleep in tomorrow, if you like. I'm coming in early."

"Tell you the truth, I'm not really in any hurry to turn in. I'm kind of worried once I close my eyes I'm going to see Junie. Or Leo. Shit, I don't want to see Leo. . . . I can't stop thinking how much blood there was. Like if you just leaned on the car seat, blood would come bubbling up around your hand. Soaked like a sponge, it was—"

"Take a drink of whiskey before you go to bed, Wayne. A stiff one. Then when you close your eyes, think about something else. Mountains. The ocean. Think about Dee." Dee was the young woman to whom Wayne was "engaged to be engaged."

"Dee. Sure. That'll work. I won't even need the whiskey. Okay. I'll see you in the morning."

"Not too early."

"Jack—hey, Jack. One more thing. . . ."

As tired and impatient as he was, Jack couldn't afford not to hear what else was on Wayne's mind. "What is it?"

"Which was worse—talking to Mrs. Bauer or Junie's mom?"

"Oh, Wayne. Jesus. I don't know."

"But which one? If you had to say."

"You don't think of it that way. You just do it."

Wayne's voice rose and threatened to crack. "But if it was me. Walking up to those doors. Which would be worse? Which was?"

"For Christ's sake, don't worry about it. Leo and June can't die all over again."

"Which, Jack? Which—if you could've gotten out of one, made me do it?"

"Wayne. Jesus, you wear me out." But an image had already wedged itself into his mind: Vivien Bauer lying on her bathroom floor, her nightgown above her knees, her shoulder bare. And now he remembered seeing what he couldn't be sure he saw at the time—the shadows, the faint shadows of Vivien Bauer's nipples showing through her nightgown.

"Mrs. Moss," Jack said. "June's mom. She was the worst."

18

JACK SLID THE DOOR SHUT, AND WHEN THE LIGHT FLASHED ON, ITS brightness gave him the same kind of headache he got from drinking or eating something cold. Once he could stop blinking and squinting, he looked up Gordon Van Allen's number.

Gordon's voice was clear but sullen.

"Gordon?" Jack was aware of his own voice assuming a false heartiness. "Jack Nevelsen. Did I wake you?"

"Yeah."

"Sorry."

"I'm used to it."

"Did I wake Patsy up?"

"She generally sleeps right through it. Can't get off the phone during the day, won't go near it during the night."

"Well, I just thought I'd fill you in on the accident. Let you know what I dug up."

"All right." A sound came through the line that might have been Gordon reining in a yawn. At least Gordon didn't say what he was probably thinking: Since when do you keep me informed about any investigating you do? I tow in the wrecks and that's it.

"I don't know if you and Leo were good friends or anything, but I know you knew him. And you were probably wondering about the accident, about how the hell he and June came to be in that car together—"

"Nope."

"No?"

"I don't wonder about such. Why the hell should I? I'll find out soon enough. I'll leave the wondering to people like you. Let you be the one who doesn't get any goddamn sleep."

"You're right about that. This is well past my bedtime. But I did a little checking when I talked to the families. Found out what was going on with those suitcases."

"What suitcases would those be?" Gordon's question was asked so deliberately Jack wondered if a trap was being set.

Then he felt a flutter of panic. Was he going back too far, making this a more elaborate construction than it needed to be? "That's right. You had already left when Wayne made his little discovery. He found suitcases in the car. A couple were June's all right, but the other had Rick Bauer's name attached. Rick—Leo's son?"

"I know Rick."

"You can imagine what was going on in our heads. Trying to figure out first of all what Leo and June were doing out there, and then with suitcases belonging to Rick and June." Jack had an impulse to stop right there and ask Gordon what arrangement he might make if he were handed these pebbles of evidence: Leo. June. Dead on Highway 284. Three suitcases, two with June's name, one with Rick Bauer's. But Jack immediately thought better of it— what if Gordon reached a different conclusion?

"So you can be damn sure," Jack went on, "the first thing I did was track Rick Bauer down and ask him about that suitcase with his name on it. Turns out him and June Moss were going to elope. Heading out for Nevada to get married and then on to California. And Leo, instead of sitting them down and talking sense into them, was helping them sneak out of town. Hiding June in Rifle Gap until Rick could get away and join her. Leo not only didn't try to stop them, he was planning on giving them his goddamn car. I tell you, I thought I knew the man, but then this happens and it all gets turned inside out. Where he got the notion it was his job to help out two young fools in love . . . Anyway. Vivien Bauer is barely holding on. She learns she isn't going to lose her boy, but she loses her husband in the deal. And June's mom. I'm not sure how she's taking it. She's got a look like she's been poleaxed. Losing her husband in the war—"

"Korea."

"That's right. Korea. Hell, if she felt like all the bad luck in the world was out looking for her, I wouldn't blame her. . . ."

Jack was generally not a talkative man, but on occasion—when he was nervous, say, or in the presence of someone who intimidated him or held power over him or was even quieter than him—Jack could begin to chatter. Afterward, he regretted these displays; although he seldom said anything downright embarrassing, the simple fact of his talking to excess was humiliating enough. At moments like those Jack felt as though he lost part of himself by squandering something that he should have saved.

He felt that way now, talking to Gordon; he heard it happening, yet he could not stop himself. This conversation had a destination, and Jack could not stop until he reached it.

"But you know, bad as it is for those women," Jack rattled on, "and Christ on a cracker, I'm not saying it's not tough—it's got to be the toughest—they're going to get help. That's one thing you've got to say about the ladies in this town: they see someone needs a hand, they're right there. What's her name—is it Mrs. Andersen? the nurse?—she's with Mrs. Bauer right now. Middle of the night she gets a call and she's right there."

Jack had talked enough that the very sound of his voice sickened him. It had risen slightly as he spoke faster and faster until it did not seem like his at all. That wasn't Jack Nevelsen on the line; this was someone imitating him and doing it badly. But he was close now, so close. Just one more small push and he'd be there.

"So if you want to go ahead and tell Patsy—" and suddenly Jack was afraid that Gordon was no longer on the line; he hadn't said anything for a long time—maybe he had hung up and Jack's voice was traveling in a circle, from his tongue to the telephone's mouthpiece through the vibrating disks and wires only to arrive at his own ear and nowhere else—"and tell Patsy what happened out there, why, I can't see any reason not to. I mean, now that we know what the actual circumstances were."

Gordon Van Allen was there. "Tell Patsy?"

"Sure, go ahead. Like I say, the ladies in town are going to get together on this sooner or later."

"You *want* me to tell Patsy?"

"You can. Sure."

Now it was Gordon's voice that seemed to rise slightly. "I know I *can*. Do you want me to? Is that what you're saying?"

"Yes. Hell, yes. I want you to."

"You want her to go over?"

"She doesn't have to. That's not what I mean."

"You just want me to tell her?"

Why was Gordon pushing him like this. Were these questions to get Jack to say something that would eventually absolve Gordon of any complicity?

"I want you to tell Patsy how the accident happened, how Leo was helping Rick and June run off. She's going to want to know so goddamn bad she can taste it, and you can tell her. Tell her no one else knows. That ought to make her happy."

Gordon did not hang up after Jack's little outburst. Instead, he simply asked, "You still want me to put the car behind the garage?"

The simplest of questions, yet Jack had trouble summoning the energy to answer. "Behind your fence, right?"

"Right," Gordon replied.

Jack ran his index finger over one of the numbers scratched into the steel shelf under the phone. Could this have been June's, gouged there by Leo so he wouldn't have to look it up? Look it up—shit! Leo would know that number better than his own. Maybe Leo etched it there with the tip of his key while he talked to June. Maybe he knew that number so well, had it so constantly on his mind, that without thinking he doodled it, scratched it, traced it, on every surface he touched. Wait—this was ridiculous. Jack could clear it up in a moment by looking up the number himself. Or by calling the number and waiting to see if the voice that answered sounded as though it belonged to the saddest woman in the world.

"How early do you think you'll be able to bring it up?" asked Jack.

"Around seven. That all right?"

"Sure, sure. I was just wondering. . . . Look, I didn't mean anything. It's late and . . . I mean, I'm going to tell Nora as soon as I get home. I'm calling right now from a damn pay phone. But I'll tell her. People want to know about a thing like this. Your Patsy—"

"So seven's early enough?"

"Seven. Fine. Maybe give me a call once you've got it up."

The conversation ended, but Jack could not bring himself to get out of the booth. A car passed, a maroon Hudson, speeding as most cars do when they are driven late at night. Jack didn't get a look at the driver or recognize the car. It could be a kid going home from a graduation party. The Concannons' perhaps. Maybe the party broke up because someone brought in word about the accident. That would be a party killer, all right. Anyway, it was just a matter of time now. Patsy Van Allen would be making her calls before breakfast. Hell, she might have the phone in her hand already.

The night must have gotten colder than Jack realized. Furnaces had come on in two of the houses across the street and down the block. Smoke rose from both chimneys. The houses were side-by-side, the same size, design, and color, and the chimney smoke, as if each plume knew it had to continue the twinship, ascended in identical straight columns in the windless air.

Jack stood and felt around in his pocket for the golf ball. He brought it out, rolled it around in his hand for a moment, gauging its heft, trying to find a way to grip it like a baseball.

He took a few steps and heaved the ball as hard as he could, aiming for the space between those two unwavering lines of smoke.

Jack listened for the golf ball's impact, since he lost sight of it soon after it left his hand.

Nothing. No crash of glass, no pock of wood. The ball might have landed soundlessly on a lawn's soft turf or in a tree's leafy branches, yet it seemed as though the ball did not come down anywhere. It flew so easily from his fingers—a missile of perfect size and weight for throwing—that he could imagine it splitting those goalposts of smoke and traveling forever through the cold windless air. But as soon as he dropped his arm to his side, a current of pain shot from his shoulder to his elbow. Throwing like that when he was cold—he was lucky he didn't throw his arm out completely.

He got into the truck quickly before he was seen and reported as a vandal. Or worse, recognized. *The sheriff is across from the Texaco station throwing rocks at houses.*

19

JACK WAS SO TIRED EVEN DRAWING BREATH SEEMED AN EFFORT, YET HE could not make himself advance past the doorway of the bedroom.

Nora was sleeping on her side, facing him. She had one hand drawn up to her chin, curled there like a cat's paw. Her mouth was set tight, a sleeping expression that always surprised him. Sleep's relaxation should have opened her lips, puffed them out. How grim her dreams must have been—or how great her determination that no unwanted words slip out, even in sleep.

If he got into bed, no matter how quietly or carefully, Nora would stir, and once she was awake he would have to tell her about the call that kept him out most of the night.

Simply saying that Leo Bauer was dead—a familiar name— would shake her completely awake. And how could he say then that Leo had been killed and not mention June? And once both names were spoken, the circumstances that linked them would have to be explained. After hearing that story, even an abbreviated version, sleep would not be possible for either of them.

No, he could not lie down in his own bed, not if he hoped for any rest in the few remaining hours before daylight.

Nora could sleep comfortably without him at her side. His job kept him from their bed too often for her not to have learned to sleep through his absence. If Jack took it in his head to run off, he could roll up a good many miles before Nora missed him. If he were not under the sheets during the night or in the morning, she would simply assume official business kept him out late or got him up early. And be grateful. Why did he feel compelled to add that thought? Was it even true? If Jack were killed in an accident, Nora would surely grieve. And if it became known that he ran off with another woman—or girl—Nora would surely feel the same anger and embarrassment that any woman would. Yet why did Jack dimly believe that Nora might also feel a sense of relief when she climbed into bed every night, knowing that his large, sweating body would not be there?

How would Vivien Bauer sleep without Leo at her side? Without his anchoring weight would the bed and Vivien drift into the open waters of sleeplessness? Would she stack pillows, fold blankets on Leo's side, then dab his aftershave on the bedding to try to deceive herself that he was still there? Or was it possible, only possible, that already, even grief- and whiskey-sick as she was, Vivien Bauer might find herself sleeping more soundly than she had since childhood?

Nora rolled onto her back and, as if she knew the bed would belong only to her, stretched an arm and a leg out into the space that would have been Jack's. She must have gotten warm—Jack had turned up the thermostat when he came in—because her movement seemed meant to free her of covers, sheet, blanket, and that fraying, leaking old quilt Nora's grandmother had given them. On her back, Nora seemed to relax. Her lips came apart, and her mouth opened and closed a few times like a baby's when it gropes and sucks blindly for the bottle or its mother's nipple.

She was wearing her winter pajamas, light blue flannel top and bottom that seemed no different in cut or fit from the pajamas sold in the men's department. For all Jack knew, they *were* men's, ordered in a smaller size from the Sears Roebuck catalog.

Soon the nights would be warm enough for Nora to switch to her summer nighties, short, gauzy affairs with thin straps that slipped from her shoulders when she squirmed and rolled in her sleep.

And just that quickly Jack's thoughts flipped again to Vivien Bauer but now not to speculation on how soundly she might sleep with Leo gone but to imagining how she looked in bed. He was not concerned with whether she lay on her back or her side, but whether her nightgown had slipped once again from her shoulder, and if, in her fitful sleep, the fabric might have slid further still. . . .

Jack retreated from the bedroom, backing slowly down the hallway until he no longer heard the tiny *cuh-cuh* of Nora's sleeping breath; then he turned and walked back to the kitchen.

Muley, perhaps deceived by his master's reappearance into believing that it was time to begin the day, rose stiffly from his station next to the stove. His tail, as if its mechanism hadn't fully awakened, wagged two or three times, stopped, twitched, stopped, then wagged again.

Maybe Muley was right. If Jack wasn't going to get into bed, he might as well give up on sleep altogether. Fix a pot of coffee and wait for Roller's Cafe to open. Roller's opened at sunup for the farmers and ranchers who had to come to town and wanted a place to eat breakfast, drink coffee, smoke, and bullshit while they waited for the bank or the hardware store or the feed store or the Ford dealer to open. Jack could go to Roller's and have himself a breakfast steak, eggs, hash browns, and then head over to the jail. Then he'd be at his desk early enough to field any calls or inquiries, to try to keep everything headed in the right direction.

He opened the door and snapped his fingers for Muley. At the invitation to go out, the dog tried to hurry and his nails skidded and clicked on the linoleum. Jack followed the dog into the night air, and while Muley sniffed his way back and forth across the yard, Jack lit a cigarette and waited on the porch.

Yes, keep everything headed in the right direction. That was his job now. Like riding herd. Try to make sure no one wandered off the trail.

He had to laugh. Riding herd. He had never ridden herd in his life. In fact, he could count on the fingers of one hand the number of times he had been on a horse.

For all his years of living in Montana, Jack had to confess to a terrible ignorance of most of what happened on the region's farms and ranches.

No, Jack was town-born and town-bred, and that was his family's background as well. His father and grandfather had both been merchants, men who sold the ranchers and farmers their supplies. On his mother's side were three generations of Bozeman dentists.

And even though when he was growing up most of his friends and schoolmates had been town kids as well, many of them had a farm or ranch in their family, an old prairie homestead perhaps that they could return to, whether it was still a working spread or not. Nora grew up on a farm that also had a few head of cattle, and her parents lived there still. Almost everyone Jack had ever been acquainted with in Montana knew the language—if not the actual working—of crops and cows.

Yet it was all Jack could do to tell a field of wheat from flax and to make the proper distinctions among the various cattle breeds. When the references became more complicated and sophisticated— to rising and falling prices, to weights and measures—Jack was lost. As a kid, he sometimes wondered if all this material was covered in school when he was absent, and as an adult, he didn't feel much more confident. He only became more adept at faking knowledge, at guessing when to nod approvingly or shake his head in sympathy. To make matters worse, unlike most males in that part of the country, he didn't hunt, not upland game, not waterfowl, not deer or antelope. Jack fished a little, but he never much cared if he caught anything or what kind of fish it was. And he certainly wasn't about to work any harder at it than to put a worm on a hook and heave it into the water.

And Jack knew he couldn't blame his ignorance on his growing up in town. After all, his father made it a point to know what the hunters, ranchers, and farmers did so he could sell them what they needed, whether it was guns or ammunition, wire cutters or posthole diggers, lariats or ax handles. Hell, his father sometimes knew what they needed when they didn't. Jack's brother, Phil, though he lived a life that didn't shape itself to any of the usual Montana conformations, was still able to talk about crop yields, the inner workings of tractors, or the stud possibilities of a particular stallion. Phil had, like Jack, worked at the family hardware store, but Phil had also worked in one capacity or another at a number of area farms and ranches.

No, nothing quite explained Jack's lack of knowledge about so much of what was at the heart of Montana life. Types of saddles, length of planting or growing seasons—knowledge of these seemed to be in the prairie air, but Jack must have found his oxygen elsewhere.

As a result, he had always felt as though he didn't quite belong up in this corner of the world. Oh, he didn't kid himself. He knew there wasn't a square of earth somewhere where he *did* belong. Outside of his years in the military, and they hardly counted in the normal scheme of things—when you were in the army you were *in* the army, no matter where in the world you might find yourself—Jack had not traveled widely. What would have been the point? Mercer County, Montana, was home, even if the business and pleasure of its men and women could be as mysterious to him as the machinery of the brain of his dog, sniffling out there from tree to bush and back to tree.

To be truthful, Jack was surprised he could be elected to public office in the county, considering these gaps in his knowledge. Hell, there were times he didn't even speak the language of the residents. He remembered once when he was caught in a conversation between two ranchers who were talking about doctoring cattle. By the time they got to talking about treatments for the bloat, Jack was so confused he couldn't even fake an intelligent look.

But he could learn. And the next time he heard a discussion of bloat, he'd know enough not to let his jaw go slack when someone suggested sticking a hose down a cow's throat. Pick up on enough of those details and before long you looked as though you belonged here as much as the next man. Fake it well enough and they might even elect you sheriff. . . .

But suppose Jack decided this small Montana town was not where he belonged. Suppose that after another day of trying to keep the wind-blown grit out of his eyes, Jack decided he had had enough. If he took a mind to, he could step down off this porch, walk over to his truck, back out of the driveway, and head out of town. North, south, east, or west—every direction was available to him.

Now, suppose he was a teenage girl with no driver's license and no money, nothing but a powerful belief that this was not the place for you. You wanted something else in your life—to go to the opera or eat Chinese food or wander around a museum or take in a big league baseball game or ride in a taxi or see water so wide you couldn't throw a stick across it. What would you do? Get on a bus or train and go as far as a ticket would take you? And then where would you be? Somewhere you might feel you belonged? Or another version of Bentrock, only this time you knew no one and no one knew you.

Would you attach yourself to someone who could take you away and deliver you to a safe place? A boy your own age wouldn't do. He might have a car and a license to drive, but what knowledge would he have of the world beyond? You wouldn't want to stand out on the highway with your thumb out until a trucker stopped and told you to climb in. That could land you in a far worse place than the one you were trying to escape. Bentrock was easy to get out of compared to the cab of a semi going seventy. And when the truck stopped, then the danger might really begin.

So maybe you might find a way to hook up with an older man, someone who seemed strong, dependable, someone who had seen more of the world than Montana, perhaps because he had been in the service. You get close to him by—oh, hell, how would she do it? By volunteering to help with the kids at Horace Mann, by working with him on the March of Dimes campaign—and then you let him know, somehow you let him know, that if he'll take you away, you will, you will . . . What could an eighteen-year-old bargain with? What could she do but point to her eighteen-year-old body and say, This, you can have this to do with whatever you like.

Was Leo the first to whom she made the offer? Or only the first to say yes?

Why didn't she just wait a few months and go away to college? That had worked for a few of the kids over the years—why couldn't June follow that route to Missoula or Bozeman or Havre or Grand Forks or Dickinson? Or take a bigger leap and land in Denver or Minneapolis? Of course, maybe June didn't have the brains or the money to go to college. Who was he to decide what she should do, or what was in her mind or heart?

For that matter, who the hell was he to decide what was best for a whole goddman town? He was a Montanan who couldn't put a bridle on a horse, and now he was leading the town in a particular direction. He had decided what the people of Bentrock should—and shouldn't—know about Leo Bauer and June Moss. He had decided what the truth would be. Had any cowboy ever tried to control a more unruly herd?

Muley had finished his business but continued to sniff around in ever-widening exploratory circles, testing Jack to see if it might be permissible to leave the property altogether.

Jack gave a short, sharp whistle, and Muley came running as if he were being hauled in on a rope.

Back in the kitchen, Jack opened the cupboard under the sink and pulled out the bottle of Old Grand-Dad, which, if he had help, Jack might work his way through in a year.

He poured two fingers in a jelly glass and lifted it to his lips. The whiskey fumes brought him up short. He couldn't get it down straight. He ran a little warm tap water into the glass and then tried again.

He drank it down in two swallows but not without a grimace and a shiver. He had no taste for whiskey whatsoever. One more Montana test he failed.

20

JACK HAD PAPERS TO SERVE.

Wally McClinton had fallen behind on payments, and now his trailer was being repossessed and his wages garnisheed. Jack had put off finding Wally—the papers had been on his desk for a week—because he liked Wally. He was a good-natured, hardworking kid with a new wife and a baby on the way. He had a decent job with a local builder, but the work was seasonal, and Wally spent too much time in the bars, not only drinking but shaking dice—a real good recipe for going through wages in a hurry. Jack hated to see Wally and his wife booted out of their home, but some people only learned hard lessons.

For that matter, Jack hated his role in the matter, but serving papers was part of the job. Besides, driving out to the construction site to find Wally would give him a chance to see if Gordon had brought the car up yet.

Jack had been in the office since before eight. When he came in, the courthouse still smelled of the floor wax the janitor applied over the weekend. But no one had called or come by to inquire about the previous night's accident.

For the first hour or two Jack had been eager to talk to people, but the longer he stayed at his desk the more nervous he became. He tried to do a little paperwork, but it was no good: he kept running through what he might say to various callers. His basic story wasn't going to change, but he might emphasize one aspect for a friend of Leo's, another for one of June's former teachers, still another for Jim Brazelton from the paper. . . . Jack was tired but so stoked up on coffee and cigarettes that his heart was racing, and he couldn't get enough air. Getting out for a while might at least slow his mind down.

Leaving didn't bring the relief Jack hoped for.

First of all, Wally was hardly glad to see him. That came as no surprise. Why would you feel any other way about the man who delivered the news that you had to get out of your home?

But when Jack turned and began to walk away, he heard Wally say, "Fuck you." He said it softly, but he said it.

Jack was next to a pile of scrap wood, small squares and rectangles and triangles of fresh-cut pine that had been trimmed away to make something fit, and he felt like picking up a block of that wood and firing it at Wally's head. Fuck *me*—why, you little son-ofabitch. It's not my fault you can't pay your bills. You'd be out on your ass a lot quicker if I'd have served those papers when I should.

But a sheriff can't go around throwing things at his constituents. Not wood. Not golf balls. Not if he expects to get reelected. He settled for kicking a chunk of wood. He caught it just right, and it flew twenty feet and came to rest at the foot of a dirt mound that looked as though a thin concrete solution had been poured over it, a gray shell over the black dirt. At least this time he saw where his projectile landed.

And Leo's car was still down there. From the road, nothing much showed but the white roof, dented and creased like a sheet of paper that had been crumpled and then smoothed out again. The roof's center was still wet where the dew—or was it frost?—had not yet burned off. Bits of grass and weeds and clumps of dirt clung to the mashed metal and twisted chrome as though someone had tried to camouflage the car and then given up.

And there wasn't much doubt—there *was* a car down there. If you drove by and looked over in that direction, you weren't likely to miss it. God damn, Jack thought, why hadn't Gordon brought it up yet? Was he punishing Jack for what he said about Patsy? He didn't want to call Gordon again, but he wanted that car out of those damn weeds. It was bad enough that everyone and his cousin was going to be driving out to see where the accident occurred; the car shouldn't be available for their inspection as well. Leave it down there long enough and sooner or later some idiot was going to climb down for a closer look. And once one person did it . . .

Jack walked up and down the shoulder of the road, looking for the spot where he had stood the night before. He found it by watching for his crushed cigarette butts, those small patches of flattened paper and tobacco shreds. He could see a few of the ornate letters of "Chesterfield"—his brand. He allowed himself to feel, only for a moment, like a good detective.

Next to the butts was a small pile of pebbles and stones, obviously pushed together by someone nervously scraping the dirt with his boot. He had no recollection of the behavior, but he knew he had done it.

He picked up a rock the size of his thumb tip, and as soon as he did, he wanted to throw it, to lob it high in the air and have it land on the roof of Leo's car. What was going on with him? Rocks and golf balls and pieces of wood—he wanted to throw everything that was small enough to fit in his hand. He dropped the stone, and with his foot nudged it back toward the pile.

He'd wait until noon. Then, on his way home for lunch, he'd drive by Gordon's station, and if Leo's car wasn't there, Jack would stop and demand to know why. If Gordon didn't want to do the job, Jack would find someone who would.

Jack had barely walked into the courthouse when Wayne grabbed his arm and told Jack he had to speak to him right away. Once they were inside the inner office, Wayne asked urgently, "Did you see her?"

"See who?"

Wayne whispered the name. "Margaret Elsey. She's sitting out there on the bench. You walked right past her."

The jail and sheriff's office were in the basement of the court-house, and in a little alcove at the bottom of the stairs was a wooden bench that had once been in the courtroom upstairs. The idea was that you were to sit on the bench and wait to be called into the office, but that corner was dark and almost tucked under the stairs, so people rarely sat there; they knew they could be too easily overlooked.

"What does she want?" asked Jack.

"She's says she's a friend of Junie's." They were alone in the office, but Wayne still looked around as if he were afraid of being overheard. "Says she wants to know something about the accident."

"She *knows* something or she *wants* to know something?"

"She wants to know, I'm pretty sure she said."

"She wouldn't talk to you?"

"I thought you'd want to do this one."

Jack walked slowly over to his desk, trying, with each step, to compose himself. Easy, just take it easy, he told himself. He knew that the work he had done the night before wouldn't be the end of it, not by a long shot. But if he stayed calm and tried simply to deal with each problem as it came up, there was no reason this whole business of Leo and June and Rick couldn't be handled with a minimum of trouble.

Jack lowered himself carefully into his wooden chair. Something in the chair's springs had broken, so if you sat down too hard or leaned too far back, you were likely to tip over backward or look like a fool stopping yourself.

Wayne had followed him across the office. "There's more," he said to Jack. "You got a couple phone calls."

Jack looked over his desk for the pink slips of paper they used to write down messages. He realized he had been holding his breath, and he reminded himself to take slow, deep breaths.

"You're supposed to call your wife," Wayne lowered his voice. "And Vivien Bauer."

In the last year Jack and Wayne had both gotten new badges. The old ones were shields, silver but otherwise indistinguishable from what the police department was issued in gold. The new badges were stars, enclosed within a circle and printed with the letters "MERCER COUNTY SHERIFF" or "MERCER COUNTY DEPUTY SHERIFF."

Wayne was wearing his badge just where he usually did, pinned to the flap over the pocket of his shirt. The shirt was one Wayne wore often, dark blue with pearl snaps and a bit of fancy stitching at the collar points. But what drew Jack's eye was the fact that he couldn't see any pinholes on the shirt's pocket flap, though certainly Wayne had pinned his badge to this shirt many times. Jesus, Jack had shirts with so many pinholes the material looked clawed. Lately he had not been wearing his badge at all. He stuck it through the outer layer of leather of his old wallet and left it there. Then he had taken to carrying the wallet in his shirt or jacket pocket. The only way Wayne could have avoided filling his shirt with holes was by pinning his badge on so carefully that he ran the pin through the same holes each time he put the badge on. Wayne's badge looked shinier than Jack's too, though they were issued at the same time.

Jack swiveled his chair, so he would not have to face Wayne and his badge. "Tell me again, Wayne, why you couldn't talk to Margaret."

"I thought . . . You know. You wanted to handle the investigation."

"And what investigation would that be?"

"You talked to Rick last night, so I figured . . ."

"You figured what?"

Wayne moved around behind Jack's back to try to get himself into Jack's line of vision. Jack swiveled his chair another foot in the opposite direction.

"Shit. You *said* you talked to Rick."

"That's right. I talked to him." Jack turned all the way back around so he faced his desk once again. His calendar was still turned to Friday, May 26, and Jack flipped the pages to bring up the correct date. "And after I talked to him, I told you what he said. Then you knew what I knew. And that's as much goddamn investigation as there's going to be."

He spun around hard to face Wayne. His deputy stood before him like a dog betrayed by its master.

"I guess investigation wasn't really what I meant to say," Wayne mumbled.

Jack sighed. "Go on. Tell Margaret I'll talk to her. Tell her I've got a couple calls to make and then I'll see her."

Wayne put a little hitch in his stride on the way out, almost like a soldier trying to step smartly for his commanding officer.

From Nora's first question, all the hours that Jack had gone without sleep descended in one great weight that settled on the back of his neck.

"Why didn't you tell me about Leo Bauer?" demanded Nora.

"And June Moss," Jack added, although later he couldn't be sure if he actually said her name out loud or only thought it. "You were sleeping. When I got home and when I left this morning."

"You *wake* me."

"From now on. Who told you?"

"Alpha. She assumed I knew." Nora was referring to Alpha Pickray, who lived across the alley. "She must have talked for five minutes before she realized I didn't know anything about it."

"What did she say in that five minutes?"

"Why didn't you say something?"

"How did Alpha hear?"

"She just knows. People know. And when it sunk in what she was talking about, I still couldn't believe it. Leo . . . Leo seemed so *alive*."

Leo? Alive? Of all the ways Leo Bauer might be described, Jack wasn't sure why his wife would choose that phrase. Alive? Of course he was, Jack wanted to say. We all are, until the day we draw our last breath. But up to that moment, slow-moving, sleepy-eyed, serious-minded Leo Bauer did not seem any more alive than the next man. Children—hopping, humming, vibrating children—

146

that was who you thought of as being exceptionally alive. But Leo Bauer? He had nothing of that vibrancy in him. Too solid, too careful, too respectable to die before his time. That was what you should think when you heard Leo Bauer was dead.

Unless, unless . . . Unless women saw something in Leo Bauer that was invisible to Jack. Something that June Moss saw. Something that Nora saw. Something *alive*.

"Have you called Vivien?" Jack asked.

"Viv . . . ? I'm not going to call her. Not now. Not *today*."

"She's having a rough time of it."

"I don't know her that well. Certainly not well enough to call her today of all days."

And yet you think of her husband as so alive. "I'm just wondering," Jack said, "who she can lean on."

"She doesn't want strangers showing up at her door."

You're hardly a stranger. Leo was so alive to you. . . . "I'm supposed to call her."

"What about?"

"Don't know." *She needs somebody.* "Of course Rick's there."

Nora made a sound as though she were shivering with cold. "That *boy*."

"What about him?"

"How he talked his father into such a scheme is beyond me. I knew his mother spoiled him, but he must have had his father going as well."

"Rick's pretty broken up too."

"You had to drag him out of a party? Is that right?"

"Not exactly. I mean, he was at a graduation party, but he hadn't any idea of the accident. Not then."

"But he knew his father was out there, trying to take care of his problems for him," Nora said indignantly. "Did you see him?"

"I was the one who found him at the party. At Concannon's."

"I mean Leo. At the accident."

Nora so seldom wanted to hear the details of his work, and certainly not the more gruesome aspects. Yet where Leo Bauer was concerned . . .

"Wayne was out there first. He called it in right away and had

147

them carted off by the time I got there. From what I understand Leo really got torn up bad. Sliced up from all the glass." Did Jack purposely serve up this information to punish her for wanting to know so much about Leo Bauer? And she hadn't even asked about June. "Wayne said June Moss got thrown from the car. Ended up so far from where Leo and the car landed that it was just luck he found her."

"It's still so hard to believe."

Jack wanted to say something more about Rick, about how hard this was for the Bauers' only child, something to elicit sympathy for the young man. Yet Jack knew that hard feelings toward Rick meant their story was taking hold. That people felt sorry for the father and hated the son was a triumph of sorts.

"I'm sorry I didn't tell you right away," Jack said.

"You *wake* me," she said again. "Or call me. I don't care when it is. No matter how late. When it's someone like Leo. . . ."

"Ah, but there's no one like Leo."

Silence followed this remark, silence so complete that Jack wondered if she was holding her hand over the mouthpiece.

"I thought I'd make a turkey," said Nora.

"A turkey."

"For Vivien. It's something you can eat for days. Meals. Sandwiches."

"You'd take over a turkey?"

"I could send it over with someone."

Jack almost volunteered to take it himself.

Nora added, "I just wouldn't feel right going over. She has good friends. . . . But I want to do *something*."

"A turkey . . . That would be something."

"I couldn't get it there for a couple days. I mean, I'd have to get a frozen one, and then with roasting. But don't you think that would work? And then she wouldn't have to worry about cooking."

"I'm sure she'll appreciate it." Actually Jack doubted that Vivien would even notice what was brought or by whom. People would be going in and out of the house, most of them dropping off a plate, pan, or platter. Only later, when Vivien saw the strip of masking tape with a name printed on it stuck to the side of the

148

empty cookie tin would she know who had brought a condolence of food. But a turkey? She might remember a turkey. . . . But if it's appreciation you're looking for, take a turkey to Celia Moss. Hell, just tear off a drumstick for her. She'll thank you as if you had brought a feast.

Jack was nervous about calling Vivien, but his nervousness was both dread—had she thought of a discrepancy in his story?—and an agreeable anticipation—perhaps she felt grateful to him for the kindness he tried to show her the night before.

This call was not what he expected either.

She did not sound like someone fighting to keep her composure. In a voice as formal, as distant as an office worker's, she asked Jack if he would be willing to serve as a pallbearer for Leo.

"I'll help any way I can," Jack said.

What the hell. By now he was used to carrying Leo's weight.

21

MARGARET ELSEY SAT ON THE EDGE OF HER CHAIR, HER HANDS TIGHTLY gripping the wooden seat. Jack couldn't decide if she hung on out of nervousness or because she was so ready to talk she had to hold herself back.

She was dressed in a white blouse with a rounded collar—Jack could never remember what those collars were called—a black pleated skirt, and white socks and scuffed loafers. The fabric of her blouse was stretched tight across her breasts, and when she sat down, little gaps like mouths opened between the buttons. Hand-me-downs, thought Jack. Margaret Elsey must have had an older, but smaller, sister. He knew the Elseys were a large family. Did one of the kids have polio? He seemed to recall a boy, younger than Margaret, in leg braces, but Jack wasn't sure. He might have been confusing them with another big family. Margaret's father, Jack was fairly certain, worked for the Knife River Mutual Telephone Cooperative.

Margaret's face was wide and round but not at all plump. She was simply large-featured. The green of her eyes reminded Jack of willow leaves early in the spring before they opened completely.

While she waited to talk, she bit down on her lower lip, and Jack watched with fascination as the color went out then came back, each time in what seemed a darker shade of pink.

"What can I do for you, Margaret?"

"It's about the accident." She took a deep breath. Her blouse stretched a little tighter. Color popped out in her cheeks as if she had just raced around the block. "What people said about what happened."

"And what did you hear?"

"That Rick and June was going off together."

"And Rick's dad was helping," Jack prompted.

Margaret nodded. "That's the problem."

Jack willfully misunderstood in an attempt to make her travel in a different direction. "That's exactly what *I* said. If Leo—Mr. Bauer—hadn't tried to help out, if he'd just let them work things out for themselves . . ."

Margaret leaned forward so it looked as though she about to rise out of her chair. "I don't believe that."

"I didn't either." He'd try to agree as long as he could, so they wouldn't be arguing, him on one side, her on the other. Then, when she saw he was not her opponent, he would gently steer her away from whatever was upsetting her. "I knew Mr. Bauer pretty well. We were in high school together. Been friends a long time. So when I started getting the details about this accident, my first thought was, that doesn't sound like the Leo Bauer I know. So I couldn't believe it either. Still can't. I can't believe he's gone. Here yesterday . . . No, I'm like you. I can't believe it either. Not about Leo. Not about someone so . . . alive."

She was shaking her head before Jack finished talking. "That's not what I mean," she said. "I mean about Rick and June. About them being a couple. I don't believe that." Each time she stopped talking, she puffed out her cheeks as if speech were taking her breath.

"You knew June?"

She nodded.

"Rick too?"

She kept that big head bobbing up and down as if she were grateful to be able to answer questions without opening her mouth.

"You graduated yesterday too?"

"Uh-huh."

"And were you at Concannon's last night?"

"For a little while."

Jack wanted to ask her if she was out in the yard when Douglas Hogue was fainting.

"Mostly I was out at Decker's." The Decker farm was south of Bentrock. Joseph Decker had just graduated, and would be heading out for army basic training any day.

"You see either Rick or June last night?"

She opened her mouth to speak, then stopped. She leaned so far forward Jack was sure she was going to stand up. "I mean," Margaret said. "I *know* Rick and June. I've known them since first grade. Like you knew Mr. Bauer maybe. But more. In high school everybody knows everybody."

Jack directed his attention to his desk. He wanted to give Margaret the impression that what she had to say was so unimportant it barely held his interest. This time he flipped the pages of the calendar back a few months. He stopped at February 6, a Monday. He had printed in pencil on that page the reminder: "PTA, 7:30."

"Mm-hmh. Go ahead," he said to Margaret. "I'm with you."

"Rick and June weren't going together." She said it as if the very idea affronted her.

"You know this for a fact, do you?"

She nodded.

"And how do you know?"

"I just know. They weren't."

"That's not what Rick says."

She puffed out her cheeks again and let out a little air for a reply.

"Rick would know, wouldn't he?" Jack asked.

She let out the rest of the air.

"Wouldn't he?"

"Rick Bauer never . . . He never went with anyone."

152

"They tried to keep it a secret. You didn't know because they didn't want you to know."

"I went out with Rick Bauer a few times. And last year to prom."

Now Jack faced Margaret Elsey, but he still tried to look uninterested. He pulled out his bottom desk drawer and rested his foot on it. "I thought you said he didn't go with anybody."

She moved her hand rapidly back and forth in front of her as if she were trying to erase a mistake from a blackboard. "We didn't *go* together. We just went out."

"Not everybody would see a big difference there."

"He's a chicken, okay? He's just a big chicken with girls. He's afraid to do *any*thing!" Large patches of color flamed on Margaret Elsey's cheeks and on her forehead.

"I'm trying to put together everything you're saying here, Margaret. But I'm not sure I—"

"I would have, okay? If he wanted to. . . . He didn't even try to kiss me."

Jack had misunderstood Margaret Elsey's blush. Embarrassment was not the source. Anger and frustration brought out that color.

He smiled at her the way he would at a small child whose trust he wanted to win. "Don't take this wrong, Margaret, but just because you couldn't get a kiss out of Rick Bauer . . ."

She turned her head away. "Don't make fun of me."

"I'm not trying to, Margaret. But two people are dead. Nothing's going to change that. And I don't see how what happened, or didn't happen, on a date with you and Rick has anything to do with that accident."

"Don't say my name all the time. You make it like I'm in school or something."

"And you're all done with that, aren't you?"

"Maybe. I might go to the business college down in Billings."

"It's getting harder to get by without more schooling. What have you got for the summer?"

"Working at the Dairy-O."

"When do you start there?"

"Already have."

"No break at all, huh?"

She shook her head.

Jack felt they were finished. He had ridiculed and demeaned her in hopes of stopping her story before it even had a chance to take shape. All that was left was to make certain she knew she had nothing to say on the subjects of Leo and Rick Bauer and June Moss. And get her out of his office.

"Did someone tell you you should come here?"

Margaret hunched her shoulders.

"You talked to someone else first?"

"My dad."

"What did he say?"

"That if I didn't think something was right, I should tell you."

"But I don't suppose you told him Rick Bauer wouldn't try anything, did you?"

She looked at him with such loathing that Jack thought her eye color changed, just the way leaves can suddenly flip up a new shade when a gust of wind hits the tree.

"I'm sorry, Margaret. Your father was right. If something's bothering you about this, I want to hear it. Why don't you back up and take another run at it."

She glared at him for a long time before she spoke. "No. I didn't say anything to my dad about going out with Rick. My dad would shit a brick if I ever talked to him about anything like that. I bet he thinks I never kissed a boy. My mom too. But I have. And more. But I never did as much as June Moss. She went all the way when she was a freshman. With Johnny Togan. So what would she be doing with a big chicken like Rick?"

Johnny Togan had been in trouble with the law most of his life. Jack himself had arrested him twice, once for drunk and disorderly and once for assault and battery after Johnny beat the hell out of a fellow who, so Johnny said, stole a gearshift from his car. After the second arrest, the judge gave Johnny a choice: jail or the military. Johnny joined the marines and had not been back to Bentrock since. He was a big, strong, handsome kid who acted as if he didn't give a damn how much trouble came his way: he was going to do whatever came into his head to do. Jack did a little arithmetic:

Johnny Togan would have been at least five years older than Margaret Elsey and Rick Bauer and June Moss. A man to that girl.

"Johnny Togan used a rubber on June Moss. Everybody knew that." Margaret finally leaned back in her chair. Jack thought he saw a smile, just the quick start and stop of one, play across Margaret's lips.

Jack shoved the drawer back into the desk and let his booted foot fall heavily to the floor. He rolled his chair closer to Margaret's. "All right. Now you listen. I talked to June's mom last night. Gave her the news about what happened to her only child. Her baby. As you can imagine, she's not taking it too good. And what she doesn't need to hear, what she doesn't need spread around, is that her daughter was easy or whatever it is you're saying."

"I just said the one time. That I know about for sure."

"Well, believe me, young lady, you're implying a whole lot more."

She crossed her legs, and her skirt slid a couple inches up her thick, tan thighs. Her exposed knee looked as large as Jack's. He put his palm on his own knee to gauge the fit of hand to knee.

"What are you getting so mad at me for?" Margaret asked.

"I'm not mad."

"You're shouting almost."

He sat back again. The last thing he needed was to look as though he was overreacting to the situation. He lit a cigarette and considered offering Margaret one but decided against it. As he began to speak he made certain he kept his voice low. "Okay, now I'm going to talk to you like an adult." He quickly added, "Which you are. You wouldn't say things to your mom and dad but you're saying them to me, so I'm going to talk to you similarly. You come in here and say something's not right about this accident. Which killed two people. Good people, as far as I'm concerned. And why do you feel something's not right? As near as I can tell, because Rick Bauer's not too forward with the girls, and June Moss was a little more experienced. That's about all I've gotten so far. Now, I don't know how you think it should be between men and women, but I remember how it was when I was closer to your age. Sometimes a shy one like Rick was drawn toward a young woman who . . . well, I don't know how people your age say it. 'Puts out,' we used to say. Who makes things a little easier for him. And then once he finds her, a little late in the game, why, his head is going to be spinning and so fast that he's likely to think he's got to marry the girl who's showed him such treasures. And sooner rather than later, so she doesn't get away.

"Now, I don't believe there's an explanation for everything in this world, but maybe this could explain how the two of them got together when they seem such a bad fit to your way of thinking."

Margaret didn't respond. She sat still in her chair. Jack could hear her breath go in and out, as slow and deep as a sleeper's.

"Who told you about the accident, Margaret?"

"Paula Walstad."

"Did Paula tell you about the suitcases?"

She simply stared at him.

"Did she tell you that Rick and June had their suitcases packed and in the car?"

Nothing.

"She didn't, did she? Maybe you ought to tell Paula about those suitcases. And let her know where you heard about them."

Why wouldn't she speak? Move? She came into his office as a woman, determined to do her adult duty and speak out on this troubling matter. It had not gone well, and now she was trying what worked for her as a child. Sulking, fuming, stubbornly refusing to speak or move from this chair until she got her way. And what would that mean, "getting her way"? Would Jack have to say, Yes, Margaret, you're right. What people are saying about this accident *is* wide of the mark. The hell. He'd carry her out of the office first.

"Was this talk too rough for you?" Jack asked. On his desk was an ashtray he had been given by a local merchant. The ashtray was glass and fit inside a miniature tractor tire, black rubber printed with white letters advertising Hagen Tractor and Farm Implement—Your John Deere Dealer in Northeastern Montana. Jack crushed out his cigarette and found that something in him caused him to keep stabbing out the butt long after there was any reason to do so.

156

But perhaps the fury with which he put out his cigarette sufficiently impressed Margaret that she spoke at last.

"I didn't call June a whore," she said.

"I know you didn't."

"June was my friend." Her lower lip trembled, and she clamped
her teeth down hard on it. When she released her bite, the color
took longer to return, but when it came back, it was darker than
ever.

"All right. She was your friend."

"Rick too."

"And Rick too." Jack turned his hands palm up as if to say,
now what? We've taken this as far as it will go.

And there they sat, looking at each other. Behind Margaret's
cold gaze, Jack was certain, lay nothing but hatred and disgust for
him. She had walked into this office expecting something of him,
and he had not even come close to measuring up.

For his part, he could not help wondering: If June Moss was
willing to run off with Leo Bauer, did that mean it was possible
that Margaret Elsey might find Jack appealing? If, that is, he could
find something to do or say that would overturn her low opinion
of him. He could think of nothing short of telling her that she
was right in being suspicious about the accident and the version
of it that was being bruited about town. And how might she feel
about him then, if he took her into his confidence?

"Can I tell you something, Margaret?"

Her expression did not change.

"One of the things I've learned in this job is that things don't
always fit together the way you want them to. Let's say there's a
crime. Somebody steals something. You know who it is. You arrest
him, bring him to trial. Now, he's guilty—no question about that.
The evidence is all against him. But there might be something
about the case that just doesn't add up." Jack brought his index
fingers out in front of him and slid them past each other. "Something that doesn't make sense. That can't be explained. I'm not
saying you think he's innocent. Not like that. You handle that
differently. I know what you do with those doubts. No, this is
something that just keeps sticking out, that you can't smooth

down. My friend Steven Lovoll—you know who Mr. Lovoll is, don't you?—the district attorney? I've talked to him about this, and he says, 'Jack, this is life. Life isn't a mystery novel. Not everything gets tied down nice and tight. You just have to accept that.' And I've been working on it. Not getting all bothered when there's a piece missing. Or one left over.

"And that's what I'm recommending to you, Margaret. This awful thing happened. You feel miserable about it. Lots of people do. The whole damn town does. But for God's sake, don't make it harder by dwelling on some little bitty thing you can't quite explain. Don't do that to yourself."

She wasn't having any of it. She wouldn't speak, she wouldn't move; her weight, her very being, seemed to increase the longer she sat there, as if an invisible pair of hands were pressing down on her shoulders, keeping her in that chair, in that spot.

Jack thought of a prisoner who once sat exactly where Margaret was now sitting. His name was Max Kidder, a greasy-haired, pimply-faced young man arrested for and charged with stealing cars. Max not only stole three or four cars, he proceeded to disassemble them and sell off the parts—hubcaps, tires, bumpers, carburetors, radiators. Max was none too bright, and he thought he could make more money selling the cars in this piecemeal fashion.

On the day of Max's trial, Jack brought him out of his cell, handcuffed and ready to be delivered upstairs to the courtroom. On the way, Jack had a moment's business to attend to, and he sat Max down to wait.

Then, when Jack was ready to go, Max would not get up. He had been perfectly cooperative up to that moment, but now he absolutely refused to budge from the chair. Sometime in the previous minute or two, Max had decided he didn't want to enter that courtroom. Jack tried reasonable talk to get Max out of the chair. He tried *please*; he tried threats. Finally Jack enlisted the help of a policeman, and together they dragged and carried Max up the stairs and into court. Max probably weighed no more than a hundred fifty pounds, yet it was astonishingly difficult to move him out of that chair. He did not flail or struggle or resist in that way;

he simply would not go along, and in his refusal he seemed to increase in size, to gain weight and mass.

Just when Jack was most worried that Margaret Elsey had found her own way to remain in that chair, Bentrock's noon whistle blew.

"I got to go to work," Margaret said.

"Hi-ho the Dairy-O, eh?"

She glowered at him another moment, then rose and walked from the office.

Jack thought he should say something before she was out the door, something that would keep her from flinging her suspicions all over town, but he kept silent because he was so relieved she was finally leaving.

Yet she had no sooner gone out the door, shutting it with just enough force to rattle the glass in its frame, than Jack was sorry to see her go.

He reached over and put his palm flat on the seat of the chair where she had so recently sat. He spread his fingers wide and felt where the wood had absorbed heat from her body.

22

JACK DID NOT NEED A HAIRCUT, BUT LATE THAT AFTERNOON HE ENTERED the barbershop in the basement of the Northern Pacific Hotel and took a seat with two other men waiting their turn in the chair.

The shop was leased and operated by Bob Langford, a loud, big man who always wore a bow tie to work and always had a cigar going. Consequently, the barbershop smelled not only of hair tonic but also of cigar smoke.

Bob had not set out in life to be a barber. He had come to Bentrock to teach history at the high school, but he met and married Mavis Tyrell, whose father had been cutting hair in the basement of the Northern Pacific for as long as anyone could remember. Then Howard Tyrell had his stroke and couldn't hold a scissors, much less a razor, so his son-in-law stepped in and took over. For the first few months, Mr. Tyrell came into the shop, took a seat right next to the barber chair, and gave his son-in-law instructions, but before long Bob was administering shaves and haircuts without assistance. He gave up teaching and turned to barbering full-time.

Someone complained to the mayor about the arrangement. A

barber was supposed to go to a special school and have a license to cut hair. No one knew exactly who was unhappy with Bob Langford taking over, but rumor had it that it was Oscar Ganrud. Oscar, who had once tried unsuccessfully to get something like North Dakota's Non Partisan League political party going in Montana, was always grumbling about something that didn't quite meet regulation. Then someone asked the question: Didn't Oscar have a son back in Minnesota or Iowa who was a barber? That sealed it. It had to be Oscar. The mayor made a statement. Bob Langford was just filling in; no matter how long he cut hair at the Northern Pacific, the job was temporary. That ended the matter, even when Howard Tyrell died.

Many people believed that Bob picked up a barber's skills so quickly because of his superior intellect. He was generally conceded to be Bentrock's smartest citizen, a title given him by virtue of his first profession, his education (it was said he had a master's degree from the University of North Dakota), and his extensive and articulate opinions on almost all subjects.

Jack did not share this view of Bob Langford. He thought Bob was a know-it-all and a bluffer, someone who sounded a good deal smarter than he was. Bob was willing to hold forth at great length, and he threw in a few little-known facts to sound even more knowledgeable. Jack sometimes doubted those facts, but they were often just odd enough to be true. Besides, on the few occasions when Bob was challenged, he brought out the full artillery, backing himself up with the titles of books and special articles and studies that no one had ever heard of and therefore could not refute.

But no matter how Jack might have regarded Bob Langford, others looked up to him and frequently withheld their own thoughts on a variety of subjects until they heard—directly or indirectly—what Bob's views were. Bob Langford probably had more influence from his basement barbershop than Jim Brazelton had from his editor's desk at the *Mercer County Tribune*.

So it was Bob Langford's status as Bentrock's unofficial adviser and opinion maker that brought Jack to the barbershop. Leo's accident had been talked around town long enough for Bob not only to have heard about it but to have developed his own take on it, and this Jack needed to hear.

As soon as Jack sat down, Bob said, "If you're in a rush, Sheriff, I can get you next. If these gentlemen ahead of you have no objection." This was no special consideration; Bob made the same offer to everyone who came in, and because of that, no one ever took him up on it.

"I'm in no hurry," Jack said. He picked up a copy of the *Saturday Evening Post*.

Jack recognized the other two men waiting. Harold Rivers, an attorney in private practice, was paging through an issue of *Argosy*. Dick Graff, a local plumbing contractor, was smoking, exhaling smoke around the toothpick he always had in the corner of his mouth. Both nodded a greeting to Jack.

"Getting a trim for the funeral?" Bob asked Jack.

"That's right."

A boy, probably no older than seven or eight, was in the barber's chair. He sat on a padded board that lay across the chair's arms.

"You'll make three," said Bob.

"Three?"

"Three pallbearers. I cut Lucky Doerr's hair at noon, and Vern Lindahl walked out of here just before you came in."

Vern Lindahl was a teacher and track coach at the high school. Lucky Doerr had his own insurance agency. Jack didn't know that Leo and Lucky had been particularly good friends.

"So you make number three," said Bob.

Dick Graff asked, "Funerals good for business?"

"The big ones. Like this one will be. Big weddings. Big funerals. Christmas. Easter. Yes, I will be doing some business on this sad occasion."

"What the hell," Dick Graff said. "Somebody might as well turn a dollar."

Jack considered asking Bob how he knew who had been named pallbearers, but Jack let it go. Vivien might have told Vern or Lucky who the others would be, and they passed that information on to Bob. Could it be that Vivien asked Jack first, and that was why she didn't mention to him who else would be lined up alongside Leo's casket?

"I heard it's going to be a doubleheader," Dick said.

"That's the plan," Bob said. "Leo in the morning. Miss Moss in the afternoon."

"Wednesday?"

"Wednesday it is."

Harold Rivers closed his magazine. "I question that. Two funerals in one day. My God."

"Why drag it out?" said Bob. "And for those folks attending both, they can put that black suit or dress on in the morning and take it off at the end of the day and be done with it. Get it done and get it behind you."

"Some things you don't rush," Harold said.

"Jews bury their dead as soon as possible," said Bob. "They've got the idea, if you ask me."

Dick Graff said, "A lot depends on family, of course. Who's coming from where. When my dad passed on, we had to wait on his sister to show up from Vermont. A sister who didn't give a good goddamn about him while he was sick, I might add."

The boy in the chair didn't move, but his eyes widened and twitched as he followed this adult conversation.

"Death in the family," Bob said. "It brings out the best in some, the worst in others." He stood back from the chair and picked up his cigar from the ashtray. Bob Langford was the only man Jack had ever known who smoked a cigar like a cigarette. He held it between his index and middle fingers, inhaled, then set it back in the ashtray. Behind the boy's back, but with the attention of the three waiting men, Bob pointed to the boy. "Little pitchers have big ears," he whispered.

"If you're talking about the worst, you're talking about Aunt Evelyn," Dick Graff said. "Jesus H. Christ, what a piece of work she is." He glanced up in Bob's direction. "Sorry."

"Vivien Bauer's got a sister coming up from Salt Lake," said Bob. "Should be here tomorrow afternoon."

"If she was a Jew, no sense making the trip, right?" said Dick. "She'd never get here in time."

Bob Langford unsnapped the cloth from the boy's neck. He swirled the cloth like a cape, then shook it, and patches of the boy's hair fell to the floor. "That's it for you today, son. Unless you wanted the shave."

The boy slid and jumped to the floor. "My dad said he'd settle up later in the week when he comes in for his."

Bob motioned to Harold Rivers that he was next. "Okay by me," said Bob. "Just don't let your dad get too shaggy."

As soon as Bob had Harold wrapped and settled and the chair adjusted to the proper height, Bob asked Jack, "I suppose you were on the scene last night?"

"I was."

Bob switched on the electric clippers, then shut them off right away. "Quite a mess, I hear."

"The car's over at the Mobil station. You can see for yourself." Jack had driven by around two o'clock and seen it there. Pulled up from the grass and weeds and put back in an environment where it might belong—sitting on the oil-soaked back lot of Gordon Van Allen's place—the car did not look so horrifying. It was, after all, in spite of all the damage, still a car, a Chevy, discernibly so, and not some specially constructed death machine. People had walked— or crawled—from worse wrecks.

Bob turned the clippers back on and moved them up the back of Harold's neck. "I'm talking about the blood," Bob said. "The way I heard, there was more blood in that car than in a butcher shop."

"God *damn*," said Dick Graff.

Bob's information meant that Wayne or Gordon or one of the ambulance attendants had been talking.

"By the time I got there," said Jack, "both the bodies had been transported."

Bob Langford stepped back and drew on his cigar. "The only dead bodies I've ever seen have already been laid out. They may not have looked too good, but they'd been cleaned up for inspection." He bent back to Harold's neck. He got so close it might have seemed as though his eyesight was poor. "I've often wondered what it would be like to look right into a dead man's eyes.

The way a man in your position has probably had to do a few times."

"That part of the job is exaggerated," Jack said.

"You'd do what you had to do," said Dick Graff. "My brother-in-law is with the fire department out in Great Falls, and he got called in on a motorcycle accident one time. Fellow ran his bike into a goddamn tree. He was okay, but the gal riding behind him got torn in two. Torn completely in two. Course she died right on the fucking spot. My brother-in-law puked his guts out, then got right to the job. You'd do the same if you were up against it, Bob. You'd do what you had to do."

Jack wondered what exactly a fireman's job might have been under those circumstances, but he said nothing. The subject had already strayed too far from where he wanted it.

"I saw a man cut in two when I was in the navy." Harold's chin was tucked into his chest, so his voice was muted and low. "I was stationed on an aircraft carrier, and one of the cables that catches and holds the planes snapped—or one of the strands of it anyway—and somebody was standing where he wasn't supposed to and he got cut in two."

Dick Graff whistled. "Sweet Jesus."

Bob Langford stepped back for his cigar, but Harold kept his head down. "The top half of him just flipped back into the ocean like he got blown in that direction. But his legs kept standing there for a second like maybe they had a mind to go the other way. Then they sort of toppled back and slid overboard too."

Jack knew the conversation could go on and on this way, each of them contributing a grisly reminiscence. (Although, since it was unlikely Harold's story could be topped, changing the subject was acceptable.) And maybe all this talk about blood meant that the accident's mayhem was its most interesting aspect rather than any scandal. But he had to know for sure.

"It's true," Jack said, "in this line of work you see things you'd rather not. But like Dick says, when it's part of the job it's different. You're already a step back. But seeing a friend, like Leo was, and a good man at that . . . I'm not too sure how I'd handle that."

The remark seemed so unlike something Jack would say that he

165

had difficulty believing it came from his brain, his throat, his mouth. But if it would do what he wanted it to do . . .

Bob, Harold, and Dick Graff were all staring at him.

"But maybe I should have seen him," Jack went on, "because I'm still having a hell of a time believing it." He let his voice trail away as if emotion prevented him from going on. "Leo . . ."

Bob Langford shook his head thoughtfully. "It's a tragedy. You hear that word used a lot, but here's where it applies. It's a goddamn tragedy."

Jack lifted his hand toward Bob in order to get him to go on.

"And I'm not going to say I saw it coming. No, sir." Bob returned to cutting Harold's hair, now working with the scissors. "Not something like this. But—"

Jack held his breath. Here it came.

"But I used to go round and round with Leo on this matter. It was my position—and I still hold with this—that he believed too strongly in identifying with the young people. He was too quick to put himself in their shoes. I tried to tell him. You've got to keep being who you are, I said, and let them come up to your standard. I know there's plenty of educators who'd say Leo Bauer's way was the way of the future, but I don't think you change just for the sake of change. Which education is notorious for doing."

Jack wasn't sure if he should breathe easy or not. What *was* Bob Langford saying?

"I always thought Rick was a good kid," Jack said tentatively.

Bob stopped cutting and stood up straight again. "Hell yes, he's a good kid. Basically. But that's my point. Your son comes to you and it's not so different from a kid stepping into the principal's office. We were talking before about doing your job. Well, a father's got a job like a principal's got a job. And it's not your job to say, Whatever you want, son; how can I help you get what you want? Now, here's my notion: If you want to hire yourself a principal—or any educator, for that matter—take a look at his kids. If they're spoiled, then by God, that's not the man for the job. Forget the degrees and that bullshit. Look at what kind of a father he is."

Jack found it interesting that this speech came from a man who had left the teaching profession and had no children of his own.

"What I can't figure," said Harold Rivers, "is why they didn't just get married and find themselves a place here in town. Jesus, they were both out of school. My grandmother was fifteen when she got married. Sixteen when she had my uncle."

Bob put his finger on top of Harold's head, leaned back, and closed one eye as if he were trying to draw a plumb line. "See, right there that tells me something. If they had to sneak off, that sure as hell means they knew people were opposed to what they were doing. Am I right? Everyone except Leo, who as I say was always identifying with people—with kids—in their plight. And when it came to that boy of his? Shit. It's a good thing he *was* a decent kid. He could have gotten away with murder as far as Leo was concerned."

"Now, in our family," said Dick Graff, "I'm the disciplinarian. If it was up to their mother, they wouldn't have to do a goddamn thing around the house but show up for meals."

As if he wanted nothing more than to offer evidence in support of Bob Langford's theory, Jack said, "Leo was going to give them his car." He looked around the barbershop. "I hope I'm not telling tales out of school."

"Doesn't much matter now," Dick Graff said.

Bob Langford walked a slow circle around Harold Rivers. "I didn't know that about the car," Bob said.

Jack slumped in his chair and stretched out his legs. The pain in his back had eased a bit. He felt now as if he could sleep. The next time Bob repeated his opinion about Leo Bauer and the accident, he would include the information about Leo giving away his car. Yes, Jack could sleep right here. The floor of the barbershop was made of small octagonal white tiles, and as he stared at them, their pattern seemed to shift. One tile seemed to rise up slightly and then another near it to sink, so the floor looked uneven. Then the tiles' borders would link and unlink, so that from one instant to the next it might seem they were connected, then scattered loosely in an approximate pattern. Optical illusions, Jack thought dreamily.

167

"Did anyone know anything about this Moss girl?" Harold asked. He was out of the chair and reaching in his pocket for money.

"I believe she worked at Nash's," Bob said. "But I could be mistaken."

Harold Rivers nodded as if to say this was precisely the information he was seeking.

Dick Graff took his place in the chair. He put his toothpick in his shirt pocket and handed his glasses to Bob. "Going to be an open casket for either?"

Bob wrapped a tissue and pinned the cloth on Dick Graff, then put his finger inside next to Dick's neck to make sure the cloth was not too tight. "Nope. And Mrs. Moss isn't even having a visitation."

Jack ran his fingers slowly through his hair. He hoped when it was his turn in the chair Bob would find something up there that needed cutting.

23

IN SPITE OF HIS EXHAUSTION, JACK HAD A RESTLESS NIGHT. SLEEP seemed a room he could only partially or briefly enter. He kept dreaming his thoughts and thinking his dreams.

At one point Jack reached out and put his hand on Nora's shoulder as she lay on her side with her back to him. From last night to this, Nora had switched from flannel pajamas to summer nightgown, and her shoulder was bare. It seemed to him that his hand on her shoulder was unusually high, and he wondered: Was Nora broader across the shoulders than he thought? Now, Vivien, Vivien Bauer had broad shoulders. He had noticed that when she was slumped on the bathroom floor. Wide white shoulders. And one exposed when her nightgown slipped and lay diagonal across her chest. Had he been thinking of Vivien when he began to drift off, dreaming of putting his hand on her shoulder? and then as he gradually woke, it was Vivien he was touching, then Nora, then Vivien, Nora, Vivien . . .

And to think of Vivien in bed was to think of Leo who lay beside her every night and who could reach his arm out and touch her wherever and whenever he wanted.

If he wanted, for example, not only to put his hand on her shoulder but to feel down the length of her arm, to begin at that pale soft flesh and reach down to the bony knob of her wrist and then go up again, higher, to turn at the shoulder and slope down to the neck and her slow, sleeping pulse. . . . But this was Nora, Nora's heart beating that rhythm, steady and true . . . that could be quickened by touch. By Leo's touch? Could Leo's fingers have traced this path, the course of Nora's shoulder? and where was the point, the precise point, where arm became shoulder or shoulder neck? or moving in another direction, where did shoulder become chest, then breast . . . ? But Leo couldn't touch. He had no pulse. You had to be alive to touch. *Leo seemed so alive.* She wouldn't sleep through Leo's touch. If this were Leo's hand here, or here, her breath would come quicker than these evenly spaced intervals.

Leo would know. If he had touched both Vivien and Nora, he would know whose shoulders were broader, whose flesh softer, paler. If he had touched them often enough, he would know in the dark. Eyes closed, barely awake, he would know. Nora, Vivien . . . Vivien, Nora. . . .

Jack took his hand away. If he didn't touch, perhaps he wouldn't dream.

He woke feeling the way he did when he was jolted out of fevered sleep as a child, ready to vomit from the way the dream-world's textures and proportions had been crazily, unbearably exaggerated and then blown apart. Now Jack put his hand over his head and rolled his knuckles against the headboard. It was wood, but his dreams had receded far enough that its hardness was a comfort. He lay in that position for a long time, moving nothing but his hand, lying still until he could be sure he wasn't going to be sick.

His nausea was worsened by a smell, strange and familiar at the same time. The odor didn't belong to the night—or did it? Jack knew he had smelled it before.

Turkey. That's what it was. The turkey Nora was cooking for Vivien Bauer. Just as she did the night before Thanksgiving, Nora had put the bird in to cook at low heat. In all the years of their marriage, had she ever prepared a turkey in any month but November? Had Jack ever eaten turkey at any other time? Yes, his mother used to make one at Easter, when every other family in town was eating ham. That survey of months and meals enabled him finally to fall asleep.

When the alarm rang, Jack felt he had to travel a great distance to come back to his own bedroom to turn off the machine. Nora was already up, but since she went to bed so early, she was often awake before the alarm.

Slowly, stiffly, Jack squinted his way to the bathroom. He swung the bathroom door shut, and as he did, he saw a dark figure appear in the shadows.

He was so startled he gasped and jerked, and the sudden movement caused him to slip on the rag rug. He stayed on his feet by catching himself on the sink, but even then his grab was so frantic he banged his elbow and felt his forearm and half his hand go numb.

The pain in his arm helped him see clearly. No one was there. His black suit, his only suit, hung from a hook on the back of the bathroom door. The sleeves were tucked into the jacket's pockets, and the suit swung slightly side to side from the force with which he closed the door.

He sat down on the toilet and tried to catch his breath. He felt a pain in his chest, but he didn't think it was his heart. This felt as though he had swallowed something sharp and it was caught halfway down and with every breath it scraped inside him. Shallow breaths didn't help. His legs were shaky, simultaneously weak and banded tight with muscle. Feeling was returning to his arm, and he clenched and unclenched his fist a few times. When he felt he could trust his legs, he stood.

Nora was in their bedroom, changing pillowcases. "I wish you'd tell the barber not to put that goop in your hair," she said. "It gets all over the pillows. And these little hairs . . ."

"Did you put my suit in the bathroom?"

"It's been hanging in that plastic bag for over a year. I thought I'd air it out for tomorrow. I'll hang it out on the line later if it's not too windy."

171

"I wore it for Angela's Christmas program."

"No. It was so cold you wore your sweater. Remember?"

She held his pillow to her chest with her chin and used her hands to pull up a fresh pillowcase. "After you take your shower," she said, "hang it on the curtain rod and let the steam take out the wrinkles."

The pillowcase was on, but she kept the pillow pressed to her as if she wanted a shield, even one of feathers, between her and Jack.

This early in the day, before shaving or having breakfast or going to work or beginning any of the day's ritual events that were done according to the clock, time felt strange, irregular, as if it hadn't quite started yet. For this reason, Jack wasn't sure how long they stood there, staring at each other. Surely something needed to be said, after a night of dreams like his, something. . . .

"You want me to come back and get the turkey and take it over?"

"Alpha and I are going over this afternoon."

"I thought— Never mind." Jack started to leave but stopped before the bedroom door. Now he remembered. He turned and looked at Nora once more. God damn, she was still clutching that pillow, and he couldn't really get a sense of how broad her shoulders were.

Something wasn't quite right about the way his suit hung there, and twice Jack put his head out of the shower to see if he could figure out what it was.

Only when he stepped out did it occur to him: The sleeves. No one ever hung up a suit coat with the sleeves tucked into the pockets. Where did Nora get that idea? He tried to think—Christ, it had been so long since he had been in a men's shop or a department store where men's suits were sold. No, he was sure they didn't display jackets that way. The sleeves always hung straight down. Why would they do anything that might wrinkle the fabric?

Leo. Jack had an image of Leo Bauer standing in a distinctive way. Feet wide-set and his hands in his pants pockets. A stance both confident and modest. But pants, hands in his *pants* pockets?

Had Nora seen Leo hang up a jacket like this? Could Leo have been alone with her in this house? Could he have undressed in one of these rooms, and as he arranged his coat on the hanger, jammed the sleeves in the pockets? Nora, watching from the bed naked under the covers, watched him and got the impression that this was the way a man liked to have his coat hung.

Jack dripped his way across the bathroom floor and jerked the sleeves from the pockets.

He was already having trouble remembering what Leo had packed in that suitcase. Was there a suit? A suit coat, to which he wore the pants? Wayne could tell him—was Leo wearing a suit when he was killed? No, he was driving; a man always takes off his coat when he has a distance to drive.

Jack usually saw Leo in shirtsleeves. A short-sleeved white shirt and tie. But of course he had a suit and probably more than one. A man in his profession had to have a suit.

Jack only had this one, and he remembered exactly when he bought it. Ten years ago, shortly after Angela's birth, he and Nora drove to Williston, North Dakota, and in the J. C. Penney store there, he bought this suit. It was wool and it was black—"so's it will go with anything," the salesman said. Jack bought it to wear to Angela's baptism, but within six months he had another occasion to wear it. His father's funeral.

Jack had never liked the suit. The armholes were snug, and he felt he couldn't lift his arms. The fabric was coarse and scratchy, especially on the inside of his thighs. Wearing the suit always made him feel as though he were in costume, pretending to be someone he wasn't. He preferred to leave it in the suit bag it came in, hanging in the back of the closet. With the sleeves straight down. On the Sundays he attended church, he usually wore an old sport coat of his father's, a baggy, light gray wool jacket with little flecks of color—red, blue, yellow—that always made Jack look twice to see if he had spilled something on himself.

He carried the suit on its hanger across the room and, according to Nora's suggestion, hung it on the curtain rod, though there wasn't much steam left in the room.

It seemed ridiculous now—having been frightened so badly by a few yards of cut and sewn black cloth. He stood in front of the

173

suit and tried to remember: When he jumped in fear and slipped on the rug, was he moving forward or backward?

He stood there a long time, until he heard a sound in the hallway and it occurred to him what a sight he must make—a naked man holding a coat's empty sleeve as if he were shaking hands with his own shadow.

24

JACK HAD NO SOONER ARRIVED IN THE OFFICE THAN HE GOT A CALL from Tommy Dunnigan. Tommy had a ranch on the south end of the county, and he wanted to report that some of his cattle had been rustled.

Jack was happy to take the call. It was a long drive out to the Dunnigan place. Then he'd have miles of fence line and acres of grassland to investigate—as if investigating would amount to anything. If cattle had been rustled, the thieves were long gone by now. And that was *if*. In the past, Tommy Dunnigan had turned in what Jack felt were false reports of stolen beef. He wasn't sure if Tommy did it to collect the insurance—which couldn't bring him much, and he damn sure didn't need the money. More likely, Tommy wanted to get someone in trouble—Indians from the reservation or those goddamn Russians who leased the place next to him—and accusing them of rustling was a good way to do it. So between driving and tramping around the prairie and listening to Tommy's ranting, a good part of the day was going to be used up. That would mean hours away from Bentrock and talk of Leo Bauer and June Moss. And worry about whether it was the right kind of talk.

The day was one more in a succession of warm, dry, sunny days. Summer vacation had begun for the schoolkids, and as he drove out of town, Jack not only remembered but felt something of what the schoolkids were experiencing on a day like this. "No more school, no more books . . ." went the chant. "Freedom!" They would shout as they burst out the doors of the schools. Freedom . . . yes, there was that. But what Jack always felt more than anything else was relief. Throughout the school year there was so much to remember—names and dates for tests, deadlines for assignments and projects—and Jack always lived with the fear that he would forget something, or worse, that he already had. For him, summer meant three months of living without that anxiety. As soon as he left Bentrock, that old summer feeling came over him, ". . . no more teachers' dirty looks."

Tommy Dunnigan was waiting impatiently for Jack at the ranch house. "Jesus Christ," Tommy said, "I was wondering if you got lost. I was ready to call out the fucking dogs. Let's get rolling."

Tommy Dunnigan was close to eighty years old, but age hadn't slowed or softened him. He had filed a homestead claim on a quarter section of land back in the late 1800s and proceeded to build a ranch as large and prosperous as any in the region. He had a reputation as a hard-drinking, hardworking man, rough and ruthless in business *and* personal affairs. He had buried two wives and a son, and he had a daughter and grandchildren with whom he no longer communicated. He was perpetually pissed off about something, and whenever Jack had any dealings with Tommy Dunnigan, Jack's only curiosity was whether Tommy's rage was merely simmering or if the pot had boiled over.

Tommy fit the image of the Montana rancher—sweat-stained Stetson, bowlegs, worn boots and leather chaps, a barrel chest that threatened to pop open the snaps of his western shirt, skin as dark and lined as leather. The only thing that didn't fit was Tommy's height. He didn't top five and a half feet, and that size perhaps explained why an old man still had a boy's name.

Tommy led the way in his truck, and Jack followed in his. They set out along the Dunnigan fence line, and although Tommy drove so fast that Jack had to keep his windows rolled up so he wouldn't choke on Tommy's dust and the ride was so rough the ache returned to Jack's back, he didn't care. The sun was shining, and he was out of town. Moreover, Jack had the feeling they had probably crossed the Mercer County line. If someone had been rustling Tommy Dunnigan's cattle, the problem would belong to Rudy Harshman, the sheriff of adjoining McKinley County.

Tommy finally stopped his truck on top of a rise and got out. He gestured for Jack to follow, then stepped between the fence's barbed-wire strands and began to walk across the sparse, dry grass. Jack pushed down the wire, stepped over slowly and carefully, and hurried to catch up to Tommy.

Less than fifty yards from the fence, Tommy stopped and pointed down. "Here it is. Here's where they took 'im."

They stood over a circle of matted grass. There was blood, a few splashes still bright red and wet high on the grass's blades but darker and congealed close to the roots and black where it mingled with the dirt.

Jack looked around in every direction. The trucks. Fence posts. A boulder humped up out of the grass, white in the sun like a leftover snowbank. Otherwise, nothing else but prairie and sky, stretching on as far as the eye could see.

"Not much in the way of evidence," Jack said.

"The way I figure"—Tommy took a few steps back and pointed toward the trucks—"they parked about there. Killed the fucker here"—he pointed again to the grass—"and hauled the carcass back out to the vehicle. Sons of bitches."

"Wait a minute, wait. You think someone carried an entire dead steer over there? Loaded it and drove away? Jesus, Tommy. That would have to be quite a crew."

"You don't think we got some professionals operating around here?"

"What are you saying, Tommy? We got a band of rustlers sneaking around here taking a cow at a time? And I don't know how the hell you reach any kind of conclusion like that from a little blood on the grass."

Tommy walked a slow circle staring down at the matted, bloody

177

grass. "Probably come in off the fucking reservation. Butchered him on the spot and threw the meat in the goddamn backseat. You see the way they treat their vehicles. . . ."

Jack bent down to catch Tommy's eye. "Do you hear yourself? You believe someone could butcher a steer out here and leave no other trace than this? No hide? No guts? Nothing?"

Tommy kept his head lowered.

Jack tried a different approach. "What else have you got? Any fence down? Any tire tracks? Footprints? I know you've been looking around out here."

Tommy said nothing.

Jack backed up and surveyed the prairie near where they stood. He couldn't see a distinct hoofprint anywhere, but the earth was soft, as if it had been trampled, and the dirt dry, stirred up, and loose; cattle probably had been grazing in the area. "Are you even sure you got a cow missing? This here . . . a coyote might have taken a nip out of one of your herd. Or brought down a deer here and dragged it off. Though there's no blood trail I can see. . . ."

Tommy lifted his head but not to look at Jack. He put his nose in the air as if he were trying to catch a scent.

"All I'm saying, Tommy, is you haven't given me much to go on."

Tommy Dunnigan pointed a crooked finger at Jack's chest. "You want something to go on? I'll give you something. You can get your ass out to the reservation and see if they ain't boiling beef today. And see if one of them fuckers ain't getting ready to make a tobacco pouch with my brand on it. Something to go on . . . Jesus fucking Martha."

Abuse went with this job. Jack knew that. He had been cursed by drunks, laughed at by teenagers, swung on by cowboys, and he usually shrugged it off. A badge can be a target, and some people are willing to unload all manner of anger, frustration, or dissatisfaction when they see one. Jack was prepared for that. He wanted as much as the next person to be liked, but anyone who runs for office has to face the fact—even if he wins—that there's a hell of a lot of people out there who don't like him. And once he sees the election returns, he's got the numbers to prove it.

But Tommy Dunnigan was getting to him. Maybe it was the fact that they were alone out there, not another soul or a structure around for miles. Maybe it was that Jack's earlier sunny mood had Tommy Dunnigan's dust clouding it over. And maybe it was just that pointing finger. Jack didn't like being pointed at.

Jack reached for his cigarettes, then realized he left them in the truck. "There's no law against boiling beef."

"My beef, there is."

"I've got no authority out there."

Tommy Dunnigan's upper front tooth was chipped, a clean diagonal break that made a neat little triangle of the stub that remained. Through that empty space, he spat at the ground. "Authority."

"Tommy, I could go out to the reservation and if I found every Indian there sitting down to a steak dinner, there still wouldn't be a goddamn thing I could do about it."

"No, you sure as fuck couldn't. But I'll tell you what I can do. I can put the word out to watch for someone who's got beef he shouldn't. Or who's got blood where it don't belong. And if I hear of such, I sure as shit don't need your kind of authority to tell me what to do about it."

Jack shook his head slowly. "I don't want to hear this kind of talk."

"And believe you me, we're going to be ridin' fence around here. And woe be to the son of a bitch I catch anywheres near that wire."

Jack moved around until he got the sun behind him and let it cast his shadow on Tommy Dunnigan. It was close to noon, and the darkness only came up to Tommy's knees. "You pull something like that, and I'll be back out here. Only it won't be for rustlers."

Tommy Dunnigan smiled at him. He didn't have much of an upper lip, and he had to lift it slowly so it wouldn't snag on that jagged tooth. "You do that. But you better bring all the goddamn authority you got. And then some."

Jack had been wondering why Tommy had brought him out here. Clearly, Tommy had no proof that any cattle had been stolen.

Or killed and butchered out here. Jack wasn't even sure Tommy believed it himself.

Then when Tommy threatened Jack—and the delivery of that threat seemed to give Tommy so much pleasure—it occurred to Jack that Tommy Dunnigan was lonely.

Had Tommy been working just to get to this moment, when he could have the company of another human being, even to threaten—or maybe especially to threaten? Had this day's loveliness dawned on Tommy Dunnigan as well, and he just had to give himself the pleasure of standing out in it with another man? One of his ranch hands wouldn't do; a moment spent with one of them was a moment taken from the ranch's work.

Call the sheriff? Hell, why not? Get him out here to keep you company for an hour. What's the reason? Wouldn't take much. A strange tire track. A little blood where it's not supposed to be. Isn't the man's job to serve the public? Well, there was no way Jack could better serve Tommy Dunnigan than to stand here and take the man's abuse. What was Tommy supposed to do—invite Jack Nevelsen out here and show him how you could live on these prairies all your life and yet on a cloudless spring day with the sun directly overhead, you might stand on one of these hills, one of these familiar hills, close your eyes and turn a few circles and then open your eyes and in the first moment of dizziness not know if you were facing the Atlantic Ocean or the Pacific? You could step down off this hill and not know if you were moving toward your home or away from it. Isn't that the goddamnedest thing, Tommy Dunnigan could say. Yes, thank God for that rock, Jack could say; thank God for your fence.

No, it was easier for Tommy to fume and curse and spit and jab his finger at you and talk about what he would do to anyone who dared come near his cattle or his fences. That was what he needed to do every now and then, and on May 30, 1957, it was Jack's job to listen.

25

A MOMENT CAME NEAR THE END OF LEO BAUER'S FUNERAL—THE PRAY-
ers were said, the eulogy read, and Corinne Holladay, the choir
director at the high school, was on the last verse of "Beautiful
Savior"—when Jack felt a sudden and unexpected surge of pride.

Thanks to me, he thought. This entire service, the packed church
(no, more than packed—overflowing; people were also seated in
the church basement and the service piped in to them over the PA
system), the heads bowed in sadness and respect, yes, especially
respect, the tears confidently shed over a good man's demise—this
is all thanks to me. Me and Rick Bauer. Without our version of the
accident, mourners would not have turned out in these numbers.

Jack could sit in the last pew with the other pallbearers and
observe all those rows of bowed heads, see the handkerchiefs flaring whitely throughout the church like flashbulbs going off, he
could hear the noses sniffing, and he could feel not just relief—
once the funeral began, he allowed himself to think, by God, it's
going to work, we're going to get away with it—but pride, and
not just the pride of accomplishment but of creation.

He *made* Leo Bauer. Without Jack Nevelsen, Leo Bauer's reputation would be shattered and lying in the dust. But Jack let Leo Bauer die with his name intact. The man lying dead up there in that mahogany casket was not who these mourners thought he was.

The feeling lasted until Jack walked out of the church, until he and the others actually had to lift the coffin.

They hadn't carried it into the church; it was already there when everyone came in, parked on a chrome cart in front of the altar by Mr. Undset and one of his sons. At the end of the service, the Undsets wheeled the coffin back to Jack and the other five men, who simply arranged themselves on each side of the cart, rested a hand on the coffin rail, and walked alongside as Mr. Undset rolled them all toward the door.

But then, to negotiate three small steps outside the church, the men had to lift. Leo Bauer and his mahogany box came off the cart, and Mr. Undset hurried ahead of them so they could once again set their burden down and roll smoothly toward the hearse's open back doors, where Mr. Undset's other son stood waiting. "Fine, you're doing fine," Mr. Undset said, as if he were encouraging the furniture movers who were maneuvering the new freezer into place.

Effortless . . . it was all so effortless. Jack had thought the job would require real strength. He imagined them lifting the coffin shoulder high, balancing carefully to keep the weight distributed evenly across their uneven heights and strengths. But it was only an honor, no real burden, and Jack walked from the church feeling nothing but that distinction and his new pride.

Until he saw Margaret Elsey.

The day was overcast but windless and warm, so even if that gray wool sky were to let drop some rain, it would bring no real discomfort. It wouldn't feel much different from standing under your own shower. A nuisance, yes, it would certainly be a nuisance. No one wanted to get wet, but a warm spring rain wouldn't stop any of the day's activities. Leo Bauer and June Moss would still be eulogized and buried, rain or no rain.

Now that he considered the possibility of rain, Jack noticed that the air smelled as if it had already begun. And who does not love that smell in spring, that odor that is really just the smell of dust that is freshly moistened? Jack looked down at the sidewalk to see if any of those small wet circles had appeared yet. No. The cement's gray was as unmottled as the sky's.

When he lifted his gaze, Margaret Elsey was still there, standing right across the street from the church.

Had she been at the funeral? She was wearing what she had worn in his office, the blouse that was too small for her and that black skirt, but many people came to church in similar clothes.

No, from his position in the last pew, Jack had been able to see almost everyone file into the church, and he would have noticed Margaret Elsey. And she could not have gotten out ahead of them, not soon enough to get across the street. She was holding a bag, a brown grocery bag, which she clutched to her chest. No one brought a grocery bag to a funeral.

She must have been walking by this morning, coming back from Nash's or on her way a little early to her shift at the Dairy-O. She saw the street lined with cars, and the hearse, so she stopped to watch. In another moment she'd be on her way.

They lined up the coffin and its cart at the back of the hearse, Mr. Undset attached or detached something at the open doors, they pushed, and the casket rolled easily into the vehicle.

Margaret was still there.

Surely she had seen enough now to know: Leo Bauer, this was Leo Bauer's funeral. And this afternoon would be the service for June Moss. But who in town did not know that?

Did she want to see who was there? Was that why she remained—to see who thought enough of Leo Bauer to leave home or office or field to come to his funeral? In this part of the country, people still used the phrase "pay their last respects." Did Margaret want to know who among the hundreds were making that payment? She didn't know Leo wasn't deserving of the respect. She didn't—she couldn't.

Maybe she wanted to see the tears. God knows, in this stiff-necked, tight-lipped town, she didn't see them often. Maybe she couldn't get over the sight of her townspeople—former teachers, kids she had grown up with, people from her church—weeping, or trying not to, right there on Third Street. There was big old Charlie Kaye, who had a shelf full of bull-riding trophies, looking red-eyed. And there was Miss Connie Reddy, the new English teacher, with salt tears raising red blotches on her cheeks. And Ivan Memke, who ran the grain elevator, acting as though he had something caught in the corner of his eye. And there, with her handkerchief pressed to her nose and mouth as if the white linen held the oxygen she needed to breathe, was the sheriff's wife. . . .

Jack walked over to where Nora stood with Alpha Pickray. Alpha had her arm around Nora as if she were afraid Nora might collapse at any moment. Jack stood in front of his wife with his hands in the pockets of his suit coat, waiting for her sobbing to subside.

Nora tried to stop by taking great gulps of air. When Angela had been hurt, she tried the same technique to stop her tears. She would cling tightly to Jack's or Nora's neck, gasp, sob, gasp, and try to say, "I'm-going-to-be-brave. Next time."

Jack looked around for Vivien Bauer. He wanted to see if the flow of her tears matched Nora's. He couldn't find Vivien, but Margaret still stood across the street.

Alpha leaned toward Jack. "Have you ever heard anything so beautiful," she whispered, "as Corinne's 'Beautiful Savior'? My God."

Nora nodded eagerly as if to say, yes, yes Corinne's voice.

"Wayne and I are taking the squad car out to the cemetery," Jack said. "Do you want to ride with us?" Jack and Nora had both walked to the church, he from the courthouse and she from their house.

Nora shook her head. "Alpha and I said we'd help set up in the basement." She took another gulp of air. "For the reception."

"That's going to be right after?"

One more little hiccup of a sob escaped before Nora spoke. "I guess. Whenever people drift back."

Jack glanced over at the hearse as if it could register impatience. "I better get going."

With her handkerchief, Nora made a tentative outward and upward move, as if she were going to wipe something from Jack's face. Then she pulled the cloth back and dabbed at her own eye.

Jack couldn't remember how to say good-bye to his wife. Some mornings he kissed her before he left the house. Most mornings, not all. But it didn't seem right to bend a kiss down to her now, not right after a funeral and in front of all these people. Besides, he'd damn near have to shove Alpha aside to get to Nora.

Oh, this was ridiculous. He could just walk away. He would see her again in an hour, maybe less. But he felt the moment called for something, a response to all her tears. He was her husband; he should say or do something.

Jack reached out and tugged the cuff of Nora's sleeve, and said "I got to get going."

Her navy blue dress. She got that dress on the same trip to Williston ten years ago when he bought his suit. And Angela got a new bonnet, the whole family buying something for the baptism. Their first outing as a family. And here they were again, him in his itchy black suit, Nora in her best dress. So as it turned out, they made that trip to Williston to buy their clothes for Leo's funeral.

Jesus, where had they come up with the money to buy a suit and new dress all in one whack? Did her folks help them out? Did his dad? Someone who saw they needed to get properly outfitted for their baby's christening?

Wayne had pulled the squad car out into the street and alongside the hearse. He was waiting for Jack so they could lead the procession to the cemetery. With Wayne parked there, Jack couldn't see if Margaret was still in the street.

Jack kept his gaze lowered as he got into the car. If he didn't look, maybe she wouldn't be there. Back in front of the church Vivien Bauer was being led toward the hearse by Mrs. Andersen and another woman Jack assumed was the sister Bob Langford mentioned. An older couple—were they Vivien's mother and father?—followed close behind. Rick was a few paces further back, his head hung low. Anyone who saw him might believe Rick was dragging along in his grief, but Jack thought you could as easily say the boy was in a sulk. Jack felt a brief tremor of panic. Rick didn't look like someone who could be depended on to help hold

185

a town together. But then, what was such a person supposed to look like?

Jack leaned forward and scanned the sidewalk across the street. Margaret Elsey was nowhere to be seen. He fell back and closed his eyes. "Don't forget to turn on the lights," he told Wayne.

Leo Bauer's grave was in the older section of the Bentrock Memorial Cemetery, an open, flat field not far from a stand of enormous, widely spaced pines, trees as old as any in the county, with the exception of the cottonwoods that grew wild along the river and in a few sloughs. Since Jack was a boy, kids had sneaked into the cemetery at night and, in those dark aisles of pines, smoked their first cigarettes or tried their first taste of whiskey. Plenty of the town's citizens probably associated their first sex with the smell and feel of pine needles. For both the sheriff's office and the police department, a regular part of the nightly patrol was supposed to include driving through the cemetery and shining a spotlight in those trees, but Jack seldom bothered. He thought his office ought to be for something more serious than interrupting kids' forays into adulthood. Let them be, he thought; who was he to stand in the way of those early experiments.

Jack stood on the side of the grave facing those pines. The coffin rested on some sort of mechanical platform that would, when the time came, lower Leo Bauer's body into the earth. Neither the platform, the machinery, nor the hole itself was visible. A heavy green drape that looked as if it had been woven from grass hung over everything, but the odor of fresh dirt was in the air. When did they stop letting us see the hole? Jack wondered. When did he turn over to the gravediggers the job of putting the coffin into the ground? What happened to the ropes the pallbearers once used to let the coffin's weight slide slowly into its earthen slot? Were there too many rope burns and slips—the casket banging into and crumbling the dirt walls? When did the practice of filling in the grave stop, everyone taking a turn dumping a handful or shovelful of dirt on the coffin? His father had died in winter, when the ground was frozen as solid as stone. Hell, snowdrifts had crusted so hard shovels could hardly cut into them, and you could scrape your fingertips across the ground and barely come up with dirt under your nails. So maybe Leo Bauer's grave didn't have anything to do with how burying was done either. June Moss was going to be buried today too. The gravediggers might have fallen behind in their work and just thrown a blanket over everything until they could get both holes dug.

On the day of his father's funeral the north wind and temperatures below zero kept people away from the cemetery. But why had so few people followed today from the church? Was there a custom or tradition that said funerals were for everybody but only those with certain qualifications were to come and stand by the grave?

Jack lifted his head to survey the small graveside group. Seeing who actually was there might answer his question about who came and why.

That was when he saw Margaret.

She was standing at the cemetery's edge, right between two of the tall pines. The trees had been trimmed over the years so that their lowest branches were still high off the ground. Margaret could have stood right next to the tree trunk, and the pine boughs would probably just touch the top of her head.

But Margaret was not standing tall. She was bending over, taking something out of that paper bag Jack had seen her carrying earlier.

He glanced around quickly. No one else seemed to notice her.

She was holding a sign. My God, that was what she had in the bag. A sign printed on a large piece of cardboard or poster board. But she wasn't coming forward with it; she just stood among the trees with that white rectangle raised over her head as if it were an advertisement or a direction that said, "EAT AT ROLLER'S," or "THIS WAY OUT."

But Jack couldn't make out what her sign actually said, only that something was printed on the board.

The members of the Bauer family were across from Jack, their back turned to Margaret. For that Jack was grateful. But suppose someone else saw the girl in the pines and pointed in her direction. Eventually every head would turn.

There was no chance Jack could get away without being noticed himself. But soon the ceremony would be over, and when the mourners backed away from the grave, someone would surely see Margaret and then everyone would want to investigate what her sign said.

If only he could shoo her away like a stray dog that was wandering too close to the family picnic—Go home, Margaret! Go on—get! This is no place for you! He looked at the ground near his feet for something to throw. There were no rocks, but the gravediggers had knocked loose a few large dirt clumps that hadn't broken apart or been stomped into the grass. He could heave one of those in Margaret's direction and hope to chase her off that way.

Pastor Ellingsen asked the assemblage to bow their heads for a final prayer, and Jack stopped squinting off toward the trees and closed his eyes along with everyone else. He didn't listen to the minister's words but tried his own petition to God. Please make Margaret go away. Please please please please.

A drop of his own sweat fell from his armpit and made a tiny, cold splash against his side. He jumped but kept his eyes clamped shut.

The problem was, he could think of nothing to promise God in return. Please make Margaret go away, and I will . . . I will . . .

". . . from dust we came and to dust we return," Pastor Ellingsen said, and Jack knew he didn't have much time to complete his own prayer. No, he couldn't. There was only one thing that God might want from Jack Nevelsen, and that he was not prepared to give.

26

As Jack walked toward the pines, the ground underfoot felt so spongy and soft that he wondered if he was crossing over a section of unmarked graves. No, more likely trees had once grown there, and they had been cut down and uprooted to make room for more graves. Although the pines looked as towering as ever, there seemed to be fewer rows of them than when he was a boy. But everything from his childhood memory seemed diminished.

Margaret held her ground, even when it became obvious that the sheriff was heading her way. And she kept holding her sign aloft, waving it back and forth determinedly as if she hoped to attract attention before she was caught.

Jack looked back over his shoulder. No one followed him. The few people who lingered at the grave were deep in their own conversations, their eyes cast downward at the earth that only a few feet away had been split open to receive one of their own. Was that Wilbur Magner, the superintendent of schools, still standing there? And Loren Waldoch, the principal at the high school? Most people walked off a few paces behind the small group composed of Pastor Ellingsen, Vivien and Rick Bauer, and their family.

Jack was relieved to find that he had to get quite close to Margaret before he could make out what her sign said. Margaret must have known herself that it would be hard to read because it looked as though she had inked over the black letters a few times, trying to make them thicker and darker against the white background. The sign said, "THAT'S NOT THE WAY IT WAS." Was Margaret left-handed? Her letters had a backward tilt. In each of the sign's upper corners Margaret had outlined a small cross.

All right, Jack told himself, all right; even if people saw Margaret and her sign, even if they were able to decipher her lettering, they would still have no idea of her message's meaning. As Margaret herself likely did not. He had to remind himself of that as well.

Margaret backed away. She brought down her sign and rolled it into a large tube, probably back into the shape in which she had carried it in her grocery bag.

Though the day was overcast, once Jack entered the corridor of pines, the air darkened even more. Margaret's white blouse glowed amidst all that shadowy gray and green, but it was her back he had to focus on as she hurried away from him. One more slight increase in speed and she'd be running.

"Margaret!" If she ran, he doubted he'd ever catch up to her. "Wait up there, Margaret."

She kept walking away.

As long as she didn't see him, he could take a few running strides to close the gap between them. He felt as if he were pursuing an animal, someone's runaway cat or dog, and if he let it know he was chasing it, it would surely panic and run.

"Margaret. Please."

She didn't slow. The trees grew closer together, and Jack had to duck to avoid catching a branch in the eye.

"Halt!" That sounded exactly like something a sheriff would shout at a fugitive. Jack wasn't sure if he had ever used the word before.

It worked. She stopped. She didn't turn around, but she stopped.

Jack got around in front of her, a position he wasn't quite sure of. If she bolted again, she'd head back in the direction of the mourners, and that was not where Jack wanted her.

190

"What's going on here?" he asked. "What are you trying to pull?"

She said nothing, as she had said nothing in his office. But she glared at him, just as a cornered animal might. Margaret Elsey could probably be pretty, perhaps even beautiful—that perfect large circle of a face—but when her expression turned as dark as it was now, something dumbly primitive took over her features, and her silence seemed not chosen but imposed. She didn't speak because she couldn't; she didn't know where or how to hunt for words.

"Did you hear me?" asked Jack. "What are you trying to prove out here?"

Margaret glanced into her bag as if to reassure herself that she still had her sign.

"Yes, I saw it," Jack said. " 'That's not the way it was.' Now, what the hell is that supposed to mean?"

She remained silent, and now Jack could stand it no longer. He ripped the bag from her so swiftly that she didn't have time to tighten her grip. The bag made a soft popping sound as it flew from her hands.

He shook the sign free and stepped back out of Margaret's reach. He held the board so he couldn't see the lettering and tore it in two. He doubled the halves and ripped them again. He threw the scraps on a small mound of dirt near which lay a loose bouquet of faded plastic flowers. Only fresh flowers were allowed in the cemetery—signs at each entrance proclaimed it so—and a grounds-keeper had probably removed these from a grave and thrown them back here. Jack kicked the grocery bag toward the torn sign.

"I can make another one," Margaret said. She might have been smiling.

"You could. But you won't."

She pushed her face toward Jack. He was ready to slap her. So help him God, if he didn't hear her apologize, back down, say *something*, he would slap that high, round cheek of hers and turn it a brighter pink than it was already.

"Do you know what's going on here, Margaret? Do you? This is a funeral. A burial. A good man died and people are taking it hard. And you've waving a sign around like this is a . . . I don't know what. A football game or something." That wasn't the comparison Jack wanted to make, but he could tell Margaret wasn't paying attention to him. She was looking past him toward the torn board, and beginning to take a few cautious, sideways steps in its direction.

He blocked her way and in return got a look from her that said she would gladly rip his throat out with her teeth if given half a chance. In that instant he felt that for the rest of his life he would have to worry about where Margaret Elsey was, that he would constantly have to check behind him to be sure she wasn't there and ready to spring. Or to hold up a sign.

"Are you listening to me?" he asked. "I mean it. You've got to stop this foolishness before . . . before something bad happens."

Something bad. How feeble those words were! Two people were dead, yet he dared threaten that something bad was about to happen?

She tried to reach around him, down toward the ground.

He didn't kick her. No one watching them could say he kicked her. He simply widened his stance, and when he did, his leg bumped her outstretched arm.

Margaret, however, stood up quickly and grabbed her arm as if she had been struck.

"You're all done with that sign," he said.

"My pen's in that bag."

"Leave it. I told you. You're not making any more goddamn signs."

"You can't stop me."

"Can't I? Maybe I can't stop you from making a sign, but I can sure as hell have something to say about where you wave it around."

"There ain't a law against it." She thrust her face forward again and cocked it to the side as if she knew how badly Jack wanted to slap her and was purposely increasing the temptation.

"I don't know where you got your legal education, young lady, but there's a law against creating a public nuisance, and you're close. You're goddamn close."

"So you're going to *arrest* me?" She didn't laugh out loud at him, but there was so much mockery in her voice she may as well have.

He would have to kill her.

That conclusion came to him not out of anger, not out of that same fierce impulse that made him want to slap the smirk off her face, but out of exhaustion, the icy weariness of no other option.

What else could he do? Margaret Elsey was going to keep making her signs. Or worse—start saying to people what her sign said. *That's not the way it was.* And before long people would ask, Well, how *was* it then? Once the weight of questions piled up, the story Jack built would collapse.

So what choice did he have? Even if he could lock Margaret up—ridiculous!—she would be barking her slogan the instant she was let out of the cage. If he could stop her today, there was still no assurance he could stop her the day after, or the day after that.

Unless he killed her.

And that might accomplish something in addition to keeping Margaret silent. A young woman's murder—the town wouldn't be able to concentrate on anything else. Whatever questions that might be lingering about Leo and June—or Rick and June—would be wiped away, replaced immediately by the much larger concern—Who killed Margaret Elsey?—and all the smaller questions that would bob in its wake—Why? Was it one of us? Is any of us safe? What kind of town is it where a young woman can be, can be—?

Strangled in the cemetery.

When would he have a better opportunity than this moment? He might follow Margaret for weeks, months, and never have her alone or out of sight of witnesses.

But he'd have to act quickly. Wayne didn't walk over to the grave site with the other mourners, and he was probably waiting impatiently for Jack to show up. Soon Wayne would come looking for him—

Now, wouldn't that be something—the deputy goes searching for his boss and finds him off in the trees with his hands around a young woman's throat! That would certainly help Wayne when he decided to run for office. There was his campaign slogan, all ready to go: "I Stopped the Sheriff from Killing Margaret Elsey."

Wayne would paint that in bold letters and post the signs all over the county. Who wouldn't vote for the man who saved a life—and made everyone forget about Leo Bauer and June Moss?

So Jack couldn't lose. Either he killed Margaret or he was stopped in the act. Either way he shut her up—why would she talk about her uneasy, uncertain feelings about Leo, Rick, and June when she could talk about the specific sensation of the sheriff's hands choking her, how his thumbs gouged into her windpipe and stopped her from crying out, how her encroaching unconsciousness made it seem as though the darkness from between the pines had seeped inside her head?

Margaret was a big girl. Killing her was not going to be easy. He recalled the photograph of June that sat in the Moss home, how her sweet, serious face sat atop a thin stalk of a neck. Now, a neck like June's—he could probably encircle it with one hand and choke the life out of it with no more effort than it would take to squeeze water from a sponge. Or snap it like a dry twig. A strong, sturdy young woman like Margaret—she was going to put up a struggle. Jack had no doubt of his ability to do her in, but he was going to get scuffed up in the process. She was going to thrash and kick and hit and try to claw her way free. He had to keep those fingernails away from his face. If he came away from this with scratch marks for the world to see . . .

He checked down the dark corridor behind and ahead of them to make sure Wayne or one of the funeral party hadn't wandered into sight. No, he and Margaret still had the spot to themselves.

Funny, just a couple days ago he had dreamed of putting his hands on Margaret in another way. How foolish and faraway those thoughts seemed now! As if there were a chance a hot-tempered—and hot-blooded—young woman would allow a stuffy married man damn near her father's age to touch her. He felt like choking himself for entertaining such fantasies.

Well, he was wasting time, then and now. . . .

Still, it was a strange world, wasn't it, where he couldn't dare reach for a woman he desired, where he didn't dare put his hands on her in a tender or loving way, yet he could do her the worst violence because it seemed as though no other option was available to him. Yes, strange indeed. . . .

"Arrest you, Margaret? No, I'm not going to arrest you, but I'll tell you what I am going to do."

When he grabbed her wrist she didn't try to twist free, but she did lean back and turn her head as if his breath was foul.

The feel of her surprised him. There was so much to Margaret Elsey, such an amplitude of flesh, that he expected she would yield softly anywhere he touched her—like Angela, whose increasing size and weight seemed still to put only layers of softness on her, as if she had not yet reached the age when sinew and bone could assert themselves in her child's body. But Margaret's wrist felt like a man's. The bones were thick and wide apart, and his fingers did not encircle her as easily as he had expected.

"What I'm going to do is . . . beg. That's right. I'm going to beg you. I'm going to beg you to please, please let this business about the accident drop."

She contorted her face as though she were trying to get out of his grasp, but she still did not pull her arm back.

"Are you hearing me, Margaret? I'm *begging* you." Jack thought he might be more convincing if he let his voice falter and crack as he made his request, but the odd thing was, he thought that after he heard his voice do exactly that. And tears—tears certainly ought to sway her, but once again they were already there.

What was happening to him? He found he could not make himself do what he believed he must, yet his body was going right ahead and doing what it wanted. The situation reminded him of high school when he sat behind Lucinda Kroeber in world history. He found Lucinda so beautiful, so desirable, that toward the end of the class period he had to keep his eyes focused on his textbook or his desktop because if he looked up and caught so much as even a glimpse of that inverted V of downy hair growing up the back of her neck or—even worse—the whiter white of her brassiere strap showing through her white blouse, he would instantly get an erection that would make him remain seated after the bell rang or else try to maneuver his way out of the room with his books and notebooks awkwardly held before his crotch. Now his body was betraying him again in the presence of a teenage female— tears welling in his eyes, his words choking like an adolescent's. No wonder Margaret Elsey was looking at him as if he were an example of a species she had never seen before.

Oh, hell, let it be; just let it be. If tears could help him convince Margaret Elsey to stop her troublemaking, then let them flow. Besides, how much lower could he go—he had been willing to contemplate murder, for God's sake! If he could face up to the fact that he was a man who would consider—even *consider*—strangling a young woman to shut her up, he could stand up to the shame of weeping in front of her.

"Can't you see how serious this is, Margaret? Did you see those people out there? Rick and Mrs. Bauer? They're doing all they can to hold on." Jack let go of her arm and tried to smile, but his mouth was still twisted down with the effort not to sob. His voice, however, unlocked itself. "Look at me, for that matter. People are busted up over this. You've got to let them grieve in peace. You come out here with that sign, you're making it hard, harder than it needs to be."

If the sight of a grown man crying in front of her softened Margaret at all, her expression did not show it. She looked as pugnacious as ever. "Not Rick, I bet," she said.

She simply couldn't let up. In another minute he would probably be ready to kill her again. "What's that supposed to mean?" Jack asked tiredly.

"Rick didn't even like his dad. He used to make fun of him all the time."

Just for the mean pleasure it would provide, Jack was tempted to ask what Rick said or did to mock his father. "I'm not talking only about Mr. Bauer. June too. Rick's had a double loss. Don't forget, that's the girl he was going to make a life with."

She didn't say anything in reply, but Jack was getting used to that. She wouldn't argue, so winning an argument with her was impossible. But her expressions, which he was becoming increasingly adept at reading, frequently stated her position. Now, for example, she practically curled her lip at his suggestion that Rick

196

Bauer's heart might be broken over June's death. Her scorn was something Jack had to address.

"Margaret, have you talked to Rick? Have you?"

"Maybe."

"Goddamn it! Have you talked to Rick Bauer?"

"Just for a second."

"What did he say?"

She hunched her shoulders.

"What did Rick say to you?"

"Just that he was pretty mixed up. He said he's having headaches. I don't get why he'd have headaches. . . ."

Jack felt the lightest tap between his shoulder blades, followed quickly by another raindrop that hit him in the forehead and then another that came down right on the top of his head. They'd been out there too long already, and now the rain would chase them away before anything had been settled. Before he could get her to promise: No more signs. Not today. Not at June's funeral. Not ever.

"So when Rick couldn't tell you anything to ease your mind, you decided to make your sign."

This time, only one shoulder shrugged, and it stayed up by her ear. "I just didn't think things were right, but I didn't know who to tell, so I thought I'd tell . . . I don't know . . . anybody who'd read it."

"Margaret, I'm going to tell you something that no one else knows. Almost no one. But you have to promise that you won't tell anyone."

She flinched but not at what he said. A raindrop had landed right above her eye. These were huge drops, the kind that made a splash on the sidewalk or in the dust the size of a quarter. At the moment Jack would have liked to try to figure out what happened high in the stratosphere that caused raindrops to vary in volume. That question seemed more soluble than trying to bend Margaret Elsey to his will.

But after she stopped blinking, Margaret nodded yes.

"Promise? You promise?"

"I promise."

Jack edged closer to the pines to get what shelter their boughs would offer. "All right. Remember, this stays right here." He looked down again at the plastic flowers. Here? Stays *here?* The rain was falling steadily enough to rinse the dust from the plastic, turning those unnatural greens, pinks, blues, and yellows to even brighter, stranger shades. Yes. Here. "June Moss was going to have a baby. You hear that? You know what that means? You understand now why she wanted to clear out of town before . . . before . . . Before she couldn't stay here any longer. So, sure. There was more to it. You were right. That's not the way it was. But you can see why we don't want that spread around, don't you? What's the point of that? June's dead. What would be gained? So we—so I—just want this to go away as quickly as possible. So people, so reputations, don't get hurt. Or don't get hurt worse anyway. Do you get what I'm saying to you, Margaret? Do you see why I want you, I need you, to stop with that goddamn sign?"

She blinked through the rain's gauzy mist as if she needed to see Jack clearly to understand what he was saying.

"I haven't told anyone this, Margaret. Just you."

She wiped her cheeks as if she were wiping away tears. "Does Rick think it was his? Is that what she got him to think?"

Jack planned to answer her. He wasn't sure why he did not. All he knew was that the longer he held his tongue, the more difficult it became to form a response, even though he had in mind to do no more than say, "Yes."

Yet before long, it made more sense to say nothing, and to make Margaret Elsey endure another's silence. That now seemed the best lesson he could offer: Margaret, not everything can be known. That was the sign *he* could hold high—a white square without a word or letter written on it.

198

27

BACK AT THE CHURCH, JACK TWICE CIRCLED THE BASEMENT FELLOWSHIP Hall, trying to find Rick Bauer in the crowd of people holding their paper plates loaded with ham, baked beans, cole slaw, rolls, and Jell-O. He finally asked Nora, at her station handing out squares of chocolate cake and pouring cups of coffee, if she had seen Rick.

"He was over with the family earlier."

"He's not there now."

"I don't wonder. With what he's put his mother through."

"Okay," Jack said. "That's where he isn't. But where the hell is he?"

At the sound of a swear word coming from him—and in church yet!—she looked sharply up at him. "How did you get so wet?"

"At the cemetery. I got stuck talking to someone."

"About Leo?"

"Not really."

She brushed at his shoulder as if the rain-soaked wool could be dried with the flick of a finger. "A couple of Rick's friends were here. Maybe he went off with them."

That statement gave Jack direction as surely as if she had pointed the way.

When Jack pulled open the door of the boys' bathroom in the Sunday school wing, two of the three young men—Mickey Windler and George Boren, both of them new graduates of Bentrock High School along with Rick Bauer, June Moss, and Margaret Elsey—threw their cigarettes into the toilet and scuttled about as if they wished the bathroom had a back door. Rick Bauer didn't move from his position sitting on the sink, and he made no attempt to get rid of his cigarette. Maybe high school graduation wasn't enough; maybe your father had to die at the same time to convince you were grown up and didn't have to hide your cigarette.

"Relax, boys. I didn't come in here to make any arrests."

The lavatory was small and seemed even smaller because of the fixtures. Since this was a bathroom for children, the sink and towel dispenser were built low, and the walls of the toilet stall were narrower than in a regular restroom. The urinal's white porcelain ran right to the floor, but its top would barely reach a grown man's crotch.

Mickey and George laughed uneasily, but Rick went right on smoking. Damned if he didn't *look* older too. Jack considered that it might be the suit, but that hadn't worked for his friends. They still looked like gawky teenagers who didn't quite know where their pockets were.

To get to the urinal, Jack moved sideways past the boys. He unzipped, and after those few seconds when he wondered, despite his full bladder, if he would be able to urinate in front of these boys, he let loose a stream that splattered noisily against the porcelain. Jack's father used to make an odd connection between the force of a man's urinary stream and his manhood. When a boy pisses outside, his father said, he just makes mud; a man digs a hole.

"Looks like you got caught in the rain," Rick said to Jack's back.

" 'Caught' is right." These were lines that strangers might say to one another, yet as innocuous as this brief dialogue was, it felt charged to Jack, as if he and Rick were talking in code.

200

Jack shook himself, zipped, and turned to face Rick. "I was talking to a friend of yours out at the cemetery." Jack paused for emphasis. "Margaret Elsey."

Rick hopped down from the sink to throw his cigarette in the toilet. "Margaret," he said. "What did she have to say?"

Mickey and George had backed up toward the door, but as long as they were still in the room, Jack couldn't say much.

"What does anybody have to say on a day like this? I guess no one can quite believe it yet."

"I believe it," Rick said softly. That was in code too, but this time only Rick knew the key.

"How's your mom doing?"

Rick glanced at his friends. Jack didn't see any signal pass between them, but George Boren said, "We're going to take off. I'll call you later."

Rick raised two fingers to his forehead in a little salute to his friends. It was the sort of gesture probably intended as a joke, but Jack didn't get the humor of it.

Rick faced the mirror, and with the backs of his fingertips he made light brushing strokes at the sides of his head. The movement was unnecessary; with his close-cropped hair nothing was out of place.

"She's okay," he finally said.

"I find that hard to believe."

Rick shrugged as if to say he didn't much care what Jack believed. "What did Margaret really have on her mind?"

"She says the two of you used to go together."

"Not exactly."

"How would you put it?"

There was that shrug again. Jack swore that boy said more with his shoulders than with his mouth. "We went out a few times."

"Well, you made an impression."

Rick leaned a bit to try to see Jack's reflection in the mirror. Jack stepped further to the side. "Doesn't take much with Margaret."

"She said she can't quite believe you and June were running off together."

Rick laughed. "Me neither."

Jack moved directly behind Rick's left shoulder so the young man could clearly see Jack's unsmiling expression. "I guess I don't see anything funny in any of this," Jack said.

Suddenly sober, Rick said, "Margaret gets worked up about things."

"Has she gotten in touch with you in the last couple of days?"

Rick shook his head.

"She might. Are you ready for that?"

The young man stepped away from his reflection and turned to Jack. "I can handle Margaret Elsey."

Jack could no longer keep track of where his allegiance should be. He and Rick were supposed to be working together on putting out a version of the accident, but now Jack felt protective toward Margaret. He had taken her into his confidence—even if it was with another lie—and he didn't like hearing this young man say he could "handle" her.

"You've been telling people about you and June? Your plans?"

"Yeah. A few people."

"How about those two that were just in here? Did you tell them?"

"Not really."

"Not really. Now, what's that supposed to mean? You did or you didn't."

"They already knew."

"Is that what they said?"

"I could tell."

"You know, Rick, we can't afford to leave anything to chance. We've got to take control where we can."

One corner of Rick's mouth slanted slightly upward. "Like grab the wheel, you mean?"

"Something like that."

Now his smirk was complete. "Take hold of the reins?"

"I'm thinking of your father. . . ."

Rick turned back to the mirror and straightened the knot of his tie that was already perfectly in place. "My father. Yeah. And June. You were probably thinking of June too. June . . . You know, we were going to have *such* a happy life together."

Jack stared down at the tile squares of the bathroom floor, marked and scuffed from the dragging heels of all those reluctant Sunday-school-goers, boys who would rather have spent their Sunday mornings in bed or on the ballfield or by the banks of the Knife River. "Of course you don't want to go to church," his father used to say to Jack and Phil, "but this is good training for you, for a life where you don't always get to do what you like." Well, Jack was back in Sunday school again, just where he didn't want to be, this time taking shit from Rick Bauer. Somewhere along the line Jack must have gotten training for that too because take it he did.

"You got another of those smokes?" he asked Rick.

"They were Mickey's." Rick turned again and stepped forward.

Jack stood between Rick and the door. For the young man to get past, either Jack would have to step aside or Rick would have to shoulder Jack out of the way.

Jack didn't move. "What about June's funeral?"

Rick stopped close to Jack. "What about it?"

"You're going."

As if he suddenly caught an unpleasant odor coming off Jack, Rick leaned away and took a backward step. "Is that a question or an order?"

"That depends on what your answer is."

Rick smiled, snorted, and shook his head. But he gave the right answer. "I guess."

"People are going to expect to see you there and see you grieving. I don't suppose you've talked to Mrs. Moss?" Jack closed the space between them that Rick had just vacated.

"I haven't seen her." The boy's voice rose slightly.

"You could have called her." As long as he had Rick backing up, Jack decided to keep pressing forward. "Don't you think that would be logical? She was going to be your mother-in-law. You could have called her, and said you were sorry. That wouldn't have been so much, would it?"

Rick put his hands behind him as if he were trying to feel where he was. He stopped abruptly at the sink. "I don't know Mrs. Moss!" His mouth twisted and puckered as if he were about to

203

spit. "I've hardly even talked to my own goddamn mother—not that she wants me to—and you want me to go calling that old bitch? Fuck that shit!"

"Keep your voice down."

"Fuck you too! Stop telling me what to do. My father's dead. I don't need another one!"

Jack wasn't quite sure what he did next. He didn't hit the boy. He was sure of that. He didn't have any desire to hit him. His action wasn't born out of any wish to inflict pain or punishment. But he did want to bring Rick under control. The boy's face was red and his features were contorted as if he were going to start bawling at any moment.

So Jack wanted to control him, to grab ahold of him just until Rick settled down, until Jack could be sure the boy wasn't going to keep shouting and swearing there in the church basement.

But when he reached for Rick—Jack had in mind that he'd grab the lapel of Rick's suit coat and that way it would be cloth he'd have a handful of and he wouldn't really be laying hands on the kid—Rick flinched and tried to twist away.

Jack had tried to grab hard. He'd admit that. Get ahold of the kid quick, that had been his thinking. So shooting his hand out fast like that might have had the appearance—and a little of the effect—of a blow, a punch.

But it wasn't a fist he was pushing out there; it was an open, reaching hand. And when Rick jerked back, Jack had to grab faster, harder, and his hand thumped against the boy's bony chest.

Somehow, the force of Jack's hand, along with Rick's violent backward and sideways attempt to get out of reach—and maybe the floor had recently been waxed and maybe the kid glanced off the sink and that hard fixture may have been like another blow, this one to the buttocks—knocked Rick's feet out from under him.

In trying to keep from falling backward and hitting his head against the wall, Rick went down sideways, landed hard on his ass, and his sliding momentum carried him right toward the urinal.

He didn't go in, but he stopped just short, right where the floor was always damp and sticky from splattered piss and careless aim.

Rick knew where he landed—he had to, he got his hands down

behind him, and they had to feel the wet. Yet he didn't hurry to
get to his feet or even to move forward a few feet.

After being there for only a second or two, Rick looked settled,
as if he were finally comfortable. No more checking his hair or
straightening his tie. No more having to be polite to people you
barely knew while they praised your father and offered their con-
dolences. He could finally relax and just sit there, the smell of
mothballs sharp in his nostrils, his trousers wet from another
man's urine.

Jack started to reach down to help Rick up, then stopped himself.
The hell with it. Let him sit. Maybe now he could get the kid
to listen.

"You're going to June's funeral." Jack realized how loud his
voice sounded in this small space, and he spoke softer. "You're
going and you'll sit right up front. Not with the family but close,
maybe in the pew right behind. And sometime, right after the
service or maybe out at the cemetery—and you're going to the
cemetery; you're going and you'll stand as close to that grave as
anyone—you're going to talk to Mrs. Moss. You're going to say
you're sorry about what happened to June. You're going to say
you're sorry the two of you acted so foolishly. And if that's too
much for you to take on, and you need an excuse, tell her the two
of you were in love and you weren't thinking clearly. And if you
can't work up a tear or two for the occasion you at least put on
the saddest face you can muster. Because, so help me God, if I see
that smirk again I'll slap it right off."

Rick moved forward a few inches. He still made no effort to get
up, only to move away from the spot where the floor sloped gently
toward the urinal.

"One more thing," Jack said. "You might hear Margaret Elsey
spreading something around town about June having been p.g. You
don't have to say anything about that. You can treat it like loose
talk, the sort that's always going to go around about a situation
like yours and June's. You don't have to deny it, and you don't
have to say it's so. Margaret doesn't have any way of knowing
these things for certain. And if you turn away from it, that's
probably what's best."

Now he reached down, but of course it was too late. There wasn't a chance in hell Rick Bauer would take his hand.

The young man stood up slowly. He made no move to wipe his hands or rearrange himself in any way. His suit coat had slid down one shoulder, but he didn't try to shrug it back on. "And then when I want to take a shit," he said to Jack, "should I call you and get your permission?"

"You can shit when and where you like. Just so long as it's not on the reputations of your dad or June Moss. I won't have that. I won't have that."

"You won't have it." Rick's mouth twisted down again as if he might cry but this time not from anger or insolence. Now he was just a boy whose pants were wet. "You won't have it. . . . You're just like my dad. You act like you're so calm and reasonable about things, but then when you don't get your way, you have to get tough."

He was like Leo Bauer? Maybe it was from hearing Leo praised all day, maybe it was from seeing how snotty Leo's kid could be, but suddenly being like Leo didn't seem such an awful thing to be. They belonged to the same generation. They were from the same state, the same town. Husbands. Fathers. They were once on the same team. Barney Gregory, Jack's high-school basketball coach—and Leo's coach—used to say the team was like family and your family comes first. You don't let anyone attack your family.

"Did your dad used to get rough with you, Rick?"

"Yeah. Sometimes. He used to. Not lately."

"I can't imagine he enjoyed it. Being a parent is tough. You do your best. . . . You try."

"He used to grab ahold of my wrist and pull it or twist it until I'd be on my knees almost. And for stupid things. Because I didn't take out the garbage. Once because the paperboy came to collect, and I told him we didn't have any money and I was supposed to say come back when my father's home. Stupid, stupid little things."

Jack reached out for the young man again but slowly this time. He delicately took hold of Rick's lapel, the same lapel he tried to grab a moment ago. Rick did not flinch or jerk away. Jack tugged the boy's suit coat until it sat a bit straighter on his frame. "Let's go find your mother. I bet she's looking for you."

Rick leaned back as if there were something wrong with his eyes, and he couldn't see clearly any object that was too close. "Do you know anything?" he asked. "Do you know anything about us *at all?*"

Us. The Bauers. They were down to only two, but they were still a family. Jack had gotten the teams mixed up again.

28

By the time Jack returned to the Fellowship Hall, almost everyone had left. A few women from the church were spreading aluminum foil over uneaten cake or putting leftover cookies into tins or plastic containers. The folding chairs and tables would no doubt remain in place until after June's funeral.

Vivien and her sister stood in the middle of the room.

If you didn't know better, you'd think it was Vivien's sister who needed comfort and support. She gripped the sleeve of Vivien's dark blue dress and rested her head against Vivien's arm. Meanwhile, Vivien acted as though she were barely aware of her sister's presence. Occasionally she would pat her sister on the shoulder, the way a mother without thinking touches her child periodically to assure the child that Mother is still there and paying attention.

The last few mourners made their way past Vivien, stopping and telling her once again—or perhaps for the first time (these stragglers may have needed all this time to summon the courage to speak to the widow)—how sorry they were for her loss, if there was anything they could do to help, anything at all . . .

To Jack, Vivien looked a bit like royalty, greeting each well-wisher with a handshake, the slightest bow of the head, and a small smile that said she was as concerned about them as they were about her. Her tears dried and put away—Jack couldn't see a wadded handkerchief or Kleenex secreted in either hand—Vivien stood proudly tall there in the low-ceilinged room, towering not only over her sister and the women who passed but over a good many of the men as well.

This wasn't his Vivien, Jack thought, then immediately chided himself for such a stupid notion. Yet this wide-shouldered, regal woman was so different from the woman he had sat with in her bathroom that he had difficulty merging the two. And since the one here now so obviously belonged to everyone—to family, to friends, to an entire town—then it followed that the bathroom Vivien belonged to him alone.

Rick, on the other hand, must not have seen any Viviens that were his because he took one look at the scene in the Fellowship Hall and left the church.

Jack didn't see Nora. That was fine. Earlier she had noticed how his clothes were wet from being caught in the rain, and he was afraid she might look closely at him again and see other changes. Then she would want an explanation. Where have you been? Have you been thinking murderous thoughts about a young woman? Have you been bullying a young man?

He waited for the last mourner, Hazel Jacobsen, to leave Vivien before he made his way to her.

She watched him approach, but as far as he could tell, the smile she wore for him was no different from the one she had shown others.

"Jack. Is it still raining?"

Her question ruined everything. He had composed a small speech—a few words praising Leo, then thanks for the honor of being chosen as a pallbearer, and finally his offer: If there's anything you need done around your place, I'm available. *I'm available.* He had thought a long time before he settled on that phrase. Just as he had gone back and forth in his mind—*need* done or *want* done? But he had decided that he would rather be available

209

to her needs than to her wants, even if he couldn't be sure how they differed.

But Vivien had spoken first, and he had to answer her question. And once he did, he wasn't sure if he'd be able to get back on the track that would lead him to the words he had memorized and rehearsed.

"I wasn't outside," he said. "I was talking to Rick—"

She didn't scowl at the mention of her son's name, as Jack thought she might. "I worry about him," Vivien said. "I know how hard all this is on him, but he's concentrating on being strong for me. Did he say anything—"

He waited for her to finish her question, but it just hung in the air between them, and Jack and Vivien both looked at Vivien's sister as if they expected her to complete the sentence.

"Oh, I'm sorry," Vivien said. "This is my sister, Vera Temper. From Salt Lake City."

"How do you do." Jack extended his hand, and Vera took it, but as cautiously, as tentatively, as a cat reaches out a paw to test if any life is left in its prey. Her hand was small, soft, and warm. She withdrew it quickly.

"Vera, this is Sheriff Nevelsen. Jack was the first one there when Leo had his accident."

"Actually—" Jack started to correct her but stopped when he saw the look in Vera's eyes. She looked relieved, grateful. "Actually, it was my deputy mostly." But how had Vivien come to believe that? Is that what Rick told her? And why—to establish Jack's credibility? *He knows because he was there.* Had he even told Rick that Wayne was the first one at the accident?

Ah, God, this story was his creation, and he even thought of it as having a simple, streamlined construction—nothing fancy, just enough to get the job done. But he felt as though others were constantly tampering with his design, hammering on details that didn't fit, screwing on an interpretation that didn't match another, cutting a notch where none belonged. . . . Gradually, the story was losing its shape, its symmetry, its purity and clarity, and perhaps soon he wouldn't be able to recognize it as his own. Was that finally preferable—that the story carry so many additions and emendations that no one could tell what it was supposed to be? Was that confusion what he should hope for?

Vivien gave no indication that she heard Jack's modest correction. "And when he brought me the news . . . It was terrible, but I could see how much pain he was in. Jack and Leo were old friends." She looked away from her sister and stared directly into Jack's eyes. "Dear Jack. Does your heart always break a little when you have to break another's?"

Did she believe this? Had she been so drunk that night that she couldn't rightly arrange what had happened or when? Was that a plea in her eyes—*Let me tell it this way; please don't contradict me?* Was she building her own version of events, and did she want him to help her—or at least not to hinder? Was this little display of tenderness, this line of poetry, something *she* had rehearsed? And for whom was it intended? Her sister? Jack? For Vivien herself?

"That part of the job," Jack said, "is pretty much exaggerated." Exactly what he had said at the barbershop.

And what part of the job was not? What was it that everyone misunderstood about the work he did?

The sheriffs of television and movies dispatched their duties with fists and guns, chasing down lawbreakers on horseback or in fast cars, and once the outlaws were dead or behind bars, the sheriff's job was finished. Jack could never watch those depictions without laughing. His biggest surprise, once he took office, was the amount of paperwork he had to do. He doubted that accountants moved as much paper across their desks as he did. Extradition papers, accident reports, court orders, expense vouchers, arrest warrants, road updates, inventories, memos, compliances, depositions, forms, forms, forms . . . in duplicate, in triplicate. To be notarized. To be delivered. To be signed. To be stamped. To be witnessed. Due by . . . on or before . . . It never ended. The jail always had space for prisoners, but they were fast running out of room for all the papers that had to be filed.

But a lie took up no space at all. It had no existence at all outside of mind. Yet there it could find a field fertile enough to take root and flourish. And that was Jack's job now, or so he saw it—to plant a lie in as many minds as possible. In order to keep this town running in the right direction—where parents could trust that teachers and principals would keep their hands off students, where older men didn't think that a high-school girl was available for their pleasure (my God, Jack could imagine men drooling over that possibility, driving around the high school in their cars and trucks in hopes of nabbing one!)—in order to keep this town civilized, Jack's lie had to blossom.

What would people say about him as sheriff if he told them the hardest part of the job was not scraping bodies off the highway or wrestling raving drunks into the tank or even breaking bad news to widows, but making sure the right lies get told? Maybe the next time he ran for office he'd use that for his campaign slogan. "Vote for Jack Nevelsen—You Can Trust Him to Pick the Right Lie for Your Town." Jesus. He wished he *could* do his job with a gun.

He hadn't considered that other people were doing his job as well. But Vivien seemed to have her own version of events: Jack brought her the news after discovering Leo's body. Rick was a loving son who helped his mother through her sorrow.

Did Vivien have any recollection of the two of them in the bathroom, of Jack draping the towel over her shoulders? What the hell; let her remember it her way. He had torn up Margaret Elsey's sign—who was he to hold up one of his own: That's Not the Way It Was.

"It was hard coming to see you," Jack said to Vivien, trying to hold her gaze long after it was comfortable to do so, "what with being Leo's friend. And you—yours. So I wanted to be sure I thanked you." Goddamn it! Here he was giving his speech after all, and as it came out, it sounded all wrong. Not *thanks*, you don't thank someone on this occasion. "For the honor of being one of Leo's . . ." And now he had forgotten the word! How could this happen? Someone who carried the corpse—no, it wasn't a corpse once it was prepared for burial. The body. Carried the body. But you didn't touch the body—you might not even see it. The box, you carried the box. And not "box"—coffin. You carried the coffin, and why would you express gratitude for being allowed to do that? Where was the honor in that?

Perhaps Vivien understood what he couldn't say. "Dear Jack," she said. There was that phrase again. He wished he could be flattered, but he couldn't find anything personal in it. He suspected that everyone who spoke to Vivien today was addressed as "dear." "Dear Jack" was as likely to be "Dear Nora," "Dear Rick," "Dear Vera." "How could I not choose you?" Vivien said. "I had to think of what Leo would have wanted."

And what—do the opposite? Jack couldn't believe that he belonged on any list of Leo's best friends, and he was certainly not among the top six. Why then did Vivien choose him? Was it for her? Was it to get him to keep quiet about the condition he saw her in that night? If she honored him as a . . . pallbearer!—there it was, that was the word!—then he couldn't betray her. Her secret was safe with him, even if he couldn't reassure her with the best proof he had of how good he could be at keeping secrets.

Vivien stepped away from her sister and came closer to Jack. With her thumb and index finger she pressed down on his shirt collar on either side of his tie's overlarge, clumsy knot. "Dear Jack," she said once more, this time so softly it could only be intended for his ears.

Back at the courthouse, Jack went into the restroom and stood close to the mirror. The points of his shirt collar had risen as if they were wings about to take flight. He never could get the damn thing to lie flat, and now it had gotten wet and worse—the tips were beginning to curl.

That must have been what Vivien was doing, pressing down his collar to push it back in place, the kind of reflexive gesture a wife or mother might make.

Nevertheless, Jack pulled loose his tie, unbuttoned his top three buttons, and spread his shirt wide, exposing a triangle of pale, hairless chest. He wanted to see if any mark might be left behind from the pressure of Vivien's fingers, a faint pink indentation perhaps, just the ghost of a fingerprint.

Of course there was nothing there, nothing at all.

29

JACK PARKED HIS TRUCK UP THE STREET FROM THE CHURCH. THEN HE moved over into the passenger seat so he had a clear line of sight straight down the block to the church's front doors. He took up his post well before anyone arrived for June Moss's funeral, but he wanted to make certain Rick Bauer attended and that Margaret Elsey did not, or if she did, it was without one of her goddamn signs.

The rain was falling harder now, not a downpour by any means, but a steady soaker, the kind of rain farmers liked to see. Or did they? Maybe they needed to get out in the fields now, and rain was the last thing they wanted. He could never keep track of what farmers and ranchers needed or when. Too hot, too cold, too wet, too dry. Too much rain. Not enough snow. Not enough sun. People who depended on the land and the weather for a living could always find something to bitch about.

Well, let it rain. It was good for his line of work. Rain helped keep people in line. It kept the kids from gathering on street corners. It kept the Indians from walking or hitchhiking in from the reservation to buy booze. It dampened tempers and cooled off troublemakers. It kept women from gossiping over the back fences and men from bullshitting out in front of the Northern Pacific Hotel. If people had doubts about the accident, maybe the rain would keep them from finding someone to whom they might express those doubts. Maybe it might even keep a teenage girl from standing outside and holding up a sign.

The rain streaked the truck's windows, making it difficult for Jack to see down the block. It also made it harder to see *into* the truck. He wasn't about to move, so he preferred that no one saw him sitting there.

If felt so natural, so familiar, sitting and watching. . . .

When Jack got out of the service—he was discharged later than most soldiers; when there was no longer much need for infantrymen, MPs still had work to do—he had difficulty readjusting to civilian life. Nothing serious. He didn't come home shell-shocked, twitching, talking to himself, or crying out in his sleep the way some soldiers did. No, when Jack finally got back to Bentrock, he felt vaguely stunned, although not by a blow but by sight. The sensation was similar to coming out of a movie theater, a matinee, and being blinded by sunlight. He just had to wait, squint, blink a few times, and soon his eyes would become accustomed to the light.

It was common for soldiers to express disbelief at how much had changed while they were away. Jack heard of soldiers saying they barely recognized their parents, their wives and girlfriends, their children, their hometowns. Especially their towns. And what seemed most shocking was not the new buildings or the absence of old ones but the alteration of scale. Everything had shrunk— the high school and the department store, the barn and the pasture, the gym and the vacant lot.

Not so for Jack. Once he was back in Montana, what he could not get over was how little had changed. It had been years, thousands of miles, and millions dead, yet there it all was, exactly as he left it: the house he grew up in, the cracks in its dirty, cream-colored stucco neither longer nor wider. The uneven squares of sidewalk in front of the post office, tilting first right then left. The hand-lettered sign in the window of Roller's Cafe—"Breakfast.

Lunch. No Supper After Seven." Ole Norgaard's tar-paper shack on the outskirts of town, out of which Ole sold his homegrown vegetables and his homemade beer and chokecherry and dandelion wine. The cars in the lot at Hench's Studebaker didn't look any newer. The roads that had been unpaved were still dirt and gravel; the planks were still loose on one end of the bridge that spanned the Knife River; the railroad underpass on the northside still flooded during heavy rains.

Of course he knew changes had occurred. Of course. He was not an idiot. His own mother had died. When he left, she was there; when he returned, she was gone. That was a fact, something he knew. But his disorientation was a matter of sight, not of intellect. He couldn't *see* what had changed.

After the war, his father told Jack he could work in the hardware store, although there wasn't profit enough in the business to pay him more than minimum wage. Elroy Munson told Jack he could come back to work for his contracting company. And Jack's brother, Phil, suggested that Jack apply at the police department; his experience with the military police would compel them to hire him.

But Jack wasn't finished blinking, and looking around.

Two blocks from the courthouse was a small park. It wasn't much—a triangular sun-baked vacant lot with a tiny flower garden in the center and a few trees and shrubs planted around the periphery. On each side of the park was an iron bench that faced the street. Jack and Nora lived then in an apartment in the basement of Ronald and Joan Simonson's home, right across the street from the park. Jack fell into a routine: He'd get up early and walk downtown, stopping for coffee at the Northern Pacific Hotel or Young Drug, maybe Roller's if he hadn't eaten breakfast, though he and Nora had so little money he felt guilty about treating himself to a restaurant meal. Next, he might look in on his father at the hardware store. Later he would walk by the Grand Street Billiard Parlor and Cigar Store, and if any of the retirees who hung out there had started their game of pinochle, Jack would watch them play. Then, on his way home, he would stop at the park and sit on one of the benches. From there he planned to observe his town as closely as he could, but he was just as likely to doze a little if the sun was warm.

One day when Jack's eyes were closed, a car pulled up to the curb, and when the sound of the car door thunking shut brought Jack around, he opened his eyes to a Bentrock policeman walking his way.

The police department had only three officers, and Jack thought he knew them all, yet he did not immediately recognize this heavy-set young man who kept glancing to the right and the left as he approached. He stopped in front of Jack as if the sidewalk were marked to indicate where he should stand. His thumbs were hooked inside his belt, but the pose did not seem casual or comfortable. He seemed to be trying to ease the pressure on his considerable gut.

He still had not looked directly at Jack when he finally spoke. "Morning." It did not sound like a greeting but a declaration.

"Good morning," Jack answered.

The policeman stopped shifting his gaze from side to side and focused on the sidewalk in front of Jack's feet. "We had complaints about someone in the park."

Jack didn't understand. These complaints occurred in the past, yet the policeman was telling Jack about them now? Why? Had it happened while he was in the service, and this young man was filling Jack in on a little Bentrock history?

"This park?" asked Jack.

The young man spread his feet wider. "Right here," he said. "More than one call we got."

Then Jack knew, or thought he did. The complaints were not in the past; they were current. But Jack had only recently left his own job in law enforcement, and he was still thinking like a policeman himself. This young man was asking Jack for help—had Jack seen anyone in the park, someone behaving suspiciously or plainly up to no good?

"I haven't seen anyone," Jack said. "Can't help you."

"I'm going to have to ask you what your business is here in the park."

There was something about the way this young policeman talked, so slowly, so seriously, so expressionlessly, that made it difficult for Jack to understand him. After this remark, for example, Jack wanted to say, You're going to *have to* ask me? So go ahead and ask. . . .

The policeman shifted his stance once again, and his shadow, foreshortened by the high morning sun, touched Jack's feet, and then Jack knew: Him, the complaints were about him. Someone had been watching him sit on this park bench and had called the cops.

Jack didn't get angry. Oh, perhaps he bristled a bit over this young man's self-importance, but more than anything he felt sad. This was Jack's town. He was born here—Dr. Snow had come to the house to deliver him—and he grew up here. He left only because he had to, and as soon as the government released him, he hustled back to Bentrock. Now, not only was he not recognized—for God's sake, he was Jack Nevelsen, Louis and Edna's boy—he was regarded as a stranger, someone who didn't belong, a threat to the town and its inhabitants.

Jack looked beyond the policeman to the house and buildings surrounding the park. He could identify many of the homes and the families who lived in them. Who was it—old Mrs. Nesbitt who lived over there with her sissy son? Had she been watching Jack? There was a little grocery store around the corner and down the block, owned by those Italian brothers—the Ferrarras? was that their name?—and one of them, the bachelor brother, lived over the store; and the other, the one with all the kids, had a house nearby. They must have had a hard time during the war. Were they trying to prove their patriotism now by reporting to the police the suspicious-looking man in the park? Or maybe it was Mrs. Ferrarra. Jack remembered her when she first came to Bentrock, a small, frightened-looking woman who spoke very little English. Over the years maybe she had learned enough of the language to pick up the telephone and ask for the police department. . . .

Jack would have to leave. That was all there was to it. He would have to leave this park and he would have to leave Bentrock. He'd tell Nora, and they'd start packing that afternoon. He'd be damned

218

if he'd live in a town where he couldn't even sit on a park bench without being rousted by the cops.

And who the hell was this young man with the big gut and the squinty eyes? Was he new in town? Why didn't he recognize Jack? Where was Russell Horton, who had been a cop since Jack was a boy and who knew everyone in town? And when had it been decided that no one was to sit in this park without being reported to the police? What was a park for? Why bother with benches? Had all these changes occurred while he was off fighting a war on behalf of a country that wouldn't even let you sit in its god-damn parks?

That was all he wanted to do—take it easy for a while, look around his hometown, laze in the warm sun.

The sun was warm. Jack was wearing a T-shirt, but the police-man wore a long-sleeved shirt buttoned to the cuff.

Of course—Chaussy Niedlinger! That was who stood before Jack. Chaussy with his long sleeves. . . .

Chaussy went to high school with Jack, though he was two or three classes ahead of Chaussy. Chaussy had been going steady with Louisa Dorner—they'd been boyfriend and girlfriend since grade school, when they lived on adjoining farms—and Louisa broke up with Chaussy right before Christmas. Rumor had it that Chaussy was so broken up that he tried to kill himself, cut his wrists, people said, and would have died if his younger brother hadn't found him. It must have been true because Chaussy came back from Christmas vacation with his wrists still bandaged, an edge of white gauze peeking out from his shirt cuffs. Jack and his friends joked about Chaussy behind his back—imagine trying to kill yourself over a girl, and someone as ordinary as Louisa Dorner at that. What a fool you'd have to be! What a sap! Yet even then Jack was secretly awed by what Chaussy had tried to do. To be so in love that you'd rather die than live without someone . . .

But Chaussy had been a tall skinny kid with an Adam's apple that stuck out like a knob on a cupboard door, and this cop was fat, solid but fat nonetheless. Roll up your sleeve, Jack wanted to say! Let's see the scars!

Yet he knew such a request was unnecessary. This was Chaussy, all right. Jack was sure of it. He should have recognized the voice, high-pitched and choked-off, damaged-sounding, as if Chaussy had tried to hang himself. Maybe Chaussy's close-set eyes gave him away or his large forehead and overhanging brow. Or maybe Jack had suddenly found the ability to see the changes that were right in front of him all along, but he could only notice them when he stopped looking.

"Chaussy?" Jack said. "Chaussy Niedlinger?"

Chaussy took his thumbs out of his belt. "Do I know you?"

"Jack Nevelsen. We were in high school together." He pointed in the direction of his and Nora's apartment. "I live right over there."

Chaussy was not about to be won over by references to good old Bentrock High. "What's the address?" he asked.

Jack told him.

Chaussy nodded as if to say, yes, there was such an address. . . .

Jack guessed there was no other way to conclude the situation, so he stood up. "I was on my way home," he said. "Just stopped to have a cigarette." He was prepared to show Chaussy the cigarette butts under the bench.

"People don't generally sit here," Chaussy said and moved off toward his squad car.

Jack had an almost overwhelming desire to call out, Hey, whatever happened to Louisa Dorner? You two ever get back together? Instead, he politely asked, "Who complained?"

Chaussy Niedlinger opened his car door before he answered. He still would not look directly at Jack. "Like I say. There's more'n one."

That evening, as Jack watched Nora prepare supper in their small, stuffy kitchen, she pulled her hair back from her face in that characteristic way of hers. Her dark hair had sprouted strands of gray as early as high school, but now a few of those strands had gathered together to make a streak that ran like a waterfall from the top of her head to her shoulders. It must have happened while he was overseas, yet he hadn't noticed until this moment. When had the spell broken? That afternoon when he had his little run-in with Chaussy? Once he recognized Chaussy under all those pounds, was Jack ready to see how everything had changed, was changing?

When he next saw his father, Jack asked him, "Have you been losing weight?"

"A couple pounds," his father said. "I didn't think it showed." In only a few months' time, Jack's father would have the first of his many operations, initially to find the cancer eating away at him and then to cut it out.

By the time Jack was sworn in as sheriff of Mercer County, the Bentrock police department had grown to four officers, but none was Chaussy Niedlinger. Chaussy moved out to Seattle to work in one of the big aircraft assembly plants. Louisa Dorner married a wheat farmer from around Crosby, North Dakota, a man considerably older than she. Nora knew one of Louisa's best friends from high school, and she said Louisa was miserable in her marriage, that she was married to a man who beat her. When Jack heard that, all he could think was, And she once had a boyfriend who loved her so much he cut his wrists over losing her. . . .

And now Jack had a job doing what he was doing years ago when he came home from the war—keeping an eye on the town, on the county, watching for changes, for anything that wasn't the way it was supposed to be, for anything that wasn't the way it was the week, the day, the hour before.

He no longer did his job from a park bench. He was more likely to do it from where he sat now, from the front seat of a car or truck, staring out through a windshield that was frequently frost-glazed or rain- or snow-smeared or dust-streaked. Around here, window glass never stayed clean for long.

But clean enough. Jack could see what he needed to see: the front doors of First Lutheran Church and the mourners hurrying through the rain.

Not many of them. Jack didn't keep count, but he knew there would be rows of empty pews.

Well, June Moss didn't have Leo Bauer's stature. Leo—yes, townspeople would feel they owed him something, something that could be repaid by sitting for an hour on a hard pew on a dark day. But now this rain . . . And this girl—who was she? Someone said she worked at Nash's Grocery, but who knew her? Or her mother, for that matter. And if you'd already attended Leo's funeral—why, would even God expect you to attend another that same day?

Was that Rick's thinking? Jack didn't see the boy enter the church—had he decided he had had enough for the day? *The hell with Jack Nevelsen and his commands; I've done my time.*

The church had a side door. Rick could have slipped in there, but Jack doubted it. He could have sprinted in while Jack was lighting a cigarette, but that wasn't likely either. The kid didn't show. Nevertheless, Jack felt he had to wait and survey the crowd leaving the church to make sure Rick wasn't among them.

Celia Moss and her family—at least Jack assumed they were her family—were first out of the church. They didn't scurry through the rain but walked slowly, heads up, eyes straight ahead—why cover or wipe away your tears when raindrops were coursing down your cheeks anyway?

Celia Moss did not need any help. She walked in the center of her small group, while the three men and three women were ringed around her as though their duty were to keep people away.

People did not linger outside the church. They hurried off to their cars, their homes, their jobs, a meal, a drink. Would anyone besides Celia Moss and her family make the trip to the cemetery?

Margaret Elsey. She hadn't attended the funeral either, although she had represented herself as a friend of June's.

In his imagination, Jack saw Margaret at the cemetery again, and this time she had company in her sign-holding. Jack saw both Margaret and Rick out there, and Rick's sign said something like, "DON'T BELIEVE WHAT SHERIFF NEVELSEN SAYS."

30

JACK KNEW WHAT ROUTE THE SMALL FUNERAL PROCESSION WOULD TAKE to the cemetery, and he drove off in the other direction, hoping his route would get him there quicker.

June's grave was on the opposite side of the cemetery from Leo's (*See*, Jack couldn't help thinking, *you weren't meant to be together*), in the newest section, a compact area on the other side of the road, where most of the tombstones were flat stones flush with the ground. You couldn't help being noticed if you held up a sign out there.

Or if you parked your truck nearby. Jack had to be content with circling the graveyard, watching for Rick's car or a vehicle that could be Margaret's. When he glimpsed the hearse approaching, he took a chance and drove into the cemetery. He sped down the road nearest June's grave, but he saw no one.

Still, he could not allow himself to relax. He had become convinced that Rick and Margaret were out there. As soon as he thought he could do so without being seen, he turned off the blacktop and steered down a narrow lane between two rows of poplars. He parked and got out of the truck. The wind had come up strong, doubling the rain's force and bringing it down in sweeping, slanting bursts. He stayed close to the trees, and each time he left their protection, another gust of rain hit him. Gradually he worked his way to a spot where he had an unobstructed view of June's grave and the surrounding area. If Rick or Margaret tried anything, he could, he could . . . What could he do? He was hiding in the trees like a sniper, but he had no gun. There was a notch in the tree where he could rest and brace a rifle, and there was the sight line he could aim down, but he had no targets.

The hearse and three cars had stopped, but no one was getting out, no mourners, no pallbearers, no coffin. Finally, Reverend Ellingsen and Harold Undset got out of the hearse and ran back through the rain to the first car. Reverend Ellingsen's surplice billowed and twisted in the wind before it took on enough water to plaster itself wetly to him.

Jack could guess what was going on. The minister and the mortician were presenting the situation to June Moss's family. Did they want to call off the graveside ceremony? Postpone it? The gravediggers weren't going to be able to do anything in this mud anyway, and the rites could be performed at another time. If it was Celia Moss they were talking to, Jack could predict the result.

Yes, just as Jack expected. The car door opened, and Mrs. Moss stepped out. She stood for a moment in that stately, erect way and looked around as though she was assessing the weather—*Yes, it's bad, but just how bad?* She had to squint from the force of the wind and rain, but she could still stand. She could walk. She could pray. *Let's get on with it.*

Celia Moss, Reverend Ellingsen, and the men and women Jack had seen surrounding Celia at the church began to make their way toward the grave site. They leaned into the wind and lifted their feet higher than usual when the claylike gumbo stuck to their shoes.

What the hell. Jack wasn't going to shoot anyone. He wasn't going to arrest anyone. He wasn't going to tear up any signs. He was already soaked to the skin. He might as well have gotten wet for a reason. He stepped out from behind his tree and walked forward to take his place with the only other people in the county who had a good reason to be out in this weather.

Celia Moss gave Jack the slightest nod when he joined their small group. She had registered no surprise when she saw him, and Jack wondered if she knew all along that he was back there, hiding behind a poplar tree. He knew he wouldn't get any more from her than that nod, but in his state he would accept it gratefully. He would take it as a blessing.

Jack tried to close the screen door gently, but a gust of wind pushed him into the kitchen and slammed the door behind him.

At the noise, Nora spun around from where she stood at the sink. She was still wearing the dress she wore to the funeral.

"Sorry," Jack said. She had to have heard him when he first pulled open the screen and turned the knob of the inner door—was she that jumpy?

"You're soaking."

He looked down at himself as if he hadn't noticed his condition until she remarked on it. "It's really coming down. And that wind . . ."

"Where have you been?"

"June Moss's funeral."

She cocked her head as if she hadn't heard him right.

He pointed to the kitchen table and chairs. "Can I sit down?"

"I didn't know you were going to her funeral."

"I didn't either. I just thought . . . I don't know. Someone should go."

As dark as Nora's dress was, there was a darker stripe across the front at waist level. She had been washing dishes and gotten the fabric wet.

"Weren't other people there?" she asked.

"Not many. Not like at Leo's." He pointed again at a chair. "I don't want to track up the floor."

"Oh, for Pete's sake." She waved him over to a chair. "Go ahead. You can't stand there all day."

He made it to his chair with two long strides. "It's getting colder, too." He wanted a drink of whiskey, and if he had to open the bottle in her presence, he wanted to have an excuse. *Just something to take the chill off,* he would say.

"Don't you want to change clothes?"

"In a minute." He reached for his cigarettes, then remembered he had taken them out of his pocket so they wouldn't get wet. "Could you get me a fresh pack?" He pointed to the carton of Chesterfields on top of the refrigerator.

She set the pack in front of him, along with a book of matches he hadn't asked for. "Did you know her?"

He looked around for an ashtray. "Who?"

"The girl in the accident."

"June Moss."

"Did you?"

"June Moss. That's her name. No, I didn't know her."

She must have seen him searching for an ashtray, because she pulled one from the dish drainer and set it on the table. It seemed to Jack she put the ashtray down less gently than the cigarettes.

Why hadn't he noticed before—Nora was wearing perfume. When she stood this close, the odor was apparent, a floral smell but with an undertone of something else, something metallic. If the earth could grow such a thing as a brass or copper flower, that would be the scent of Nora's perfume.

So she wore perfume to Leo Bauer's funeral. He tried to think of other occasions when Nora might wear perfume. The Christmas party at the country club. The New Year's Eve party the Lovolls hosted every year. Maybe one or two other wingdings that might be dress-up affairs. Jack didn't even know—did Nora wear perfume to church? Well, she wore it today. She wore it for Leo Bauer's funeral.

Nora took a step back, and that was enough distance for Jack to lose the scent. That was all right; she hadn't put it on for him in the first place.

Where did she put her perfume anyway? He remembered her dabbing it behind her ears. In the hollow of her throat. On her wrists? Could that be right? Her wrists?

Let her come close again . . . He could catch her by the arm and bring her wrist right up to his nose. He'd find the smell on her. He'd spin her around and unzip her dress, press his face to the back of her neck, behind her ears, and then inhale. He'd pull her dress down off her shoulders, her arms, right down to her waist; then he'd run his nose along her collarbone and down the cleft between her breasts. Like a dog, he'd stay on the scent until he discovered every secret place she touched herself. For Leo. Where she touched herself for Leo.

Then . . . then he'd get the smell off her somehow. He'd rub it off if he had to. He'd lick it off. He'd cover her with his own sweat, his own sour odor. He'd strip her naked and haul her out in the backyard. He'd hold her out there until the wind whipped the smell of perfume off her and the rain washed her clean. She'd struggle to get free, but Jack would hold her tighter while the wind raged around them. For Leo! he'd shout—you put this on for Leo! He can't smell a thing! You're wasting your perfume—why not pour it down the drain? Better yet, pour it on the ground. It'll come to Leo's nose quicker that way than dabbed behind your goddamn ear!

Jack breathed deep, and Nora, as if she knew that his very act of drawing in air was a threat to her, backed all the way to the sink.

He tore the cellophane and foil from the pack, tapped out a cigarette, and brought it to his lips. No windows or doors were open, but hell, this wind could find the cracks in the tightest house. The wind—that would explain why the match flame wavered as it did. The wind, and not his shaking hand.

The odor of sulfur had not completely faded when the acrid aroma of burning tobacco filled his nostrils. He drew the smoke in hard and deep and held it as long as he could. He'd be fine. He'd smoke his cigarette and wait for Nora to leave the kitchen. When you put your nose in a glass of whiskey the smell was so strong it filled your whole head. It not only drove out every other smell, it barely left room for thought.

"I just wondered if you knew her," Nora said softly. "Since you went to her funeral. . . ."

"The truth of it is, I only went to the graveside service."

Nora nodded.

"Did *you* know her?" Jack asked.

Nora hunched up her shoulders. "Someone said she worked at Nash's. I suppose I saw her when I shopped there. But I can't think of who she was."

"Thin girl. Long, skinny neck."

Nora shook her head.

"Doesn't matter." He almost added, *You knew Leo though, didn't you?*

"Did you have lunch?" she asked.

Jack shook his head.

"I can fix you a turkey sandwich."

"Turkey?"

"Vivien brought it to the church, and then left it there. She probably had too much food. Alpha said I might as well take the turkey home. There's enough for supper too."

"Where's Angela?"

"She's at Bonnie's. She's going to eat over there." Nora held up her hands as though they were covered with a substance that she might spread to another surface if she weren't careful. "Just let me change out of this dress, and then I'll fix you a sandwich."

Jack thought of following his wife. He even considered that she might be extending an invitation—Angela out of the house, both of them needing to change out of their funeral clothes . . . He'd wait a moment and then walk quietly down the hall to their bedroom. He hoped he could catch her when she was bent over and rolling down a nylon stocking. He'd see her from the side—her dress would be off, her slip, her brassiere, and he could see her bare back, its curving line interrupted by the tiny knobs of her spine, her breasts made fuller, heavier by her bent-over posture—

What was the use? His shoes were soaked, and if Nora heard the squeak of wet leather, she'd cover herself before he got to the door. Besides, he didn't know the order in which she removed her clothes. For all he knew, maybe she took her nylons off first. And she wasn't going to take off her brassiere and maybe not her slip either. She might shrug out of the dress only and then button on one of her housedresses. He didn't know what kind of perfume she wore or where she dabbed it, and he didn't know how she dressed or undressed herself.

He crushed out his cigarette, and the ash made a sizzling sound because Nora had given him an ashtray that was still wet. He put the just-opened pack in the pocket of his suit, then, with one long stride in case his shoes were muddy, stepped over to the kitchen sink.

From the cupboard under the sink he took one of the paper grocery bags they used to line the garbage can, and he put the bottle of whiskey in the bag. With two more long steps he was out the door. This time, anticipating the wind's strength, he held the door tightly and pulled it shut quietly.

31

JACK WOKE TO THE SOUND OF ICE CLICKING AGAINST HIS OFFICE WIN-
dow. The temperature had continued to fall throughout the afternoon and evening, and sometime—probably after dark—the rain
had changed to sleet.

He got stiffly out of his office chair and went to the window.
In the circle of light cast by the streetlamp behind the jail, he
could see the tracers of ice coming down in slanting lines. He could
tell the freezing rain was trying to turn to snow. Here and there
fat, wet flakes fell with almost the force of rain. While he watched,
the flakes multiplied. Soon it would all be snow.

Here it was, tomorrow the first day of June, and it was snowing.
It wasn't unheard of. In his years in Montana he'd seen snow in
every month but July. The weather up here on the northern plains
was nothing if not unpredictable. You could freeze your ass one
day and fry it the next. His father and other old-timers loved to
use the line, "If you don't like the weather in Montana, just wait
a minute."

Now it looked as though it was turning back to ice. Yes, he
could hear it crackling against the casements. The sound alone was

enough to give him a chill, and he turned away to put his shirt back on.

When he came into the office, he took off his shirt and his suit coat and draped them both over the backs of chairs near the radiator. He put his wet shoes on the chair as well. He made sure the door was locked, then went back to his desk, and poured his whiskey into his coffee cup. He put his feet up, lit a cigarette, and began to drink.

He was retraining himself. He found that by taking small sips of whiskey and rinsing it in his mouth with his saliva, he could get past its hot, raw taste. And after the first glass, something cooled and healed over, and he could toss it back without difficulty. It still gave him no pleasure to bring the whiskey to his lips, but then it was an end he was after, not a means.

Oddly enough, he found himself thinking about his mother. Or maybe it wasn't so odd. Maybe every man who drank alone sooner or later thought about his mother.

Jack's mother was a lifelong insomniac, yet she never admitted to her condition. She went to bed early, just as his father did, even though she knew she would not be able to sleep. She would lie awake for two, three hours, before giving up and getting out of bed. Then, often after midnight, she would begin one of her projects. Jack could remember waking during the night to the clink and clatter of his mother cleaning out or rearranging the silverware drawers, the medicine cabinet, the pantry. Occasionally she would tackle an even larger job. When he was in high school, he came home late one night and found the living room furniture pushed into the middle of the room and covered with drop cloths. It was after midnight, and his mother was going to paint the living room. From her perch on the stepladder, she greeted Jack and tried to convince him that it made perfect sense to paint at that hour; she would be least likely to disturb the family if she painted while they slept.

But there wasn't work enough to fill all those sleepless hours, so she would often simply sit in her favorite chair—the platform rocker—and read and smoke until close to sunup.

That was the image Jack fell asleep to in his office chair—his mother sitting next to the window, paging through a copy of *Photoplay* or *Silver Screen*, reading about lives so far removed from her in northern Montana she might as well have been looking at *A Thousand and One Arabian Nights*.

Then he woke to ice tapping at his window. *Wake up, Jack, wake up! It's about to snow, and you don't want to miss that!* Montana could work its own magic. . . .

He wasn't sure how long he had been asleep. The whiskey had relaxed him, and he began to drowse, gradually losing the sense of himself as a physical being, tilted back in a barrel-backed wooden chair with his stocking feet up on his desk. . . .

In his mind, he had been talking to his mother, telling her about Leo Bauer's accident, and what her son had done in its aftermath. Why would he tell his mother, of all people? She could not tell him if he had done right or wrong. As she herself freely admitted, most of life baffled her. Perhaps because she had such difficulty sorting her own whirring thoughts (she would often say, "Sometimes I think I think too much"; then she would laugh and add, "And now I'm doing it again!"), she wouldn't presume to know what motivated the actions of others. Just so. What Jack longed for was someone to talk to who would not judge, someone—like his mother—who would listen to what he had done, what he had decided must be done, and say nothing, nothing more than shrug her shoulders, widen her eyes, and turn her palms upward, someone whose expressions and gestures would register exactly the bewilderment he felt.

Sleeping in the chair had not done his back any wonders. The pain now, however, was high, between his shoulder blades, where it felt as though the muscles had somehow crossed themselves and become attached in the wrong places. He leaned up against the wall. If he could only press his back hard enough, maybe the bunched muscle would spring loose. As loose as his thoughts . . . which kept rolling from subject to subject. That of course was the whiskey, still doing its duty.

It was the whiskey, for example, that let him entertain the fancy that the snow was Leo Bauer's fault. Leo had disturbed the order of things by attempting to leave Bentrock, to sneak off with a young woman not his wife. Once the other men in town figured out what Leo had been up to, what would keep them all from running off? Why should anything remain as it had been? Why should children go to school? Why should the baker prepare loaves of bread? Why didn't everyone say, Fuck it, if I want a drink of whiskey in the afternoon, why not have it? And June—why not allow June to be an equal partner? Why wouldn't the other young women follow her lead and seduce the town's older men? Why wouldn't other women lure husbands from wives? Why would husbands and wives stay true to each other? Why would the schools stay open? Why would the dough rise? Why would the weather obey the seasons? Why wouldn't it snow in May? In June, July, and August, for that matter? No, he couldn't bring himself to blame June Moss. He turned again to the window. That snow—flakes now as big as half-dollars and sticking wetly to the blades of new grass and then sticking to each other—that was Leo's. Only Leo could turn rain to snow.

Wait! This snow wasn't Leo's triumph—it was Jack's! The thought burned away the whiskey fog. Snow was going to finish Leo Bauer. All over town tonight people were going to look out their windows and see what was falling from the sky—"Honey, come here and look at this!" "God damn—snow, and it's almost June!" "Take another look at the calendar—is it December?" The snow might as well be falling inside their skulls; they wouldn't be able to keep their thoughts on anything else. And tomorrow—over the table, the fences, the hedges, the desks, the corrals, the stable stalls—the talk would be of nothing else: "June, and winter's not done with us yet." "Are we going to have fireworks for the Fourth of July or snowballs?" "By God, we've picked a hell of a place to live, haven't we?" Best of all, the weather was a safe subject—people could wrap themselves in it as if they had been shivering without it. Talk of weather was something everyone could participate in—no matter what your age, your politics, your background, your occupation. In this barely populated part of the world, where you couldn't keep from knowing too much about the lives around you and therefore had to keep your jaw clamped on too many topics, talk of the weather came as a relief, as welcome as a rain that ended summer's drought. Weather didn't ask you to take a side, or have an opinion; it didn't require you to have any more education than you got with your own senses.

This snow was falling with the weight of history. Tomorrow, next week, next month . . . a year, ten, twenty years from now, people would remember the last day of May 1957 as the day snow fell on Bentrock. Right now, it was working to cover the graves of Leo Bauer and June Moss; it would cover the memory of their death as well.

Jack's father used to keep a diary of sorts. It was in Phil's possession now, but Jack had looked through enough of the leather-bound books to know what his father thought worth recording. The entries for most dates carried nothing but the day's high and low temperatures, with an occasional note about unusual weather phenomena—the severity of the wind, the depth of the snow, the proximity of the lightning strikes. The only entries that weren't meteorological concerned major expenditures: every car and the amount paid, the house, the remodeling for the hardware store, a water heater, a refrigerator. Perhaps Jack's father trusted his mind to hold on to birthdays and anniversaries, because none was noted in the diaries. And though Jack knew his father attended his share of confirmations, baptisms, weddings, and funerals, he saw no need to record their dates and times. But if snow fell, he wrote down when and how much. . . .

So let it come down! Let it fall through the night! Let it stack up over the county so you couldn't tell a highway from an open field. And in Bentrock Memorial Cemetery, with no headstone or cross rising out of the snow, nothing would identify the new graves of Leo Bauer and June Moss. And on the highway, where the white crosses were not yet pounded into the soft dirt of the roadside, nothing would reveal that here two people died. Ah, let the snow fall all night, let it fall all summer long, let it bury Mercer County like Leo Bauer and June Moss were buried, let its white weight smother every thought but the thought of snow itself.

The knock on the door was so faint—the click of glass on glass—that Jack thought at first the snow had turned back to ice. Then, when he realized someone was outside the office door, he called out, "Just a minute!"

He grabbed his shirt and was buttoning the third button when he opened the door and saw Nora standing there. As soon as she saw Jack, she carefully looked past him, but with an expression that said she was afraid of what she might see.

Jack stared at his wife. She was still wearing her dress—what had happened after she went to the bedroom to change clothes?—but she had zipped on her thin spring jacket, and its collar and shoulders were wet from the rain and snow. She was hatless, and her hair clung wetly to her forehead and cheeks. But Jack was searching for what she used to tap on the glass of his office door—her fingernail? her wedding ring? Had she knocked so lightly because she didn't expect him to be in there?

He opened the door wider, but Nora showed no inclination to enter.

"What about this snow?" he asked, then immediately regretted speaking. His voice sounded too loud, too exuberant. "In May," he added softly. "Snow in May, I mean." Then he wasn't sure that was what he wanted to say. It had occurred to him that he had no idea of the time. He fell asleep when it was light and woke when it was dark. It may have been after midnight. It may have been June.

"Celia Moss wants you to call her," Nora said.

"About what?"

Nora shrugged but did not lower her shoulders. A quick, tiny tremor shook her.

"You're freezing. Come in here and warm up." He backed away, aware that it may have been the smell of whiskey on his breath that made her reluctant to enter the office.

She took a small, tentative step forward, still looking around as if she expected to find someone else in the office with her husband.

"The heat's on," he said. "Go on over by the radiator."

She walked over obediently, her wet shoes squeaking on the tile. She was wearing the crepe-soled shoes that she wore in spring and summer when she worked in the garden and the yard.

"You didn't walk over, did you?" he asked.

235

She shook her head. "I parked in front." The primary entrance to the jail and his office was at the rear of the courthouse.

He hurried over to his desk for two reasons. He wanted to make certain he had put the whiskey bottle back in the drawer and he wanted to check the clock. No, it wasn't past midnight: ten-thirty. Still May. Nora was usually in bed by this time. But here she was, wet and shivering in the sheriff's office and looking far more frightened to be here than Margaret Elsey had. The sheriff's wife, nervous in his office, in his presence.

"Mrs. Moss didn't say what this was in regard to?"

"She just said she wanted to talk to you. That was why she called the house. Because she needed to speak to you personally."

"I can't imagine what this could be about." The only light came from his desk lamp. Nevertheless, she could see into all the room's shadowy corners and know that Jack was alone. Or perhaps she wanted to avoid looking at him, her husband alone in his office, in his stocking feet, disheveled, stinking of whiskey, giddy over a snowfall.

"I've had these reports to get to," he said. "I've fallen so far behind . . ." He waved feebly toward his desk.

"You've got your job to do." Nora said this as though she knew it was her job to be understanding, even about matters that she could not understand.

Earlier Jack could not remember how he parted from his wife. Now he could not figure out how to talk to her at all. The urge to speak was there—he could feel it like a physical sensation. His tongue flexed upward, his lips parted, something deep in his throat, at the top of his chest, opened then closed, as if he had another mouth down there, but the apparatus in his brain that formed the words would not produce anything.

So they simply stood there, at opposite ends of the room, Jack near the light, Nora backed up close to the heat.

"Shouldn't you call her?"

"I should."

"She sounded . . . I don't know. Urgent." Nora furrowed her brow as if she knew that wasn't the right word. "Important."

"I wonder why she didn't call here." Jack looked at the phone on his desk as if to confirm—yes, he could receive calls here. Even asleep, even drunk, he could hear it ring. Even with his shoes and shirt off, he could pick up the phone. He could do his job.

"She wants to talk to you."

"Didn't you tell her to try here?"

"I wasn't sure you were here. I told her I'd try to find you."

Jack wanted to ask: Was this the first place you looked? If you hadn't found me here, where else would you have gone?

"Well, you found me. You did your job."

"Just call her, Jack. I'll leave and you can call her." She pulled up on the zipper of her jacket though it was already zipped as high as it would go.

"I don't mind if you stay."

"Angela's sleeping over at Bonnie's. You know what happened last time. She got sick and had to come home. I have to be there in case she calls." Three or four times in the past Angela had called during the night from a friend's house where she was supposed to be sleeping over and asked to come home.

"She wasn't really sick."

"She thought she was. It's the same thing."

"Maybe we should make her stick it out."

Nora snapped. "Is that how you would've wanted your parents to handle it? Make you—" She waved her hand as if she were batting at an insect. "Never mind. We can discuss it later. You see what Mrs. Moss wants." She headed toward the door.

"Wait! Nora, wait."

She stopped with her hand on the doorknob, but she would not look in his direction.

"Take my coat," Jack said. He grabbed his suit coat off the back of the chair. "You've just got that thin jacket. . . ." He glanced back at the window. The snow was still falling.

Nora didn't move as he draped the coat over her shoulders. "You'll need something if you go out," she said.

"I've got a warm coat over in the jail." It was a lie, but they both let it pass.

As he snugged the coat about her, he thought he felt a shudder pass through her. Was it occasioned by his touch? Could it have been arousal? Revulsion? Was she still shivering with cold? Since he didn't know, he couldn't act.

At that moment, he wasn't sure what his duty was: to call Celia Moss or to go home with Nora, where they could spend the night alone together. They might make love, and after, marvel at the snow falling on the grass that he had already mowed this spring.

She stepped away from his touch. "I made you a turkey sandwich," she said. "It's in waxed paper in the fridge."

"I might be right home. Depending on what Mrs. Moss wants."

She turned to face him. She looked tiny in his suit coat, like a child dressing in a parent's clothes. She brought her arms up and shook them to get her hands out from all that material. Once her hands were free, she had nothing to do with them.

32

"MRS. MOSS? JACK NEVELSEN." HE SWIRLED THE WHISKEY IN THE glass. He had poured a small amount, barely more than a mouthful, but he promised himself he would not drink it until he found out why Celia Moss wanted to talk to him. "My wife said you were trying to reach me."

"Sheriff. Yes. I think we've got some trouble on our hands." Her voice sounded different, as if her mouth was dry and she was having trouble sliding the words out.

"What kind of trouble?" He put the glass down and pressed his fingers against his closed eyes until streaks of light appeared.

"My brother-in-law. He's taken off after the Bauer boy."

"Your brother-in-law?"

"Calvin's brother. My husband, Calvin?"

"I didn't see him at the funeral."

"He got to town after. Drove up from Colorado."

"And what? He's *chasing* Rick Bauer?"

"He's . . . I meant to say he's looking for him. He heard the story about what happened to June, and it set him off. He was her godfather, and he thought the sun rose and set on that girl. When he used to come around more often, he'd bring her presents and—"

"Does he know where to find Rick?"

"That's the thing. He banged out of here without looking up the address. So we're not sure how he knows where to look." She was talking faster, and Jack wanted her to slow down, for his sake as well as hers.

"You said, 'we.' Who's there with you?"

She paused as if she were surveying who was in her house at that moment. "I got family here."

"Your brother-in-law . . . What did he say about finding Rick?"

"He kept saying, 'It's not fair. It's not fair that the one who caused all the trouble gets off scot-free.' I tried to tell him this is hard on the boy too, but Ralph wouldn't listen."

"Ralph's your brother-in-law?"

"I might as well tell you, Sheriff. He's been drinking. He already had been when he got here."

Jack looked down at the whiskey in his own glass. It occurred to him that if he didn't take that swallow, if he didn't drink any more that night, he might be a better match against Celia Moss's brother-in-law. A sober man always had the advantage over the man who'd been drinking, no matter what the endeavor or arena. That was a truism Jack believed in as devoutly as any, and his years in office only strengthened that belief. Nevertheless, he also knew that as soon as he hung up the phone—and perhaps before—he would drink that whiskey. What the hell—an amount that small—it wouldn't matter if he drank it or poured it back in the bottle.

"But he doesn't know where Rick lives? You're sure of that?"

"I don't know how he could."

Jack knew. Ralph Moss could look up the Bauer address in the same phone booth from which Jack called Wayne and Gordon Van Allen.

"You'd better tell me what your brother-in-law looks like. And what kind of vehicle he's driving."

"He's . . . he doesn't look anything like my husband. Do you remember what Cal looked like?"

Jack remembered him only from the photograph he had seen in the Moss home. "Yes."

"Ralph's shorter. Sort of wiry. Jumpy. Like he can't sit still. And dark. He always looks like he needs a shave. He's driving—just a minute." Celia Moss put her hand over the phone, but Jack could still hear her call out the question. "Does anyone know what kind of car Ralph's driving?"

It took a moment for Celia to answer, too long for Jack to rely, with any certainty, on any answer he got. "My brother thinks a Ford or Merc. Maybe a 1950 or '51."

"What color?"

"Black. I saw it when he drove up. Black."

"All right, Mrs. Moss. That helps. I'll go out and see if I can't track down your brother-in-law. Night like this, I can't imagine there's too many folks out on the streets."

"Ralph's got a good heart, Sheriff. He drinks too much, and he gets a wild hair now and then, but he's got a good heart. It's what's getting him in trouble now. He just thought the world of June."

"And he'll probably turn up back at your door any time now. But I'll get out there and check around all the same."

Celia Moss let out an expulsion of air that sounded like half a sob, half a grunt of exasperation. "Oh, damn it to hell! He's got a gun! Ralph's gone looking for that boy with a gun." Now she breathed in sharply. "He's got a—" This time she didn't bother to cover the phone. "What kind of gun did you say Ralph was waving around?"

Jack closed his eyes and waited for further information.

"A Luger," Celia Moss said. "He's got a German Luger."

It occurred to Jack that he might tell Mrs. Moss that Lugers were always German. Instead he said, "I'm glad you thought to mention a gun. That's the kind of information we want to have."

"I don't want anyone getting hurt, Sheriff. Please. We've had too much of that here already."

By "here" Jack wasn't sure if she meant in the town or in her home.

"No one's going to get hurt, Mrs. Moss. Don't worry. I promise

241

you. No one will get hurt." But if someone had to be, he wanted to ask—if it could not be avoided, whom would you choose for pain: Rick? Ralph? Me? If you could go further back, days perhaps, and pick one person out of this whole mess who had to die, who would that be? Surely not June . . . but would Leo still be dead? But why should it be up to Celia Moss? Why not keep the power himself? If he had to kill someone for everyone else to live—whose life would he sacrifice?

He put down his glass and shook his head to clear away the foolishness of this thinking. Sacrifice! My God, where had that come from! But another part of his brain kept on playing and provided an answer: *Leo. Make it Leo.*

Celia Moss said, "My brother wants to know if you need him to help you look for Ralph."

"Tell him thanks anyway. He should stay put for the time being. I'll probably check in with you a little later to see if your brother-in-law's come back. And if I drive by and see a black Ford in front of your place and no lights on, I'll know everyone's settled down for the night."

"I'll tell you what, Sheriff. If Ralph comes back, I'll turn off the porch light. That'll be the signal."

"That sounds fine. Now, you don't worry. This whole business is going to last about as long as that snow out there."

For a moment, Jack considered going over to the Bauers', instead of calling. It was late, but this was an emergency. Even if Vivien had already gone to bed—had already put on her nightgown—he would be excused for ringing the bell at this hour. A man with a gun was looking for her son—what greater urgency could there be?

No, no—this *was* urgent. Ralph Moss might be on his way there right now—he could be pulling into the driveway while Jack sat at his desk wondering about the nightgown that Vivien might wear on a night when rain turned to snow. On the night of the day she buried her husband . . . Jack reached for the phone.

Jack did not recognize the voice of the woman who answered the phone.

"Viv—Vivien? Is Vivien there?"

"Call I tell her who's calling?" The sister. That's who it had to be. Vivien's sister taking care of Vivien by screening her calls.

"This is Jack Nevelsen. Sheriff Nevelsen."

"It's so late. Is this . . . personal?"

Vera—that was the sister's name. The woman who clung to Vivien's side at the church. Well, Vera was a bulldog now. "This is county business," Jack said. "It can't wait."

"I'll get Vivien. It might take a minute or two."

"Sure." Had she already gone to bed? Was she in the bath? Was she too drunk to come to the phone? Maybe he should have asked for Rick. . . .

But Vivien came to the phone almost immediately. "Hello, Jack," she said. "Vera said this was important. Is something wrong?" In spite of her sister's hesitation about the hour, Vivien sounded bright, unconcerned, almost cheerful. She probably believed that nothing worse could happen to her.

"We've got sort of a funny situation here, Vivien. Is Rick home?"

"Funny? He just went to bed. Was it Rick you needed to talk to—"

"No, no. Let him be. As long as he's there. Vivien, probably nothing's going to come of this, but I thought I'd better let you know: I got a call from Celia Moss. It seems her brother-in-law's in town, and he's out looking for Rick."

"He's looking for Rick? I don't understand. . . ."

"He's upset, Vivien. Mad at Rick for . . . I'm not sure what for. For being alive. When June's not. He was the girl's godfather."

"He doesn't even know Rick. How could he—? I really don't understand."

Jack could hear the bewilderment in her voice as she strained to understand what she was being told. But he could also tell she had no comprehension of the situation, and he knew he had to say something to help her.

"He means to do Rick harm, Vivien."

Bentrock was so small Jack sometimes thought he could stand

in the center of town—in the middle of Third Street right in front of the Northern Pacific Hotel—shout out a piece of news, important or trivial wouldn't matter, and before long, every man, woman, and child would know it. A good many would hear his shout, especially if it gave townspeople a chance to gather; the rest would get it in due time from the initial listeners. However, in the last few days it seemed as though so many important conversations had been conducted quietly, darkly, through these black wires, one mouth to one ear. He could feel himself becoming more skilled at this hushed talk. He could hear now, for example, in Vivien's silence, how her mood had switched again, how the bewilderment that had replaced her brightness had changed to fear. Oh, yes, he was becoming very good at this. He could even imagine how she had twisted the telephone down from in front of her mouth to her throat so she wouldn't breathe her fear into the mouthpiece. She may have brought her hand to mouth, fingertips clasped tight to her lips.

"But it's not going to happen, Viv. You hear me? Rick's home and you keep him there. He'll be all right. Just don't let anyone in you don't know."

"Here?" Vivien said weakly. "He's coming *here?* How does he know where we live? Did Celia—"

"Whoa. Hold on. I didn't say that. I only meant if a stranger should show up—"

"Jack. You've got to do something! You've got to arrest him before— Not my boy! He's after my boy!"

"*Sshh!* Viv. Easy. I told you. It's going to be okay. I'm going out right now to find this fellow. I'll swing by your place from time to time to make sure no one's lurking about who shouldn't be. But you make sure Rick stays put—you hear?"

"I can't believe this is happening. . . ."

"Who's still there with you? Your sister? Anyone else?"

"They all left late this afternoon."

"I hope they don't run into snow," Jack said and winced. He didn't mean to add to her store of worries.

"Jack. My God. What kind of place do we live in?"

Did she mean the snow? A place where it could snow when it was almost summer? Where a stranger with a gun could come after a young man for no other reason than that he was alive when someone else was dead?

Jack took a guess. "He's not from here, Viv. He's up from Colorado."

33

ONCE JACK WAS OUT AND DRIVING AROUND, HE FELT SUDDENLY CALM, and he wasn't sure why.

Maybe it was simply because he was doing something. At last. In the aftermath of the accident so much seemed to depend on waiting. Get the story out there and then wait to see if it takes hold. Wait to see if Rick does his part. Wait for Patsy Van Allen to spread the version he wanted out there. Wait to see how far it went the first day, the second. . . . Wait for some evidence, some contradiction, to surface. Wait to see if any suspicions flared, caught, and started their own slow burn through the community. Wait for the car to be hauled up; wait for the bodies to be put down. . . . Wait, wait. And Jack knew—he didn't want to dwell on it, but he knew—that the waiting would never be over.

So now he had a job to do, a mission. Get out there and find a black Ford with Colorado plates. Get out there and make good on his promises to Celia Moss and Vivien Bauer that no one was going to be hurt.

Promises he shouldn't have made. He had broken one of his own rules when he did. Don't promise if you can't be sure you'll deliver—his father used to say it all the time, and Jack took it to heart, and tried to make it his policy, whether he was making a campaign speech or responding to one of Angela's requests about what they might do on an upcoming weekend. But here he'd gone and promised these two women something he could not absolutely guarantee.

It had been a show-offy thing to do, especially with Vivien. He wanted to calm both women, but Vivien he wanted to impress as well. Don't worry; I'll take care of everything. Prideful. He was taking too much on himself. Before he left the office, he wondered if he should call Wayne in on this, and perhaps the police department. The more people out looking for this Moss fellow the better the odds of someone spotting him, and sooner. Jack could also have suggested that someone be stationed outside the Bauers', in case Celia Moss's brother-in-law should find his way there.

But no, he had decided to do this alone, to keep it to himself. For himself. If he could make good on his promise, the credit would all be his. If he couldn't . . . He wasn't quite ready to think about that.

Besides, this situation with Ralph Moss not only gave Jack a chance to get off his ass and do something—even driving around was better than sitting and drinking—but it gave him an excuse to get out in the snow. Jack loved the snow. If he hadn't had a reason to go out tonight, he would have made one up. And since the pleasure he took in the snow was a child's pleasure, any experience with it—whether he was kicking his way through it or shoveling it—felt a little like play. He had probably spent more hours romping with Angela in fresh snow—sledding, building snowmen and snow forts, making angels—than in all their other father-daughter activities. He sometimes wondered what would happen when she got a little older and could no longer be so easily recruited for snow play. No, unlike other Montanans, Jack was not one to curse the snow, though he was usually careful to keep his delight concealed, especially in the presence of those for whom fresh snow meant anything from inconvenience to outright disaster.

But if you hated snow, Jack often wondered, why would you

choose to live in northern Montana, where it was quite possible snow would cover the ground six months of the year? Then again maybe you didn't choose. . . .

During all his years in the state, Jack had become something of a connoisseur of snow, and he could quickly judge, on the basis of only a few flakes, to which month each snow should belong— whether November's icy pellets or December's airy fluff or January's or February's fine-grained, swirling dust or March's or April's waterlogged fat flakes. Tonight's snow, for example, was heavy, and wind-driven, a strange hybrid of a season's first and last snows. June snow it was, for it was probably past midnight by now.

It looked as though it might well last into the following day. It was beginning to stick not only to the lawns and the open, weedy fields but to the paved and blacktopped sidewalks and streets as well. As he drove through town, Jack could see tire tracks and know not only if someone had driven down a particular street but how recently. And the only vehicle that had gone past Bauers' in the last hour or two was his. More than once.

That was what prevented his search for Ralph Moss from being more efficient; he had to keep looping back to drive by the Moss and Bauer homes. It felt a bit like eating a sandwich by taking a small bite from a different corner of the bread every time.

Yet a sandwich would eventually get consumed that way, and sooner or later he'd cover all of Bentrock. And its outskirts.

He was moving farther and farther out now, having begun close to the town's center. He was searching beyond the tracks on the north side, and he was almost to the Knife River on the east. He had turned around once less than a mile from the spot where Leo and June went off the road, and maybe the next time he drove out that way he'd keep right on going. Stretch the rope so tight it would snap, and he'd be on his way. . . . Oh, hell, it was a big county; he could drive a long time in any direction and still be in his own jurisdiction. When he got beyond the town's limits, out where there were as many open fields as houses or buildings, yet there was the shelter of trees or even a fence line, the snow had begun to drift, and the truck bumped a little as it rolled over these snowy fingers stretched across the road.

He no longer felt the whiskey's intoxicating effects, but he had one hell of a headache. One more reason he shouldn't drink. One or two drinks were enough to leave a hangover in their wake. Then his head would feel achingly full, and the bones of his skull would seem to throb. Breathing became difficult, and he had to take in air through his mouth to get enough oxygen.

Tonight, however, he welcomed his headache. It satisfied a need he felt for punishment. My God, what he had stooped to in the last few days! The lies, the schemes, the dark thoughts—murderous, lustful, suspicious. . . . He wished he could say this wasn't him, that if Jack Nevelsen was anything, he was honest, trusting, faithful, gentle. And he was no liar. He wanted that to be so more than anything. But the evidence was against him. Without Jack's lies, Ralph Moss wouldn't be out there looking for Rick, and Jack wouldn't be peering through this snow to try to find Ralph.

Where *would* Jack be? Home, he imagined. Probably asleep by now. Hell, he might not even know it was snowing. He'd wake tomorrow morning, and there it would be—frosting on the first day of June.

That prospect wasn't satisfying either. Sleeping through it—he didn't want that. He wanted to be out in the snow. . . . This was an extraordinary occurrence, a phenomenon, and he wanted to be part of it.

The question was, would this headache be punishment enough? There was the matter of Ralph Moss's gun, his "German Luger," as Celia Moss had felt compelled to point out. A man with a gun was always dangerous, and finding and confronting Ralph Moss was not a matter to be taken lightly. This was a far more hazardous endeavor than sliding around these snowy curves. "Sheriff Killed in Shootout with Colorado Man." "Sheriff Wounded in Gun Battle. . . ." If Jack were to be shot sometime in the next few hours, would Jim Brazelton have time to get it in the evening edition of the *Mercer Country Tribune*? Would Jack get a headline? Yes, certainly if he were killed; possibly, if he were only wounded, but a lot would depend on the severity of the wound.

But Jack was getting the wording wrong for the headline any-way. There couldn't be a "gun battle" because Jack was unarmed. He had left his office so quickly he didn't think to bring a weapon with him. And what would he have brought? There was a pistol in his desk drawer, a rusty Italian-made .32 automatic that had been left there by someone who held the office before him. Jack couldn't remember ever taking it out of the drawer, and he doubted he ever would. Besides, the gun seemed like something that be-longed in a woman's purse, not as the sidearm of a county sheriff. Jack still had the .45 automatic that the army issued him. . . . No, that wasn't right; the gun that rested on the closet shelf at home wasn't his. Jack had turned his in, as he was required to. He hadn't, however, been asked to give up the .45 pistol that he had confis-cated from a drunken noncom who had indicated that he might use the weapon on himself. That was the pistol at home. And Jack couldn't bring himself to carry it on the job either. It was a sol-dier's weapon, made for using on the enemy, not on your fellow Mercer County residents, on your neighbors, for God's sake. So most of the time he was without a weapon, unless you counted the tire iron that clanked around in the back of the truck or the Winchester lever-action .30–.30 that was in the trunk of the squad car and which he had never removed from its scabbard.

Yet this matter of being armed or unarmed wasn't of real con-cern to Jack because the truth was, he didn't really expect to run into Ralph Moss, with or without his German Luger. Jack wouldn't give up his search, he wouldn't stop looking for an out-of-state license plate or a dark-colored Ford or Mercury, but at some time he had stopped expecting to see the man. What wouldn't surprise Jack would be to see that car parked in front of Celia Moss's house the next time he drove by. He couldn't exactly say why, but this entire business with Ralph Moss had the feel of something that wouldn't amount to much.

He had to laugh. He remembered one of the first calls he got after taking office. It was a Friday night, cold, blustery, and Mrs. Foyle—Harry Foyle's widow—called to say someone was in her farmhouse. She had come home from visiting a neighbor and saw someone in the upstairs bedroom.

When Jack drove up to farmhouse, the shivering Mrs. Foyle was waiting for him in the driveway. She was sure the intruder was still in the house; she hadn't seen anyone leave, and now it looked as though someone might be moving around behind the living room curtains.

Had Jack armed himself before entering the house? Oh, yes. He picked up a brick from Mrs. Foyle's porch and stepped inside. He moved from room to room, turning on lights, looking behind furniture, in closets. The search was scary. The Foyle house was three stories of dark hallways, parlors, pantries, sewing rooms, and bedrooms. Each time he walked through a doorway or opened a closet door, his heart beat faster and it felt as though a cold wind blew across the back of his neck.

He found no one, and Mrs. Foyle accepted his assurances that it was safe to go back into her house. Still, he remained outside in his parked car for an hour, watching to make certain the prowler did not return. Jack took his brick with him, and when he put it on the car seat, he could see, even in the faint illumination provided by the dome light, the marks his sweaty fingers had made in the brick's orange dust.

The next time Jack responded to Mrs. Foyle's call about someone in her house, he walked through it empty-handed. He still felt uneasy when he went down her narrow basement stairs but nothing like the chill of fear he felt the first time. By the third and fourth calls, he knew the floor plan of the Foyle house by heart, and he could conduct his search by proceeding quickly and systematically from floor to floor. What the previous sheriff should have left in the desk drawer was not that fussy little Italian automatic but a note about Mrs. Foyle and her false alarms. Ah, well, even if he had known, Jack would still have driven out there. Putting old women at ease was as much a part of his job as apprehending prowlers. Still, if he had known about Mary Foyle, he could have saved himself some adrenaline.

None was pumping through his system now. He was tired and this search for Ralph Moss had taken on the same dutiful feel as walking through the rooms of Mary Foyle's house.

Then that cold wind breathed down his neck again.

Just outside Bentrock, in the snow-covered parking lot of Little Sam's Roadhouse, was parked a 1951 Mercury—dark blue or black, it was hard to tell—with out-of-state plates.

Jack pulled right up behind the Merc so his truck's headlights shone on the license plate. Snow had piled up and packed itself between the bumper and the license, but Jack could still read the numbers and the state. Colorado.

34

JACK HAD NO TROUBLE PICKING OUT RALPH MOSS FROM THE GROUP OF men at the bar. Celia Moss's description was right on the mark: her brother-in-law was swarthy and hadn't shaved for a couple of days. Ralph Moss's features were out of proportion. He had a narrow face, a long nose, a wide mouth, and small eyes that were so far apart his look reminded Jack of an animal with eyes on the side of its head. He was dressed in a heavy wool suit and wide tie, an outfit that looked as if it had been bought in the 1920s. He wore a wool cap with a peaked, short bill, and it settled low on his forehead.

But even without a description and in the dim light of Little Sam's, he would have recognized Ralph Moss because Jack knew the other men at the bar.

To Ralph Moss's right were the Gow twins, Charles and Chester, beefy-faced, fat men in their sixties, both of them retired railroad workers. It wasn't surprising to find them out on a night like this. They were heavy drinkers, but they lived with their mother, and Harriet Gow, ninety-two years old, wouldn't allow liquor in the house. As long as she was alive, the boys—and they were still referred to as the Gow boys—had to do their drinking in Bentrock's bars and taverns, where they matched each other beer for beer, shot for shot. Whenever one of them rolled himself a cigarette from their tin of Prince Albert tobacco, he automatically rolled one for his brother too.

They were cheerful drunks, and neither had ever given Jack or anyone else in town, a minute's trouble. The other man in the group sat on a stool behind the bar. This was Delbert O'Keefe, the bartender: Del had once been a top hand on a big North Dakota ranch until a horse landed on top of him and broke his hip and both legs. Little Sam was a cousin of Del's wife, and he gave Del a bartending job even though the pain in Del's legs was so bad he had to sit most of the time.

Del's limited mobility didn't prevent him from being a perfectly adequate bartender. The job didn't require much. Little Sam's was a small establishment, a metal Quonset hut that had once served as housing on a military base and which Sam had relocated to this spot—a small space hacked out of a stand of trees that a long-forgotten farmer had once planted as a windbreak. Sam slapped the building down on a concrete slab, installed a bar and two tables, a cooler for beer, a gas heater, and he was set for business. Little Sam's was for dedicated drinkers. There was no pool table, no jukebox, no shuffleboard, no food (unless you counted the jars of pickled eggs and venison jerky, which Little Sam's wife, a full-blooded Blackfeet, made herself). The beer came in a bottle, and Del didn't have to know how to fix anything fancier than whiskey and water, and most of the time he didn't have to bother with the water. The parking lot was never full at Little Sam's, and there were always empty stools at the bar. Nevertheless, somebody came in almost every night, and Little Sam had been in operation much longer than bars that did a brisker business, at least initially. Part of the reason for Little Sam's steady trade was that it had never been known as a bar that catered to any particular clientele. It was not a cowboy bar or an Indian bar or a businessman's bar or a farmer's bar. If you had the money to pay for your drinks (no one ever ran a tab at Little Sam's), and if you weren't out to make trouble, you were welcome at Little Sam's. Jack wondered how Ralph Moss found his way here, out of all the county's bars. And he wondered why Ralph Moss had his gun, his German Luger, out and on the bar in front of him.

Something about the position of the pistol, its distance from Ralph Moss, the way its grip was turned, put Jack at ease. Yes, the gun was within Ralph Moss's reach; yes, he could grab it at any second. You would have to say, strictly speaking, considering the gun's proximity, that Ralph Moss was armed, and an armed man was always dangerous, to use the phrase so often applied to suspects and fugitives. Yet Jack felt somehow the gun had been set aside, whatever use or interest it might have held now gone. Ralph Moss also had before him on the bar a bottle of Budweiser, a glass, and a stack of five silver dollars, and he gave these more attention than the gun. He held his glass of beer angled forward. With his other hand he kept lifting the coins and letting them fall on top of each other. Their clinking noise made Jack think of ice breaking away and falling on more ice.

Del was the first to greet him. "Jack. What brings you out on a night like this?"

He sat down, leaving an empty stool between himself and Ralph Moss. "On the job. Same as you."

"Well, we got an excuse," Dell said. He nodded in the direction of the other three men. "Not like these Honyockers."

One of the Gow brothers raised his glass to Jack. "No excuse what-so-ever," he said happily. If Jack had been closer, he could have told which twin had spoken. Chester had a small, red bump near his ear, and Jack used that bump to differentiate the twins. The bump reminded him of a blister, "blister" rhymed with "Chester."

"If you got to be out on this night," said Del, "least we can do is stand you to one. What can I get you?"

Jack pointed to Ralph Moss's bottle. He could as easily have been pointing to the gun. "What the hell. Cold night. Might as well go all the way. Make it a cold beer."

"You got it, Sheriff."

Did Ralph Moss's eyes widen when he heard Del address Jack as "Sheriff"?

Jack pushed aside the glass that Del put on the bar and took a long swallow of the beer. It was so cold its chill replaced the whiskey headache he had been nursing. He was aware that he was breaking one of the few lessons his father had taught his sons: Beer on top of whiskey, mighty risky. Whiskey on top of beer, never fear.

Jack lit a cigarette and decided he better get to it. He pointed to the Luger. "Someone here expecting trouble?"

The other Gow twin leaned forward. "You know who we got here, Sheriff? This here is the Colorado Cat Man. Himself."

Ralph Moss smiled sheepishly and waved off Mr. Gow's remark.

The second twin picked up his brother's enthusiasm. "Go ahead. Tell 'im. Tell 'im how many cougars you collected the bounty on."

"Shit," Ralph Moss said. "I wouldn't know. I didn't keep any kind of running count."

Charles or Chester said, "Show 'im the picture. Show 'im."

Ralph Moss shook his head embarrassedly, but he reached into his suit coat's inside pocket and brought out a photograph. He slid it down the bar, and out of the same motion he reached out his hand to shake Jack's. "Ralph Moss," he said with a thin-lipped smile. "From Colorado. But I reckon you got that part."

"Got it."

The photograph was taken a good many years ago, but there wasn't much doubt that the man in the picture was Ralph Moss. He could have been wearing the same wool cap and the same suit that he wore now. In the photograph, however, he wore a pair of hunting boots that laced almost up to the knee. One foot rested on the bumper of an old truck, and the roof, the fenders, even the hood, were draped with the carcasses, and perhaps pelts—the photo wasn't clear enough for Jack to see the difference—of mountain lions, mountain lions lying on top of mountain lions. If Jack had wanted to try to make an accurate count, he would have concentrated on the heads, the dark, shining, open eyes or the gaping mouths with their glistening, useless fangs. Jack was more interested in what was in Ralph Moss's hand in the picture. He was holding a German Luger.

Jack put his finger on the pistol in the photograph. "That the weapon of choice?" He slid the picture back toward Ralph Moss.

"That's the thing," Ralph Moss said, "hunting cats ain't like hunting antelope or elk. You don't get to sit a mile off with a thirty-thirty and a scope. You run 'em up a tree with dogs and then blast 'em off a limb. Like I was telling these boys, it's not something you do for sport. I did it to make a living. And back then there was a living to be made at it for a few of us. There's easier ways, God knows, and I tried most of 'em." He picked up the photograph and put it back in his pocket. "I was telling Del here I used to pour drinks right here in Bentrock. Bar called Staples? Across from the old Studebaker dealership?"

Jack nodded. "It's just off-sale now."

"But old man Staples is still there?"

Jack looked to the Gow twins for help. They knew the town's liquor establishments and their history better than he did. Charles or Chester said, "That's the oldest boy running it now."

Jack said, "But it was June brought you here this time, wasn't it?"

Ralph Moss let the heavy coins clink a few more times. "What is it about you Montana folks and silver dollars? God damn, you like your money heavy enough to rip out your pockets, don't you?"

Del wiped his rag along the edge of the bar. "Most of us don't have the weight to worry about."

The Gow brothers both laughed, and one of them said, "I ain't ever had to sew up any of my pockets!"

"Me either," his brother added.

The other twin pointed his thumb toward Ralph Moss. "He done time too."

"That so?" Jack said. "Deer Lodge?"

"None other," Ralph Moss replied.

"What did they put you away for?"

Ralph Moss swirled his beer. "Oh, this and that."

Let it go, Jack thought. Let the night play itself out like this, five men drinking at the bar and bullshitting about the weather and silver dollars and hunting and any other matter that wouldn't cost one of them a wink of sleep tonight. Ralph Moss wasn't going to find Rick Bauer, much less do him any harm. So why not let it all pass, Celia's and Vivien's fears, the gun sitting out there in the open . . . let it go. Raise your glass and simply let yourself be one of the men at the bar, but not the sheriff and not the man

257

preserving Leo Bauer's reputation. The beer was cold, the bar was warm—Del had the gas heater turned up—let it go. . . .

But those women . . . They were out there, and he could hear their questions, their accusations: Vivien asking what Jack was doing to look out for her boy's safety. Celia Moss wanting him to make certain that no other Moss name was connected to tragedy. Margaret Elsey holding up her sign declaring that's not the way it was. And behind them all, Nora, waiting at home, saying nothing but her expression plain to read: If you're not out there doing your job, why aren't you home with your daughter and your wife? And June Moss? What would she ask of him? What would she say if she could speak and point her finger at him? Jack wasn't sure, but he knew the answer would be worse than confronting Ralph Moss, with or without his Luger.

Ralph Moss held one of the silver dollars up against the light from the Hamm's beer sign over the bar as though the blue neon would allow him to see through the coin. "Every time I come back from Montana I've got a few silver dollars in my pocket. Don't always know how the hell they got there, but I always put 'em away. Only way I've ever been able to save a goddamn dollar in my life."

Jack persisted. "How much did you miss the funeral by?"

He spun the silver dollar on the bar, and only when it stopped spinning, wobbled, and toppled over did he speak. "Shit. An hour. Less. They barely got their coats off when I pulled in. I drove like a bastard to get here. I had car trouble in Wyoming or I would have made it."

Del asked, "You run into snow anywhere else?" Did he know Jack was going after something else, something deeper, darker, and was Del's question his way of trying to keep everything proceeding down the well-lit, easily traveled roads? Jack sympathized, but he hadn't spent all those hours looking for a black car only to ignore it now.

"Celia's worried about you," Jack said to Ralph Moss.

He kept looking right at Jack, but it was Del's question Ralph Moss answered. "Rain. Didn't see a snowflake until here. Not even in the high country."

"Celia called me," Jack said. "She asked me if I could find you."

Ralph Moss smiled his wide, wolfish smile. "And you tracked me down."

"Fresh snow. You know how easy that makes tracking."

"You always get your man, Sheriff? That the kind of lawman you are?"

Ralph Moss gripped the bar so he could lean back on his stool and look Jack over from head to foot. "Man your size, I bet you don't have any trouble at all bringing down the criminals."

"How long have you been away, Mr. Moss? It's quiet up here. We don't have much in the way of trouble. Or troublemakers."

Jack hoped that remark would be warning enough, but apparently Ralph Moss wanted to go further: "You probably don't even need handcuffs. Just put 'em in a fucking headlock and haul 'em off to the hoosegow."

Well, Jack had pushed and now Ralph Moss was pushing back.

Jack should have known better. Not in a bar, not even one that felt as calm and companionable as Little Sam's did tonight. Bars did something to men and women, a kind of electricity was there in all that barroom smoke, an electrical charge that just waited for bodies to get close enough so the spark could leap across the gap. Ready to fight. Or fuck. It wasn't the liquor alone, but, God knew, it was a big part of it—flammable enough to let those sparks catch fire.

During his time in office Jack had only once been injured—and deliberately injured another—and that occurred in a bar. It was on a warm breezy autumn night that he got a call from Bob Pinckney saying that a kid from Canada was tearing up the Full Moon Saloon out on Bessie Creek Road.

Jack walked in unarmed that night too. Maybe Ralph Moss was right, maybe Jack did have a confidence about his size and his ability to handle disturbances with bulk alone.

Bob Pinckney had it right. The place *was* torn up. Broken glasses and bottles everywhere. Chairs, stools, tables overturned. A pinball machine lying on its side. The felt on Bob's beloved snooker table torn and flapping over the side.

The part about a kid was accurate too. Wedged in a corner was

259

a slender young man who looked boyish enough to be a teenager. His blond hair and white shirt were both soaked and sticking to him as if he had just stepped out of the shower.

Bob Pinckney was the only one left in the bar besides the kid, and when Bob saw Jack, Bob said, "He had ID! I checked! I swear!"

When Jack got close to the young man and said, "Let's go," the kid took off. The Full Moon wasn't large, but Jack chased the kid all around the place. Every time Jack got near enough to make a grab for the boy, he put on a little spurt that put him just out of reach. Once he had ahold of the kid's shirttail; then Jack stepped on a pool cue, and his feet went out from under him. He hit his head on the pool table and opened a gash over his right eye that shed so much blood that the kid got scared and stopped running. He gave himself up by dropping to his knees in front of Jack.

By this time, Jack was in a rage. "Seeing red"—he had heard the expression all his life, and now his own blood *was* obscuring his vision, and the effect was maddening. He was frustrated too from all those futile efforts to catch the young man.

Jack grabbed the kid's shirt collar and hit him hard, twice, three times, right on the top of the head, and though Jack used his fist, he protected his knuckles and struck him with the meaty part of his fist, as if he were pounding nails into the kid's skull.

Dr. Snow had to shave Jack's eyebrow to put three stitches into his forehead. The swelling went down after a few days, but the discoloration lingered. Jack made quite a sight, but it was his behavior more than his appearance that embarrassed him—so much so that when the kid's father, a minor government official in Saskatchewan, showed up, Jack told him just to take his son home, all charges dropped.

So Jack had his scar to show what could happen when you didn't watch your step in a barroom, yet here he was, locking horns with a man who could reach out and put his hands on a pistol.

35

YET IT WAS DEL O'KEEFE, WHOSE INSTINCTS FOR WHAT MIGHT HAPPEN in a bar were no doubt sharper than Jack's, who picked up the Luger.

"You pulled this out," Del said, "and I thought, Shit. Here we go. War stories. More goddamn souvenirs and more goddamn war stories."

"That's right," one of the twins said, nodding vigorously. "Yep. That's right. Official sidearm of the German army. That's right. There it is."

Del held it by the grip, but he didn't have his finger inside the trigger guard. "It looks nasty, you know?" He held it higher. "Not all guns do. But, you got to admit, this one just looks like a mean fucking piece of hardware."

Ralph Moss had turned away from Jack and was keeping his eye on his pistol. "It's too bad that's all people think of in regards to that gun. Nazis. The Luger's got a long history."

"Yeah?" Del said. "Then why'd they make it so fucking ugly?" He turned it back and forth. "It looks like it wants to take a bite out of you."

Jack hadn't been in office very long when Olive Shadlow came into the jail one morning. She was carrying three guns, a single-shot 16-gauge shotgun, a bolt-action 30.06, and a .22 pump. She put them down on the desk and told Jack, "It would be better if we didn't have these around the house." Jack questioned her, but Olive refused to say any more. The guns obviously belonged to her husband, Mason, a vice-president at the bank, but Jack never knew if Olive wanted Mason's guns kept from him because he might do harm to himself, to Olive, to one of their four sons, or to someone outside the family. Or was it possible Olive wanted the guns kept away from herself, that she had been contemplating a use for them? Mason Shadlow never came in to claim his guns or to report them missing.

Montanans knew their guns, their make and caliber, and they knew exactly which one was right for each type of destruction. And they knew whose hands they should be kept out of.

Jack wondered what Del's thinking was in picking up the Luger. Was it impersonal—merely making certain that if these two men got into it in Little Sam's that one of them couldn't start shooting up the place? Because, as Del surely knew, when guns were fired, damage was going to be done, and it wasn't always possible to predict where bullets would go. Misfires, ricochets, poor aim—everything and everyone within range was in jeopardy.

Or did Dell have Jack's welfare in mind? Did he pick up the gun so Ralph Moss could not get to it first and turn it on the sheriff? Even that motive may not have been personal. Ralph Moss was an outsider, and even if Del O'Keefe didn't vote for Jack—didn't even like him—he and Jack still came from the same spot on the map.

Whatever the reason, Jack felt his breath come a little easier with the Luger in Del's hand.

He pointed to the gun. "Is that what you were going to use on Rick Bauer?"

Now Del O'Keefe had one eye closed as if he were sighting the pistol, but since he was holding the gun sideways, his action looked more like a carpenter checking the bubble in a level than someone aiming at a target.

"Is that what you had in mind?" Jack said. "Chasing Rick down like one of your big cats and then blowing him out of the tree?"

Two expressions crossed Ralph Moss's face in rapid succession. The first was recognition. Obviously he knew whom Jack was talking about. The second was pain. His smile lost its width, and his upper lip peeled back in a quick wince as if some chronic condition had suddenly revisited him. "June's boyfriend," he said.

"That's right," Jack replied.

The hurt remained in his eyes. "That's what you think? I'd go after a boy?" He pointed to his pistol. "With that?"

"That's what Celia thinks. That's why she called me."

Ralph Moss shook his head sadly. "Celia don't know shit. She's always had a low opinion of me." His smile came back, a bit ruefully this time, as if to say that he knew Celia Moss's view of him was not entirely without justification.

"She was worried about you too. Not just about what you'd do."

"Yeah? God damn, that's hard to believe." He poured the last of his beer into his glass. Jack was surprised to notice that he'd finished his own. "How come she's worried? This kid, what's his name again? He really someone to reckon with?"

"Rick Bauer?" Jack recalled the sight of the young man sitting in front of the urinal on the floor in the lavatory in First Lutheran Church. "No, he wouldn't give you any problems." He pointed to the pocket where Ralph Moss had put the photograph of himself and his bounty of mountain loins. "No sharp teeth or claws on that kid."

"Hey, I told you. Those days are long gone."

"What are you doing now?" Del asked. He had put the gun back down on the bar, but he placed it closer to his side of the bar than Ralph Moss's.

"Shit. It's embarrassing. Stockin' shelves at an auto-parts store. I done a lot of hard work in my time, but unloading and stacking car batteries damn near beats it all. It's hard and it's boring." He turned toward the Gow twins as if he were continuing a conversation with them he had started earlier. "This is what gripes the hell out of me. I could've been retired by now. Sitting on my ass and collecting a fat fucking check every month. Me and my brother had a chance years ago to get in on the ground floor with some oil speculators. But we took a pass, and they hit it big, let me tell you."

"This was around here?" a twin asked.

"Over by Scobey. Where we're from originally."

"I don't know anybody here got rich in the oil business."

"Little Sam owns some minerals rights," Del added. "Doesn't amount to much."

Ralph Moss turned back to Jack. "That's why Celia's got it in for me. She knows it was her kept Cal from throwin' in with me on the oil deal. So she knows it was her kept them poor." He shrugged as if to say that it was his nature to forgive and forget.

"I take it this was not recent," Del said.

"Oh, no. Hell, no. Cal was killed—when?" He arched his eyebrows at Jack as if Jack would know the answer. "Fifty-one? Fifty-two?"

Jack shook his head.

Ralph Moss mimicked Jack's action. "Me neither. I can't keep track of fucking years anymore."

The Gow twins were losing interest in this talk of family relations. One of them rolled a cigarette, while the other assisted his brother by holding the fixings.

"Celia says you were real fond of June," Jack said.

Ralph Moss looked around, and when he saw that Jack seemed to be the only one listening—Del was moving bottles around under the bar—Ralph leaned closer. "In the Moss family, out of the five of us"—he held up his hand with the fingers spread wide—"Cal and me and our three sisters, Cal's the only one got married and had a family. Think of that, Sheriff. Out of five, only one to carry on the bloodline. What are the odds of that? So you're damn right we paid attention to June. All of us. Especially after Cal was killed."

Jack shook a cigarette out of his pack, and Ralph Moss asked, "Can you spare one of those tailor-mades?" He sniffed the air that was filled with the sweet aromatic smoke from the Gow's cigarettes. "I can't handle those hand-rolled jobs."

He took one of Jack's Chesterfields, and though he held it strangely, pinched a little too tightly between his thumb and index finger like an inexperienced smoker, he drew the smoke in deep and held it. With a protracted sigh he began to speak, the words riding out on a stream of smoke. "I think June sort of looked up to me." He tugged roughly at the sleeve of his suit coat as if he were aware of the garment's shabbiness, its age and poor fit. "God knows. Being the big-city uncle and all, I suppose. 'What's Denver like?' she was always asking. Like she wanted to know what was on the other side of the wall. And I'd tell her. Just like everywhere. Only a hell of a lot more people." He turned his head to see if the Gows and Del O'Keefe were paying attention. "Though presently I'm living in Hargrove, which is east of Denver a ways. Out on the flatland. Not so different from the country around here, though we don't get the iron-ass winters like you do. If I moved back here, I wonder if I could take another of those fucking winters. And like this—snow goddamn near the year around. Christ almighty. It's no wonder Junie wanted out.

"She asked me once. Twice, no twice. Once in a letter. Could I bring her down to Denver? she wanted to know. And live with me? An old bachelor like me? Scared the shit out of me, just the idea. Wait, I told her. Just wait. Get your education. Finish high school. Like none of your aunts and uncles ever did, I could've said.

"She wasn't above putting a little pressure on either. You're my godfather, she said. My dad would've wanted you to. Whoa, I said. Plunking you down in Denver ain't something he'd want me to do. And to tell you the truth, I'm not so sure about being her godfather. I know I was there, for the baptism and all, but I can't remember exactly if I was part of it or just watching. Seems to me it might've been Celia's brother and maybe his wife. Either way, I guess it shows I don't keep too good a track of such things."

Ralph Moss looked up and down the bar at the glasses and bottles in front of the four men. He said to Del, "What about one more round here?" He put his cigarette between his lips and

265

pressed his palms on the bar on either side of his stack of silver dollars. "On me," he said.

Del nodded in Jack's direction. "We're past closing already, but I reckon if the sheriff here says okay, we don't have to worry about getting into trouble."

"What the hell," Jack said. "Let's make it a special occasion. How often do we get snow in June?"

The Gow brother farthest from Jack leaned forward. "Four years ago. At least in the northern part of the county they got a few flakes."

His brother nodded in eager assent. "We was fishing."

Jack took the news of a June snow in times so recent as a defeat. Snow in June only four years ago? It was that common? He had no recollection of the event. But if it could happen every four years, it was no more rare than a presidential election. That wouldn't be enough to keep people's minds from the accident, so it surely wouldn't be enough to dominate their talk. The inside of his mouth felt stale and faintly acidic. The taste of too many cigarettes. The taste of defeat.

"All right then," Jack said. "How about this—two funerals in one day? Goddamn it, that ought to be special enough for anyone."

Del O'Keefe recoiled slightly from Jack, as if he couldn't quite be sure his sheriff was saying this.

Ralph Moss, however, had no problem with Jack's assessment of the occasion. "Good enough." He slapped the bar.

Del brought out the bottles of beer, but he kept looking at Jack.

"How about pouring shots with those?" suggested Ralph Moss. "Finish the night off right."

Del finished levering open the last beer by smacking down harder than necessary on the bottle opener. Then he stood with his hands on his hips and stared at Jack.

"Pour 'em," Jack said.

Del set shot glasses down in front of the four men. From a bottle of Four Roses, he filled each glass right to the rim. "Pour yourself one," Ralph Moss told Del.

"A little late for me."

Jack didn't dare pick up his whiskey. He didn't trust the steadiness of his hand. Down the bar, the Gow twins, as if they had been given a signal, bent simultaneously toward their shot glasses. With their mouths only an inch or two away from the whiskey, they lifted their glasses and, in a sudden movement that looked as if they were catching the liquid in their mouths just as it was spilling upward, swallowed all the whiskey. The brother furthest from Jack shook his head after drinking. Only in that movement did his action differ from his brother's.

Ralph Moss held his own full glass aloft and watched the Gows. "Jesus. You two are something else. You do everything together?"

"Damn near," the head-shaking brother said.

" 'Cept shit and jerk off," said his brother.

"That's because the outhouse is a one-holder," the first twin added.

As hard as Ralph Moss laughed at the twins, the whiskey in his glass did not waver. Right in the midst of his laughter, he tossed back his shot with one swift motion. He kept his head tilted back and closed his eyes. *"Whoof.* Feel that heat," he whispered.

While Ralph Moss's eyes were closed, Jack quickly put his lips down to his shot glass and sipped out enough whiskey so he could then lift the glass without spilling.

Ralph Moss took a swallow of beer, then resumed talking to Jack as if there had been no interruption. "But godfather or not, Cal was my brother, and since he ain't around, I figured I got to at least make some noise like I'm going to do what a father would do, under the circumstances.

"So who's responsible for Junie's demise? Got to be the boy, right? The one who was going to run off with her—What'd you say his name was?"

"Bauer."

"Jesus, why can't I remember that name? Anyways. It looks to me like the finger's got to point to that little bastard. And he's the one still walking around. So am I right? I bet you got kids. Isn't that what a father would do? Find this Bauer boy and kick his ass?"

"That's not going to do anybody any good."

Ralph Moss helped himself to another cigarette from Jack's pack.

"Yeah, well. What the fuck. Like I say. I was just making noise."
He shrugged. "Maybe trying to impress Celia. Show her I'm not
such a fuck-up. Show her I could do right by Junie. Hell, maybe
I'm the one's to blame. If I'd have taken her down to Denver,
maybe she wouldn't have had to trick that little bastard into taking her."

Del O'Keefe had resumed his chores behind the bar, preparing
to close down Little Sam's for the night. The Gow twins were
engaged in their own quiet private argument. Jack couldn't be sure
what the dispute was about since the brothers were muttering their
complaints simultaneously, but it seemed to have something to do
with the keys to their car.

"Is that what you think?" Jack asked Ralph Moss. "That June
tricked this boy?"

"Did you know Junie?"

Jack shook his head.

"She could do it, let me tell you. She could be tricky. She almost
had me goin'. If I wasn't Cal's brother . . ." He shook himself
away from this line of thought. "Hell, it was probably just a
way to get out of Celia's house. So I wouldn't have to keep
looking at her sorrowful goddamn face. And not a drop of liquor
in the house . . . Hey, that ought to be a lesson for men everywhere. You want out of the house, start waving a gun and hol-
lering about revenge. They'll stay the hell out of your way, let
me tell you."

"Sounds pretty drastic," Del said when he came back to the bar.

Ralph Moss ignored Del's remark. Instead, he pointed his finger
right at Jack and said, "And then Celia goes and calls out the
dogs. . . ."

Before Jack could think of something to say in response, Ralph
Moss spun himself around to face Del and said, "But you want
war stories? Hey, I'll give you fucking war stories. Let me tell you
about all the dangerous piles of potatoes I had to peel."

Jack pocketed his cigarettes and stood up.

"You taking off?" asked Del.

"Way past my bedtime." He took a step toward Ralph Moss to

shake his hand in farewell. "Well, good to meet you. Enjoy the rest of your stay."

Ralph Moss didn't look at Jack or extend his hand. "It ain't going to last much longer."

Jack's bottle of beer sat untouched on the bar, and he started to reach for it, then decided against it. Beer on top of whiskey, mighty risky. . . .

36

WHEN THE BULLET STRUCK JACK NEVELSEN, HE WAS RIGHT IN FRONT of his truck. He had been walking slowly, gazing up toward the pole light planted in the road next to Little Sam's driveway. The snow seemed to have stopped, a fact that Jack was trying to verify by watching that cone of light closely to see if any stray flakes were still falling.

When the bullet struck him, his feet flew out from under him, and he fell forward and to the side, hitting his head on the truck's front bumper. Later, he would wonder if he lost consciousness for an instant because he could never find the tiny sliver of time that seemed to belong somewhere between his being on his feet and his being on the ground.

When the bullet hit him, time, as in the order of events, immediately became a problem. It was as if all the knowledge of what had just happened to him was printed on little thought-cards, and though he could tell what each card said, he couldn't be sure he read them in the right order.

The gunshot, for example. He heard the gunshot quite clearly. The wind had died down, and the snow cover muffled the night's usual sounds but amplified the pistol's booming crack.

Yet Jack didn't associate the gunshot with something that *had* happened to him but with something that *might*. He had fallen. There had been a gunshot. Was that the order of things? Was Ralph Moss trying to shoot him while he lay on the ground? Somewhere in the gun's echo Jack could hear the grunt and curse—"*Uhnh!* Shit!"—that he uttered when he fell. So the gun fired first? Did its sound startle him, causing him to lose his footing? The ground wasn't frozen, but it was rutted, slushy, and snow-packed in the tire tracks, and you could easily slip if you weren't paying attention, if you were looking for falling snow, for example.

But there *had* been a gunshot, without question, and Jack's most urgent concern was to head for cover, to interpose something between him and the direction from which the shot came.

What *was* that direction? Reason told him that it had to be from Little Sam's, that Ralph Moss must have grabbed his Luger from the bar, come outside, and fired a shot. Yet Jack had hit his head so hard on the truck, and the blow and subsequent pain had so clotted his thoughts, that he didn't quite trust what reason told him. The shot didn't sound as if it came from behind him. It sounded as if it came from the trees that ringed Little Sam's on the south side, the direction that Jack was now facing. He didn't want to move the wrong way.

But maybe, reason argued with sense, maybe the sound coming from the trees was the shot's echo, and since nothing was happening in quite the right sequence—or he wasn't remembering in the right order—maybe he heard the echo *before* he heard the gunshot.

Reason convinced him. It had to be Ralph Moss, Ralph Moss behind him firing his pistol, and Jack decided it would be best to crawl along the side of the truck, keeping the truck between him and Little Sam's. That strategy would also bring him closer to the door of the truck and maybe he could get inside, stay low, and start up the truck.

Only when Jack tried to push himself forward across the snowy ground and found his right leg would not work the way it should, did he realize he had been shot. Even then, the awareness seemed to come to him not as a discovery but as a memory. *Oh, yes, I forgot; I've been shot.*

Even while the realization embarrassed him, he almost welcomed it. He'd been shot! Of course! How could he be so stupid, so foolish, as to not know he had been shot! Jesus, it was one thing not to know where a bullet was coming from; it was another not to know when it had hit you! Jack even considered that if he didn't die as a result of this occurrence, he might one day tell about it as a joke on himself: *Oh, yeah, after a minute or two passed I knew I'd been shot. Not too swift, I guess you'd say.* Still, he knew now, and a measure of relief came with knowing.

That explained so much.

He hadn't slipped and fallen; his leg had been shot out from under him.

The shot came from behind him and preceded his fall.

He had noticed, while he was on the ground, that although the slushy snow was soaking through his clothes—Jesus, how many times today was he going to get wet!—he hadn't felt the moisture as cold but as warm. Blood. Sure. That was it. He lay in his own hot blood. . . .

And his right leg wouldn't work the way it should not because he had twisted or strained or banged it when he fell but because a bullet, a large-caliber bullet from a German Luger, had slammed into it.

But right on the heels of this discovery came another doubt: Had he been shot anywhere besides the leg? The pain in his head, in his forehead and the right side of his face, was worse than in his leg—was it possible he had been shot in the head as well? That he hadn't heard a gunshot and an echo but two shots? It didn't seem likely. After all, he could still think, even if his thoughts were shuffled, he could still hear, he could still see. He was alive. Yet he remembered hearing during the war horrific stories of soldiers having parts of their skulls, their brains, blasted away and continuing to talk, to breathe—at least for a short time.

Blood. That would give him the answer. He felt around his face and when his fingertips came away without any dark splotches or streaks, he breathed easier. Then, just to double check, he pushed his face into the snow. The impression he left was not darkened or discolored in any way.

So he had some additional material to add to his story—his joke—about how he lay on the ground and didn't know he was shot. He lay there, Jack would say, and conducted an inventory: Fingers and toes—all there. Sight. Hearing. No holes in the head that weren't supposed to be there. Arms working. Legs—wait! Problem there!

He knew if he reached down to the back of his leg, and perhaps the front too, right above the knee, his hand would come back bloody. For that matter, he could scoop up snow from down there, and if the warm blood hadn't melted the snow back to water, the snow would be stained bright pink or deep rose.

But he didn't put his hand down there. Not yet. He didn't want to do anything to disturb that leg. Whatever damage the bullet had done he felt would be made worse by moving. The pain reminded him of an injury done to muscle or tendon or bone rather than to skin and blood. His leg had stiffened like a bad sprain, though only seconds had passed since the bullet hit him. His leg felt pinned down as well, as if something had not just passed through it but was still in there, something long and narrow, a sliver perhaps, a sharpened sliver longer than the thickness of his leg and which went in the back, came out the front, and then stuck into the ground.

Shit, what if it was his leg bone that was poking him! What if the bullet had shattered bone, and it was a broken-off splinter of bone that he felt? That might have been why he didn't want to move his leg—because any movement would cause more bone to break away. And was that why he kept the muscles in that leg flexed tight—because he was trying to keep everything in place? Yet he could also hear an admonitory voice in the back of his mind saying, Relax your leg; just relax it. "I can't," Jack answered back, and it scared the hell out of him when he spoke out loud. Talking to his own mind—that was not a good sign, though he wasn't sure what it meant. Was he getting shocky? Was that it? Was he growing as pallid as the snow he was lying on?

The possibility of being in shock gave him an even worse fear:

he could bleed to death. He knew there were major arteries in the leg that could pump your life blood out so fast you couldn't do a goddamn thing about it. Wasn't that what happened to Marge Flightner's husband, Walt? He shot himself in the leg, and that was it, that was all she wrote, and the next thing, Jack and Father Howser were running after Marge to break the news.

Then Jack heard something that made him put off even this worry of bleeding to death. A car started, and then as its driver gunned the engine, the car's tires spun, trying to find traction as they burned their way down through snow, ice, mud, and finally got down to the gravel that clattered up against the car's undercarriage.

That had to be Ralph Moss, and Jack believed Moss was coming for him, planning to finish off with the car what he had started with his gun.

Jack tried to scramble out of the way by getting under the truck, an awkward maneuver at best but further complicated by the fact that he couldn't decide if he should crawl or roll under, and he ended up trying to do both and doing neither. He hit his head on the running board, a bump that caused the pain from the earlier injury to come back in full force. His legs somehow got crossed, the wounded leg on top, and it felt as if he would never get himself righted.

Ralph Moss, however, was not coming in Jack's direction. The sound of the roaring engine was not coming closer, and Jack got himself turned around in time to see the black Mercury fishtailing out of the lot's other exit.

Jack had been so instantly convinced that Ralph Moss would try to run him over that he experienced a moment of bafflement when it didn't happen. For that matter, why hadn't Ralph Moss fired again at Jack? He had been a near stationary target on the ground, and Ralph Moss would only have had to take a few steps to have a clear shot at Jack. And why the leg? Why would Ralph Moss shoot Jack in the leg? He was marksman enough to shoot mountain lions out of trees, or so he said. Surely he could have given Jack a graver wound than the one provided by putting a bullet in the back of the leg. Was Ralph Moss so drunk that he carelessly snapped off a shot and didn't much care where it hit? Then why not finish the job?

Del O'Keefe's voice interrupted Jack's thoughts. "Jack? Hey! Are you still out here?"

"Over here!" He surprised himself; his voice didn't sound as though it belonged to a man who had been shot off his feet.

At the sound of Del O'Keefe's approach, Jack decided he had to get to his feet. He wanted to show Del he was not hurt badly, and he wanted to prove it to himself as well.

He got his back up against the truck's running board and, braced there, with the aid of his hands, arms, and good leg, slid himself upward. As soon as he could, he reached down and pulled the loose material of his trousers tight around his injured leg. He was thinking less of a tourniquet and more of a brace. It seemed important to keep the leg properly aligned, to keep whatever was in there that had been broken loose, whether bones or nerve or blood vessel, as close to its original position as possible.

Jack was surprised at how easy it was to stand up. How long had he been down? A minute or two at most, yet it had come to seem as though down was the direction where he belonged and snow and slush the environment in which he would remain. Now, however, gravity seemed to want him up, so much so that as he finally drew himself to his full height, his head felt as though it would keep on rising, weightless, floating up into the night sky.

In the next instant, the pain in his leg, like a counterweight, yanked him down, down, and from that yo-yoing sensation, as if he were in an elevator that could instantly change direction, his vision darkened, and it seemed as if the only thing that kept him from losing consciousness was that he had to stay awake to vomit.

He convulsed violently because he had next to nothing to bring up, just beer, whiskey—mighty risky—and his stomach's juices. He heard Del's voice again—"Jack! Jesus, Jack!"—but it barely came through his own strangled, choked retching.

Then Del had a gentle hold on Jack's shoulders, and after one more shudder Jack felt himself settle down, still standing upright and no longer floating or falling in place.

"Hey," Del said softly. "Hey, are you going to be okay?"

Jack leaned back against the door of the truck. "*Ahh*, the son of a bitch shot me."

"Yeah. . . . Christ, I'm sorry, Jack. He grabbed the fucking gun and was out the door before I could do anything to stop him."

Jack shrugged himself out of Del's grasp so he could bend over and spit in an attempt to get the sour taste out of his mouth.

Alongside the truck where they stood, the snow had already melted down to bare ground in patches. Body warmth and body fluids, Jack thought.

When he straightened up, he saw the Gow twins ten feet in front of him. How long had they been there? "God damn. I'm seeing double. . . ."

They both grinned, and one of the brothers, nodding enthusiastically, said, "Seeing double!"

Del lowered his head and looked up at Jack. ". . . then we heard the shot, and I got to tell you, Jack, we was scared to come out."

Jack waved away Del's apology. "You did right. You don't want to go charging into a gun."

"And when Chester seen him drive off, we came out, but we didn't see you anywheres. . . ."

"Did he say anything?" Jack asked. "Before he came out?"

Del winced and smiled ruefully. "He said, 'Cocksucker,' and just grabbed the gun. He was out that door in a flash."

"Yeah, well. I guess he knew what he wanted. . . ."

Del moved in closer. "You're not looking too good, Jack. Maybe we better get you inside. Call the ambulance."

Jack shook his head. "Tell you what you can do. Call Wayne. My deputy. Let him know this Ralph Moss fellow is out there and see if we can't do something before he gets too far. If you can't get ahold of Wayne, call the police. No, call them anyway. Call them both. And tell Wayne I said call the highway patrol. *Cocksucker*. . . ."

Jack opened the door of the truck and got in backwards, getting his ass up on the seat first and then swinging his legs in.

Jack wanted to spit once more before he closed the door, but Del stood in the way.

"You going after him?" asked Del.

"I was thinking about it." He pulled the choke out a half an inch and turned the key. The truck coughed and shook itself to a start. "But maybe I'll go check myself into the hospital first."

He was not about to ride in the ambulance. No, sir. The last occupants of that vehicle had been June Moss and Leo Bauer. (Did they ride together? Hell, why not? Even if there wasn't room for two, what did it matter once they were dead? They could stack them on top of each other.) And Jack was determined that he would not travel in the manner of Leo Bauer when he made his last trip, strapped to a stretcher. No, sir. He'd drive himself and drip a trail of blood all the way to the hospital if he had to.

Besides, Jack had a little detour in mind that he doubted he could persuade the ambulance driver to make.

The thought had occurred to him, as belatedly as the earlier realization that he had been shot, that perhaps Ralph Moss had put the bullet in Jack's leg and not his back because he only wanted to slow Jack down, not kill him. Maybe Ralph Moss was still planning to hunt down Rick Bauer, and he wanted to make certain Jack couldn't interfere.

En route to the hospital Jack had to go only a few blocks out of his way to drive by the Bauers'. And if he left the lot traveling in the opposite direction as Ralph Moss, Jack could probably get there before that son of a bitch.

37

JACK WOULD PROBABLY NOT HAVE BEEN ABLE TO DRIVE IF HE HAD BEEN shot in the left leg. As it was, he could keep his right foot on the accelerator only by keeping his leg straight—he didn't dare flex his ankle—and lifting it up and down from the hip. He worked the clutch and the brake with his left foot, shifting into a lower gear and letting out the clutch when he needed to slow down and throwing the truck into neutral when he had to stop.

Jack did not come across a single car moving through the streets of Bentrock, and when he came to the block where Vivien and Rick Bauer lived, Jack saw no sign of Ralph Moss and his black Mercury. Jack had trouble remembering: Many of Bentrock's blocks were bisected by alleys—did one run behind the Bauers'? Could Ralph Moss be parked back there? No, the alley on Fourth Street was on the other side of the street. If Ralph Moss was looking for the house, he hadn't yet arrived.

Then Jack couldn't decide: Should he park right in front of the house and thereby warn off Ralph Moss? Or should he stay a distance away, trick Ralph Moss into stopping, and then pounce once he did?

Pounce? *Pounce?* Who was Jack kidding? He was not only un-armed in the face of Ralph Moss's Luger, Jack wasn't sure he could get out of the truck without assistance, and if he did, he might pass out as soon as his feet hit the ground. Better to remain visible.

He left the truck's engine running. Right now the pain in his leg was bearable. In fact, it had already acquired the kind of famil-iarity that chronic pain frequently took on. This leg will hurt for-ever, Jack thought; as long as I draw breath, the ache will be there. This realization was a kind of crazy comfort. If the pain had kept spiraling upward, he would not have been able to entertain the thought of living with it. He wasn't sure why he wasn't concerned about losing blood. He had gingerly put his hand near the wound, and his fingertips came back wet. He knew, however, that blood was not gushing or spurting out of him. Earlier, he considered that perhaps he should wrap a tourniquet around his leg, but he dis-carded the idea almost immediately. For one thing, he already felt a tightening sensation around his leg. Swelling, he thought. Like spraining a knee and now it's puffing up. But another kind of tightening was going on, closer to the surface, as if the skin was puckering, the way a cut did around its edges when it began to heal. Nevertheless, he knew he'd have to get himself looked at before long, and once he decided to head for the hospital, he'd want to get there quick. He couldn't take a chance on the truck not starting.

Yes, there was another reason. . . .

The Bauer house was dark, but maybe Vivien would hear the truck's chugging engine, look out, and see Jack. She'd grab her coat, throw it on over her nightgown, and come out to him. The snow would soak through her slippers, but she wouldn't notice. And once she found he'd been shot, that he'd taken a bullet to protect Rick, to save the entire Bauer family, she'd . . . she'd . . . He couldn't keep the goddamn fantasy going! He could see Vivian running out of the house, coming out to the truck—he'd roll down the window—and . . . Then nothing. His imagination sputtered and died.

Of course it did. Jack didn't get shot for anybody. That bullet was meant for him. He deserved it.

He wanted Vivien to see him as a hero, but the truth was, he was the villain of the piece. If it weren't for the story he and Rick concocted—the story he coerced Rick into going along with—Ralph Moss would never have started cruising the streets with his Luger. Oh, maybe he would have found his way back to Staples where he once tended bar, and there he would have bought himself a pint of Four Roses and tried to soak his sorrow, alternating his swallows of whiskey—first one for poor Junie, who never found the way out of Bentrock, and then one for Leo, the middle-aged fool who said he'd take her away.

Hell, no wonder he couldn't imagine Vivien doing anything beyond walking out to the truck. If his thoughts went any further, they might bring out a Vivien who knew the truth, a Vivien whose surly son might have gotten so scared when she told him why he had to stay in the house tonight, why the doors had to remain locked, that he might have told her the truth ("Those were Dad's clothes! He took my suitcase!"), a Vivien who, armed with that knowledge, knowledge more dangerous than Ralph Moss's Luger, might come out only to curse him, a Vivien who, if she found him dead in his truck, might say, good riddance, for all the anguish he caused. It made sense that the engine that drove his fantasies broke down when it tried to put Vivien's arms around Jack—the man doing the imagining was not the same one she would be embracing.

He'd wait a few minutes longer to see if Ralph Moss turned up. A cigarette, he'd wait as long as it took to smoke a cigarette.

Careful not to disturb the angle of his hip and leg, Jack turned on the radio. Nothing but static on that station. Probably long since off the air. The middle of the night, however, a signal was bound to come in from somewhere. He started to reach for the dial to tune in another frequency then stopped. He reminded himself again. Angela might have the radio set for the station she wanted. He kept the static on but turned the volume down until it sounded like nothing more than a drawn-out raspy sigh.

He wished he could hear her music now, that the static would suddenly stop to inhale, and then there it would be, Angela's music, something with a rhythm so fast you couldn't snap your fingers fast enough to keep up. Or somebody singing about his baby. His baby, he lost his baby. Angela was Jack's baby, and it wasn't that many years ago when she used to sit on his lap while he drove the truck. When she got a little older, she asked to drive, still on his lap, and Jack would put his hand over hers on the shift lever and let her think she was putting the truck through its gears. To help her pretend she was steering, he would put her hands on the top of the steering wheel while his hands, hidden at the bottom of the wheel, were actually in control. Well, she couldn't be with him now. Not this late. Not while he was working and especially not while he was waiting for a man with a gun. Not while he was bleeding. . . .

It was a good thing he didn't give a damn about the truck's interior. He was soaking the upholstery and floorboards with bloodstains that would never come out. Not that it would continue to look like blood. Over time, that deep bright scarlet would darken and fade until the stains would look more like rust than blood. . . . Funny, Wayne had gotten so upset over all the blood Leo Bauer shed in his car, so much blood that the cloth seats became saturated with it. Jack had assumed Wayne had gotten squeamish over the sight of the blood, but maybe what really bothered him was the destruction of the car. Not only was the body beat up, the interior was ruined as well. There was no way bloodstains could be washed away. . . . Might as well sell the truck. Or try to. Neither Nora nor Angela would be willing to set foot inside after the mess he made in here tonight. Would he be able to find a buyer, for that matter? Oh, hell, this was Montana; if the price was right and if the truck ran decent no buyer was going to be put off by a little dried blood.

He rolled the window down a few inches to let the smoke out. Along with the breath of cold air—the truck's heater blew hot air on his feet and legs while his forehead felt the sudden chill—came an odor that Jack at first could not place. It was a spring fragrance, that mix of rain and damp earth, but there was another smell, chemical, stringent, that puzzled his nose. For a moment, he wondered if his sense of smell was out of whack, if when he banged his head more damage had been done than the golf ball-sized lump that stuck out above his left eye.

Ah, no—he knew what the problem was. Snow, it was the strange winter smell of snow lying on top of spring. . . .

He had concentrated so hard on the odor that he found it difficult to get his mind back to where he was and why. Vivien's. He was parked in front of Vivien Bauer's house. Like a high-school boy waiting for his date. But the house was dark. She wasn't coming out . . .

. . . and Ralph Moss wasn't coming either. Jack had no reason to be here, a realization that came to him with a cold shiver. Then another. And another. He rolled up the window, but he couldn't stop shivering.

Disordered thoughts, uncontrollable shaking, a chill that couldn't be warmed—shit, he knew what this meant. It was time to get himself to the hospital while he could still find the way and steer the truck.

He jammed the truck into gear, gave the Bauer home a little wave, and drove away.

Jack knew nothing could come of it, but he took a little side trip on the way to the hospital and drove by Celia Moss's house. Even if the Mercury was parked there, Jack wouldn't stop—he didn't *think* he'd stop—but he'd know where Ralph Moss was. That was all Jack wanted now, to know, just to know . . .

He drove slowly down Celia's street, letting the truck lug along in second gear. No . . . no black car. But the porch light was on, and the light in—what was that? the living room? the kitchen? Waiting up. Waiting up for Ralph. Jack wondered if he should stop, only for a moment, just long enough to tell Celia to go to bed, get some sleep. To tell her Ralph wouldn't be walking through her door again. Not tonight. Not ever.

Jack parked as close as he could to a side door that he was sure led to the hospital's emergency room. There was no sign over the door, however, and for a moment he wondered if he was in the right place. But he wasn't about to go around to the front door. He wasn't about to drag his bloody leg into the lobby of Good

Samaritan Hospital and scare the hell out of whoever was on duty at the front desk.

He hobbled up to the side door and tried the handle, half expecting it to be locked. It opened onto an empty, dimly lit corridor. Jesus, where was he? A storage area? Maintenance? He didn't smell that familiar cheesy, antiseptic hospital smell but instead an odor that was more like baking bread. And cinnamon? Had he gotten the wrong building? He was going to bleed to death in a goddamn bakery with the smell of cinnamon rolls in his nostrils.

"Hey," Jack called out. "Anybody here?"

He moved forward a few steps then stopped, leaning against the wall. "Hey!"

Down the hall he spotted a flash of white, there and gone so quickly he couldn't be sure if it was a nurse.

He tried one more time. "Hey. Am I in the right place?"

She leaned out the doorway again, and this time Jack saw enough of the white cap and uniform to be sure. "I've been shot, goddamn it."

"Sheriff?" the nurse asked.

"I don't believe I can go any further under my own power."

"My lord," the nurse said and bobbed back inside the doorway. In a moment she came back out, this time on a dead run and pushing a wheelchair.

The nurse was an older woman, in her late fifties or sixties perhaps, a pretty woman with ruddy, veined cheeks and a comforting smile made all the more shining by her gold-filled teeth. Jack recognized her. She was Adeline Keogh, and she used to be old Dr. Snow's nurse. Jack could remember as a child receiving both a shot and lollipop from Adeline Keogh when he visited the doctor. She talked tough, but everyone knew that Nurse Keogh loved kids. Jack would have guessed she had retired when Dr. Snow closed his practice, but by God, he was glad she hadn't. Jack couldn't imagine that there was a face he'd rather see if he had to go to the hospital.

Adeline Keogh swung the chair around. "Sit yourself down, Sheriff. Now, tell me. What have you been up to on this godforsaken night?"

"Trying to stay out of trouble." He tried to lower himself into the chair, but he was already too stiff and had to drop his weight down. "Not doing a very good job of it either."

She came around to the front of the chair, lifted and locked the footrests, and, with little assistance from him, got his feet up. "Well, we're going to take care of you now."

Adeline Keogh reached up and very lightly patted his leg right above his wound. Her touch seemed calculated to reassure him: See, your leg doesn't look so bad; it doesn't bother me to put my hand on you. For his part, Jack had assiduously not looked down.

Adeline Keogh hurried down the hall toward the room she had come out of.

Jack closed his eyes. "Mrs. Keogh, do you suppose I could get you to call my wife for me? And tell her real quick that I'm okay before you tell her where I am."

"Honey, I know how to make that call. Don't you worry." She pushed the wheelchair with one hand so she could stroke his head with the other hand.

Jack opened his eyes, hoping that would keep the tears blistering behind his eyelids from spilling over and running down his cheeks.

38

THE DOCTOR WHO EXAMINED JACK WAS MALCOLM HALLETT, A MAN Jack knew mostly by rumor and reputation. Hallett had been in Bentrock for little more than a year, a new resident there to practice surgery in the new hospital. An outdoorsman, he had left a practice in St. Paul so he could be closer to the hunting and fishing he loved. He had already bought riding horses for himself, his wife, and his three daughters, and he stabled them at Les Harney's place. The word was the doctor was looking to buy a small ranch.

Dr. Hallett was Jack's height, and he had a wild, thick, red beard, and a manner so rough Jack had heard more than one person wonder if the doctor had been kicked out of the city he came from.

He poked around in Jack's wound, turning Jack from his back to his side on the examining table, before he spoke. "So you got yourself shot," the doctor said. It sounded to Jack like a reproof.

"It wasn't something I planned on." He was trying not to grunt in pain from the doctor's rough probing fingers and instruments.

"You know who did the deed?" the doctor asked.

"I know."

"Arrested him?"

"Not yet."

"Well, don't be too hard on the bastard. He did a damn good job on your leg."

"How's that?" Jack almost twisted away from the doctor; it felt as if he were putting his finger deep into Jack's leg and then wiggling it.

"Bullet went right through and didn't shatter any bone. Maybe took off a little chip. Didn't tear up any major arteries or vessels. If you've got to be shot, this is the way to have it done."

"I'll be sure to thank him."

"I'm saying you're lucky, Sheriff. That's all. Don't get pissed off at me. I'm the one who's going to clean you out and plug you up."

"Have I lost too much blood?"

Dr. Hallett coughed out a laugh—*Kuh-kuh!* "Too much blood? Well, shit, in the course of the day we're not supposed to lose any. But you're not in danger. The bullet sort of sealed things up on its way through. Which will sometimes happen. Could be you're a quart low though. We'll get you topped off."

Adeline Keogh came back into the room. She bent down and put her face close to Jack's. Her breath smelled of wintergreen. "Sheriff, can you hear me all right?"

The doctor answered for Jack. "He can hear you."

"I talked to your wife." Jack must have had an uncomprehending look because the nurse raised her voice. "I talked to Nora. She knows you're here. She knows what happened, and she knows you're going to be all right." She glanced quickly up at the doctor, no doubt to confirm that Jack's condition was not grave. "She's going to be here in a few minutes."

"She better hurry," Dr. Hallett said, "because we're putting this fellow to sleep shortly."

"Like a dog," Jack said weakly.

"Heard the line before, Sheriff. No, I only treat humans." He pulled a wad of gauze off Jack's leg. As soon as it came away, Jack felt the sting of cold air on the spot. "Ad," the doctor said, "you want to step out here for a moment, and I'll tell you what I want set up. Our friend here has some things torn loose in his leg, and we'll see if we can't get them reconnected."

Once Jack was alone, and he had no need to impress anyone, he brought both hands up under his head and closed his eyes once more.

Almost immediately he felt himself fading, but this was not just the vanishing of consciousness that accompanied sleep's onset. It seemed to Jack as though he were somehow losing himself, as if the lines, the boundaries, outlining his body, containing part of him—no, no, not a part, *him*, his self, his soul—were leaking out, dissolving in the room's bright light, mingling with the rest of the hospital's antiseptic molecules. He wondered if there was a way he could hold on to himself, stop the slippage—if he wrapped his arms around himself, or curled up tightly there on the examining room table—but the feeling of dissolution was so strong he could not even concentrate on those thoughts of panic or prevention.

Then Nora was in the room, and like Adeline Keogh, she bent down to Jack and brought her face close to his. She put her hand on his shoulder, and though he could feel her hand's chill right through his shirt, he wanted to tell her to keep her hand right there, don't move it, because as long as it was there it confirmed his body's shape. If he were vanishing, her hand would not be able to rest in place. . . .

"I guess I should've gone with you," Jack said.

She smiled at him, a brief half smile that was no doubt the best she could muster under the circumstances—tears were running down her cheeks and her lips were so chapped and dry a wider smile might have cracked them open.

"Does Angela know what happened?" Jack asked. "Does she know I'm here?"

Nora shook her head.

"She's sleeping over, right? At Bonnie's?"

Nora could do no more than nod in assent.

"Morning's soon enough. You can tell her then. Or maybe I can. No need to wreck her night."

Nora started to move her hand, and Jack reached up quickly to hold it tightly in place. "I bet she's going to be embarrassed by her old man," Jack said.

"She won't be," said Nora.

"Tell her she's going to have to take Muley out the next few days. And make sure she does it."

"Wayne's here," she said. "He wants to know if he can talk to you before you go up to surgery."

"Did he catch the guy"—Jack hesitated; to say the next thing seemed as bad as uttering an obscenity in Nora's presence—"who shot me?" The fact of it felt as vulgar in speech as it had in thought. The self-dramatizing quality of the phrase further embarrassed him.

"He didn't say," Nora replied.

"Then he didn't. Tell him to keep trying. He knows who—" Jack stopped himself. If Ralph Moss was caught, he would be questioned, not only about his deed but about his motive, and not only by the authorities but in open court. Ralph Moss's lawyer might even put Rick Bauer on the stand, and once the boy put his hand on the Bible and swore to tell the truth, who knew what might come flooding out of the kid?

"Okay," Jack said. "Send Wayne in."

Nora stood and folded the collar of her winter coat tightly across her neck. Jack raised himself on his elbow in order to look down. Yes, just as he thought; the hem of Nora's nightgown, an expanse of blue-and-red plaid flannel—the night was cold—hung down below her coat. When she heard what happened to him, she had hurried from the house without getting dressed. Satisfied, Jack lay back down, crinkling the tissue paper that covered the examining table. He pushed a thought out to Nora as she walked out the door: Make sure you keep that coat buttoned; the world's full of men who'd like nothing better than to get a look at a woman in her nightgown. . . .

Wayne kept moving around behind Jack, and from the small sounds of clicking and scraping, Jack guessed that Wayne was looking over the equipment and supplies in the room.

"Doc says I'm supposed to make this quick," Wayne said. "He's going to operate."

"It's not a big deal," Jack said. Trying to place Wayne only by hearing made Jack sick to his stomach. He saw what he guessed was a bedpan on a counter across the room. Maybe he could ask

Wayne to hand him the pan, and Jack would use that if he had to vomit again.

"But surgery, Jack. Jesus. An operation."

"Wayne. It's not like they're taking out my gallbladder."

"You look so damn pale. I got scared when I first seen you."

"It's been a long winter. Everybody looks pale. Now, listen—"

"Can I ask you something first? Getting shot—what's it like? When we were kids we used to play this game: Which would be worse, getting stabbed or getting shot? Almost everyone picked stabbed. You know, because you can feel the knife right in you and all. But I always said getting shot would be worse. Because a bullet's hot, right? So the goddamn thing burns its way right through you. That's what got me. I mean, a bullet tears you up, but it burns you too, right?"

"Wayne—"

"Did it? Did it burn?"

Jack couldn't recall any sensation but the bone-deep throbbing ache he felt now. It seemed as if something had been hammered into his leg, pounded in from both front and rear, yet this pain now seemed to be caused by Dr. Hallett's steel probe rather than Ralph Moss's bullet.

"Yeah," Jack said. "It burned like a sonofabitch. Like a red-hot poker was in there." The image was completely made up for Wayne's benefit, yet once Jack offered it, trite as it was, it immediately became his own, so much so that he thought of himself lying by his truck outside Little Sam's, his red-hot bullet wound melting the snow beneath him until he lay in a pool of water. Hereafter, this might be his memory. . . .

"That's what I used to say to those other guys," Wayne said. "Hot. It had to be hot."

"Then I didn't have to go get shot just so you'd know for sure, did I?" Jack propped himself up again so he could turn around and see Wayne. The deputy was slowly working a forceps back and forth, as if only by carefully watching its movement could he figure out its function. "You talked to Del O'Keefe?" asked Jack.

"He was the one told me what happened. Then I went out there and got a statement."

Jack wondered why Wayne felt it had been necessary to talk to Del twice, but Jack didn't ask. "So you know it was Ralph Moss?"

"Yep." Wayne kept clasping and unclasping the forceps. "Doc said they got to clean out your leg. Said there might be thread from your pants and all kind of shit in there."

"I guess he'd know. Now, about Moss—"

"Police know. Highway Patrol too. I gave them descriptions of him and the car. Unless he gets across the border, I figure we got the bastard." He opened the forceps, clamped its teeth onto a hair on his wrist, twisted and yanked out the hair. "Called the Canadian authorities too, but they always act like they don't give a shit."

Jack collapsed his weight back down on the table. For once, Wayne was doing his job and doing it well. It was too late to call him off, and besides, what would Jack say? It would be better for all concerned if Ralph Moss was not captured?

"You know what's going to happen when we catch up to Mr. Ralph Moss, don't you?" Wayne asked his question as casually as he might ask Jack if he knew what happened when a ball was thrown into the air. Down, it had to come down. "He so much as spits, he's going to get blasted out of his fucking boots. Hell, he puckers to spit and he'll get it. Shoot a cop . . . you ain't got a prayer."

Oh, where might Jack begin to correct Wayne's thinking! He was not, strictly speaking, a cop. A sheriff was not a cop. . . . Ralph Moss wore brogans, not boots. And no matter who eventually pulled the trigger—Bentrock police officer or Montana Highway Patrol or Canadian Mountie—no matter who fired the bullet that killed Ralph Moss, his blood would be on Jack's hands. But how could he explain that to Wayne? How could Jack explain that it was his own fault he had been shot? And how could he banish this new guilty thought: If Ralph Moss was killed, he could not be questioned, and Rick Bauer would never be called to testify. . . .

"Is somebody over at the Bauers'?" Jack asked.

"Leo's?"

"Rick. That's who Ralph Moss is out for. Because he's alive and June's dead."

"That don't make sense."

"Just get your ass over there. Watch the house to make sure

Moss doesn't show up. And if you can't be there, find someone who can."

"He ain't going over there. Not now." Wayne was talking to Jack, but his attention seemed to be focused entirely on the tip of the forceps. He held it up to the light, perhaps to examine better the hair he had plucked from his arm.

"You don't decide what he is or isn't going to do. Sit yourself outside Vivien's and keep watch."

"You said Rick's."

"It's the same house, Wayne. The same goddamn house."

Nurse Keogh opened the door and leaned in, exactly the way she had stuck her head out into the hallway when Jack first came into the hospital. Come in, he thought; come all the way in.

"Are you almost finished, Deputy?" she said. "Doctor needs to work with the patient."

"Yep. About done," Wayne said.

As Adeline Keogh backed out the door, she kept watching Jack. Stay, Jack said silently to her; please stay, a request he had not made with either thought or tongue when Nora was with him. But best not to make too much of that. After all, Mrs. Keogh was a nurse; she could save Jack's life.

Wayne hesitated before the door; Jack knew something else was on his deputy's mind. "Now what?" he asked impatiently.

"I was wondering . . . Do you reckon I ought to get sworn or something? I mean, while they're operating, you're going to be knocked out, and it'll be like we ain't got a sheriff. . . ."

If he believed Wayne's question was prompted by ambition, Jack would have become angry, but Jack knew Wayne was concerned only with making certain that the correct procedures were followed. Just doing his job. . . .

Jack waved Wayne away. "It's like I'm out of town, Wayne. I'm out of town but I'll be back soon. . . ."

The last words Jack heard in the operating room, right before his loss of consciousness was complete, were "June's here already."

In his mind, Jack answered, "I am too." But late, too late. If he had only gotten to the hospital well in advance of June Moss's arrival, he could have told them how to care for her. You have to support her head, he might have said. Her neck is broken, and she hasn't the strength to hold up her head without help. Like a baby, like holding a newborn baby, you've got to keep your hand or the crook of your arm under that heavy head. But Jack didn't have the chance to say any of these things, so he knew that if he looked across the room, he'd see June Moss lying on a table like the one he lay on, but her neck would be stretched beyond its already considerable length and her head would be lolling off the table, her sightless eyes bulging wide and aimed accusingly in his direction.

Still, Jack thought, even if he was too late to save her, he knew what she needed. She needed to be held, the way a baby needs to be held. She didn't need a man's—she didn't need Leo Bauer's—body pressing down on hers. And didn't Jack's knowledge count for something? Even if he couldn't save June Moss, couldn't he get credit for being a man who didn't hurt or use her? "I'm not a bad man," Jack said.

Or did he say it? Perhaps he only thought the words. No one else in the operating room gave any sign of hearing him speak. But Nurse Keogh brought her brown eyes, those eyes that shone dark with bottomless kindness, close to his. Had she heard him speak? She seemed to look searchingly to him. If he had not uttered a declaration but asked a question—"Am I a bad man?"— she might have answered him. Of course, she may only have been peering into his eyes as part of the preoperative procedures, checking perhaps to see how quickly the anesthesia was taking effect.

Later, when Jack Nevelsen saw other brown-eyed nurses in Good Samaritan Hospital, he knew that he couldn't even be certain that it had been Adeline Keogh in the operating room with him. After all, the woman was wearing a mask, a surgical mask. . . .

Even worse was the embarrassment Jack felt when he realized that the words he heard—"June's here already"—referred to the calendar and not to June Moss.

39

NORA STOOD WITH HER HAND ON THE SILL OF A WINDOW THAT WAS not supposed to be there. The sun that was not supposed to be shining struck Nora full on, bathing her in light. Her eyes were closed not, Jack was sure, because of the brightness but because the sunlight's warmth must have felt so good.

But the examining room where he last remembered being did not have a window. Their home didn't have a window, not like that one. No room in which Jack and Nora belonged looked like this one. He might as well shut his eyes too, since his sight was no help in telling him where he was.

The image of Nora stayed with him. The look on her face . . . it was like a woman in ecstasy. Sunlight? Sunlight could do that to a woman? And her husband in the hospital. . . .

Jack opened his eyes. Yes, he was in the hospital. But no longer in the examining room. They must have moved him to his own room, a room with a window. Where Nora stood. But her hand was no longer on the sill, and the sunlight no longer washed over her. Jack didn't know how much time had passed since he last saw her, but he knew he still had this power. He could close his eyes and all units of time—seconds, minutes, hours—would pass without differentiation. This was better than sleep; this was sleep that wiped away the world and all its measurements.

Nora's eyes were open, and now she looked outside with a worried expression.

"Is it still snowing?" Jack asked.

She didn't seem startled at the sound of his voice. Perhaps he had been talking in his sleep.

"That's not what I meant," Jack said. "I mean has the snow melted?"

"How are you?" She smiled at him, but her smile did nothing to banish the concern from her eyes. Was he worse off than he thought? Had the doctor misled him? He looked down the length of his body. Under the white sheet and the not-quite-white hospital blanket was a lump that indicated the presence of two legs. He curled the toes and flexed the ankle of his good leg first, then his bad one. The movement brought forth a sensation in his injured leg that reminded him of the freshening pain you got from pressing your tongue into the cavity of a bad tooth. It turned the ever-present pain from a pale blue to an inky blue-black. But all right: the leg was there and he could move it.

"Tired," he said to Nora. "Can't keep my eyes open."

Her smiled widened but brought no more joy to her face. "Go ahead and close them," she said. "Sleep. The doctor says it'll be good for you."

"How long have I been out already?" He tried to sit up but found he couldn't. Sitting up called for too much concentration; the process seemed too complicated. Then he became frightened and a little sad. If sitting up was more than his mind could manage . . . Was there any part of life that henceforth would not seem too daunting for him?

He followed Nora's advice and closed his eyes. As he slid toward sleep, these thoughts held tight: Was this what life felt like for Phil—simply too complicated—and was that why Jack's brother lived jobless and alone in a dilapidated trailer, picking up possessions by watching for what lay on the ground, because a life that asked or gave more would be too much? Stitched into those

294

thoughts of his brother was another question that Jack knew would trouble his sleep—Why wouldn't Nora tell him if the snow had melted?

He woke in the middle of the night, alone in his hospital room. At least he assumed the room was only his. Earlier, he had looked to his right, to Nora and the room's tall window, but maybe if he looked to his left, he'd see another bed and another patient. Maybe he was in a ward—there might be a long line of beds and patients next to him. He knew that wasn't so. A wall loomed not far from the foot of his bed; a hospital ward would be larger on the sides as well. Besides, he would know if others were in the room, even if they were sleeping. That was something he had trouble adjusting to in the army, sleeping in the barracks. God, men could make noise in their sleep. Snoring, sure, but much more: groaning and farting and whimpering and grunting and gasping and whistling. How he used to lie awake at night listening to that choir! And what church would that choir belong to? Well, that would be the Church of Life, wouldn't it? The Church of the Holy Moaners, the Sacred Snorers, the Faithful Farters. . . .

Jack was alone; he was sure of it. Still, to make it official, he turned his head. A nightstand. A door. Only the bed he lay in. He wanted to enjoy these moments when no one was asking him questions, when he had no duty to perform but sleep. Sleep—ah, that world was even more attractive than the darkened solitude of his room.

In his dream, however, Jack was not alone. Leo Bauer was in the hospital, roaming from corridor to corridor. He was not there as a ghost or a walking dead man, but as someone who had an official connection to the hospital. Jack wasn't even sure how he knew Leo was present since Jack never saw him. Perhaps, however, Leo was looking for Jack. Was that Leo's reason for being there, to find Jack? He would not be difficult to locate because his hospital room, like a room in a doll's house, had walls on only three sides, and his bed lay exposed to the hall and anyone walking by. The bed itself had been stripped of all its sheets and blankets. Jack's body, clothed in an ankle-length brown duster designed especially for patients who had no bedding, was stretched out on a mattress stuffed with—was this possible since he felt no chill?—snow.

In his dream Jack felt no fear or uneasiness over the prospect of meeting Leo Bauer. Leo and he had, after all, been friends for many years; they would have no trouble landing on a subject they could talk about companionably.

Jack was worried, however, that Nora would come while Leo was still in the building. They must not meet; Jack knew that, yet he couldn't think of any way he could get a message to Nora. It seemed to him there had to be a way he could use the powers of his office to keep her away, but what they might be, he couldn't say. The longer the dream went on, the greater his anxiety became.

When Jack woke, his brother, Phil, stood over the hospital bed. It was daylight once again, but Jack had no idea of the hour. Neither did he have any feeling for how long he had slept. He felt rested, yet he knew that if he closed his eyes, he could be asleep again in seconds.

"Hey, little brother," Phil said. "You in there?"

Jack's mouth was dry, and it took him a moment to find the moisture he needed to make words. "Has the snow melted?" he asked.

Phil pursed his lips and nodded thoughtfully. "Gone by noon yesterday. Except for back in the trees and in the ditches." Jack's brother smiled, and his close-set eyes, always slightly crossed, opened wider. "And on the north side of my trailer. I'll probably be making snowballs out there on the Fourth of July."

"Snow in June . . ."

"Life in Montana."

Phil tilted his head from side to side as if he could find a way to see through his brother's bedding. "I hear the surgery got kind of complicated."

"Doc says I'm probably going to walk with a limp. Nothing serious."

Phil nodded, and then Jack and his brother had nothing more to say to each other. There were no hard feelings between them— indeed, Jack had been pleased to look up and see his brother's face—but neither had they ever been particularly close. Phil was ill-at-ease in virtually all human company, family included. As soon as Jack could think of something to say that would excuse his brother from the hospital room, Phil would happily take his leave.

"How long you been here?" Jack asked.

"Me? Oh, I don't know. Couple hours maybe. It ain't visiting hours, but I thought I'd just sneak in here and spell Nora while she went home for lunch. Take your time, I told her. Lay down for a while maybe. While you been doing all this sleeping, she's been staying awake. She'll probably poke her head back in here any minute now."

"She doesn't have to sit here all the time."

"That's what everyone's told her. It's not like you're going anywhere. But you know Nora. There's no keeping her away."

You know Nora—it was strange to hear Phil say that because Jack would have guessed that his brother didn't know Nora very well at all. For that matter, beyond recognizing him on the street, Nora probably didn't know Phil. She certainly had not heard Jack talk much about his brother, or their childhood together. Yet Phil had used the phrase . . . What the hell. Jack had his brother here, as sure a captive as if he were the one in this high bed with the rails locked in on each side. Why not make use of this time they were forced to spend together?

"Do you?" Jack asked his brother. "Do you know Nora?"

Phil kept smiling but worry clouded his eyes. Perhaps he wondered if his brother was out of his head. He'd been out for a long time, and maybe his mind hadn't completely cleared. "I was at your wedding," Phil said. "I was your best man. . . ."

"So you think I did right, marrying Nora?"

"She's been . . . She's worried about you."

"Because, you know, we never did talk before the wedding. You never did tell me what you thought I was getting into."

Phil looked nervously toward the door. Then he began nodding so eagerly that his movement seemed as though it could be an affliction. "Nora? She's . . . Jesus, Jack, she's . . . she's a peach, a peach of a girl."

Jack had to smile. Their father's words had gotten into Phil's mouth. How many times had Jack—had both of them—heard their father say of a female, *She's a peach.*

"So you think I've got a good woman?"

"Hell, you don't need me to tell you that." Phil's nodding slowed, but he took a couple steps back from the bed.

Jack sat up as if he were preparing to pursue his brother. "What I *need*—" He was surprised when he slid his legs up along the sheets, how easily his bad leg moved, as if it were lighter than it had been when he entered the hospital. "What I need, is to hear you say whether you think someone else has had that good woman."

Phil's face took on an expression of horror, but Jack wasn't willing to read too much into that. What no doubt frightened Phil more than anything was talk this intimate. There was no remark about the weather or about cattle prices he could make that would extricate him from the moment. Hell, Jack might as well have locked Phil in an embrace he couldn't get out of.

"I can get more specific, if that'll help," said Jack. "I can give you a name—how would that be?"

Phil raised his head and moved it from side to side the way you sometimes see blind people do to make certain they catch every sound floating in the air. What was he listening for? Jack wondered. A far-off alarm—something that meant visiting hours were over? The sound of footsteps—a nurse coming to take Jack's temperature? Nora, returning to resume her vigil? A voice from the heavens, telling Phil how to answer his brother?

"Leo Bauer," Jack said. "What do you think? Leo and Nora—that ring any bells for you?"

"Leo . . . Leo's dead. Just."

"Well, now this would've been *before* he was dead." Jack sat up straighter, and as he got his back off the pillows, he felt how sweat-damp his back was. "Ah, come on, Phil. Goddamn it, you're my brother. Why don't you see if you can be some use to me for once?"

"What you're talking about," Phil said softly, "I never heard anything like that. Never."

"Somebody else then. Nora and somebody else?"

Phil shook his head.

"But then you wouldn't, would you? You'd be about the last person to hear talk like that."

"That's right," Phil said, his voice softer still.

Jack looked away from his brother. Hanging on the wall next to the door was a small, framed photograph. Although Jack could only discern its general outlines, he was fairly certain he knew what was pictured: it was another mountain scene, and he believed he could name it even more specifically. Those peaks were in Glacier Park, photographed from the Going-to-the-Sun Road. One of the few vacations his parents took Jack and Phil on when they were children was to Glacier Park, though Jack was so young when they made the trip he had no memory of it. His mother had shot rolls of film of the mountain scenery, and for years after she loved to show her sons the photographs. After each snapshot, she would ask Jack—implore him, beseech him—"Don't you remember? Don't you?" Eventually Jack gave in and admitted to memories he didn't have. Phil had said all along that he remembered, but Jack had always wondered if Phil was only trying to please their mother. Jack had never asked Phil. And what would be the point of asking now? They were both of an age when it was practically impossible to differentiate between actual childhood memories and the photographs in the family album.

Jack asked his brother, "Do you see an ashtray over there?"

Without hesitation, Phil opened the drawer of the metal cabinet next to the bed. He brought out a battered, scorched, green metal ashtray and set it on top of the nightstand.

"You see my cigarettes in there?"

Phil shook his head.

"You got one you can spare?"

Phil threw his hands in the air. "Gave 'em up!"

"No shit." Jack fell back on the bed. The pillows felt as though they had been waiting for him. "When did this happen?"

"Couple of months ago. Decided I couldn't afford 'em."

"You could roll your own."

"Tried that. Just couldn't get the hang of it. Tobacco kept falling out."

"Well, good for you. Could you check around and see if my

clothes and things are here someplace. I had a pack of Chesterfields when I came in here.''

At Jack's request, Phil looked immediately toward the door, of all places, and his look was so wistful that Jack said, "Forget it. I don't need a smoke. Maybe I'll see if I can sleep a little more. Or maybe I'll quit too. What the hell.''

As soon as Jack closed his eyes, he could hear his brother back away. "I'll check back later," Phil said. "You sleep.''

Jack nodded. He heard the door open but then quickly sigh shut. His brother was still in the room. Jack knew it.

"Don't think that about Nora," Phil said. "Really. It's not true. It couldn't be true.''

He waited, and when he did not hear his brother leave, Jack said, "Anything can be true, Phil. Almost anything.''

40

DURING VISITING HOURS THAT NIGHT, ANGELA CAME IN, WEARING HER father's red-plaid wool jacket with the collar turned up. Because the hospital's policies said you were supposed to be fourteen to visit, Angela was trying to disguise herself, and she huddled close between her mother and grandmother. Nora had told him earlier that she would try to smuggle Angela in, and Jack had been waiting all day for her visit. Now the three of them stood at the foot of Jack's bed. Jack wondered if they would look any more somber if he were lying in his coffin.

"Hi, sweetheart." He hoped his hoarse, weak voice wouldn't alarm her.

She walked hesitantly around to the side of the bed. Jack glanced back at Nora and her mother to see if one or both of them had urged Angela forward. In that instant, when he saw mother and daughter together—Nora and her mother were the same height and had similarly slender frames, and both had assumed exactly the same posture, hands clasped just below their waists—Jack believed his brother was right: *That couldn't be true of Nora; she could not have had an affair with another man.* She and her mother wore identical expressions, both their faces tight with worry but with a measure of bewilderment thrown in as well. Passed down from mother to daughter was the lesson that life already held too much—stick close to home and don't add to the confusion. They belonged on these quiet treeless prairies, where even natural beauty was carefully, sparsely rationed. Seeking more pleasure would make no more sense to them than asking for more pain—an ounce more of either might be the weight that unbalanced them completely.

"Hello, Lillian," he said to his mother-in-law.

"You're doing better, I see." He heard the wish in her words: Say, yes, just say yes.

"Oh, I've been worse. I can't complain." Jack was stalling. He knew Angela was at his side, but he wasn't ready to turn to her. Suddenly, after seeing those two generations at the foot of his bed, he no longer knew what he wanted for his daughter's life. Certainly not their fearful, withheld lives, yet for the moment the only alternative seemed to be June Moss. . . . Let the answer be there, he thought, there in my baby's eyes.

When he looked at her, she smiled tentatively as if she weren't quite certain what emotion was appropriate for the circumstances. Without thought, he smiled back at her.

"Did you get shot in the butt?" Angela asked him.

"No, honey. In the leg. I got shot in the leg."

Angela stared at him as if she not only didn't understand what he said, but as if she wasn't sure of his identity. Then she looked anxiously to her mother for help. What was wrong? Jack wondered. Hadn't Angela been told what had happened to him?

Then it came to him. When Angela was six years old, she had been sick with tonsillitis, and Dr. Snow had given her a penicillin shot. The injection had not only been physically painful but had also hurt her burgeoning sense of dignity and modesty. From that incident a joke developed between Jack and Angela. Whenever the mood of either one of them seemed low, the other would try to jolly him or her with the words, "What's the matter—did you get a shot in the butt?" *A shot*—that's what Angela had asked him; she was trying to cheer him, and he had not heard her correctly.

"But they gave me a shot," he rushed to say, "in the arm." He bared his teeth in a grimace of pain. "And it hurt like *anything!*"

Her expression brightened as if Jack had just returned from a long absence. "Did you cry?"

"Uh-huh. I cried so hard the nurse told me I wouldn't get supper unless I stopped."

Angela giggled, a little squirt of laughter that sounded like the squeak of rubber-soled shoes on a freshly waxed floor. "Did you get spanked?"

"Oh, no. I've been good. But when I ate supper, I almost started crying again it was so bad."

"Vienna sausages?"

Jack stuck out his tongue. "Chipped beef on toast. And green Jell-O with little slivers of carrots."

Angela gave a little shudder. The first food he mentioned was the one he disliked most (Vienna sausages were a close second), but the Jell-O was something Angela hated. "I'll make you a milk shake when you come home," she said.

"Extra thick?"

"When are you coming home, Dad?"

"I'm not sure, hon. I've got a little temperature, and the doctor says I can't go home until it's back to normal. In the meantime"— he made another face—"green Jell-O."

"A fever?" Nora asked. "Infection?"

Jack shrugged. "He's not sure. Maybe. He doesn't think it's anything to get worked up about."

"He didn't say anything to me."

"Me neither. I got this from the nurse."

"I wonder why he didn't say anything."

Nora's mother crooked her fingers to Angela and whispered, "We'll wait in the hall."

Jack didn't want his daughter to leave. "She's okay," he told his mother-in-law.

"Give your father a kiss," said Nora.

"I'm walking okay," Jack told the two women. "I can get to the bathroom on my own. Limping, sure, but . . . okay. My leg's okay."

"We better skedaddle," Lillian said to Angela, "before the nurse comes."

"No one minds," Jack said. "No one's going to say anything about her being here."

"It's the rule . . . Give your dad a kiss."

Angela puckered and leaned forward slowly as if she weren't quite sure how far her lips would have to travel before they reached their destination. When they touched Jack's cheek, she simply let them rest there for a second. Her lips were warm and dry. The breath from her nostrils whistled across his face. He could smell his daughter, that odor that children have, as if their youthful heat had caused some fermentation process to begin. The sound of her kiss was like a tiny, dry pop.

Jack grabbed Angela's wrist, and she began to pull back.

"I want to tell you what happened, honey."

"She knows," Nora said, stepping around the bed to stand beside her daughter.

"But I want to explain. . . . I want her to know how—"

Angela tugged again, but gently. She was not trying to jerk herself violently free of his grasp but was simply leaning back, back, as though she was trying to get away from her father and yet at the same time not hurt his feelings. Jack let go.

She backed away, and as she did, Jack told her, "This wasn't supposed to happen, Ange. I know you used to worry about something like this, but this was different. It couldn't ever happen again because it wasn't supposed to happen in the first place. It was—" He stopped himself. How could he ever make her—make anyone—understand that it was his own goddamn fault that Ralph Moss shot him in the leg?

"You make sure you have some ice cream on hand," Jack said. "And some chocolate syrup. Because I'm going to want that milk shake as soon as I get home."

Angela waved to him by closing her fingers down over her palm, exactly how she had first waved good-bye when she was little more than an infant.

*   *   *

Alone again, Jack was surprised to find how tired he was following Angela's visit. He could feel his heart thudding in his chest as if he had been toting a heavy weight. Last summer when water flooded into the basement following a rainstorm, they had decided to throw away the big square of linoleum that had been on the concrete floor since they moved into the house. By the time Jack got the soaked, moldy-smelling roll of linoleum to the top of the stairs, his heart was pounding so hard—as it was now—that he was afraid he was going to have a heart attack. Maybe he should tell his doctor and the nurses that visitors shouldn't be allowed, not even family. His heart wasn't up to it.

But as soon as visiting hours began that next afternoon, Wayne showed up. He was wearing a white shirt and a tie, and he brought Jack a gift: a deck of cards. "As long as you're just sitting here," Wayne said, "not sick or nothing, I thought you might like to play solitaire. Or deal yourself some poker hands. Blackjack. Whatever."

Wayne had not come to visit but to report on what was happening in the search for Ralph Moss. Nothing. A report had come in that he might have been spotted near Lander, Wyoming, but nothing had come of it.

Jack was not surprised. During his time in the hospital, he had given himself over to the belief—cautiously, optimistically—that Ralph Moss would never be caught. From his hospital bed he let his mind travel any escape route Ralph Moss might take, and in every direction from Bentrock, there was so much space, so much emptiness, that it was all Jack could do to keep his thoughts from circling around and running into themselves. Then, when the blank space of the plains ran out, the Rocky Mountains took over. Or the North Dakota Badlands. Or the Black Hills of South Dakota. It was not difficult to suppose that a man could escape into that country. Or a man and a woman, as Leo Bauer and June Moss must have joyfully concluded. . . . Finally, however, when in his mind Jack got Ralph Moss to freedom, it was back in his home state. There, Jack imagined Ralph Moss roosting safely and contentedly on a mountain slope, high in the branches of a yellow pine tree, looking down on the world below like one of those cougars he used to hunt.

"Keep looking," Jack told Wayne. "He might turn up. And keep watching the Bauers."

As soon as Wayne left, almost as though he had been waiting his turn in the hall, Steve Lovoll came in. He too brought a gift, a paperback novel by Erle Stanley Gardner, whose books Jack had often heard Steve deride as laughably implausible. Nevertheless, Steve read them. Jack did not.

They had been friends since childhood, but now that Jack lay in the hospital bed, Steve seemed uneasy in Jack's presence. He kept pulling down at the cuffs of his shirt, as if Jack would judge Steve harshly if he did not have the right amount of white sticking out from the sleeve of his dark suit. Hell, Jack remembered when they were kids and used to take pride in changing their clothes only when their mothers insisted their uniforms—T-shirts and dungarees (and flannel shirts in the winter)—had to go into the wash.

"When are you getting sprung?" Steve wanted to know. He sat across the room on the window ledge. Beside him he set his cream-colored Stetson, the hat he had been wearing with his suits since he ran for state's attorney. Steve rested the hat on its crown, which he insisted was the right way to do it, though Jack had never seen anyone put a hat down that way.

"Any day now," Jack answered.

"You're up and around all right?"

"Just stiff."

Steve tugged at his cuffs again, then with his index finger scratched at the scar that curled down his forehead and stopped dangerously close to his eye. Jack remembered too how Steve got that scar. When they were in the fifth or sixth grade, they had been playing football during recess, and Steve fell and hit his head right where the playground ran out and the blacktop began. His skin flapped open, and he shed so much blood that a classmate of theirs—Harriet Adams, God, how did he remember her name?—fainted at the sight of Steve. Jack knew Steve's fidgeting meant he had something on his mind. Was he wondering if Jack would still be able to carry out the duties of his office?

"I don't know if you know it," Steve said, "but folks in this town are talking about you."

Jack resolved that he wouldn't ask. He picked up the paperback Steve had given him. The cover illustration was of a man and a woman standing on either side of a table. On the table was a revolver, and both of them were reaching for it. There was no way of telling who would get to it first. The woman's hair was a shade of yellow that Jack believed did not exist in nature. Her shoulders seemed unusually broad.

"You want to know what they're saying?" When Jack did not respond, Steve answered for him. "They're saying you're a hero. Oh, they don't use the word. God forbid someone should come right out and say it, but that's what they mean. Wounded in the line of duty and all."

Jack wondered if the illustrator had a model before him when he drew this woman or if he drew from memory or imagination. Or maybe her shoulders were simply a mistake. He extended the line too far, and rather than change it, he decided: She would have broad shoulders; a woman could, after all, have broad shoulders.

"You've got yourself quite a store of goodwill built up in this town," Steve went on. "In this *county*. I'm not just talking about votes here. Though there's that too. I think it's fair to say you can be sheriff here as long as you like. And down the road you can maybe set your sights higher, if that's something you're interested in."

Mercer County used to limit to three the number of consecutive terms a sheriff could serve, but since the policy was changed a few years back, it was theoretically possible for a sheriff to stay in office—as long as the voters wanted him—for life.

"A hero, huh? Let me tell you what kind of goddamn hero we're talking about. I turned my back on a drunk with a loaded gun, and I damn near got my ass shot off for my trouble. Is that the kind of man people want for a sheriff?"

Steve Lovoll stared at Jack for a long time. Then he lifted his hat and put it on so carefully it seemed as if he might hurt himself if he got the angle wrong. "You know what, Jack? You're no fun. You're no fucking fun at all."

Nora was his last visitor of the day, and she returned just before dark carrying a small white paper bag. From it she extracted a tall, sweating paper cup and a straw. She had brought him a chocolate milk shake from the Dairy-O.

"You said milk shake, didn't you?" Nora asked. "Not a malt, a milk shake?"

Jack lifted its cover. Some time had obviously elapsed since the milk shake was prepared because the ice cream had melted and the shake was not much thicker than milk. Thick, he liked them thick. . . .

"No, that's right," he said. "I told Ange I wanted a milk shake."

"Well, that's what I got."

Or perhaps the milk shake was exactly the consistency it had been at preparation. Perhaps Margaret Elsey had concocted this milk shake and, knowing it was for Jack, made no effort to make it something that would please him. Hell, if Margaret made it, she might have loaded it up with rat poison.

He dropped in the straw and sucked. Not much effort was required to bring up a mouthful of liquid. Thick, he liked them thick.

Someone left a newspaper in his room, and Jack was able to see that he got his headline in the *Mercer County Tribune*. Marching across the top of the newspaper's front page were the bold black words, "LOCAL SHERIFF AMBUSHED," and below, in slightly smaller type, "Jack Nevelsen hospitalized with gunshot wound." There was a photograph of Little Sam's Tavern taken from the road in front. The picture was none too clear, but Jack couldn't see any traces of snow around the building or in the parking lot.

Considering the size of the headline, the accompanying article was quite brief. Beyond saying when and where the incident occurred, there weren't many details. Jack's words were in the story and in quotation marks, although he could not remember being interviewed, in person or over the telephone, by Jim Brazelton or anyone else from the newspaper. But apparently Jack told someone that "the assailant's identity was known but his name will not be released because it might jeopardize the investigation." The article emphasized that the gunman was not a local citizen. Wayne was quoted as saying that "a widespread manhunt is under way, and there is every confidence that the suspect will soon be apprehended." The words did not sound like Wayne's, but Jack guessed that Wayne might have been trying out a vocabulary for the day when he ran for office. Dr. Hallett said that Jack's wounds were "of a serious but not life-threatening nature." No motive was offered for the attack; however, the newspaper speculated that alcohol was involved.

More than the fact that he could not remember talking to anyone from the *Tribune*—he already sensed how tattered and partial his awareness and memory would be following this hospital stay with its blurring of time, its fog of anesthesia and pain, its parade of visitors all asking the same questions—Jack was troubled by the paper's use of the word "ambushed."

It was a word out of Wild West days, and it conjured up a place where outlaws and assassins lurked behind rocks and trees, waiting to rob or murder the unsuspecting citizenry. That was not Bentrock! This was a peaceful town where people left their doors unlocked and felt safe walking the streets any hour of day or night. Jack had worked too hard to uphold this view of Mercer County only to have it undone by a journalist's irresponsible choice of words. Ambushed indeed! Why couldn't the newspaper use a word that accurately described what happened? "SHERIFF SHOT," "SHERIFF WOUNDED"—what was wrong with a headline like that? Jack wished he could call up Jim Brazelton and tell him the truth. Look, Jack could say, this was no "ambush"—I brought this on myself.

It was after eleven o'clock when Nurse Keogh looked cautiously into Jack's room. He had napped so much during the day that he was still awake. That was all right. He especially liked being in the hospital at night, when even the building itself seemed to observe those signs posted on the street outside: Quiet—Hospital Zone. Somewhere in the building a machine—a furnace? a fan?—ran all

day, and at night its sound, faint but distinct, like a continuous
exhalation of breath, ceased. Into that silence, the hushed late-
night voices and footsteps of the nurses suddenly became clear.
Jack liked to fall asleep with the light on over his bed. He would
wake during the night and be reassured by its soft illumination,
yet by sunrise it was always off, though he never knew who turned
it off or when.

"Sheriff Nevelsen?" Nurse Keogh whispered.

"Yes."

"I'm sorry. I should have brought this in earlier." She held up
an envelope. "Someone dropped this off. I guess it got shuffled
around when shifts changed."

She handed it to him but did not leave his bedside. "Doctor says
you can probably go home tomorrow."

"Really? He didn't say anything to me."

"If your temperature is still normal. He doesn't like to say anything in case he has to change his mind. Patients can get so
disappointed."

"I can handle it."

"I know you can."

On his palm he tapped the envelope on which were penciled the
words "SHERIFF JACK NEVELSEN." He was in no hurry to open
it. "And will you come home with me?" he asked Nurse Keogh.

She smiled her warm, gold-backed smile as if she knew he wasn't
joking. "I talked to your wife. She knows all about changing your
bandages. What to watch for. Oh, she'll take good care of you.
She and that daughter of yours are going to spoil you rotten." She
began to back away from his bed. "Buzz if you need anything."

Inside the envelope was a letter from Celia Moss written on
lined paper torn from a notebook.

Sheriff—

I'm sorry what happened to you. I told you Ralph was a
hot head but I didn't think he would do something like that.
He will go to hell for sure for what he did to you, on top of
other things.

I'm going to Spokane to stay with my sister a while. If

310

you need me for anything her name is Louise Jennings, 1022 Beacon Ave.

Can you keep an eye on my house? Someone might get a bad idea if they know its empty. Kids maybe.

Celia Moss

Jack was not sure if the words he silently repeated qualified as prayer. He did not, after all, invoke God anywhere in his plea: *Please don't let Vivien leave. Please don't let Vivien leave. Please, please. . . .* Yet who but God could see to it that such a request would be granted?

41

IN HIS FIRST WEEK BACK ON THE JOB, ONLY TWO INCIDENTS REQUIRED Jack to act in any official capacity, and both of these were in response to complaints that came from people living along the same dirt road northeast of Bentrock.

The first call was from Anna Fechtig, a woman in her seventies who came to Montana from Germany as a teenager and who still spoke with a thick accent. Her sputtering anger made her even more difficult to understand, but Jack eventually figured out what was bothering her. She was missing twelve books of S&H Green Stamps, books she said she had bundled into packets of four, secured with two thick rubber bands, and left on top of the refrigerator. When she had two more books, she planned to redeem them for a floor lamp. The culprit, she was certain, was a young woman who worked as a housekeeper on a neighboring farm. As far as Jack could tell, the only reason Mrs. Fechtig suspected this young woman was that her name was Patricia Rough Surface.

Jack had less than a mile to drive to visit the other complainant. May Newbold was much less angry than Mrs. Fechtig; in fact, Mrs. Newbold was apologetic for having called Jack in the first place, but she didn't know what else to do. The Newbolds' neighbors had a new dog, a beagle, and they could hear it baying off and on throughout the day and into the night. It wasn't so much the fact of the baying that bothered Mrs. Newbold but its peculiar quality. It didn't sound like a dog at all but like a human, like an old man, and an old man moaning at that. The sound, said Mrs. Newbold, was something she could not ignore. She kept thinking someone was in distress, in pain.

As different as these complaints were, Jack handled them the same way. He told both women that he would take steps right away to solve their problems. Mrs. Fechtig could count on getting her stamp books back, and Mrs. Newbold would not have to keep hearing that dog's unnatural bark. Neither woman asked him what exactly he intended to do.

And he did nothing. His assurances placated them, at least for the moment. Then Jack told Wayne to look into both matters, and Wayne cheerfully assented.

Since Jack had been hospitalized, Wayne had taken over almost all the work of the sheriff's office, and certainly every task or duty that required physicality. Although Jack could get around fine, he limped noticeably and he used a cane (largely for peace of mind, but once he began carrying it, he somehow believed it would be with him the rest of his life). Jack had not initially asked Wayne to assume any extra duties, but neither did Jack protest when Wayne eagerly stepped forward to do almost everything that needed to be done. Before long, every time Wayne asked, "You want me to handle that?" Jack simply nodded. Over a few weeks' time it gradually evolved that Jack had only two sets of duties.

He would act, first of all, as a reference person for whatever paperwork needed to be done in the office. As it turned out, Jack knew better than anyone where all the necessary and appropriate forms were filed, and he knew what kind of language was called for in filling them out. Even Jean Hofer, who had worked as a secretary in the office for close to five years, still had to ask Jack about finding or completing certain kinds of reports, requisitions, or correspondence.

Jack also did his share of going out on patrol, at least the kind of patrolling that could be done from a vehicle. The squad car had an automatic transmission and would have been easier to drive with his bad leg, but Jack preferred to use his truck, for reasons that were at least partly ethical: when he was driving the county roads and the city streets, his primary mission was not entirely department business.

Oh, he kept a casual eye out for troublemakers, for speeders, for drunks, for vandals, for poachers. He watched at night to see if a light was on in a store when it was supposed to be dark, or if it appeared as though a shopkeeper had left open a door that should have been locked. He was confident that he had been in office long enough that alarm bells would go off in his head if he saw something amiss, and he was further confident that he could spot this trouble without really looking.

But what Jack watched for most closely were teenagers, high school kids—or recent high school graduates from Bentrock High. Jack had come to believe that if any voice of dissent was going to challenge his version of the circumstances surrounding the deaths of Leo Bauer and June Moss, it would come from young people.

He simply didn't see any evidence of doubt, suspicion, or disbelief among the town's older citizens. They might shake their heads or cluck their tongues over the waste, the stupidity, the tragedy of the accident, but no one demonstrated any inclination to think that anything had happened any differently than the way Jack said it had happened.

For that matter, had he even said what had happened? Yes, he knew he let certain things be believed, but wasn't it possible that people might have come to that belief, or something similar, on their own? Leo Bauer had a reputation in the community, and wasn't it possible that given the circumstances of the accident—and the presence of a suitcase with Rick's name on it—that people would construct a story of *how* and *why* that was consistent with their image of Leo as solid, respectable, decent, reliable? If you wanted to make a movie about an older man running off with a teenager, you'd never cast Leo Bauer. You'd want someone with a lopsided, fuck-if-I-care grin. Or you'd go the other way and find an actor with a desperate, haunted look in his eyes. But Leo Bauer?

With that oversize, firmly-set jaw and that wide, blank forehead? All wrong for the part.

As the weeks passed, Jack allowed a tiny shard of doubt to enter his own mind: How certain was he that the clothes in the suitcase were Leo's? Wasn't it possible that Rick might have been going off to start his adult life dressed as his father dressed for his? Rick was his father's son—why wouldn't he wear his father's brand of aftershave and take a Bible just as he'd seen his father do? Or maybe Leo had helped Rick pack that suitcase. Here, he'd say, you're going to need white shirts, and he'd throw in a few of his own, even though they were too large in the neck. You want to make a good impression out there and a clean white shirt will help you do that. . . .

Sure, why couldn't Jack be right, and why wouldn't people believe him? Besides, he took a bullet for them. . . . Wasn't that the way it happened? They elected him to be their sheriff, they chose him to stand between them and danger, and he had been shot in the line of duty, out investigating a report that a stranger—a man with a gun—was in their town intending to harm one of their own. And there was Jack, still limping, still showing the effects of that gunshot wound. Yes. Why wouldn't you believe him? Why indeed?

But the young people . . . Rick and his friends. Margaret Elsey. June Moss's friends. . . . They were a different story. Leo wasn't one of them, so they weren't inclined to believe the best of him. A school principal—they'd probably get a kick out of splashing mud on his reputation. As for Jack—hell, they didn't vote for him. He was their parent's sheriff. Wounded or whole, he wasn't someone whose version of events they would necessarily trust.

What if Rick and Margaret started dating again? What if they compared the conversations they had had with Jack? Suppose Rick got a few beers in him some night and decided to tell his buddies about how the sheriff dragged him out of a party on graduation night not just to tell him his father had died in a car accident, but to enlist him in some bullshit story about Rick and June Moss planning to get married?

And Margaret—Jack had torn up her sign, but maybe she

still had the impulse to tell the world, "That's not the way it was."

But maybe, just maybe, if Jack kept his eyes open for any congregation of young people, he could stop that kind of talk before it got started.

So night after night, Jack made his circuit, paying particular attention to those spots where kids were likely to gather. If he couldn't order them to disperse, maybe his appearance would be enough to scatter them or, at the very least, keep them from talking about him.

He drove, therefore, past Roller's Cafe and peered through the plate-glass window toward the booths in the back corner where the kids liked to sit because Andy and Stella Roller would let them smoke and order nothing but refills of Coke and coffee.

He crept over the Knife River Bridge, trying to see if people were gathered in the area under the bridge where the brush was cleared away and where kids sometimes hunkered down, smoked, drank, or necked.

He swung out past Ole Norgaard's shack because Ole would not only sell his homemade beer or wine to kids, he'd let them drink it in the fields next to his home.

Jack drove out north of town, along that stretch of gravel road that ran past the area known as The Haystacks, long a favorite spot for keg parties.

He drove past the golf course because he knew the young men with cars liked to gather there late at night and mark up the parking lot with the rubber from their squealing tires.

He crawled along in second gear past The Hut, trying to see if there were carloads of kids pulled up to the drive-in for a reason other than hamburgers and malts.

He cut his lights when he drove into the cemetery, then turned on the high beams just when they flashed down that long aisle of pine trees where he'd had his conversation with Margaret Elsey.

Jack circled the high school endlessly, though he knew no one would be there during the summer, day or night.

And Jack drove past 611 Fourth Street so many times he

wouldn't have been surprised if Vivien Bauer called the police department with her own complaint: *Can't something be done to prevent this man from cruising up and down our street in his pickup truck?* On occasion, Jack saw the silhouettes of moving figures behind the drawn curtains of the Bauer home, and one afternoon he saw Vivien carrying a bag of groceries in through the garage, but he never saw Rick, not around the house and not on the streets of Bentrock.

He frequently saw Margaret Elsey, however, as she waited on customers at the Dairy-O. And once, he saw her after the Dairy-O closed at ten o'clock, and after that night, Jack allowed himself the cautious belief that Margaret Elsey could be trusted not to make trouble.

The Dairy-O's outside lights, a row of bulbs running along the store's overhang and a neon tube outlining a giant ice cream cone, were turned off, but a light still glowed inside. Margaret cleaning up after closing, Jack figured. He had long since memorized Margaret's work schedule not only by driving by but also by parking and watching the shop, as he did now, from Lincoln Street, where he had a clear view of the Dairy-O's back door and its parking lot.

Although the shop was closed, a car was still parked in the lot, and a young man dressed in faded jeans, a white T-shirt with the sleeves cut off, and battered straw hat, leaned against the car. Jack believed he recognized the young man as Mike Rand. Mike had graduated from Bentrock High School three or four years ago and went away to Bozeman to attend the state university. He lasted only a year or two; then his father had a heart attack, and Mike came back to run the family farm. He was a good kid, hardworking and dutiful, and the farm had been doing fine since Mike took over.

The Dairy-O went completely dark, and both Jack and Mike Rand looked to the back door where Margaret was likely to exit.

She came out, padlocked the door, and then ran for Mike Rand. The big girl's feet slapped against the asphalt, and when she hurled herself into Mike Rand's embrace, her momentum bent him back and knocked off his straw hat. Mike let the hat lie at his feet while he concentrated on kissing Margaret.

But it was not the embrace, not the kiss, not the fact that Mike Rand slid his hands easily, confidently under Margaret's white blouse (which had come untucked during her hours of scooping ice cream) and held her close by pressing the warm bare skin of her broad back. It was none of those actions that convinced Jack that Margaret Elsey had found a young man who would do with her the things that Rick Bauer would not, a young man who would one day soon marry her and take her off to live with him on the ranch that he would inherit, a young man who would give her children, children who could make her forget about June Moss and make it impossible for Margaret to try to figure out the Way It Was because she would be too busy to concentrate on any signs but those around her, the signs that said, This Is the Way It Is Now.

No, what told Jack that Margaret Elsey might not do anything that would disturb the pattern of life in Mercer County, because doing so might mean disturbing the life she was likely to have with Mike Rand, was a small gesture that Mike Rand made as they broke off their embrace. He pulled his hands out from inside her blouse, but the shirt—perhaps because it stuck to her perspiring flesh or perhaps because it was too tight—wouldn't fall back down on its own, so Mike Rand reached behind her and gently, thoughtfully, possessively pulled down her shirttail so no part of Margaret's back was exposed.

At that moment, Jack permitted the birth of a small hope: Perhaps he could stop worrying about Margaret Elsey.

Jack turned away. When he witnessed that gesture, he felt as though he had gotten a look deep into the private lives of these two young people, and that had not been his intention, not at all. He had only wanted evidence that he could stop worrying about Margaret and the possibility that she could still upset the applecart. Now that he had what he believed was that evidence, he wanted to slip quietly away. But if he started the truck now, the noise would surely draw their attention.

While he waited to hear them drive away, he kept his head turned and pretended to search through the newspapers, maps, and gasoline receipts that littered the truck's front seat.

What he finally heard, however, was not the sound of Mike Rand's car, but Margaret Elsey's voice.

"Sheriff?"

Jack turned to see Margaret Elsey standing in the middle of Lincoln Street. His impulse at first was to start the truck and speed away, but he held tight.

"I know you been watching me," Margaret said.

Jack said nothing.

Margaret tugged at the hem of her blouse, though it was already pulled down as low as it would go.

"I seen you out here before."

Jack stuck his head out the truck's window, and though he could see no cars approaching from either direction, he said. "You better get out of the street, Margaret."

She could have taken his command as an invitation to go back to the parking lot where Mike Rand waited, but Margaret stepped forward until she was close enough to the truck to reach out and touch it.

"I ain't going to make any more signs."

"No?"

"I said I wouldn't and I won't."

"That's good to hear." Margaret spoke in normal tones, but Jack kept his voice lowered, hoping that Margaret would take the cue and not talk so loud.

"I saw your cigarette butts." Her voice was no softer.

Jack cocked his head as though he had not heard her quite right.

"Your cigarette butts," Margaret repeated and pointed to the pavement alongside the truck. "You always park in the same place and dump your ashes here. I walk by and there your cigarette butts are. There and where they blow into the gutter."

Jack looked down at the street but remained silent.

Just as she had that day in his office, Margaret puffed up her cheeks and let out a long exhalation of air before she spoke. "What I'm saying is, you don't have to keep watching me."

"No?"

She glanced quickly over her shoulder. Mike Rand was still leaning against his car. Her cheeks filled again. "I mean, I ain't going to say anything to anybody about June or Rick, if that's what you're worried about."

"That's given me some concern, yes."

"Well, I thought about what you told me." Now she stepped closer and spoke softer. "About June being p.g. and all? I never heard that before. Before you told me at the funeral. I mean, I was her friend, and I never heard. Not about her and Rick either. So I figured—"

Now it was Jack's turn to hold on to a mouthful of air.

"I figured maybe I didn't know June as good as I thought. Maybe we weren't such good friends. Is that possible, do you think?"

He let out a tiny sigh. "It's a hard subject to bring up. Even with your best friend."

"We weren't best friends, June and me. I never claimed that. Not like some did. But maybe I was feeling something about her condition all along. And that's why I thought—" A car came down Lincoln Street, and Margaret stepped closer to the truck. The car was well down the street before she resumed talking. "That's why I just kept thinking something wasn't right, even though I didn't know what."

Jack sat behind the wheel of a motionless vehicle, yet he felt he was being taken somewhere, and Margaret was doing the driving. She was leading him to some point of agreement, and though Jack didn't know where that would be, he was just as sure he would soon be there. This conversation reminded him of the one he had with Rick the night Rick's father died, but then Jack had been the one in control. Jack was no longer sure if Margaret knew something or not. Was it possible that June had told Margaret about June's and Leo's plans, that Margaret had that knowledge all along and withheld it only because no one else would step forward with her? Oh, this Margaret Elsey was an impressive young woman! Jack wondered if Mike Rand or any man in Mercer County was a match for her.

"Plus I keep thinking about something else you said. About how things don't always fit together just right?"

"I remember."

"So I'm just saying if you been following me because you think I'm going to say something, I'm not. Hell, I can't even remember now what I was so worked up about."

"It was a hard time for a lot of folks."

"And you getting shot and all . . . I was sorry about that."

Her apology struck Jack as odd, as though she somehow counted herself to blame. "A misunderstanding," he said. "Wasn't your fault."

" 'Course not. I just meant I felt bad." She leaned forward and looked at herself in the truck's side-view mirror. Her action seemed caused by curiosity rather than vanity, and she bared her teeth at her own reflection.

"Mike's worried he's the one you're after."

"Why would that be?"

"A few weeks ago he got all pissed off at old man Gammon for always driving his cattle down Mike's folks' road, so he run over the Gammons' mailbox."

"And what's he going to think now—that you're over here turning him in?"

"No. That I'm getting you to stop trailing us. Like I said I would."

Jack nodded slowly, and when he did, it seemed as though his head's weight had increased so that a simple nod required effort. "Okay, Margaret. Go tell Mike you succeeded."

Her first step back was so quick it was like a little hop. Before she was halfway across the street, Jack stopped her. "Margaret? One more thing."

"Yeah, Sheriff?"

"Are you and Mike getting married?"

As she backed away, she nodded and smiled widely. "He just don't know it yet."

Jack kept track: in the month following his return to work, he put almost three thousand miles on his truck, driving the roads and streets of Mercer County as systematically as a farmer plows his field, working from the outside in. As the circuit became shorter and shorter, he always made certain that he concluded by driving down the 600 block of Fourth Street. For none of those miles did he turn in a voucher for reimbursement. In addition to increasing the mileage on his truck, Jack's consumption of cigarettes doubled. He went from smoking a pack of Chesterfields a day to two.

42

FROM THE DAY JACK RETURNED HOME FROM THE HOSPITAL, SLEEPING arrangements in the Nevelsen household were altered.

First of all, Nora was inordinately worried about bumping or kicking Jack's injured leg during the night, so she had them switch the sides of the bed they usually slept on. But even with his bandaged leg on the side furthest from her, Nora still tried to keep as far from Jack as possible, and she slept huddled so close to the edge he was afraid she might topple out of bed.

The first time they tried to make love after he was shot, Nora's concern for his leg acted as a check on her passion and, eventually, his.

She insisted they place towels on the bed so no blood would stain the sheets if his dressings came loose.

She lay down, careful not to disturb the arrangement of the towels, and then she immediately got back up again. Jack was afraid she had changed her mind—perhaps the thought of him as a wounded, damaged man, or the image of the clotted hole in his leg made it impossible for her to go through with the act.

No. She rose so she could lift her nightgown over her head and go back to bed with nothing on.

Jack wished he could believe that this action was a gift for him, not only a quick, shadowy glimpse of her lithe, naked body before she secreted it under the sheet, but also her wish to press together the entire length of their bodies, with nothing between her flesh and his. Similarly he wished he could believe that the width she spread her legs expressed her desire to envelope him completely, to take him as deeply into her as she could.

But Jack feared Nora took off her nightgown for the same reason she put towels under them: to make certain the barely scabbed-over holes in his leg didn't leak, soak through their layers of gauze, and dot her white nightgown with blood. And he feared that she arranged her legs so she could be sure she wouldn't bump him.

As it was, during the act itself, when Jack straightened his arms and rose above Nora and, plunging deeper into her, sighed aloud with pleasure and effort, she abruptly stopped her own movement, opened her eyes wide, and asked, "What is it? Did I hurt you? Did I hit your leg?"

Jack assured her she had not, but she seemed to recede from the moment nonetheless. She clung tightly to him and stayed well within her own modesty and worry, far from the borders of abandon and ecstasy. When Jack resumed his own rhythm, he simply rode toward release, forgoing his concentration on the pleasure of the instant in favor of reaching the conclusion.

Soon, because of Nora's uneasiness about being in bed with him and his bad leg and because he was often out so late on his extended patrols, it made more sense for Jack to fall asleep on the couch or in the overstuffed chair with his feet on the ottoman, his emptied whiskey glass and ashtray on the table beside him. Then, if he woke stiff and aching from sleeping in the single, unchanging position that the living room furniture enforced, he could stretch out in Angela's bed, which was sometimes empty when he came home at night.

Shortly after Jack was shot, Angela began to have nightmares. She was afraid to go to sleep, and once she did, she would often wake up screaming. She was reluctant to talk about her dreams, but Nora got her to tell this much: In the bad dream, she was with a group of people, family and friends, in a strange house. Angela believed she was safe in the house because others were present, but suddenly she was in a room with "something bad," and when she looked around for the others, she found she was alone. She cried out for help and that usually woke her. To calm her, Nora would take Angela into their bed. When Jack came home late, he first looked in Angela's room. If her bed was empty and the blanket and sheet twisted and tossed back, he knew she had awakened with a bad dream. If the bedclothes were smooth, he knew Nora had simply let Angela fall asleep in Jack's place. Either way, he knew the narrow child's bed would be available if he wanted it.

And once a week, he had his choice of any surface in the house for his slumber. During the summer, Nora would take Angela, almost always on a Sunday, out to her parents' farm, where they would spend the day and the night. Nora used to ask Jack if he wanted to go, but she had long since stopped. She knew what his answer would be. On those nights when his wife and daughter were at the farm, Jack wouldn't spend much time at home either. He took advantage of their absence by putting in even more hours patrolling the county, returning home only when he became so tired he was in danger of falling asleep at the wheel. One night he dozed off while he was driving, drifted to the right, and woke with a start when the gravel on the shoulder of the road clattered up against the truck's wheel well. He pulled over immediately and tried to nap in the truck, but by that time his heart was pounding so hard with fear there was no possibility that he might sleep. Leo? Jack thought, could that have been what happened to Leo the night of his accident? He had been so excited, so tense, so worried about running away with June that when the moment finally came, when they finally escaped, Leo relaxed completely and fell asleep when they were barely outside the town limits. June wouldn't have let that happen, would she? Wouldn't she wake him before he left the road? But on that road, where the curve came up so quickly, even a second's sleep could be deadly. . . .

Jack was sufficiently concerned, however, about Angela's dis-

325

turbed sleep—crescents of dark shadows appeared under her eyes—that he adjusted the hours he was out on patrol. He stayed home in the evening until Angela went to bed, or occasionally, he did not go out at night at all. On those days, he substituted an expanded daylight patrol, concentrating more on the spots—the sandbars of the Knife River, the baseball diamond, the corner outside Young Drug—where young people were likely to gather in the day's heat.

It was on one of those sunlit tours, just as he first turned onto Fourth Street, that he saw Vivien Bauer and she was gesturing for him to stop.

The day was hot and windy, and the sky so cloud-free that the sunlight seemed to be bleaching the color out of everything. Every surface glinted like metal.

Vivien stood by the curb. She had been mowing the grass along the berm, the sparse brown strip between the sidewalk and the street where passing cars kicked pebbles up on the lawn and then the mower churned up these small stones and threw them back out like projectiles. Vivien's legs were bare—she was wearing, for God's sake, a sundress; she was mowing her lawn in a yellow sundress with nothing but thin strips of fabric on her shoulders.

Jack supposed that she must have seen him turn onto her street, and then shut off the mower and waved for him to stop. Yet it seemed as though she had been waiting for him, expecting him, leaning on the handle of the mower until he drove by, just as she knew he would.

He pulled up to the curb, and shifted the truck into neutral but did not shut off the ignition.

Vivien Bauer pushed the lawn mower up onto the sidewalk before approaching the truck. She stepped into the street in order to walk around to Jack's side of the truck. She peered past him as if she were checking to make sure no one was in the passenger seat.

Without a preliminary, Vivien said, "Teach me to drive."

Since her hand rested on his truck, her fingers inside his open window, Jack thought for a moment that she wanted him to point out the means by which a vehicle such as his was operated. He didn't know what to say.

"Rick's car." She nodded toward her driveway and garage. "He left his car here, and I don't know how to drive it."

"He left his car?"

"That college he's at. They don't allow the kids to have cars. Not their first two years anyway."

"Rick's gone away to college? Already?"

"Weeks ago. He and the boy who's going to be his roommate. A boy from Billings. Rick met him a couple years ago at a Luther League convention, and they kept in touch, and this summer Pastor Ellingsen set something up so they could both go early. He got them jobs as junior counselors or something. They're already living in their dorms. He said in his last letter they've got a whole big building to themselves."

Rick away at school already . . . That was information Jack wished could be made public. He had heard a report, weak at best and made weaker by the fact that it came to him third-hand— Wayne's cousin to Wayne and Jack—that a man who fit the description of Ralph Moss was spotted near McCoy, North Dakota. Jack doubted the rumor could be true. Still, if it was generally known that Rick Bauer no longer lived in Bentrock, Ralph Moss would have no reason to sniff around.

"So you're all alone. . . ."

She moved her head to the side so she could look around Jack again. As she came closer, he could smell her, an odor mingling freshly cut grass, gasoline, and sweat. Her time in the sun had brought out a fresh outbreak of freckles up and down her arms, on her chest and shoulders, across her cheeks and nose. She was sunburned as well. A pink flush brightened her skin under those freckles, and on her shoulders, those lovely wide shoulders, Jack could see the series of tiny white bubbles that meant her skin had not only burned but blistered and would soon burst and peel away.

". . . mowing my own lawn. Can you imagine?"

"Someone would do that for you, Viv. You know that."

"I had to ask Charlie Reese how to get the lawn mower started. I asked Mr. Lucas first, but he's never used anything but the push kind."

She stood and adjusted the strap on her shoulder. Jack could see a white strip of skin where the strap shielded her from the sun. She looked down the street as if she were expecting someone else, another car, to come into view. "Before he left I should have had Rick take me through the house, the garage, and show me how to work things. I never realized how much he did around here." She bent down and looked Jack in the eye again. "So now I've got this car that I don't know how to drive. I need someone to give me lessons."

Jack turned his own gaze down Fourth Street. He didn't want Vivien to think he was trying to stare down the front of her dress. Not that he could see anything. Rows of elastic had been sewn into the fabric so that the dress fit her snugly on top.

"What is it about Rick's car—" Jack began to ask.

"It's got a clutch." She levered her hand helplessly up and down in the air to indicate the difficulties of shifting a car. "If it was a—what?—an automatic? an automatic transmission?—I could probably figure something out on my own. I've tried. I took the keys one day and got in, but I just sat there. I didn't have any idea how to get going."

"You've never driven a car?"

Vivien shook her head. "The Chevy was an automatic. I was going to learn on that."

"And what is it Rick's got? A Plymouth? What year?"

"Nineteen forty-eight, I think. Leo wanted him to have a manual transmission. If Rick learned on that, he could drive anything, Leo said."

The introduction of Leo's name into the conversation made Jack even more uncomfortable, but he hung in there and even spoke Leo's name himself. "Leo was right about that."

Vivien tapped her hand impatiently against the door of the truck. "I'll pay you. I mean, I don't expect you to give up your time teaching me how to drive and not get paid. I should've said that before."

"No, no. I wasn't thinking about that. Gosh, no. No, this would be part of my job."

Vivien stood up straight again. "Is it? Giving driving lessons to widows . . . ? That's some job you have, Jack."

"That's not what I meant. I meant . . ." He slid his hand around the steering wheel as if the motionless truck could carry him over this difficult stretch of talk. "I'd be happy to teach you how to drive, Viv. Or try to. I don't know how good a teacher I can be."

She smiled. "Just don't yell at me when I make a mistake."

Jack filed away a point to remember: someday he would ask Vivien if Leo used to yell at her.

Vivien stepped away from the truck. Jack shut off the ignition and got out.

"Not today," she said. "I didn't mean we had to start today."

"Now you're going to do something for me," Jack said, stepping stiffly toward the curb. "You're going to go inside and put some salve or something on those shoulders. You've got a helluva burn already. You stand out here any longer and you're going to have a serious case of heatstroke. I mean it. Go on. I'm going to finish up your lawn."

To verify Jack's diagnosis, Vivien looked down at her shoulder. She pressed two fingers against the skin and when she took her fingers away, two white spots briefly remained.

"See?" Jack said. "If you put some lotion on right away, maybe you can keep from peeling."

He unwound the cord that he'd use to start the mower. "Have you got plenty of gas?"

Vivien nodded. "Should you be doing this? With your leg?"

"Doctor says I'm supposed to treat it like normal. When you baby it, that's when it causes trouble. It sort of seizes up. The muscles get weak."

"You're sure?"

"Go on. I can use the exercise."

Vivien had mowed the front and side lawn and most of the berm, but the entire backyard was left for Jack. That was fine with him. He could push the mower around back there and not worry about being seen. On the other hand, maybe it would be better if he were out in front, visible to anyone driving past. As it was, what were people going to think when they saw his truck parked in front of Vivien Bauer's but didn't see him?

The hell with what people thought! He wasn't doing anything but a good deed, mowing the lawn of a widowed woman who had difficulty handling the job herself. Nevertheless, Jack wanted to remind himself that when he gave Vivien her driving lessons, it might be best to leave the truck at the courthouse and walk over here.

He cut Vivien Bauer's grass exactly the way he drove the roads of Mercer County: he started on the outside and moved toward the center in ever-tightening geometrical shapes. The angles remained the same, but the distance he covered—and the time it took him to do it—decreased with each circuit. But what do you know—in both cases he ended up where he was now—at 611 Fourth Street in Bentrock, Montana.

43

JACK WAS AMAZED AT HOW QUICKLY VIVIEN LEARNED TO DRIVE, BUT then she approached the entire enterprise with a determination and dedication that were close to maniacal.

From the very first lesson, she carried a small spiral notebook in which she jotted down every bit of instruction and information that Jack passed on, no matter how offhand or inconsequential it might be.

She diagrammed the H pattern that the gears—reverse, first, second, third—made.

When Jack offered a gentle correction—don't crank the steering wheel so hard when you make a left turn, let the driver on the right go first when you arrive at an intersection simultaneously, leave a little more room between the car and the road's shoulder when you're driving on the highway—Vivien would at the end of the day's lesson draw a star in her notebook and then write an abbreviated version of his criticism.

But she didn't need much advice, and she seldom needed to be given a bit of instruction more than once.

Vivien Bauer adjusted the rearview mirror, clamped her hands on the steering wheel—at ten o'clock and two o'clock, according to Jack's suggestion—kept her eyes fixed on the road ahead, and drove, just drove.

She stepped down too hard on the accelerator, she jammed on the brakes too soon, she let the clutch out too fast, and she ground and clashed the gears as she shifted, but these excesses were part of what enabled her to learn so quickly. She didn't worry, as beginning drivers so often did, about what she might do wrong. Instead, she simply concentrated on making the automobile do what it was intended for: moving from one location in space to another. Vivien Bauer was in a hurry, and late one afternoon when they were driving south of Bentrock on State Highway 41, she told him why.

The day was hot, and they had the windows and vents open, including the one in front of the Plymouth's windshield that popped up and sucked in prairie air and blew it back at their feet and legs. Once in a while a gust rippled the hem of Vivien's dress, and she absentmindedly smoothed it back down over her leg. She wore a scarf on her head to keep her hair from blowing in her eyes. The scarf's knot wasn't centered under her chin but tied up close to her ear.

"How many miles is it possible to drive in a day?" she asked. With the windows open, she had to raise her voice.

"Possible? I'm not sure if I know what you mean. Possible. It depends."

"I mean if you were taking a trip. A long trip. How far could you go in a day?"

"Oh, five, six hundred miles is a good day. A long day, if you've got no one to spell you. But you can do more. A buddy of mine and I once drove straight through to Stevens Point, Wisconsin, for a wedding. I'm not sure how far that was, but it was close to a thousand miles." Jack paused to do the arithmetic in his head. "Hell, maybe more than a thousand. But, you know, roads were good, weather was good. We were young. It all depends. Why—what kind of a trip are you thinking of?"

Although Vivien was tall enough to see over the steering wheel without difficulty, she still stretched out her neck and tilted her head up as she drove. With her head up in the air like that, Jack had a good look at her profile. She was still showing the effects of her time out in the sun. Her sunburn had faded a little, but she was still pink and freckled, and the skin on her nose had peeled, leaving behind a patch of paler pink outlined in white. "Salt Lake City," she said. "I'm planning on traveling to Salt Lake City."

"That'd be a long haul, all right. When do you plan to make this trip?"

"When you say I'm ready."

"Whoa. Now don't go putting that on me. I give the lessons. I don't give out the license." When they drove in town, Jack usually sat leaning toward Vivien, ready to reach over and grab the wheel or help with the gearshift should it become necessary. Out here on the open road, however, especially a stretch as straight and level as 41 south of Bentrock, Jack felt confident enough about Vivien's driving to stay on the passenger side, today with his bare arm crooked out the open window. Evening out his tan, he thought. This spring and summer, he had spent so many days driving around with his left arm hanging out the truck window that that arm had baked deep brown while his right arm remained pale. "Are you planning to go by yourself?" He didn't look at Vivien when he asked this question; he asked it out the open window, to the wheat field stretching away to the west.

Vivien usually did not turn her gaze away from the highway, but she cast a quick glance in Jack's direction before she answered. He looked back just in time. "Unless," Vivien said, "I can talk someone into making the trip with me."

Keep your eyes on the highway, Jack wanted to tell her, but the advice would have been more a reminder to him. Even when the road looks as untroubled as this one. "Salt Lake City. That's home for you, right?"

"I grew up there. Yes."

"And your sister's there? Vera?"

"You have a good memory. Vera. That's right."

And am I right about this as well, Jack thought, you're inviting me to go with you? And how will we get to the actual, spoken invitation? If we keep heading in this direction, will we both simply know when we've arrived? Will you ever say it aloud? Or will I have to ask?

"What about Rick?" Jack asked. "Would he be interested in driving down there with you?"

Vivien shook her head and smiled. "I told you before. Rick's gone."

"I thought, maybe . . . You know, he might be back later this summer. Before school in the fall."

Her smile turned to laughter. "You don't understand. Rick's gone. I have every reason to believe his move is . . . permanent. No, my son is one of those young men who, once he goes, goes for good." She reached out and patted the car's dashboard. "And making this mine for good."

"Jesus, Viv. I'm sorry."

"Oh, don't be. You're a parent. You know how it is. We raise our children to leave. That's how it's supposed to be. It's not like a husband leaving."

A husband *leaving*—that was the word she used. Not a husband dying. My God, what did Vivien Bauer know? What had Rick told her before he left? Nothing. He had probably told her nothing. Indeed, that was likely why he left. Rick believed—no doubt with cause—that his mother hated him, that she blamed him for her husband's death. No wonder Rick wanted to leave, and no wonder his mother didn't seem heartbroken with him gone. How difficult it must have been for them to live together in that house, each of them biting back words. Vivien's of accusation and blame, Rick's of denial and truth.

Jack could put another mark on his personal scorecard of responsibilities: he had come up with a plan that destroyed a relationship between a mother and a son and that drove that boy from his home.

"How long would you be gone," Jack asked, "on this trip of yours?"

Her laughter this time must have struck her as inappropriate and excessive because she stopped quite suddenly. "My goodness. I'm not doing a very good job of making myself understood, am I. I don't mean a vacation. I don't mean that kind of a trip. No. I would be moving to Salt Lake City. This would be permanent. Like Rick, I would be leaving for good."

Jack glanced over at the speedometer. Vivien was doing a little over seventy. Montana had no posted speed limit—"reasonable and prudent" was the only restriction—and no one would say Vivien Bauer was driving too fast for this section of highway. Maybe for her experience but not for the road. Her ability to keep her speed constant was quite remarkable in a beginning driver.

"Vivien. This is your home."

"Now, what was it you asked me just a minute ago? You asked me if Salt Lake was home. See, you think it too: I don't belong here. Not anymore."

A car approached, still far in the distance, yet Jack didn't want to say anything until it passed. As it came closer, he recognized first the car, then the driver. Behind the wheel of that big Buick Roadmaster was old Marcus Fenton. What's more, Jack knew where Mr. Fenton had been. His wife was in an old people's home down in Glendive, and she'd been there for over five years, ever since her senility became so advanced that she could no longer live at home. At least three times a week, sometimes more, weather permitting, Mr. Fenton made that long journey down to Glendive to see his wife, a trip close to three hundred miles, round-trip. Mrs. Fenton no longer recognized her husband, but he kept up with the visits nonetheless. Now, as he drove past Vivien and Jack, Mr. Fenton turned his head stiffly to see who was speeding away from the city he was speeding toward.

Since these lessons began, Jack and Vivien had been seen together before. How could it be avoided? Someone learning to drive had to practice, at least initially, in daylight, and she couldn't learn only on backcountry roads. Besides, if they never drove around in town together, it might seem, once they were spotted, as if there were a reason to be secretive about what they were doing. Vivien Bauer wanted—needed—to learn to drive, and Jack, as a county official as well as a family friend—a friend to Leo *and* to his widow, let it be remembered—was teaching her. What was wrong with that?

Jack had never acted as though they had anything to hide. If

335

they drove on the quieter streets, it was only because he thought Vivien would be less nervous where she had fewer cars to contend with. But certainly they had been seen together. Certainly. From the passenger seat of Rick Bauer's Plymouth, Jack had looked out at his fellow Montanans, seeing them just as they were in the act of seeing him, and if he did not wave or acknowledge them in any way, it was only because he wanted to look as though he was paying attention to his job, which at that moment meant watching Vivien to make sure she steered straight and shifted into the right gear.

He had even told Nora about the lessons. Well, in a sense he told her. "Vivien Bauer wants to learn how to drive. Isn't that something—our age and not knowing how to drive?"

Nora didn't look up from the peas she was shelling. "I think she's older. You and Leo were the same age, weren't you? And she was older than Leo."

"I just meant learning something new when you're grown-up."

"My grandmother used to say"—Nora looked up at him and smiled—"you're never too old to learn." Jack wasn't sure if the smile was for him, as they shared an amused recollection over an old woman whose every utterance seemed to be a statement so self-evident it never needed to be said in the first place, or if the smile was occasioned only by the memory of a woman Nora loved. "She proved it too," Nora continued. "She took up knitting when she was in her seventies." She turned back to the stack of peas. "She was a demon for knitting. . . ."

"Knitting's not like driving a car." The remark seemed worthy of Nora's grandmother.

"Well, there's no sense having Rick's car and then letting it sit there."

Since Nora knew so much without being told, Jack reasoned, it wasn't necessary to tell her that Vivien had already begun her driving lessons, and that Jack was giving them to her. He had said enough, enough so that when one of Nora's friends mentioned that she saw Jack and Vivien driving around together and Nora asked him for an explanation, he would be ready: I told you about that, he would say; I told you she wanted to learn how to drive.

Then again, Nora would never ask.

Jack had to correct her on one issue however. "Leo was older than me," he said as he left the kitchen. "Two years older." Which made Vivien how much older than him? he wondered.

To Wayne, Jack said he was actually giving Vivien driving lessons.

"Yeah?" Wayne replied. "That's hard to believe."

"Well, she didn't know who else to ask."

"I mean, never learning how to drive. Can you imagine. Going through so many years of your life not knowing how to drive. Jesus. How helpless can you get?"

"She's catching on pretty quick," said Jack.

"I suppose. Just riding in a car you probably pick up on a lot. But not being able to drive yourself . . . God damn."

That was the extent of Wayne's reaction. He was on his way out of the office, heading upstairs to meet with Steve Lovoll over Wayne's testimony in an upcoming trial.

So Jack had covered himself. Marcus Fenton could go back to Bentrock and tell anyone who would listen that he had seen Sheriff Nevelsen and Vivien Bauer out on Highway 41. All Mr. Fenton was likely to get in response was a shrug and perhaps the information that Jack was teaching her to drive.

Vivien said nothing about Marcus Fenton; her mind was much further south. "Have you ever been to Salt Lake City, Jack?"

"I never have."

"You'd love it. I know you would. You like the mountains, don't you? Salt Lake is snugged up tight against the mountains and then the Great Salt Lake out to the west. Really. It's beautiful."

"Mountains, huh?" Jack stared out at the flat, sun-struck landscape. He had a sudden impulse to defend his own region, but he could find nothing out there worthy of praise, certainly nothing to match the grandeur of mountains. "Sounds great."

A minute, perhaps two passed, which meant, at Vivien's constant speed, miles passed as well, but neither of them spoke. Another sign, identifying and numbering their highway, went by, and when it did, Vivien asked, "Is this the route I'd take to Utah?"

Jack twisted around in his seat to look behind them, though he knew perfectly well what road they were on. "Let's see . . . Forty-one. Yeah, you could take Forty-one. I mean, you've got to head south eventually; you might as well start right out in that direction." He turned back to face the front again. "But maybe you'd lose a few miles that way. Your best bet might be to go west. To Scobey, then cut south. That would take you through the reservation, of course, which some folks would just as soon avoid—"

"Jack. Jack, that's all right. Relax. I'm not talking about now. I'm not going to kidnap you. Haul you off to Salt Lake City against your will."

He glanced over at the gas gauge. Over half a tank. What the hell, he wanted to say, let's go. We still have a few hours of daylight—let's make a run for it. And once night falls, I can drive. Or we can find a motel for the night.

"I'd have to look at a map," Jack said, "to figure out the best route."

"I still have a lot to do," Vivien went on as though she hadn't heard what Jack said or sensed what he thought. "I don't want to leave until the house is sold. I've talked to Gary Zehm about putting it on the market, but he still hasn't gotten back to me about an asking price. Oh, there's so much. When I look around the house at all that needs to be packed up . . ." She gave Jack an appraising look—too much time for her to be taking her eyes off the highway, except on a road as flat and undeviating as this one. "I still have most of Leo's things. You're welcome to look through them and help yourself."

What about the contents of that suitcase? Jack wondered. Surely Rick would have gone off to college with the suitcase that bore his name. Had he sneaked his father's possessions back into the closets and drawers where they belonged? Or maybe Rick wasn't up to that task, and he had left it packed—in which case it was ready to go, ready for Jack to pull it out from under Rick's bed, throw it into the trunk of the Plymouth, and take off. Now, there was a thought—Jack Nevelsen going off to start a new life with Leo

Bauer's widow, Leo Bauer's shirt, Leo Bauer's toothbrush, Leo Bauer's Bible.

"I wouldn't feel right about that, Viv."

She nodded as if she understood.

"Anything else I can give you a hand with, let me know."

Without signaling, Vivien made a hard left turn onto a dirt road and stopped. She had to hunt for reverse, but when she found it, she backed the car out onto the highway and then they were heading back toward Bentrock. The setting sun now was shining in her window, and she didn't quite know how to handle its glare. She couldn't shade her eyes because she had to keep both hands on the wheel. She finally settled for driving with her head cocked slightly to the side. "Just tell me when I'm ready, Jack. Just tell me when I drive well enough to take the test."

44

As long as it was going to be up to Jack to decide when Vivien Bauer was ready to drive away from Bentrock, then he'd make sure she was good and ready.

He made the driving lessons, the practices and maneuvers she had to perform, increasingly difficult.

He insisted she learn to parallel park, though when she took the actual driver's test, the examiner would not ask her to do more than park the car diagonally along Bentrock's Main Street.

He encouraged her to try downshifting, letting the clutch out to slow the car going into curves or down hills.

On the highway, he made her pass other cars, no matter how fast they were going. "Okay, step on it," he would say, and Vivien would tromp down on the accelerator and pull out in the other lane. Jack wasn't sure if Vivien even looked to see if the way was clear, or if she was simply obeying his command, blindly trusting that he would not tell her to pass when an oncoming vehicle was too close.

To teach her to steer the car in reverse, he had her back the car up over fifty yards in the high school parking lot and then swing the rear of the car into a narrow slot by the school's back door.

To give her practice in driving on different road surfaces and under varying conditions, he made her drive along the gravel and soft sand of a road that ran along the course of the Knife River. He had her drive on unpaved farm roads that were little more than two parallel dirt tracks hemmed in and almost overgrown by prairie grasses. He ordered her up and down a trail that ran through a corner of Marv Hennigan's ranch, a trail that rippled like a washboard and rattled every screw, knob, and dial in the car.

No matter where Jack told her to drive—even when it appeared there was no access available for an automobile—Vivien Bauer made no complaint. She put the car into gear, gripped the steering wheel hard, and moved forward. The road might bounce her around the Plymouth's interior as if she were on a bucking horse, but she kept her head tilted up, she held tight, and she drove. She drove along the edge of a plowed field that was as heavy-going as winter snowdrift. She drove the broken blacktop of old County Trunk T, where the cracks and potholes were deep enough to ring and bang the Plymouth's wheel rims.

She drove the twisty, hilly section of Highway 284 that ran right by the Sprull ranch, and when she came to the curve where her husband ran off the road and killed himself and his passenger, she said nothing and looked neither left nor right, so she did not see the two white metal crosses that marked the site of two traffic fatalities.

But Jack saw them and wondered how he could have missed them before. He had driven by here on his own so many times he doubted that the crosses could have been planted much earlier. Yet they didn't have a fresh or recent look either. They were partially obscured by the wild mustard and hawkweed that grew thickly along and to the height of the crosses. Furthermore, they were flecked with rust, as if they had long been exposed to the elements.

The next time he was out alone in his truck, Jack stopped by the crosses and got out, hoping a closer investigation would tell him how long they had been there.

They weren't stuck in the ground on the road's shoulder; they were a few feet down the slope, not far, but with his bad leg Jack didn't dare step down there. That would be his luck—step into the weeds and get stuck, unable to crawl his way up to the road. Call the tow truck! We're going to have to winch the sheriff back up to the highway!

Had the crew in charge of pounding those crosses into the ground been told that Leo Bauer and June Moss ended up off the highway, down by those cottonwoods, and so they dug their iron posts into the side of the ditch to be closer to where the deaths actually occurred? Or had they struck rock here beside the road and moved off to softer ground? But stuck here in tall grass and below the road's surface, the crosses might be missed by motorists, as Jack had missed them. And after all, those stakes weren't like grave markers—no one was buried here; they were supposed to serve as a warning, and a warning sign was no good if it wasn't seen.

Jack decided it was the location of the crosses that had kept him from noticing them earlier. Sure, he had driven by twenty, thirty times, but he had always been behind the wheel before, and just those few feet—from driver's side to passenger's—could be enough to prevent him from seeing the white crosses. Plainly, they had been there awhile. Could they have been stuck there as early as Jack's stay in the hospital? Those few days and his ensuing recuperation at home constituted the only extended block of time when he hadn't driven by the accident site.

Had Vivien been out here before? Had she asked Rick to bring her before he left for college? When her family came for the funeral, had they made an expedition of it, all of them piled into the car to go see where Uncle Leo met his death?

Or was it possible, that Vivien Bauer didn't flinch when she drove by here because she didn't know that the accident happened at this spot? She didn't see the crosses from her driver's seat, or if she did, she didn't know one of them was for her husband. That could be. Before Vivien began her driving lessons, she stayed close to home, whether she wanted to or not.

Jack wasn't sure what he had expected to result from making Vivien drive past the Sprull ranch. Was he hoping she'd break down, that she'd become so distraught that she could no longer drive and, having pulled over, fall into Jack's arms because he was the only available support she could grab ahold of in order to keep her collapse from being complete? Or were his directions to Vivien to drive this stretch of road a way of testing her, of finding out just exactly what she was feeling now, weeks after her husband's death? And had she failed or passed that test? Jack wasn't sure about that either.

Before he got back into his truck, Jack had a strange thought: If he could negotiate his way down the slope—and really, it was less than two yards—how difficult would it be to pull those crosses out of the ground? Grab ahold of the crosspiece and lift—the dirt was soft there, surely that iron stake would come free. Then what? Here Jack's thoughts were even stranger. He'd throw them into the back of the truck, drive over to Vivien's, and then call her out to have a look. See, he would say, see what I did for you this time? Now there won't be anything out there reminding people of what happened to Leo—and nothing there to set people to speculating on what happened to Leo. But would he be doing that for Vivien or himself?

Jack didn't run back to his truck, but he moved—empty-handed—the fastest that he had since he was shot.

Vivien told Jack that many of Salt Lake City's neighborhoods were exceptionally hilly, and that gave him the idea for another test of her driving ability.

He instructed her to drive east of Bentrock, out to an area of hills and buttes where he and Phil used to look for arrowheads when they were kids.

A road—no, not a road, a path, a rutted, rocky path—wound up one of the steepest hills, and Jack told Vivien she should drive halfway up the hill, stop exactly as though she had come to a red light, and then proceed on to the top of the hill. If she wanted to drive in a city that was as up-and-down as she said Salt Lake City was, then she had to learn to stop on hills, and, even more difficult, she had to hold the car there at a full stop, then drive on—letting go of the brake, dropping the clutch, and stepping on the gas, almost simultaneously—without allowing the car to roll backward, not even so much as a foot, since on a city street, another car might be right behind her.

Vivien was game. She listened to Jack's instructions and nodded without taking her eyes off the hill in front of them. She gripped and regripped the steering wheel as if she suddenly could not find the grooves to fit her fingers.

It was early afternoon, and the sun beat down on the treeless hill. The air was so breathless the tall dry grasses stood without motion. Two hills away, three horses grazed. When Vivien gunned the Plymouth's engine, one of the horses turned in the car's direction, but the other two did not lift their heads or twitch their ears at a sound so out of place on these acres of shadowless prairie.

Vivien made it halfway up the hill without difficulty. She started in first gear, then shifted easily into second when the slope decreased. The road curved around an outcropping of rock—a sudden reddish orange blaze of scoria that popped out of the grass as if the earth's interior had thrust a fist through to the surface—and there Vivien chose to stop.

It was a bad decision. The road to the top of the hill was straight, but the incline had steepened considerably.

"Okay," Jack said softly, "now see if you can put your heel on the brake and your toe on the footfeed. There. Now give it some gas and let the clutch out slow. Okay. Head out."

The first time, Vivien stalled out the Plymouth. She let the clutch out too fast, and the car bucked and died. She had to shift into neutral to start the car, and that complicated the entire process. She didn't get into first gear, so while the car's engine roared, the car didn't have a chance to move forward. She let up on the gas, and the car died again.

"Easy," Jack said. "You can do it." He had devised this torture for her, and now he not only felt sorry for her but felt ashamed of himself.

On the next try, the car began to roll backward, and Vivien panicked, jammed on the brake, and both the car and the engine stopped.

She ground the starter hard, but the engine refused to turn over.

"Easy now," Jack said again. "You don't want to run down the battery."

Vivien pumped the accelerator repeatedly.

"*Easy.* You're going to flood it. Then we'll never get off this hill." He put his hand in the crook of her arm and gently pushed her back from her frantic attempts to start the car. "Just wait a minute. *Wait.* Then try it again. But don't give it any gas. Don't."

Vivien let go of the steering wheel and leaned back. She had not said a word since she started up the hill, but now Jack could see tears coursing down her cheek. She tilted her head, and the wet streak altered its path and ran back toward her ear. The knob of her jaw bounced in a rhythm that could have been timed to her pulse.

"Shit," Jack said. "This was a lousy idea. What the hell was I thinking? Here. Let me drive us to the top. Then we'll turn around and go back and . . . We can quit for the day. Or go find a little hill somewhere. A starter hill. Not this. . . . Here. Come around here, and I'll get behind the wheel."

Vivien got out the car, but she did not walk around to the passenger side. Instead, she began to climb the hill, walking in one of the wheel tracks almost as if she were balancing, stumbling, leaning forward, swinging her arms to find some momentum to carry her up the steep grade.

Jack slid over into the driver's seat. It took a moment for the car to start, but he kept his eye on Vivien while he turned the key. She hit a patch of loose rock and skidded down to one knee, but she was back up immediately. Jack leaned on the horn to signal her to stop, but she didn't look back.

Jack felt he had to get to the top of the hill before Vivien. He had a vision of her reaching the summit, then leaping off the precipice to her death, a death for which he would be responsible. Absurd. She was not scrambling to the top of a cliff. From up there she could do nothing but look down another grassy slope.

Jack released the clutch and crept up the hill in first gear. Soon he had the Plymouth's front bumper only a few feet behind Vivien. Surely she could hear the engine growling at her back. Her scarf had come untied, and she trailed it loosely in her right hand as if it were the flag she would plant to mark her successful climb. And if the final yards of ascent should become too difficult, Jack could use the car's power to nudge her to the top. . . .

In what seemed her own desperate attempt to reach the top of the hill before Jack, Vivien veered off the curving path and made for the summit. She let go of her scarf, and that square of almost weightless fabric opened, rode a current of air, and floated back toward the car. Through his open window, Jack grabbed for the scarf, but it hung just above and beyond his grasp. A killdeer, scared into flight by Vivien, burst out of the grass with a piping cry and flew off in the opposite direction from the scarf.

45

JACK PARKED THE CAR NEXT TO VIVIEN ON TOP OF THE HILL.

She stood on a rock not much larger than the fat dictionary that Jack remembered resting on its own stand in the Bentrock High School library when he was a student. Vivien balanced on her perch as if roiling seas surrounded her and not waves of prairie grasses.

Jack got out of the car but left his door open. "Vivien. Jesus. I'm sorry. I said this was a bad idea. I should never have—"

She stepped off a quarter turn on her rock and pointed to the north. "Is the river over there?"

"More in that direction. Not far."

Vivien turned to where Jack pointed. "All these years of living here, and I still get confused. . . ."

"I shouldn't have brought you here, Viv. This was no kind of test."

She stepped down from her rock as carefully as if she were testing the water's depth. Jack noticed a thin strand of blood that ran down her leg and stopped above her ankle.

"You're bleeding, Viv."

She lifted the hem of her dress and looked unconcernedly at her reddened knee and the small puncture where the blood originated. She must have scraped and cut her leg when she stumbled climbing the hill. She did nothing more than swish her dress in the direction of her injury, as if a little cooling breeze were all the treatment she required.

"Let me take a look at that for you," Jack said.

Vivien walked over to the car, but she stopped alongside the hood. The engine still ticked and softly, rhythmically hissed from the heat and effort it took to get up the hill. Vivien trailed her fingernails along the hood's cooling metal.

"I take it," she said, "all this would be easier if the car was a—what do you call it? A hydromatic?"

"Easier? What would be easier?"

She looked back down the hill she had just come up, but her gaze was so unfocused she might have been trying to figure out another compass direction. "You know," she said, "driving uphill. Or maybe I should say *stopping* uphill."

"An automatic. That's what you mean. An automatic transmission. Sure, it's easier. You know, you can keep one foot on the brake and one on the gas pedal if you need to." Jack glanced into the car's interior as if he were confirming its transmission capabilities. "But you'll get the hang of this. Someday it'll click for you, and you won't even have to think about what you're doing behind the wheel."

"I wish," Vivien said, still stroking the Plymouth's hood, "I wish Leo would have taken this car."

"The Chevy was an automatic? Yeah, I think you mentioned that."

"But I suppose he thought—oh, who knows what he thought. That since he was leaving me the house and the furniture and everything else, then he was entitled to the car? After all, why leave me the car when I didn't know how to drive? That wouldn't make sense."

No! No! If only they weren't out here, Jack thought, out here under all this empty sky, surrounded by all this open land, if only they were someplace enclosed, in a car or a kitchen, in an office

348

or a cafe, someplace where behavior was regulated, where it wasn't possible just to say anything, the way Vivien was now, someplace where she couldn't throw out her words heedlessly, certain no one would hear them but Jack Nevelsen.

"You're getting it mixed up, Viv. Leo wasn't leaving you. He was coming back. Leo was coming back. I don't think he was even going to switch cars with Rick, the way some people say."

As he spoke, Vivien began to shake her head. Her hair, free of the scarf's enclosure, whipped back and forth in front of her face.

"The Chev was going to be yours, Viv. Yours and Leo's. It was going to be parked in the garage. In the driveway. You'd look out and there it'd be—"

"No, Jack."

"I can just see Leo out there. Washing it every week. Jesus, did he take good care of his cars. I remember he'd even scrub the sidewalls with an S.O.S. pad. Shamed me, the way I neglected my own vehicle—"

"Jack. Jack, why does it matter so much to you? Leo left *me*." She smiled tenderly at Jack as if she hated to be the one to bring him this bad news. "He ran off with another woman. With a girl, a child, I should say. He drove off in the Chevy, and the only way he would ever come back here was the way he did return. To be buried. I think you know this, Jack."

Not so much as a breath of wind blew—and of how many days could that be said in their corner of the state?—nothing to catch Vivien's words and sow them all over the county. Maybe it wasn't too late. He could reach out and clap his hand over her mouth, and if she didn't say any more, maybe the words she had already spoken would be too weak to stand on their own.

But the car door stood open between them. He could not possibly stop her in time.

"Did she drive?" Vivien asked. "The Moss girl? Was she going to drive the Chevy? I kept wondering about that. Was Leo going to let her drive? Then I thought, God, maybe she was driving. He let her drive, and she was going too fast around that curve. . . . Was that it? Did you try to keep that from me too? Was she driving?"

Jack walked around to the front of the car where Vivien stood, but he proceeded slowly, holding on to the car door. Perhaps this hill did have a precipice he didn't know about, a sheer drop he could step off if he weren't careful.

He stood before Vivien and began to count off on his fingers the points of his argument, although he was soon aware that the sequence of fingers popping into the air bore no relation to the words tumbling faster and faster from his mouth. And once he began to speak, Jack found he was unable to say anything that sounded in the least convincing. All he could do was repeat, reflexively, hollowly, disconnectedly, the few facts on which he had rested his entire elaborate construction for the past weeks.

"First of all, Leo was driving. That's a fact we're sure of. We know that. June Moss didn't have a driver's license. We know that. So Leo was the driver of the vehicle. He was driving her, delivering her, more or less, for Rick. Rick has confirmed that he and the Moss girl were going away together. We took Rick's suitcase out of the car. We know for a fact the suitcase was Rick's because—"

With a swiftness and dexterity that surprised Jack, Vivien covered his mouth with one hand and with the other she wrapped up his frantically ticking fingers. Her touch on his lips felt cool and dry, while the hand gripping his hand felt warm and moist, although that could have been his own heat and sweat his fingers were sliding in.

"*Sshhh*. Jack. You don't have to convince me. I know. I know Leo was leaving me. I knew that night. I just didn't know about the girl. Until the accident. Then when I heard two people were killed, I knew about her too."

She slid her hand away from Jack's mouth, and as soon as his lips were free, he began to speak as rapidly as he could. "It might have looked like that at first, like they were together, but that's why we kept digging, because we know Leo wouldn't . . . he wouldn't—"

This time Vivien's hand pressed hard enough against Jack's mouth to push his head back. She leaned right after him and got her face close enough to his that she could be sure his eyes were locked on hers. Out in the bright sunlight, her pupils seemed not much larger than the lead of a pencil.

"Leo told me, Jack. He told me he was leaving me."

Did his own eyes widen then, in shocked comprehension at what Vivien was saying? Is that what she was waiting for before she went on, a sign that he wholly understood what she had told him?

"Actually, he told me he *left* me. I didn't find out until he was already gone." She fell back from Jack and let the car's front fender catch her weight. "He left me a note. Does that sound like Leo? Does that sound like the man who loved to give those little speeches at school-board meetings, at church suppers? At any opportunity at all to hear the sound of his own voice. He used to rehearse his talks on me. He'd work for hours writing them, memorizing them, and I'd have to listen to them over and over. . . . But when it came time to leave me, he couldn't be bothered with a speech. Was it because he couldn't rehearse with me? I used to wonder. Wouldn't that girl let him practice on her? Was that it— she didn't want to listen because it made her think someday he might say those words to her and they'd be *meant* for her?"

"What did the note say?" Jack held on to a small hope. Maybe he would hear something in the way Leo phrased his farewell, something ambiguous, something that could be interpreted more than one way, and Jack could point out to Vivien that she had misread the note, that Leo meant something completely different.

"I can tell you exactly what it said. I still know it by heart. 'I need a change from life in Montana, and I am leaving Bentrock for good. I don't know where I'll end up or even which direction I'll go, so don't try to follow me or find me. Everything we owned together you can have. This is something I have to do. Good-bye. Leo.' I didn't mean to memorize it, but it was so short and I read it so many times. . . ." She began to cry, but as in the car, her tears came without the accompaniment of sobs. And, as in the car when she could not make the car do what she wanted it to, her tears seemed to flow from a pool of frustration and anger rather than sorrow.

"I'm sorry, Viv. But maybe what Leo meant was—"

"Oh, no, wait. Please. There's more. Before you go off defending him. Tell me. Where do you think he left this note? Where do you think he left it so I would be sure to find it? But not too soon, he couldn't take a chance I'd find it too soon. Come on, Jack. You're a man. Think. Where do you suppose he left his note for me to find?''

"I don't have any idea."

"No? Well, maybe if you had more time. Maybe if you could think for a while you could come up with a place as clever as the one Leo thought up. He pinned it to my nightgown. That way I wouldn't find it until I went to bed. So he'd have that much of a head start. I already knew he'd be late that night. He said he was going to help Loren Waldoch with records over at the high school, something they did every year right after graduation. So I wasn't looking for him. I wasn't going to be worried. He and Loren would probably have a drink after. They'd gossip about the kids graduating, and the ones coming up to replace them. Did you know that about Leo? That he loved to talk about kids, especially about their personal lives? But he wasn't doing it out of concern, was he? He was going over his prospects, trying to find his likely candidate, someone he could seduce and persuade to run away with him.''

"It was probably the other way around, Viv. From what I understand about this June Moss—''

"Please, Jack. I know something about the man I was married to. Not as much as I thought I knew, but still . . . Besides, I haven't finished telling you about the note. Didn't I say pinned to my nightgown? But there's more, so much more. Leo was so clever. He put it *inside* my nightgown. He safety-pinned his little note inside, right about here." Vivien placed her hand just above her right hip. "That way I'd actually have to put the nightgown on to find it. Now, what do you suppose he was thinking? That if he pinned it here"—she touched the elastic neckline of her dress—"or the strap"—she tugged at the fabric covering her shoulder—"that I'd find it too quickly, that I might still be dressed then, and I'd run out of the house after him? Do you think that was it, Jack? Is that how his mind was working that night?''

She fell silent and looked into the distance. Jack watched her carefully. If she decided to run again, as she had from the car earlier, he wanted to be ready to stop her.

"I don't know," she went on, "maybe I didn't know him at all." Her voice became toneless, as if it no longer mattered that someone was listening to her. "Because I certainly didn't know the man who could think to put his good-bye note inside his wife's nightgown. . . . I didn't discover it until I was in bed. I read for a while, and then when I turned off the light and rolled over on my side . . . I think I heard it before I felt it. You know, when you're in bed you don't expect to hear paper rustling. Even after I figured out something was there I still had to take my nightgown off to get at it. Then I lay there, reading it over and over and over and over. I never even got out of bed. I went to bed and got this news, and it wasn't too long after that Rick came home with even more news, that Leo had not only left me but had left this world completely. And does this make me a bad person?: When I heard Leo was dead, when I finally understood *that* from the complicated, confusing, ridiculous story Rick was trying to tell me, I thought, *Good. Bastard. Son of a bitch.* You deserve to die. I thought other things, but I did think that. I definitely did."

Less than ten yards from where Jack and Vivien stood, a tree limb, stripped of its bark and as long as a man's leg, lay in the grass. The hill they were on was mated to a smaller hill on each side, but on none of the three hills did a tree grow. From where, then, had this branch come? Who—or what force—brought it to this height and why? How long had it lain there, bleaching under summer sun or winter snow? These were questions to which Jack knew he would never have answers, as he knew he would never have an answer to what Vivien was leaving out of her story. What about the whiskey? he wondered. What about the whiskey he smelled on her breath that night in the bathroom? If she didn't get up after she learned her husband was gone and do her drinking then, and if she didn't have time to have a drink after Rick came in, that meant—what? That Leo could have taped his note to a whiskey bottle, certain that Vivien's uncapping it that night would be as inevitable as her pulling on her nightgown? Jack would no more pose these questions to Vivien than he would ask questions of a tree branch.

"So then Rick knows—"

Vivien pinched her lips tightly shut and shook her head so violently from side to side the motion seemed convulsive. When the shaking wouldn't stop, she turned away from Jack and braced her hands on the car.

Jack gently touched her back. "Viv? Are you okay?"

She scuttled away from his hand. "I didn't tell him."

"When? That night, you mean? When he came in?"

She shook her head again, although not as vigorously as before. He reached out to touch her hair, but she shrank away again.

"Viv?"

"I never told him."

This time it was Jack who took a step backward.

"It wasn't something I planned." Vivien spoke to her own reflection in the car's finish. "When Rick first started telling me what happened—'Dad's gone'—I thought Leo had given Rick a note too, or had talked to him. But then Rick said there was an accident, a bad accident, and you were waiting outside, and something about a suitcase and this, this girl and how they were going away together, and then I realized he was talking about himself, that he and—God, I don't know why I can't say her name—that they wanted to run away, but there was an accident and they were both dead, but Rick was there, in front of me, so that meant— Oh, I don't even know when I finally understood what he was telling me."

She glanced up at Jack, and the calm smile she gave him was even more frightening than her earlier head-shaking.

"I had the note there in the bed with me," she said. "I could have simply pulled it out from under the pillow. I could have put my arms around him and held him tight, held him the way I haven't held him since he was a baby. I could have told him he didn't have to go on with this . . . this fiction. Not for me. Not for his father. Certainly not for his father. For the girl? I confess I didn't give a thought to what became of her and her reputation.

"But I couldn't. I just couldn't. He looked so, so helpful. The

354

look in his eyes . . . He was scared and sad, but he was begging me. I could see that. Please, Mom, please believe this. Please don't say you know it's a lie. Please don't say Dad already talked to you. . . . Please . . ."

She stood up straight but still looked down at the car. She traced an invisible figure eight over and over again on the hood.

"Yes. Another confession. Yes. I thought about how I would be served by this story. I could let Rick's story stand and then I wouldn't be the woman whose husband left her for a teenager. Maybe I even thought of Leo. Then Leo wouldn't be this crazy, lovesick middle-aged man who thought he could make a new life with a girl young enough to be his daughter. Lovesick . . . See how even now I want to make this pretty? I was the sick one, but I don't know what sickened me more—disgust over what Leo had done or disgust with myself, for what I was going to allow my son to do." Now she looked up at Jack. "As for that suitcase you keep talking about. That was Leo's. It had Rick's name on it because he borrowed it last summer when he went to the Luther League convention out in Seattle. Leo never took Rick's name off."

Jack had a sudden vision of the Bauer house, that trim, tidy box with its shining stove and its bathroom with one white towel and in the air the lingering aroma of overcooked vegetables, and in his mind that dwelling now seemed miniaturized, shrunk, a pretend-house, large enough to contain the flesh-and-blood bodies of Vivien and her son but much too small to hold their lies. No, there wouldn't be air enough to serve their lungs and their lies. Of course Rick had to leave. Of course Vivien was planning to leave.

"Viv. Listen. What you've just told me. It stays right here. On this hill. You don't have to leave Bentrock. Nobody has to know any of this. I'm not telling another soul. There's no reason for you to. Not now."

Vivien's laugh carried easily to the adjoining hills. "You don't understand. I *want* to tell."

46

Vivien pushed away from the car and began to turn in slow, wandering circles, as though she were trying with her body to remember the movements of a dance she knew long ago.

Jack made a halfhearted grab for her hand or wrist, but when she twisted out of his reach, he gave up. He'd watch. He'd sit on the hood of the car, smoke a cigarette, and watch Vivien Bauer twirl and spin across the hilltop. He could think of worse ways to spend the afternoon.

"See," she said, as she came near him on one of her circuits, "I've told you, and I feel better already."

"So what's the plan, Viv? Are you going to march up and down every street in town, knock on every door, and then let people have it with the truth about this affair, just let them have it with both barrels?"

She stopped her circles, but even as she stood in place she still swayed back and forth. "Here? I didn't mean *here*." She laughed again. "That's why I'm leaving. I want to go someplace where no one knew Leo Bauer. I want to live where I can meet someone new, and when they ask if I'm married, I'll say no—my husband's dead. 'Oh, I'm sorry,' they'll say. And then it will be my turn. 'You don't have to be sorry,' I'll tell them. He was a shit. That's what he was. A shit, who took up with a child, who ran out on his wife. And his job. And his son—who he left behind to clean up his father's mess with a preposterous lie. And because they won't have any idea who Leo was apart from what I tell them, they won't try to argue with me. They won't try—like you do— to convince me that I've made a mistake. That I've misunderstood. They'll accept my version of Leo and of what happened to him. Now, admit it, Jack—doesn't that sound wonderful? To have that kind of freedom?"

"What about Rick? Where does he figure in all this?"

"Rick knows the truth about his father."

"But he doesn't know you know."

"That's right. He thinks he saved me from the truth."

"And?"

"And what? Let him think that. He believes he did something pure and noble, risking his own reputation to save his father's. I'm not going to take that away from him."

Jack dropped his cigarette into the dust and quickly jumped down after it. He ground the butt hard with his boot heel. "So Rick gets sacrificed . . ."

Vivien shrugged. "That's not a word I'd use."

It was odd. For weeks Jack had contemplated a moment like this one, when the secret he had worked so hard to keep hidden might suddenly be revealed. When he thought about something like this occurring, he was never quite certain how he would feel. Would he take it as a defeat and come away shattered and ashamed? Or would the relief be so welcome that nothing else would finally matter?

Instead, his emotion was closer to sorrow. He had tried so desperately to keep from Vivien something she had known all along. All his scheming and manipulating amounted to nothing as far as Vivien was concerned. Jack looked down at the chalk-dry dirt they stood on. No point in trying to plow and plant a crop in soil like this. The tufts of sere grasses would provide a little grazing, but the earth wasn't good for much more than that. Jack's story, that he coerced Rick into promulgating, seemed a waste now, something that did about as much good as it would to pour a tumbler of water into this thirsty ground.

Waste, waste . . . For weeks, Jack Nevelsen and Vivien Bauer had been drinking alone when they could have been raising their glasses of whiskey to each other, trying to ease Vivien's misery, moving perhaps toward the moment when they could laugh at Leo's folly, even if the laughter would be drunken. Waste, waste . . .

"Besides," Vivien said, "if Rick lives with his story long enough, maybe he'll believe it's the truth."

"Is that the way it works?"

"You know it is."

It was Jack's turn to shrug. "You might be right," he said. He looked at Vivien's leg. The narrow strip of blood seemed to have crept further down toward her ankle. "Come over here, Viv. It looks like your leg is bleeding again."

As docilely as a child, she walked back over to the car. She positioned herself precisely with her back to the front tire and leaned back against the fender.

She seemed almost to have braced herself, as if she were expecting a critical surgical operation to begin. Something in her posture and attitude reminded Jack of a scene from a movie . . . a white woman lashed spread-eagle to a wagon wheel while the Indians prepared to torture her. Well, maybe we have made some progress, Jack thought; look at the wheels we put on our vehicles today—too damn small to tie anyone to.

He took out his handkerchief and dropped stiffly down to a kneeling position in front of Vivien. Without being asked, she lifted the hem of her dress above her knee.

Jack was wrong. The bleeding had stopped, and the red trail down her leg had already dried and begun to darken. Although he knew it would do no good, he carefully dabbed and wiped at the blood. Some of it came away but in patches, the way old paint flakes off a board. The borders of the blood-trail remained, but the middle wiped away, leaving two faint, fine lines going down her leg where before there had been a single, broader stripe.

Vivien's entire knee was abraded, but the flesh was broken in only one spot. Right over her kneecap the skin was punctured and lifted slightly in a small triangular flap. From this cut—caused no doubt by a stone's sharp point (could it have been one of the arrowheads he and Phil used to search for?)—the blood had begun to flow.

But flowed no longer. It had clotted almost to black.

With one hand behind her ankle, Jack gently lifted Vivien's leg a few inches off the ground. To make up the rest of the distance, he got his other knee down on the ground and bent himself lower.

As if the bloody cut had been placed there as a target for his lips, Jack kissed Vivien Bauer's knee.

Immediately he regretted his action. Wrong! Wrong! This was not what happened between a man and woman; this was something an adult did to a child—kissed a hurt to make it feel better.

But no adult kissed a child's injury with such open-mouthed passion that he actually tasted the blood, its moist coagulum salt upon his tongue.

And no child ever answered an adult's kiss the way Vivien answered Jack's, by bending over and caressing the back of his neck, then letting her fingers slide down a few inches inside his shirt to press hard against his spine.

Thus emboldened, Jack put both of his hands on her leg, and when she stood up straight again, he slid them even higher, past her knee, up her thigh.

He had one hand running up the inside of her leg and one up the outside, and he was sure he could feel differences in temperature. The hand on Vivien Bauer's inner thigh touched flesh that was warm, damp. Furthermore, he believed he could feel gradations of heat as his hand traveled higher.

Jack leaned forward and pressed his face into Vivien with such force that he could, if he wished, inhale the thin fabric of her dress. He could take it between his teeth and rip it, tearing his way to bare flesh.

Surely Vivien could feel right through her dress Jack's breath on her abdomen. . . . Was that what prompted her to reach down once again, to grab his jaw on each side as if that shelf of bone were there for her hand to grip, and lift, to pull him up toward her?

In the first instant of their kiss, Jack wondered if Vivien could taste her own blood on his lips. It could be the taste of their secret, their shared knowledge of the truth of Leo Bauer's death. . . .

But Jack did not wish to linger with that thought or with Vivien's lips. Her shoulders . . . he had to get to her shoulders.

Her summer sundress had a neckline of gathered elastic, and he got his hand inside the fabric and pushed until it stretched off her shoulder. Then only the thin white satiny strap of her brassiere . . . He slid that off and down her arm.

He tried to uncover her other shoulder as well, but as long as she had that arm raised and wrapped around him, he couldn't make the elastic stretch far enough.

He'd content himself then with just one of Vivien Bauer's bare shoulders, the same shoulder that had freed itself from her nightgown the night she sat on her bathroom floor while Jack stared down on her.

Now, however, her flesh was not as pale white and unmottled as it looked that night. Now it was burned to shades of pink, and a brighter pink where a layer of skin had peeled away. And here he was, trying to pull Vivien Bauer's clothes away, further exposing her to the sun's blistering rays.

She must have realized that he was staring at the aftereffects of her sunburn, because she said, "For you, Jack." Her voice came in husky intervals, between her heavy breaths. "That's from standing. Out in the sun. Waiting for you. To drive by."

He had to readjust his thinking, and in place of the image of the happy accident—Vivien mowing just while he was going by— he had to insert a picture of Vivien standing day after day under the sun, burning herself raw while she watched for him. But my God, didn't he drive by her house every day?

Now he felt responsible for the damage done to that lovely shoulder, and he covered it with kisses, keeping the touch of his lips as light as he could.

Jack himself was burning, but neither the heat of sunlight or lust alone was enough to explain what he felt.

He was desperate to get inside Vivien Bauer. Ever since the night Leo Bauer died—since the night Jack had first felt himself moved by desire for Leo's widow, desire that he thought he had to quell—he and Vivien had held in their separate minds the truth of Leo's death, and now that the secret was open and shared, nothing need keep them apart. Jack wanted, needed, to make them one body—the taste of blood would not be enough.

Jack reached down as far as he could and grabbed a handful of Vivien's dress and tried to pull it up. The weight of his own body against hers prevented him from lifting her dress above her waist. His other hand he fumbled up along her thigh toward her buttocks, pressed tight against the car.

"Jack . . . Jack. Not here. . . ."

Her head was thrown back and to the side. He ran his lips along the long exposure of her neck, and he spoke into the paler flesh at the base of her throat. "In the car then."

When she put her head down, her chin knocked against the top of his head. "Not like this, I mean. Out here."

He could not understand her reluctance. Only three horses were near enough to hear the deepest moan or the loudest scream. How many places on the earth would offer them the privacy they had on this sunlit hilltop?

Sunlight . . . Was that the problem? Was she afraid of baring some new portion of skin to the sun's punishment? Or was it merely the presence of the sun—the sky's searchlight—and not what its rays could do?

Before his mind could come up with an answer, much less construct an argument that would overrule Vivien's objections, she got her arm between them, and with the heel of her hand she pushed against his chest.

There was nothing frantic or frightened in her action, and he might have ignored it and tried to overcome Vivien with her own passion or his strength, pretending that his ardor was so great he could do nothing but press on.

But he did not. At the first pressure of Vivien's hand he broke their embrace and stepped back.

He was ready to apologize, but Vivien spoke first. "I can't . . . Not here. Not in the car like—" She pulled her dress back up on her shoulder with a movement so deft Jack wondered if she had to think to perform it. "We're not a couple teenagers, Jack. We don't have to sneak around in the backseats of cars. We're grown-ups. We—"

"When?" The urgency in his voice surprised him.

She continued to smooth her clothing. "Tonight? I've got that whole house."

"What time?"

"You tell me. No one expects me to be anywhere at any time."

"After ten. I'll come over sometime after ten."

She touched her hair as if only now did she realize she was not wearing her scarf. She looked around where she stood and back over the hood of the car. "I'll be waiting."

Vivien drove back down the hill with such skill and authority that Jack had a moment's doubt about whether her earlier difficulties were real or feigned. Of course, driving downhill was far easier than driving uphill. . . .

"Viv, let me ask you something. When you said you were waiting for me—"

"Oh, God, some of the things I did to make it look like I actually had a reason for being out there! Mowing was one thing. I could do that. But you can only mow your lawn so many times. One day I stood out there with a tool—an edger, I remember Leo called it—and I didn't have the slightest idea what I was supposed to do with it."

"It's for digging a little trench along the sidewalk and the driveway." He tapped her shoulder. "Slow down a little."

"A *trench?*" She laughed as if the word itself were hilarious.

"It's so— Never mind. I mean, when you were waiting for me, what were you waiting for?"

They were almost at the bottom of the hill, and Vivien leaned forward over the steering wheel to see exactly where the path turned. "I was waiting for you to come along and take me away. Either that, or teach me to drive so I could take myself."

And did you have a preference, Jack wanted to ask, for one or the other?

"Take a right down here," he said. "That's it. You're doing fine."

47

JACK LEFT HIS HOUSE THAT NIGHT AT TEN-FORTY, AFTER FIRST MAKING certain that both Nora and Angela were asleep, each in her own bed.

He had ninety-six dollars in his wallet, twelve left over from his last paycheck and eighty-four he took from a cigar box in the sheriff's office. This amount had accumulated since last December and represented the department's coffee fund. Jean Hofer brewed an urn of coffee when she came to work in the morning, and workers from other offices in the courthouse refilled their cups throughout the day. Most people were honest enough to pay the nickel they were supposed to contribute for each cup of coffee; as a result the department was able to buy the coffee out of the fund and pay Jean a bonus at Christmas. At the end of each month, Jean put the pennies, nickels, dimes, quarters, and half-dollars into rolls and exchanged them at the bank for paper money. Although she knew the money would be hers at the end of the year, she always left the full amount in the cigar box.

Jack took the money on the off chance that when he went to Vivien Bauer's she might suggest that they hop into the Plymouth, then or early in the morning, and head for Salt Lake City and a new life together. He wasn't kidding himself, he knew ninety-six dollars wasn't much to build on, but it could buy gas, a few meals, and a night or two in a motel. At least he'd be contributing something. . . .

He planned to walk to Vivien's, and not only because he didn't want anyone to see his truck parked there late at night. (Funny, when he pulled into that driveway on the night Leo was killed, it never occurred to Jack that an unseemly thought might result from the presence of his truck. And what had changed since that night? Everything. Nothing. Leo Bauer was dead then. Vivien Bauer was his widow now.) If he left town, he didn't want Nora to have to go over to Vivien's to retrieve the truck.

If he left . . . *if.* In spite of these preparations, Jack didn't think it was likely. Vivien hadn't yet sold her house—there wasn't a For Sale sign stuck in the lawn. She hadn't packed her possessions. He wasn't even sure how much money she had to her name. Leo of course carried life insurance, and she had probably received payments on his policy by now. A portion of it she had no doubt set aside for Rick and his education. Still, if Vivien could get her house sold and her goods auctioned off, she'd have a fair stake for starting over in Salt Lake City. With or without an additional ninety-six dollars.

Jack wondered: The money was in his pocket now, but if he and Vivien didn't need it and he returned the full amount to the cigar box before anyone discovered it missing, was he still a thief? That question led him to speculate further: Was he already an adulterer, convicted on the basis of what happened between him and Vivien on the hilltop, or did he need the rest of the night to attain that status?

Jack had to laugh. Those were exactly the kinds of questions he used to bother Steve Lovoll with back when Jack first took office. Jack had worried that as sheriff he wouldn't be able to make the proper discriminations between the guilty and innocent. "You just haul them in," Steve told Jack, "and let me or the judge or the jury decide the rest. Don't make the job more complicated than it has to be."

The evidence was certainly mounted against Jack now. Here he was, sneaking out the back door, dressed in a clean shirt, freshly shaved, and smelling of the Old Spice that Angela gave him last year for Christmas. And if bodies could register fingerprints, his would be found all over Vivien Bauer.

All he could offer in his own defense were the pants he wore. It was ridiculous, he knew, but he imagined that when he got to Vivien's she was going to ask to see the scars on his leg from where he was shot. She hadn't visited him in the hospital, and she hadn't said anything about what had happened that night when Ralph Moss was on the prowl for Rick. Tonight . . . Jack had convinced himself that it would happen tonight. That afternoon he had checked the wound on Vivien's knee, and tonight she would ask to see the scar on his.

In anticipation of that moment, Jack had deliberately dressed in the pants he usually wore with his sport coat. They were gray wool and loose-fitting enough that Jack could hike them up over his knee, high enough to reveal the two fingertip-sized, brownish pink circular indentations (one slightly smaller and less ragged than the other) that indicated where Ralph Moss's bullet passed through his leg. If Jack had worn other trousers, he would have to unbuckle them and drop them down around his ankles to show off his scars. Show them off? Is that what he would be doing? He could never quite decide how he felt about the holes in his leg. Was he proud of them—the insignias of a wound he incurred in the line of duty? Or were they an embarrassment, the shameful scars of an unnecessary incident, and an incident that Jack himself had instigated, in a fashion? Hell, he might as well have shot himself in the leg—and that was nothing to be proud of.

Jack was getting ahead of himself. Maybe Vivien had no interest in seeing his scars. Maybe Jack would be taking off his trousers— no matter which ones—in a darkened bedroom, and he'd drape them over the same chair Leo used when he undressed at night.

The walk to Vivien's was only a few blocks, so Jack left his cane at home. He might have been willing to hike up his pant leg and show Vivien his scars, but he didn't want her to see him entering his house with a cane. Not tonight.

And when he went to the office to get the money in the coffee fund, he left his badge on his desk. He wasn't sure what that act was supposed to signify, but the badge belonged to the county, and if—there was that *if* again—he and Vivien left town together he didn't want to have to mail the badge back. So there it was. If need be, Wayne could pick it up, pin it on, and business would go on as usual.

On the sidewalk leading to Vivien Bauer's front door Jack Nevelsen hesitated. Then he decided. He turned and walked up the driveway and toward her backyard.

During the walk from his house to Vivien's, he had noticed a shimmer, low in the northern sky, as if a smokeless fire were burning far off, miles up in Canada, not only outside Jack's jurisdiction but beyond his county's border. Of course, no heat accompanied the light from this fire. Even the most vivid, colorful displays of aurora borealis—and Jack had seen them glow red, green, and gold—always seemed more like the flare of ice than fire.

Tonight the show had been, at first, a modest one, the lights flickering low and limiting their color to a greenish white, but in the last few minutes they had started to attain some height, shafts of light shooting up to the first quadrant of heaven's dome. Jack wanted to watch a while longer, just in case they flared even higher or—better still—took on color. Vivien's backyard, removed from the interference of streetlamps and porch lights, offered a better view. He considered going to get Vivien, but he thought he would first watch in private. Then, if the show became impressive enough, he would invite her out to watch with him. But if these were merely the final flames before the fire died out completely—well, why bring her out when there was nothing to see?

Jack could still remember the most impressive exhibition of northern lights he had ever seen. It had occurred when he was six or seven, and he and Phil sat out in their yard on a chilly summer night—they brought blankets from the house to wrap themselves in—and stared at the show, spear after bright spear of light, greens and pinks predominantly, streaking and blazing all the way across the sky. They *ooh*ed and *aah*ed as if they were watching a fireworks display, each explosion of icy light more spectacular than the one before. The show went on and on, but they couldn't stop watching, even when they had to lie back on the grass because their necks ached from gazing upward. At one point, Jack could feel himself becoming frightened. How long was this going to continue? The heavens simply weren't supposed to behave like this.

Did Phil sense Jack's fear? Was that what prompted Phil's idea? The night had gotten so bright that Phil thought there was enough light for them to play catch. The boys got out their gloves and a baseball and gave it a try.

Of course it didn't work. The light was not constant or focused, so the ball seemed to go in and out of light and shadow, brightly illuminated in one instant, then disappearing, then coming back into sight looking like a flat, dark disc.

Nevertheless, Phil and Jack persisted with their game, holding their gloves far away from their bodies and turning their heads so they wouldn't get hurt when they inevitably lost track of the ball's flight and missed it.

Soon they dispensed with trying to catch the ball altogether and simply took turns throwing it straight up, heaving it as high as they could and trying to see how much of its ascent and descent they could trace by the waving, flaring light.

Tonight a ball would have to be large and bright indeed to be visible in this sky. Yet as unassuming as this show was, Jack could not tear himself away. Occasionally, a column of light, as if caught by a gust of cosmic wind, would suddenly blaze up, then quickly die back down, but leaving behind the suggestion that more might follow at any moment.

He knew Vivien was waiting. Or was she? He didn't see any lights on. Was it possible she didn't expect him to show up at all? Perhaps she was asleep in her bed by now, confident that when she pushed him away that afternoon, it was not for the moment but forever. And, finally, what did it matter what Vivien Bauer expected? Jack would appear at her doorstep or he would not, independent of what she thought.

Something moved along the shrubbery bordering the yard, but Jack did not bother turning around or lowering his gaze from the northern sky. If he had been asked to account for that sound, he would have explained it as the rustling of a cat or dog checking to see if the lids were loose on any of the garbage cans behind Vivien Bauer's garage.

Similarly, if Jack had been quizzed about the other distinct sound that came from behind him, he would have said, No, it couldn't be the click of a Luger's safety being thumbed off, this sound was too soft—the softest *tsk* tongue and teeth might make—to be anything mechanical. But then Vivien's neighbor had left his sprinkler on, and its watery hiss muted and liquefied every night sound.

On that snowy night when Jack was shot, the pistol's loud report had confused him, both in location and sequence. This time he knew exactly where the gunshot came from—directly behind him and, considering the metallic echo, from next to Vivien Bauer's garbage cans as well. He also knew immediately what effect the bullet had, and although his head snapped down from its upward gaze, Jack didn't have to look to confirm what touch had already told him: the bullet had struck him in the back and exited his chest. When he clapped his left hand over the wound, he felt not only the warm gush of his own blood, but also something sharp, a splinter of rib or shard of breastbone poking out, and something cool, his breath—no, more, air, all the air he needed to hold in, whistling out the hole his hand couldn't seal. His pain seemed connected to this escaping air, as if the hurt came not from what made the hole—the spike driven through him back to front—but what came spooling out of him.

In the instant after he was shot, Jack's mind, which he could feel trying to tear itself away from his shattered, leaking body—but where was his mind going to go without him?—could only register small ironies and incongruities, observations that could each have begun with the word "funny" or "odd" or "strange."

Funny, when he was shot in the leg, a minor wound from which he had nearly completely recovered, he had fallen and briefly lost consciousness, yet this time he was able to remain on his feet and alert, even though his wound was surely fatal.

Odd, that he should be able to think so clearly when he was dying, considering the many times in his life when he could not coax his thoughts into any clarity whatsoever. Now each of his thoughts came out completely enclosed and separate from all others, each locked in its own crystalline cube of ice. He knew too how quickly they would melt and what he would be left with then.

Strange, that Jack could go through a war and never hear a shot fired in anger, and now to hear two such shots fired in his own hometown—and at him! Both at him!

Funny, that Jack would be relieved to hear a voice and to learn that his approaching death was all a mistake.

"Hey, boy," Jack heard Ralph Moss say, "you didn't think Junie was going to die and you get off scot-free, did you?"

Rick. Ralph Moss thought he was killing Rick Bauer. . . . A strange comfort at this late hour. . . .

And yet Jack felt he should be allowed to go back in time, to undo what had just been done, by pointing out a mistake of another kind. I can't be shot, he wanted to say, that's already happened to me.

The next shot Ralph Moss fired struck Jack less than two inches from where the first bullet went in. As it exited, the slug tore off Jack's left index finger at the second knuckle.

Now Jack could no longer remain on his feet. He pitched forward, pulled down, or so it felt, in the wake of everything—blood, bone, and air—streaming out of him. When he hit the ground, his cheek slid on the grass, already wet with dew.

Somewhere on the block a dog began to bark, a small dog by the high, sharp, perfectly spaced series—*rark-rark-rark-rark*. At the gunshots? Jack wondered. Was the dog barking at the commotion of a gun fired late at night on this quiet street? Or at a man—Ralph Moss—running through the hedges and across the lawns as he made his escape. Jack thought he remembered a story someone—his father? Phil?—told about a dog who barked at the northern lights.

A screen door slammed. Not Vivien's. Jack could see Vivien's back door. *Don't come out!* Jack tried to think as clearly and forcefully as he could and to throw his thought as far as it would go: *Don't come out! There's a man with a gun out here!*

Jack had his own escape to make. He was dying, and he didn't want to do it in Vivien Bauer's yard. Home, he wanted to make it home, but he knew it was impossible. If he could just get across Vivien's property line . . .

He could only crawl forward on his knees and his right arm, and that movement was becoming increasingly difficult because his brain was rapidly losing the ability to make its wishes understood by the rest of his body.

Jack got as far as the lilac bushes at the end of the yard when he collapsed. He tried to poke his head through to the other side of the shrubbery, but when he braced his legs for that final drive, they seemed to push back against nothing but air. Yet he was on the ground; he knew he was on the ground. . . .

Now he heard the bark of another dog, and from the sound of it, a much larger dog and close, so close it could have been standing right over Jack. He lifted his arm, hoping that this dog—Muley? could it be Muley?—might take his wrist between its teeth and drag him farther from Vivien Bauer's home. In the next instant he knew the true source of the barking: those were the sounds of his own gasping, honking breaths, breaths he knew would be his last.

If there were only enough time . . . He reached for his pocket, hoping that he could get his wallet out and throw it far from his body, so that he would not be found with the money from the coffee fund. Yet by the time his hand reached his pocket, there was no longer a signal telling the hand what to do.

Strange, that we simply called the night "dark" when it had so many degrees, as now when Jack's vision looked out at what might have been auroras of darkness rather than light.

White Crosses
by Larry Watson

ABOUT THIS GUIDE:

The following questions are intended to help your
reading group find new and interesting angles and topics for discussion. We hope the following interview
and author biography will enrich and enhance your
group's reading of Larry Watson's *White Crosses*.

QUESTIONS FOR DISCUSSION:

1 The motives behind human behavior are seldom simple or singular. What motivates Jack Nevelsen to act as he does? What about other characters in the novel?

2 The novel's action takes place in 1957. Could it have happened in the 1990's?

3 The 1950's are often characterized as a buttoned-up, repressed decade. In what ways can *White Crosses* be read as a novel about repression?

4 What role does the community of Bentrock play in influencing the behavior of various characters?

5 Jack Nevelsen concocts a lie because he believes the truth will damage his community. What is the source of his belief? Does it come primarily from his knowledge of the town and its citizens or from his own character? From what you learn of the town, is his belief justified?

6 Telling a lie seems to release something in Jack Nevelsen's nature. What is it? Why does it?

7 Much of the novel is concerned with Jack Nevelsen's perceptions, which are wrong almost as often as they are right. What are examples of both his accurate and inaccurate perceptions?

8 Through the course of the novel, what aspects of his own personality is Jack Nevelsen forced to confront?

9 How might the relationship between Jack and Nora Nevelsen be described?

10 Why does Jack Nevelsen suspect his wife of having had an affair?

11 How would you characterize the lie that Jack Nevelsen devises? Is it naive? Desperate? Evil?

12 In the classical Greek tragedy, the hero, through pride and arrogance, brings about his own downfall. Is this true about Jack Nevelsen?

AN INTERVIEW WITH THE AUTHOR:

Q: What gave you the idea for *White Crosses*?

A: This novel, as with any novel I've written, had its genesis in the confluence of a number of seemingly disparate ideas and incidents, most of which do not appear in—indeed, do not even bear any resemblance to—the finished work. In this case, two odd and unrelated experiences came together to make me start asking of myself—what if? The first was my half-sister's death in a car accident many years ago. She died alone, and there was no real mystery about the accident and how it occurred, yet there were a couple of small unanswered—and unanswerable—questions about the circumstances. Second, my wife told me about a boy she dated in high school. When she talked to him on the telephone, his father frequently took the phone and began to flirt with her—behavior that the father continued to exhibit in person.

Q: Two of your other books, *Montana 1948* and *Justice* also have sheriffs as protagonists. Why are you drawn to writing about this occupation?

A: The quick and easy answer is that both my father and grandfather were sheriffs, albeit in a small North Dakota community and not in Montana. The answer doesn't go quite far enough, however, when you consider that both served their terms in office before I was born, so that I have no memory of those men working as law enforcement officers. Neither do I have any recollection of stories they told about their experiences in office. Consequently, my sheriffs are wholly fictional, as are the plots in which they importantly figure. Beyond that autobiographical connection, I know I'm also drawn to writing about sheriffs because I'm interested in exploring moral questions—how should humans rightly behave? Certainly all of us are confronted with such questions in our everyday lives, but perhaps few of us have the matters pressed on us so urgently as those sworn to enforce a code of conduct. Considering how such a vow might carry over into a private life seems to me full of potential for both outer and inner conflict.

Q: When you began *White Crosses* did you know how it would end?

A: I didn't. I write, at least in part, in order to make discoveries about my characters and the world they inhabit (and, directly, about myself and my world). Writing, for the writer as for the reader, offers an opportunity to experience something vicariously. If I knew how the story came out, I might not feel as though there were anything left to uncover and learn in the act of writing. Of course, as the story progresses, as human action leads to human action, as in life, the range of possibilities for a story's resolution dwindles, and some endings take on a feeling of inevitability. Given certain circumstances, certain stories can only end one way.

Q: *White Crosses,* like *Montana 1948*, is set in an earlier era. What is it about the decades of the 1940's and 1950's that appeals to you as a fiction writer?

A: I'm interested in writing about the human heart in conflict with itself, to steal a phrase from Faulkner. Stealing another phrase—this time from Woody Allen, by way of Pascal—the heart wants what it wants and it seems to me that in the post-1960's world, the heart more often gets what it wants, with fewer conflicts. The more tightly wrapped America of fifty or sixty years ago better suits my fictional purposes. And now that I've said that, I have to confess that I'm currently working on a novel set in the 1990's.